how to keep a boy
from kissing you

how to keep a boy
from kissing you

TARA EGLINGTON

thomas dunne books   st. martin's griffin ❧ new york

THOMAS DUNNE BOOKS.
An imprint of St. Martin's Press.

HOW TO KEEP A BOY FROM KISSING YOU. Copyright © 2016 by Tara Eglington.
All rights reserved. Printed in the United States of America. For information,
address St. Martin's Press, 175 Fifth Avenue, New York, N.Y. 10010.

www.thomasdunnebooks.com
www.stmartins.com

Designed by Anna Gorovoy

The Library of Congress Cataloging-in-Publication Data is available upon
request.

ISBN 978-1-250-04953-7 (hardcover)
ISBN 978-1-4668-5053-8 (e-book)

Our books may be purchased in bulk for promotional, educational, or business
use. Please contact your local bookseller or the Macmillan Corporate and
Premium Sales Department at 1-800-221-7945, extension 5442, or by
e-mail at MacmillanSpecialMarkets@macmillan.com.

Originally published in Australia in 2013 by HarperCollins Publishers.

First U.S. Edition: October 2016

10 9 8 7 6 5 4 3 2 1

WOODSON

For my grandmother Heather,
fellow bibliophile and kindred spirit,
and my father, Peter,
who had unfailing belief in the book
from the day I began work on it.
Your love and support has always
been of a level immeasurable.

how to keep a boy
from kissing you

1 operation stop kiss

How do you stop a guy from kissing you?

I know this sounds like a ridiculous question—obviously there are a multitude of options available to the almost-kissee. But Bradley Scott's lips were eight inches away from mine and I was seriously in search of an etiquette-appropriate response. Without, you know, resorting to physical shoves, screams, or other emotionally scarring options.

Normally I'm completely on my game when it comes to preemptive measures—that is, avoiding any situation that could lead to a guy going in for some lip action. Stargazing, fireworks watching, or even brief contemplation of a city nightscape has, in my opinion, a Stendhal syndrome–like effect—only, rather than fainting in response to the spectacular scene in front of them, boys seem to fall lips-first in my direction with little to no warning. I can't count the number of times a fireworks display has forced me to end a night early.

The other key moment to steer clear of is the awkward good-night ritual at the end of a date. Notions of "expected" first moves confuse the male mind, and no matter how clear a stay-*away*-from-me vibe a girl tries to give out, the majority of the species will make an ill-judged lunge for the lips. I've learned that the only way to avoid postdate fallout is to implement an effective avoidance tactic at the good-bye point. Having a person waiting at your front door (ideally giving a big friendly wave to your date as you arrive) works well, particularly if they're a parental. No teenage boy is going to want to go for the clinch while under keen observation by your relative. My other fail-safe is a phone call received just at the moment of romantic inclination, whether this is in your date's car or on your doorstep.

Unfortunately, this fail-safe option had fallen through for me tonight. I had sent a panicked text message at the usual spot—as Bradley Scott's car passed the corner store (exactly five minutes from good-bye time)—to my best friend, Cassie Shields: *PUT OPERATION STOP KISS INTO ACTION!* But the crucial time had come and my phone was completely silent. It was too late to employ Option 2: Evasive Maneuver (carrying a drink so you can take a sip as the lips approach), because I had no beverage available; and Option 3: Distraction, which involved asking a question (*So, how about this election?*) or pointing out something important (*There's a spider on your shirt!*), was also useless. Nothing would distract Bradley now except a nuclear bomb. No, this was the end of playing it cool and collected. I could feel Bradley's breath on my face, meaning I had approximately ten seconds before the torpedo hit the target.

As Bradley's arms moved to encircle me, I lunged for my seat belt, frantically pushing at the release button. The belt slackened and I threw open the car door, tumbling out just as Bradley's lips kissed the cool air where my lips had been, precious seconds before.

I felt an overwhelming sense of relief for a second—a wondrous second—before I landed with a tremendous splash in the ever-present puddle in our driveway that my father refers to as "Loch Ness."

The cold water must have shocked me, because I sat there motionless as the brown water soaked through my clothes, watching Bradley react to the disappearance of his hoped-for make-out partner.

He leaped out of his seat and raced around the front of the car. "Aurora! Are you all right?"

I couldn't speak for a moment. After all, it wasn't every day I found myself taking a twilight bath in my front yard.

I pulled myself together as Bradley reached down to haul me out of the water. This beyond-cringeworthy situation had only come about because of his darn touchy-feelyness, and I'd had just about enough of it for one evening. Pushing him out of the way (and leaving dirty handprints on his white shirt in the process), I wearily got to my feet, releasing the ten liters of puddle water that my used-to-be-white-before-this-epic-disaster dress had collected. The ringlets that I'd painstakingly created now lay flat and dripping down my back. I was close to tears.

"Bradley, thank you for an interesting evening." I pushed past him.

"Aurora, wait! Let me unlock your door or find you a towel or something!"

He followed me, right on my dripping heels. I summoned as much dignity as someone with gravel-encrusted knees possibly could and turned to face him. His misty blue eyes were showing complete confusion. Obviously, this wasn't your run-of-the-mill end to a date.

I forced a smile onto my face. "Really, Bradley, I'm fine."

"You don't look fine," he said, taking in my increasing resemblance to a swamp creature.

My date was now repelled by my physical appearance. Could this night get *any* worse?

"Uh, yeah, happens to me all the time."

Was that really the best I could muster?

"For real?" Bradley was staring at his mud-splattered shirt. "I know Leos can be clumsy."

Oh, no. Now he was back to his favorite topic: astrology. I'd already heard an in-depth analysis of my star sign and his star sign and various planetary influences, all through our meal at La Bella Donna, an Italian restaurant in town. I'd barely been able to appreciate the tiramisu amid Bradley's insights about my moon sign and its apparent ability to make me an impatient and often selfish lover.

"Look, I think the stars have indicated that we should end our date here," I said, as convincingly as I could.

"My horoscope *did* say there would be a strong presence of water today," he mused.

You'd think that, along with all of his other insights into our future, he could have shared that one with me.

"Don't worry, Aurora." He grabbed my hands reassuringly. "For our next date, I'll make sure that Venus is in a favorable position!"

I pulled my hands away. "Great . . . next time. Call me, okay?"

Bradley wandered back to his car, looking dreamily up at the heavens. I breathed a sigh of relief and hobbled up our too-long driveway. My mother had insisted on its length to give our place "atmosphere" (i.e., it made it look impressive).

What a night. So much for my aim to exude an Audrey Hepburn–like elegance. And why hadn't Cassie called me? I couldn't believe she'd failed me.

"Another successful date, hmm?"

Hayden Paris, my neighbor, former childhood playmate, and ever-reliable bane of my life, stood grinning on his side of the not-high-enough fence that separated our properties. His hazel eyes danced with amusement as he spun a basketball between his hands.

Was Hayden to be witness to every embarrassment of my dating life? Just three weeks ago, he'd seen Daniel Benis get stabbed in the eye when I'd employed Option 2: Evasive Maneuver as Daniel tried to kiss me on my doorstep—unfortunately forgetting that my drink had a second straw sticking out the other side.

"At least it was you that got injured, not your date this time, so he can't press charges."

Please. Daniel had been such a baby about it. He'd worn an eye patch for, like, six days afterwards. Bravery was now one of the crucial characteristics I was looking for in a date. At least Daniel had been so embarrassed about the cause of his temporary blindness that he hadn't breathed a word to anyone.

I rolled my eyes. "Funny, somehow I knew I could rely on Mr. Zero Compassion to humiliate me even further."

"Come on, Princess." He drummed the basketball against the ground, wearing his constant smirk. "You have to admit it was funny. Bradley kissing the passenger seat while his date tumbles into the water? His ill-judged attempt at chivalry resulting in a mud-covered shirt and a girl scrambling away from him? Priceless! Best part of all? His face when he realized that your white dress is see-through when wet—"

"*What?*" I screamed, looking down at my dress. The outline of my lacy white bra was plainly visible.

Hayden tossed me his jacket to cover up. "Mr. Bradley Yes-I'm-a-Sensitive-Sagittarius may say he focuses purely on the spiritual things in life, but I'd swear on my unblemished academic record that his mind was very much on physical things at that moment. I wanted to give him a piece of my mind."

"Enough!" I yelled. "Listen here, Hayden Paris. This unnatural interest in my dating life? There's a word for it: *spying*." I knew I must be turning red. I hated the way Hayden wound me up. It was like every time he opened his mouth I completely lost it. "How would you like it if I made it my special interest to offer a running commentary on *your* dates?"

Hayden raised an eyebrow. "I have a basketball hoop here, remember?" As if to prove his point, he sent the ball straight through the net. "How can I help it if I'm out here sinking a few baskets and accidentally witness your dramatics, using tonight as an example, exactly sixteen feet away?"

"Accidentally? Who plays basketball at ten p.m.? You can't even see out here!"

"Your logic's a little off tonight, Princess." Hayden sank another basket. "One minute you're accusing me of spying on you; the next you're claiming it's too dark out here to be witness to anything, accidentally or on purpose." He grinned, his impossibly perfect teeth showing.

"Well, all I know, *Paris*, is next time you have a date, I'll be sitting out here on the excuse of catching some rays at ten p.m., okay?"

"I'm afraid you won't have much opportunity," Hayden said. "I'm not dating at the moment. You could say I'm hyperaware of the dangers involved, both emotional and physical." He mimicked Daniel clutching his eye in pain.

I refused to respond to his mockery of my maimed date. "Well, the female populace is safe for now. Excuse me while I spread the good news." I gave him a little wave and turned and walked away with dignity. Well, as much dignity as I could manage with squelching shoes.

I was almost at my front door when he called after me. "Hey, by the way, Princess? Your mascara's not waterproof. Just thought I'd let you know."

"Arrgghh!"

I slammed the front door. I'd never get the last word with Hayden Paris.

Once inside, I stopped and did the covert listening thing, praying that the NAD (New Age dad) wasn't home. As of right now, only three people had witnessed my date-turned-nightmare, and I wanted to keep it that way. Luckily, there was no sign of him.

My dad's been going through a midlife crisis thing that involves, as he puts it, "a critical examination of my core values and the societal construction of my self-identity." He told me this when I caught him *destroying* his interior-designed bedroom and office. He called it "freeing himself from baggage," which seemed to involve tossing out a large number of personal belongings, including several Ralph Lauren jackets and some Tiffany & Co. cuff links. I'm grateful I've been able to keep him away from the rest of the house. I mean, the minimalist look can be stylish, but the NAD's taking it *way* too far. Since he stripped his office of all its furnishings, he's been forced to do any after-hours work sitting cross-legged on a hemp cushion, with his laptop perched awkwardly on his knees. Personally, I consider the laptop to be a complete contradiction of his new philosophy, but when I asked him about it, he muttered something along the lines of "the unavoidability of conformity in the modern world," while his new CD played soothing whale sounds in the background. Conformity must be the reason he's still wearing his Armani suits to work at the advertising agency, where he's a creative director. I'm keeping my fingers crossed the changes are just a NAD fad and everything will return to normal, including the decor.

Seeing the NAD was out, I could dash straight to the bathroom. As I caught sight of myself in the full-length mirror, I let out an involuntary shriek. Without Hayden's jacket, my dress was undeniably see-through, my modesty barely preserved by the sporadic sprinkling of the small pebbles and blades of grass I'd picked up in the puddle. The look was topped off by massive black rings around my eyes. I looked like a waterlogged panda.

When I stepped out of the shower, it was like I'd been on one of those makeover shows, except it was the old me—sans mud and dishevelment—staring out from the mirror.

I generally try not to think too much about my appearance— okay, that's a slight lie. I am a teenage girl (sixteen and six months, to be exact), so a fair amount of my time is spent on grooming and choosing outfits. But I like to focus on my inner self and improve what really matters—mind, heart, and soul. What's the point of a fifty-dollar haircut on a fifty-cent head, right? I want to know who Aurora Skye really is.

That's my full name, and it totally sounds like the NAD was responsible for it, but it was my mother who named me. She likes herself (her name is Avery) and anyone associated with her to stand out from the crowd. Despite the schoolyard teasing that inevitably comes with standing out from the crowd, I like my name. It means "dawn sky," which sounds very poetic and inspiring. It's also a great name for an author, which I plan to be. Lately, I've been thinking of penning a self-help book for teenage girls, since—as you can see from my sad example—our lives are fraught with peril, and the answers to our most important questions about love, life, and meaning don't get taught in school.

As I made my way up our thickly carpeted stairs to my bedroom, my presence was met with two meows.

"Hello, my precious pumpkins!"

I picked up Snookums, my marmalade tomcat, and his purr motor started on cue. Bebe, my Birman, wrapped herself around my legs.

"How are you guys doing?"

I worry that my cats, due to being left alone all day, may feel deprived of mental stimulation. I recently saw this great ad for a DVD with over three continuous hours of fish and bird scenes to engage the feline mind. I think it would fast-track Snookums's and Bebe's synaptic development, but I haven't worked up the nerve to ask the NAD for something new at a time when he seems to be parting with just about all unnecessary (in his opinion) material possessions. I don't want to interfere if he's at the crux of self-realization.

Snookums (obviously not named by my mother) has been my pal since I was six. One morning I found this tiny bundle of orange fluff meowing his hardest at our front door. We were only supposed to keep him till he could be relocated (as my mom called it), but I wasn't letting my furry friend go anywhere, and I begged until my mom agreed he could stay, "but only as an outside cat." Snookums now sleeps in a satin-lined basket in my bedroom. Dad bought me Bebe when he and Mom split up. That was four years ago. One Sunday, Dad and I came home from bonding time at the mall and Mom wasn't there. I figured she was at Yogilates or the beauty salon or something, but as we found out from our answering machine, she was actually in London. She said she needed to breathe.

It sounds weird, but the first thing to come out of my mouth was, "Couldn't she just have gone down to the park for some fresh air?"

My dad got the strangest look on his face before he let out an odd, choke-like laugh.

The answering machine message was followed by a series of postcards from various points across the globe, with hastily scribbled explanations such as *I felt stifled* or *Being a wife or a mother never came naturally to me.* None of those statements—totally at odds with the cheery scenes depicted on the postcards' fronts (*Greetings from Ibiza!*)—made my dad or me feel any better or any less confused, but perhaps they helped Mom to heal. For ages after she left, I had this weird fear that one day I'd come home and my dad would be gone, too.

Anyway, a month after the Answering Machine Incident (as it became known), Dad came into my room holding Bebe, a purebred seal point Birman (a beautiful longhaired cat with chocolate tips and white paws). She was crazy expensive—a fluffy guilt gift, I guess—but taking care of her resplendent-bordering-on-excessive hair and making sure she was happy (she's a very fussy cat) was an effective distraction. I slowly stopped feeling so sad. After all, my mom had never been very maternal. Most of the time she'd been preoccupied with new home furnishings.

After she left, Dad replaced just about everything in our Spanish-style house. Freedom Furniture's profits must have soared that year, since every time the thought of my mom crossed his mind we'd head on down there and load up a new couch or lamp. Now, four years later, my mom had returned with a Spanish boyfriend, and Dad, the NAD, was off-loading everything.

Despite the attentions of Snookums and Bebe, I was starting to feel a tad down after my disastrous date. I was thankful when the phone rang.

"So, did it go fabulously? You have to tell me every single detail, okay?" Cassie cried, before I'd even said hello.

I sighed. "Does that include an unwanted kiss, an almost-drowning, and an ego-crushing run-in with Hayden Paris?"

"*What?* I thought you guys were planning to go to La Bella Donna. How'd you end up at the beach with Hayden?"

"The beach? All of this happened in my driveway!" I briefly filled her in on the night's unfortunate events, knowing her to be the soul of discretion. "Where were you, Cass? What happened to Operation Stop Kiss?"

"Where was your text? I was watching out for it, but it never arrived, so I figured your date was a true meeting of souls."

"You never got my text?" A feeling of horror ran through me. "Oh god. If it didn't go to you, who did it go to?"

It had been nearly impossible to see in the car, and I'd been trying to be discreet while Bradley jabbered on about astrologically favorable locations.

I rifled through my still-damp evening bag. My cell lit up with ONE NEW MESSAGE.

"Please let this be non-Operation-related," I whispered as I pressed OPEN MESSAGE.

No such luck.

Operation Stop Kiss? How about Operation START KISS? Oh baby!

Great. Ryan Danfield, whom I'd brushed off two months ago because of his unappealing thriftiness (our finest dining experience was at McDonald's), had taken my text as fresh encouragement. I'd only just managed to get free of his endless phone calls and e-mails.

"Arrgghh!" I sank back into my chair. "Why Ryan?"

"Don't worry. Ryan may be worryingly cheap, but he's harmless enough," Cassie said. "What was wrong with Bradley Scott? Bradley could totally take on Zac Efron in a hotness contest. And he's deep—look how he's always talking about destiny and the meaning of life!"

"He got a little too deep when he claimed he was actively practicing astral travel in the hope of achieving greater intimacy with intergalactic beings."

"What?" I could hear the giggles rising up in Cassie's throat.

"Evidently I don't hold much appeal, if Bradley's prepared to travel several light-years to find a better match." I burst into laughter. "I wanted unique, and I certainly got it!"

Uniqueness is one of the qualities I deem necessary in a prospective partner, and I'm always really careful to make sure that potential candidates possess it before saying yes to a date. I'd said yes to

Bradley Scott because he was always talking about the stars and the universe. Little did I know he viewed it as a galaxy-wide dating pool equivalent to match.com. I'd been impressed that Daniel Benis wrote poetry, although I discovered later that this consisted purely of odes to his new Ford Falcon. And Ryan Danfield had seemed like the strong, silent, Heathcliff from *Wuthering Heights* type, until I realized the reason for his silence was a lack of activity in the cerebral area.

"Oh, Cass," I said, turning serious, "I really am tempted to call off the search for a while. I think my soul mate is a long way from Jefferson High."

"Aurora! You're always telling me that it's only possible to find your true love if you put in the dedication, right?"

"Right . . ."

"So now is not the time to give up! You know what they say about frogs and princes."

"Huh?"

"You fell right into the home of the frogs tonight—literally! Prince Charming must be within sight. He's probably calling out for you right now!"

I could almost hear something!

"Cass," I said dreamily, "there *is* a sound."

"Do you mean that buzzing noise?" she said.

"Yes!"

"Oh, that's just Andrew. Mom and Dad have left me in charge again, but there's nothing I can do to stop him joyriding up and down our street."

Cassie's brother recently saw *Rebel Without a Cause* and was so inspired he started up his own neighborhood motorcycle gang.

"I don't know why your parents don't just take the bike away from him," I said.

"They're proud that he's showing some leadership qualities."

Cassie's parents are psychologists; hence the interesting parenting philosophy.

"Oh no, I've got to run," Cassie added. "Old Mrs. Barker's yelling again—I think the guys just knocked over her garbage can."

"Cass, first day back at school means the opportunity to meet Potential Princes. Remember to wear your best!"

"Gotta go!" she cried, as the buzzing in the background got even louder.

Thank god I'm an only child.

Cass is the only person who knows my deepest, darkest secret, one that could make me the laughingstock of our entire school. I'm sixteen and I've never been kissed.

It all has to do with Sleeping Beauty. Yes, the fairy tale. When I was five, I was completely obsessed with it—partly because the princess and I share the name Aurora, but mostly because of how romantic it is. A beautiful maiden, asleep in a crumbling, rose-filled tower, waiting for love's first kiss. A prince fighting through a forest to get to her, then falling madly in love within seconds of beholding her. And then that all-powerful kiss—able to bring the princess back to life, to transform her, to awaken her. Even at five, I realized that locking lips was a very powerful thing.

And so, ever since, I've saved my first kiss for my Prince. I've opted out of truth or dare, spin the bottle, and all other lip-orientated high school games, and I've ducked and maneuvered my way out of a multitude of good-night smooches. It hasn't been easy. Most guys try to make a move on the first date; thus the creation of Operation Stop Kiss. The only problem is, my dedication to saving my first kiss for my Prince seems to be leading to no end of embarrassing situations.

I groaned, thinking again of tonight's near miss. If only boys would give you a little more warning of an imminent kiss. A yell of "Incoming!" or something.

It was getting late. I fed Snookums and Bebe their evening meal, then traipsed back into my room. I reflected on my conversation with Cassie. As always, she'd restored my peace of mind and strengthened my focus, like only a childhood bestie can. Dating can certainly drag a girl down, especially if the pressure is on to set an example for others.

I haven't told you yet about one of the most important aspects of my life: the Find a Prince™ program (FPP). It's a self-help program for teenage girls, which I designed myself. Over many years of negotiating the minefield that is the high school dating scene, I've seen girls get their hearts maimed by boys left, right, and center. Consequently, I decided that any investment of my heart had to be soundly investigated beforehand. Call me calculating, but I want to invest my time and emotions in a guy who thoroughly deserves them. Aka a Prince.

Now, many girls would probably get sarcastic at this point and say that the whole idea of Prince Charming is ridiculously outdated. However, my Find a Prince™ program has nothing to do with glass slippers, poisoned apples, or talking woodland animals. It's about us girls valuing ourselves and saying no to guys who use or abuse us. Guys who play around with our feelings like it's a form of sport. Guys who consider a relationship to be code for gaining a more intimate knowledge of our bra size. It's about realizing we deserve better. The FPP's chief decree is that every girl deserves to be treated like a princess. And who better to do that than a Prince?

A Prince:

- has **P**rinciples. He stands up for what he knows to be right instead of going along with the crowd.
- **R**ecognizes your worth. He understands how special you are and treats you with respect and kindness.
- possesses **I**ntegrity. He's genuine with his feelings and won't mislead you for underhanded or selfish purposes.
- **N**ever doubts that you're the only one for him.
- is **C**onstant. He stands by you through the sunshine and the shadows.
- possesses **E**ndurance. He's willing to overcome considerable obstacles to win your affection.

This list might sound slightly full-on, but I don't think any girl should compromise when it comes to how a guy treats her.

That's not to say we should lie around waiting like some damsel in distress. Part 2 of the FPP is realizing that a modern princess makes her own destiny. I always keep my eyes open for Potential Prince candidates (PPCs) and take advantage of dates to assess a guy's prospective princely qualities.

So far, only Cassie and I are following the program, though I plan to take it to the next level once we've gotten results. It's taking some time, which I put down to the often abysmal choices provided by high school boys, who, sadly, have their minds on spitballs instead of soul mates. I hoped that this year, heading into junior year, things would be more promising.

2 the glide-by

"How do I look?" Jelena asked.

Cass and I carefully studied her as the three of us stood by the school gate the next morning.

"Amazing, as always," I replied, looking at Jelena's long, sleek black hair, navy-blue eyes, and alabaster complexion—features that have longing male gazes following her like children after the Pied Piper. Jelena has an exotic air that I'm convinced comes from her Russian ancestry.

"You're positive?" she said.

Normally Jelena wouldn't even consider the possibility that she might look anything other than perfect (and with her looks, it's completely understandable), but today was a crucial day. A day when an outfit could make or break a girl. The first day back after summer break.

Summer is a transformative time for any teen—just consider the movie *Dirty Dancing*—and there's always a touch of uncertainty, a hint of fear, the essence of possibility in the air on the first day of the new school year. The entire social structure of a high school can revolutionize itself in those six short hours. I knew that Jelena wanted to be dead certain that her social status was secure for another year.

Jelena possesses such fabulous qualities as confidence, never-ending energy, and an innovative mind, but she has something of an obsession with being popular. Her goal is to be CEO of an international company in ten years, and she thinks Jefferson High is the perfect place to practice using her influence. Ever heard the phrase "an iron fist in a velvet glove"? Well, that's Jelena. On many an occasion I've had to talk her out of implementing a system of serfdom. It's thanks to her that our group is, as she puts it, "akin to reigning tsars."

Jelena looked at me critically, gesturing at her form-fitting cream-colored dress. Attending a school where free dress is permitted meant the stakes were especially high. "Are you absolutely sure, stake your future on it, that I look like a teen queen?"

"Yes!" I said. "And Cass, you look fab, too."

Cassie wore dark denim short shorts, a baby-pink top, and a diamanté headband atop her fairest-of-fair blond curls. Those curls, along with her fawn-colored eyes, petite features, and voluptuous pout, would probably enable Cass to get away with murder. However, she's as good as she is beautiful.

"So let's head on in," I said. I was dying to see what was new on the first day back.

"I don't know." Jelena arched a brow. "It's important to build anticipation."

"Don't you want to be the first to check out any new talent?" I asked.

If there's one word that motivates Jelena, it's *first*. She views life as a battleground in which she must be the constant victor.

"Let's go," she commanded.

We clicked our identity rings together, a gesture left over from primary school but one we can't help resurrecting every so often. The rings reflect how we like to see ourselves. Cassie's ring reads "Angel," Jelena's is "Power," and mine, naturally, is "Princess." Hayden Paris happened to catch sight of the ring years ago and now refuses to call me anything else. Probably in the hope of embarrassing me. There's no knowing what goes on in that disturbed mind of his.

We smiled at each other and stepped onto the school grounds. Jelena gave a satisfied nod smile as she did a perimeter scan. "Fantastic. There's no one capable of challenging our status."

I spotted Hayden sitting among a group of guys underneath the big pine. Two of them were playing guitar. When Hayden caught sight of me, he sent me a cheeky grin.

"Hayden's looking at you," Cassie announced in a singsong voice.

I groaned. "Don't remind me. He's probably replaying the image of me sitting in that puddle, again and again, like some sweet reverie."

Cass, Jelena, and I are really close, but we also have two other girls who make up our group: Lindsay and Sara. They joined us at our surveillance spot at the edge of the school grounds.

Lindsay is petite, with wavy chestnut locks, dark eyes, and year-round bronzed skin, which half the school is jealous of and attempts to replicate with Ambre Solaire, with varying success rates. The other important thing to know about Lindsay is that she's part of TylerandLindsay, which isn't two businesses joined into one super-company but a couple who have been going out for so long and so seriously that the entire student body views them as a single entity. I was surprised that Tyler wasn't glued to Lindsay's side. I looked around and saw he was sitting nearby. Lindsay was blowing I-can't-believe-we're-separated kisses to him, and he was making a show of catching each one in his palm. Oh, brother.

Lindsay's identity ring will come as no surprise—it reads "Love."

Sara was telling some long, involved story, as usual. "And then they told me that they were discontinuing that brand, so I said, 'Well, how am I going to manage without it? Youths with significant expendable incomes are looking to this pharmacy to provide different options!' And then he got all self-righteous and so I demanded to see someone more superior and—"

Sara's ring reads "Diva." Everything about her is dramatic—from her bright-red hair to the way she handles situations. To get out of PE last year, Sara didn't complain of PMS or a strained ankle; instead, she fainted and had half the basketball team carry her to the nurse's office while the other half ran for water and smelling salts. It's virtually impossible to keep up with her constant level of hysteria, so I tune her out when she's not actually experiencing a real crisis. I think most of us do, to tell you the truth.

"HS." Jelena's voice was loud and clear.

We had a hottie spotting.

"Where?" Cass glanced everywhere, not so subtly.

"Don't make it so obvious!" Jelena hissed. "Twelve o'clock!"

We all looked straight ahead, toward a group of guys from our grade. Among them were two new, highly attractive faces. The one on the left had sun-streaked blond hair and a wide grin that displayed dimples in both cheeks. Even from a distance, his baby blues were very striking.

"Potential Prince," Cass breathed to me.

The guy on the right had something no other guy in the school had: a goatee. That alone was impressive. He leaned against the brick wall, showing off his muscular arms to perfection. Every so often he'd run his fingers through his dark, perfectly styled hair.

"Guy on the right looks potentially egotistical," I said.

"Girl standing next to me obviously hit her head when she fell last night, because guy on the right is godly," Jelena replied.

"Exactly—looking down on the rest of us mere mortals," I retorted.

"If he's conceited, he has every right to be," Jelena said. "Look at him! Should we approach?"

Sara was still going on with her pharmaceutical sob story, and Lindsay had obviously decided she couldn't take the separation from her beloved any longer, since she and Tyler were now sharing a swing, so the three of us looked at each other and made a decision.

"High heels?" Cass asked.

"Check!" we all cried.

"Time for the Glide-By," Jelena said.

The Glide-By, like scarlet lipstick, is based on evolutionary tendencies—though it's likely Darwin never saw this one coming!

In the Glide-By, you wear an eye-catching outfit but pair it with *loud* shoes. This is because, although a guy's sight is his primary sense when it comes to attraction, you often need to combine the visual with sound to really make an impact. Back in caveman days, men were trained to focus on their direct line of sight in order to spot prey. This evolutionary tendency is still part of the modern man's makeup, so he might not pick up on your presence, no matter how gorgeous you are, if you happen to be slightly out of his line of sight.

This is where the loud shoes are vital. They announce your presence. The minute a guy hears a loud sound, such as a pair of heels among the near-silent scuffing of sneakers, he will almost always turn his eyes toward it—an instinct from the days when responding to a sound could mean life or death for him and his tribe. Once his eyes are on you, the gorgeous outfit will have its desired impact. And, if your glide-by is successful and he becomes smitten, he may even learn to recognize the exact sound of your particular heels in a crowd, the way penguins recognize a partner among thousands of identical birds.

We headed up the path toward the guys, our heels drumming an ancient arrival call. As we hit the spot, five yards away, all eyes lifted from various Hacky Sack games and skateboard tricks. The boys looked at us; we looked at them. There was this moment of intense silence during which we mutually evaluated each other. The Glide-By was running smoothly so far.

Just when it looked like we would attempt an approach, Cass, Jelena, and I smiled simultaneously, turned abruptly, and headed for the history and arts block. We could feel the gazes following us. The Glide-By was a success.

You should never speak too soon.

"Hey, Princess!" Hayden's voice boomed out across the schoolyard, instantly destroying any intriguing aftereffects of the Glide-By. "When am I going to get my jacket back?"

"In medieval England, beer was often served with breakfast," Mr. Bannerman, our history teacher, announced.

His announcement was met with loud cheers from the male students. Several guys punched their fists in the air.

"Man, these historical dudes had it good!"

I love history. It has all the good stuff—intrigue, corruption, love affairs, characters full of good, characters full of evil. If I'd lived back then, I would have been the one watching everything and jotting it all down on parchment with a quill pen.

"Now, I'm sorry to tell you, Aurora," Mr. Bannerman said, as if he had read my thoughts, "that with your statuesque height, you might have had trouble finding a husband, since the average man was only about five foot six."

Okay, there would have definitely been some downsides to life back then.

"She would have had to bend down to kiss him!" Jeffrey yelled.

Now the whole class was laughing. Hayden Paris turned around in his seat and gave me a wink.

Hayden has sat directly in front of me for ten years now. I don't know who came up with the idea of alphabetical seating, but if I had a time machine, I'd go back, ascertain their identity, and then sue them for inflicting mental and emotional anguish. Maybe I could sue for physical pain as well, since I'm sure I've strained my arm as a result of all the years of hitting Hayden with a ruler when he's too impossible to deal with. Which, if you know Hayden Paris, is just about always. I'm too mature and poised to use the ruler anymore, so I have to rely on my wit.

Luckily, my embarrassment was brought to an end by the arrival of the new blue-eyed boy we'd seen earlier this morning. He leaned on the doorframe, sliding a lock of sun-streaked hair back behind his ear.

"Is this the eleventh-grade history class?" he asked.

"None other," replied Mr. Bannerman. "Hope you're ready for bloodshed, Mr. . . . . let's see . . . Scott Ryder."

Blue-eyed boy smiled a confused but still delicious smile. Cassie, who sat on my left, could barely conceal a squeal of delight.

"Scott Ryder!" she whispered to me.

My guess was we'd soon be seeing that name scrawled on Cassie's books.

While Mr. Bannerman verified Scott's details, Hayden turned around and leaned his elbows on the front of my desk.

"So, pretty soon I'll be trumping you in history tests."

"Hayden, I beat you every week last semester—"

"Not every week. We tied, in that one about Charlemagne, re-member?"

How could I forget? It had been so embarrassing seeing our names up on the board together, like an engagement announcement or something.

"Whatever," I said breezily. "Why would I stop that amazing run now?" I smiled in what I hoped was a superior way.

Hayden just smiled back and stayed silent.

"Well, *why* then?" I demanded.

He shrugged. "Well, with all the dating you've been doing, you're bound to get distracted. Drift off into Harlequin Romance fantasies. Potent stuff. Naturally, your studies will suffer. Since I'm not par-ticipating in the dating game, I think it's safe to say that it'll be top of the class for me all this year." He raised his chin in a smug gesture.

"Paris, if I haven't let your incessant ramblings distract me all these years, a date or two isn't going to have a chance against my iron-willed focus. And," I added, "you know nothing about my fantasies."

"No, I don't," he agreed. "But knowing you, they'd be something highly original."

I looked at him suspiciously. Was he saying I was a creative thinker, or warped in the head?

Before I had a chance to reply, Mr. Bannerman pointed Scott to the seat next to Cassie. All the girls in the class looked at her with envy. At least alphabetical seating was having a positive effect on someone's life.

"Now, a small assignment," Mr. Bannerman said, pausing at the window. Everyone groaned. "I said *small,* people. We've got to get those sleepy brains buzzing again after such a long break. I would like you to research one aspect of medieval history that interests you and present it to the class next Tuesday."

I already knew what I'd research. I wrote the words *courtly love* on my notepad in swirly script, then caught Hayden peering at it.

"Courtly love? Sorry, Princess, but I think I've already got that one in the bag."

"I think you'd better think again, because I've already claimed it," I replied.

"You just said you're not the Harlequin type and, technically, courtly love could be considered historical romance." He grinned. "Because you don't want to pollute your mind with any clichéd topics, you should probably leave that one to me."

"You? Discussing romance? Ha!"

Hayden put on a hurt face. "I think I might be all right at it. After all, I've been doing a lot of observing lately." He gave me a significant look.

"Observing?" I repeated, curiosity getting the better of me.

"Well, you keep accusing me of spying on your dates," he said and shrugged. "So, technically, I guess I'm learning about romance firsthand. It seems kind of brutal, judging from the good-night ritual I saw last night."

My blood wasn't boiling, but it was pretty warm. Despite that, I was not going to lose my temper. I was determined that, this year, Hayden Paris wasn't going to destroy my composure.

"But I haven't seen the whole picture," he went on. "I was thinking I could sit in on the restaurant part of it; help you assess your dates. I would have given Bradley Scott a strike right off the bat."

"My dates are none of your business!"

"If I'm doing the study, they are."

"Study something else!" I hissed, just as Mr. Bannerman arrived at my desk.

I smiled. "Mr. Bannerman! I have the best idea for this assignment—"

"Aurora, I'm afraid I'm going to have to remind you that drawing on school property is not allowed," Mr. Bannerman interrupted, looking serious.

"What?" I said. The last time I defaced anything was when I was four, and my mother's reaction to my mural on our dining room wall had stopped me from sketching on anything ever again.

I took a closer look at where Mr. Bannerman was pointing. There was a heart drawn on the front of my desk. I struggled to read the scrawled black words inside it. "I love . . . HR?" I guessed.

"HP," Hayden put in helpfully. "I never suspected you had such intense feelings for me, Princess."

"W-what?" I stuttered. Then it dawned on me. "You!" I cried. "You graffitied my desk!"

"Nothing you can do will ever make me admit it," Hayden said, as solemnly as someone can when they're suppressing a smile. "Don't worry, Mr. Bannerman," he added, "it's nonpermanent. Aurora can take advantage of the situation to get me alone at break and help me clean it off."

"You're driving me crazy!" I cried.

There went my composure. The whole history class turned to look at us.

"A person can only drive you crazy if you give them the keys," Hayden said with mock serenity, like some sort of Buddhist monk.

"You've *stolen* the keys!" I yelled.

He just looked at me and raised his eyebrows.

The bell rang before I could kill him.

3 contact established

If you guessed that I didn't stick around to help Hayden Paris clean my desk during break, you'd be dead right. Instead, I watched him through the window. Seeing him furiously scrubbing my desk with a bottle of heavy-duty cleaning fluid and rags soothed my anger slightly. For once, justice had been served.

"What was the deal with you and Hayden in history?" Cassie said, pulling me away from the window. "It seemed to get pretty heated."

"Heated? This went beyond heated years ago. An accurate picture would be a deadly battle."

"A deadly battle? Ooh, tell me more!" Jelena came around the corner. Instead of history, she took business studies. As you can imagine, she was acing the subject. "Who with?"

"Someone who doesn't fight fair," I said.

"Hayden again," Cassie whispered to Jelena.

"One of these days, you're going to discover why Hayden Paris gets you so worked up," Jelena said, swerving around a game of handball going on in the corridor.

I clenched my jaw. "I know why he gets me so worked up! He's deliberately set out to persecute me ever since he moved into the area. When I was six years old, he pushed me into the pool at the get-to-know-the-neighbors barbecue his parents threw. I could have drowned!"

"It was a wading pool, Aurora," Cassie said, in what I considered a very uncaring way.

"Pool, wading pool, what's the difference? He still had devious intentions."

Jelena made a pained face. "Not to be insensitive here, but can we please drop the Hayden subject? For two reasons: the first being, Aurora, no offense, but to the general public you seem to be bordering on crazy when it comes to Hayden—"

"Hey," I said, feeling hurt.

Jelena's voice dropped several decibels. "And the second is obvious if you study the boys positioned at three o'clock."

We all pretended to look over at the school fountain, but what we were really studying was Scott Ryder and the other new guy we'd noticed in the schoolyard earlier that morning.

"Did you get any info on Goatee Guy?" I asked Jelena.

"He wasn't in business studies. I'm hoping for some kind of alignment in our schedules somewhere."

"Scott Ryder sits next to me in history!" Cassie said excitedly to Jelena.

"Have you established contact?"

"I felt way too shy to say anything."

"See, that's where guys have it easy," Jelena said. "They can just toss a pencil or paper ball at us to get our attention."

The moves of high school boys—Casanova had nothing on them. I tried to imagine Cassie lobbing her pencil at someone.

"So," I said, breaking into my friends' daydreams, "plan of approach?"

As the FPP specifies, a girl's got to actively seek out her Prince. Once she spots him, it's important to take action.

"I think Lose an Earring would work well," Jelena suggested.

"Who's doing the losing?" I asked, even though I already knew the answer. Cassie always plays the role of the loser, since she's so sweet and innocent-looking. No one could ever suspect her of setting up a fake situation.

Our plan was off and running. Cassie handed me one pink dangly earring and we started walking toward the two boys. Just as we were about to reach them, Cass's hat brushed against a branch of the fig tree and fell down over her right ear.

"Oh no!" she cried in a slightly louder than normal voice, putting her hand to her ear. "I think I've dropped an earring!"

She and Jelena dropped to their knees and started combing the ground with their palms. Scott Ryder and Goatee Guy looked over at them, then at each other, then leaped off their lunch table to join in the hunt.

Scott dropped down next to Cass. "What does it look like? Did you just notice it missing? Is it expensive?" The questions were exhaled in one breath.

While the girls were explaining just how the earring had been lost and giving its exact description, I discreetly dropped said item just to the right of them. Yes, it's a highly calculated maneuver, but if it helps you make contact with a crush and establish a friendly rapport, can it really be harmful?

"It's pink," Cass said, gazing at Scott's face instead of where she was supposed to be looking. Luckily, Scott's eyes were on the ground.

"Pale pink, bubblegum pink, or hot pink?" he asked.

Cassie looked at him in shock.

"I have thirteen-year-old twin sisters," he explained. "I've heard them painstakingly discussing the shade of a new nail polish."

I was impressed. A boy who knows his colors demonstrates that he pays attention to detail.

Just then, Scott spotted the earring. Both he and Cassie moved toward it at the same time and collided, knocking heads.

"Oof!" Scott said.

"Ow," Cass moaned.

They stood up, both rubbing their heads.

Jelena took control of the situation. "So, to whom do we owe our endless thanks?"

Goatee Guy smiled and extended his hand to her. "Alex West." He gave her a wink. "This is my trusty friend of two hours, Scott Ryder. Fresh meat has to stick together."

"Jelena Cantrill." Jelena took his hand and shook it confidently.

"Aurora Skye." I gave them both a little wave.

Cassie just stood looking dazedly at Scott.

"You're Cassie Shields," he said, smiling at her. "I saw your name on your pencil case in history."

He'd noticed! Majorly good sign.

"I like your sneakers," Jelena said, checking out Alex's up-to-the-minute footwear. "Do you play a lot of sports?"

"I don't just play," Alex said. "I *live* sports. At my old school, I was captain of the soccer and basketball teams. Both ended up in the nationals last year. I also played for the U-17 soccer team—"

Scott turned to me, smiling. "You said your name was Aurora Skye, right? I already know all about you through a friend."

Word of how fabulous I am had obviously spread throughout the land.

"I'm an old friend of Hayden Paris," Scott went on. "He's part of the reason that I transferred here."

What do you know? Hayden had actually come in handy for once. Thanks to him, Cassie had a Potential Prince at her fingertips.

"I saw you sitting behind him in history but only just put two and two together now. I think my brain's still running a little slow after the holidays." He smiled, flashing those incredible dimples.

Cassie and I grinned back at him. Dimples like that excused any lapses of memory.

Scott glanced around the crowd. "Hayden said he'd meet me where Alex and I were sitting before. I wonder what kept him away?"

Graffiti and its removal came instantly to mind, but there was no way I was going to get into that with Scott. Who knew what Hayden had told him about me? I was going to have to do my best to make a good impression, for the sake of Cassie's romantic future. Friends are a powerful influence upon dating decisions. Any further talk about Hayden's and my tumultuous relationship could inhibit Scott's favorable opinion of Cass.

Luckily, I was saved from any Hayden-related chat as the bell sounded for class.

"Yes!" As soon as the boys left, Jelena punched the air triumphantly, making several heads turn. "Contact has been established."

Cassie didn't say anything, but her ear-to-ear grin spoke for itself.

"Play it cool, Agent J," I said. Nothing gets Jelena more excited than a successful power play. "Remember, at this stage it's important to evaluate the subject impartially."

"Impartially speaking, he's gorgeous and a champion athlete."

"What about the bad points?"

I remembered how Alex had carefully looked us over before he talked to us. I suspected he was making sure we were the "right type" to associate with.

"Oh, I'll think of the bad points later," Jelena said breezily. "Did you know he has an interest in social structures, too? He asked me lots of questions about which groups were which. I, of course, indicated modestly that we belong to the most socially desirable one."

Oh, brother.

"This is shaping up to be one fabulous start to the semester," Jelena said, sweeping her fingers through her hair.

"That's for sure," I said as I looked at Cass's happy face.

As Jelena and I headed for the performance room where our first dance class was to be held, my heart felt so light I could have floated away. Normally I hated gym, but dancing might actually be fun. I pictured myself waltzing around the room with a dashing partner. He was just telling me how divinely I danced when reality cut in. The other members of our class had stopped at the doorway of the performance room and were peering in with wide eyes. Curious, I did the same.

A woman with the longest brown ringlets I'd ever seen, wearing a wispy white dress, was standing in the center of the room, her arms raised in a dramatic arc. The scent of sandalwood floated through the air, along with the soft strains of flute and harp coming from the speaker system.

"You may enter," she said.

Everyone looked at each other dumbly. Was this even the dance class?

"Anyone who is late will receive a mark against their name."

Okay, she was obviously a teacher. We all filed in cautiously.

"Welcome," the woman said in a soft voice. "My name is Dana DeForest."

"Is that your real name?" Jeffrey Clark asked, curiosity obviously getting the better of him.

"No, it is my soul name, one that resonates more strongly than the name I was given by my parents, Mr. . . . ?"

"Oceanus," Jeffrey said.

Everyone snickered.

"You are here to expand your consciousness," Ms. DeForest continued, unperturbed, "through interpretive dance. I am here, as your teacher, to lead you along the path to enlightenment."

I wasn't sure I wanted to be led along Ms. DeForest's path. It looked like one trodden by people who spent a lot of money on incense.

"Now, if everyone could move into a circle, we'll start some relaxation exercises. I want you all to loosen up from the waist down. Pretend you have an oversized backside and you're shaking it around."

What?

I wasn't the only one standing with my mouth open in shock.

"Do I have to remind you, class, that participation in these exercises makes up forty percent of your mark?" Ms. DeForest hit a button on the iPod and the harp music switched to a fast tribal beat.

Everyone got moving. With all the gyrating, the room looked like an MTV music video. Next thing you knew, we'd be wearing hot pants. I jiggled halfheartedly to the tribal music before deciding that I'd had it. It was time to put a stop to this.

"Why are you pausing, Miss . . . ?" Ms. DeForest stood in front of me, displeased.

"Aurora Skye." I put my hands on my hips. "I'm pausing because I think this is a derogatory exercise for women. I don't want everyone looking at my butt. I want them to listen to what I have to say as a person!"

Ms. DeForest's response was cool. "Ms. Skye, you've got to let go of your attitude that everyone is focusing on you. Everyone is concentrating on the exercise. *No one* is looking at your butt!"

"Actually, I was looking," Jeffrey said.

"Yeah, I was, too," Jesse Cook added.

A few other male voices joined in with further confirmation.

"Sorry to say, Miss, but as red-blooded men, we were studying all the girls' butts," Travis said.

The female element of the class let out a collective shriek and clamped their hands over their backsides.

"*Enough!*" A vein was throbbing in Ms. DeForest's forehead. My guess was that she was going to need a lengthy meditation session to get over this class. "Next exercise! I want you to use your bodies to demonstrate emotions. Joy!"

Everyone ran about as if they were skipping through buttercup meadows.

"Fear!"

We all dropped to our knees, covering our heads like a nuclear bomb was about to drop.

"Lust!"

Jeffrey grabbed his crotch in a Michael Jackson–style move.

"Keep it clean!" Ms. DeForest screamed. All signs of her formally peaceful demeanor had vanished.

"It's lust!" Jeffrey said in a hurt voice. "How *can* you keep that clean?"

"Rejoice in it, people! Feel the air vibrating with emotional intensity!" Ms. DeForest called out.

The air of emotional intensity was broken by the sound of the bell. Thank god.

"Now, I don't have you again till next Friday," Ms. DeForest announced over the stream of students stampeding out the door like prisoners being released from Alcatraz. "During that time, I would like you to remember a traumatic experience from your past and create a two-minute dance using this memory. You will perform this for the class next week."

"Was that ever one heck of a class!" Jelena blurted, as soon as we were out of earshot. Her hair was mussed up at the back from lying on the floor. "I don't think this school is ready for Ms. DeForest's revolutionary methods."

"I don't think the *world* is ready for her methods," I said.

4 finding religion

"And then my heart with pleasure fills / And dances with the daffodils." Mrs. Kent, our English teacher, wiped a small tear from her eye as she finished reading Wordsworth's poem "Daffodils" during our Friday afternoon class.

Mrs. Kent always encourages us to surrender ourselves to any emotions provoked by works of literature. Last year, when we watched Baz Luhrmann's *Romeo + Juliet*, I cried my eyes out during the scene when Romeo and Juliet first set eyes on each other by the fish tank (the emotional intensity heightened by my favorite song of all time, "I'm Kissing You," playing in the background). Mrs. Kent had just smiled and handed me a box of tissues. Rumor has it that she's a closet Harlequin Romance author.

"So, class, because you've now been exposed to the many forms of poetry," she said, "from sonnets to blank verse, I would love it if you took the next two weeks to create a poem of your own. It can be in any form and on anything you like. Look at it as a chance to express yourself in a new way. Presentations will be on Valentine's Day."

I loved the idea of expressing myself. The only trouble was choosing what to write about. Mrs. Kent's assignment left the poem's topic wide open. Hayden Paris, in his usual spot in front of me, was smiling to himself as he wrote the assignment down. You had to wonder what he was going to write about. I was rather curious about his deepest thoughts and emotions. Perhaps I could find a weak spot to use to my advantage during our battles of wit.

The bell sounded and I headed across the courtyard, dashing quickly from pool to pool of shade. Today's sweltering weather seemed capable of causing a mirage if you stayed out in it too long.

"Hey, Aurora, where are you headed?" Jelena appeared at my side.

"Bathroom."

"I'll come, too."

Guys always wonder why girls go to the bathroom in groups. The truth is, all the interesting stuff happens there. It's where you discuss what's going on outside the bathroom, help others out by lending them some blush or listening to their horror stories, and prepare yourself to go back into battle. You never know what you might find out in a bathroom.

Today was no exception. As we walked in, we found Lindsay clutching the sink desperately and sobbing her eyes out.

"Tylererabrokubbbmeee!" she wailed.

We rushed forward, grabbed her by the arms, and sat her down on the bench by the wall. Her sobs grew heavier and she collapsed like a rag doll.

"What happened?" Jelena gasped.

Lindsay's normally bronzed face was pale and her dark eyes had a hollow look to them.

"Did your heel break or something?" Jelena asked.

I frowned at her. Did she really think a broken heel was worthy of semi-hysteria?

"No one died, did they?" I asked, frightened.

Lindsay just cried harder.

"Lindsay, *please* tell us what's wrong so we can help you," Jelena begged.

"T-t-t-t-t . . ." Lindsay stuttered, taking choking breaths.

"Breathe, Lindsay. Try to think of each word before you say it." I stroked her hair reassuringly.

"Tyler." Breath. "Broke." Breath and sob. "Up." Choke. "With me-e-e!"

"What?"

This was unbelievable. Tyler and Lindsay had been going out for three years.

"When?" Jelena cried.

"This mor-ning. At br-eak," Lindsay said, wiping her eyes with the back of her hand. Jelena ran to get toilet paper.

"Why?" Jelena and I both asked, hardly able to wait for a reply.

Lindsay's eyes widened with pain. "He said he needed some freedom so he could spread his wings and fly like an eagle."

"What?" I said again. This wasn't a typical breakup line.

"He won't be doing any flying once I get my hands on him." Jelena was squeezing the toilet paper roll so tightly that it was nearly flat.

"Don't tell me you've spent all day in here by yourself, Lindsay?" I said.

"I couldn't leave!" Lindsay put her head in her hands. "I didn't know what to do. I don't even know how to cope on my own! I'm hopeless!"

"Linds, you are *not* hopeless!" But I could tell that she wasn't listening. She was in shock.

I was in shock myself. To see something as strong and solid as TylerandLindsay crumble sent my faith reeling. If *they* couldn't make it, who could?

I snapped out of my quickly darkening thoughts. It was time to take action.

"Jelena, take Lindsay to the school nurse and demand that she be allowed to go home," I said. "You've got a free period this afternoon, so both of you jump in a taxi and head to my place. Here's my key." I handed it over. "There's no one home right now. Run Lindsay a bath, okay?"

Jelena nodded.

"I'm going to organize a get-over-him party. I have a mother–daughter meeting this afternoon, but I'll pick up supplies afterwards. I'll aim to be home at six, but I'll get everyone else to come by earlier to assist with moral support."

Jelena and I lifted Lindsay to her feet.

"I can't face everybody," Lindsay wailed, but Jelena had her out the door and halfway down the hall before she could protest any further.

Still reeling from the news, I headed toward my locker. On the way, I happened to glance up at the bulletin board. In among the notices about lost calculators and dress code regulations was one that grabbed me right away:

SIGH NO MORE, LADIES (AND GENTLEMEN!). SIGH NO MORE, FOR THE AUDITIONS FOR SHAKESPEARE'S MOST LIVELY COMEDY, *MUCH ADO ABOUT NOTHING*, ARE TO BE HELD ON TUESDAY, FEBRUARY 4! ASPIRING ACTORS, COSTUME DESIGNERS, AND BACKSTAGE CREW ARE ALL INVITED TO BE A PART OF THIS YEAR'S BIGGEST AND BEST PRODUCTION!

The notice went on to give the exact time and place of the auditions and backstage sign-up. My eyes skimmed over it excitedly. Here was something to take Lindsay's mind off her breakup. Our whole group could get involved!

Excited by the prospect of our new group project, I was full of energy when I arrived in the city center to meet my mother at 3:30 p.m. As I reached the Macy's perfume department (our usual meeting spot), I saw her approaching from a distance.

Everyone always tells me how much I resemble my mother, but if you look beyond a few short glances, you'll see we're actually very different. We both have fair hair, but my mother's is the type of blond that you see on really young children: pure spun gold. Her eyes are emerald and her features are finer than mine. Today she wore a cream-colored designer suit that fitted her in an impossibly perfect way. Everyone took notice as she walked past.

I have to admit that my mom, like those scarily popular girls in teen movies, intimidates me. Even when I was three, I think she somehow expected me to talk to her like an adult. Thirteen years and an extended period of absence later, I am still on my best behavior.

"Hello, Aurora," she said, giving me an air kiss so as not to mess up her lipstick. "How was school today?"

We started walking toward the women's fashion area.

"We got an assignment to write our own poem!" I said. "Isn't that cool?"

My mother didn't answer. She was trying on a pale lavender hat. "Mom?"

"Wonderful, darling," she said, examining her reflection from all angles.

When my mom first came back from overseas, I didn't want to see her. Then I read a book about the fundamental importance of the mother–daughter relationship; apparently it can permanently affect a woman's sense of self. I'm now making an effort to be friends with my mother, but sometimes I feel like all the things that we can't talk about have formed a big, gaping hole between us, a crevasse that I'm always trying to skirt around or leap over with my eyes shut.

But I'm not one to give up. I'm going to fill in that hole.

I decided to talk about things that interested my mother. I ran through the list in my head: Carlos, the new Spanish boyfriend (we were *not* going to discuss that); designer brands; home furnishings; relationships. I decided to go with the last one.

"Mom, guess who broke up?" Her eyes flickered with interest. We had a sign of life. "Tyler and Lindsay." Yes! I'd managed it as three separate words.

"Lindsay . . ." Mom mused. "Is she the pretty blond who likes to wear denim?"

"No. That's Cassie. My lifelong best friend?"

I couldn't help being a little sarcastic. Cassie and I had practically grown up at each other's houses. She must have registered on my mom's radar *once or twice* in eleven years.

"Darling, you can't expect me to remember every tiny detail of your life." Mom raised her perfectly shaped eyebrows. "So who broke up?"

I decided not to make a scene in a heavily populated department store. Time for a subject change.

"Never mind. The best thing about today was that I found out they're holding auditions for *Much Ado About Nothing* at school."

"Now, that is great news." Mom took the hat up to the sales counter. "Who's the female lead in that play?"

Mom wants me to be in show business. I've told her that writing is part of the arts, but she never really listens. The cashier took her credit card.

"Beatrice—" I began.

"Beatrice." My mother put in her pin code to authorize the transaction. "She's that argumentative character, isn't she?" She frowned. "Why don't you go for the part of Hero? I'm sure she'd get a gorgeous costume."

"I don't want to act. I want to help out backstage."

"Why on earth would you want to do that? Someone like you should be out front and center."

"But—"

"Promise me you'll audition, Aurora. Then I can come and watch my daughter on stage."

The idea of my mom taking an interest in any non-fashion-related aspect of my life was intoxicating. I could try out for a small part and still help out backstage, couldn't I?

"Sure, Mom," I found myself replying.

My mother beamed at me. "Wonderful!"

She grabbed my hands and danced me past women's underwear. There's something exhilarating about my mother when she's happy. Suddenly she stopped dancing and looked at her watch.

"Oh no. Aurora, I've got to go. Carlos and I are hosting a dinner party tonight."

She became Avery again: elegant and unattached.

"Next Wednesday, yes?" She didn't wait for my answer as she breezed out of the store.

I've never been to my mother's new house. She holds a dinner party just about every second Friday. Sometimes I hold my breath, hoping she'll extend an invitation to me. She never has.

I felt a twinge of sadness before I realized that it was almost time to meet the girls for our get-over-him party. Tonight was about Lindsay's pain, not mine. I grabbed get-over-him supplies—nail polish, face masks, a DVD, a blank diary.

As I walked into the supermarket in search of cookie dough, I almost ran straight into Hayden Paris's mother, Jennifer.

She gave me a big hug. "Hey, hon. We're just shopping for a weekend away." She gestured toward Mr. Paris, who had a bottle of champagne in his arms.

I always love seeing Mr. and Mrs. Paris together. They've been married for nearly twenty years and still hold hands any chance they get.

"Keep an eye on the house for us, won't you?" she asked. "Hayden's staying with friends for the weekend."

No Hayden Paris for two days? Things were looking up!

5 the get-over-him party

By seven p.m. the get-over-him party was in full swing. Upbeat music was pumping on the living room stereo system and Lindsay, Jelena, Cassie, Sara, and I were in the kitchen making chocolate chip cookies.

"She's getting tears in the batter," Jelena whispered to me, nodding at Lindsay, who was crying again.

We'd been doing our best to keep the conversation light and funny, but it clearly wasn't working.

I needed to provide a better distraction than cookies. I was going to have to make a suggestion I really didn't want to make.

"Hey, baking in a heat wave was a seriously bad idea," I say, putting down my ball of dough. "I've got a better one—how about we go swimming?"

Next thing I knew we were attempting to scale Hayden Paris's back fence, wearing our bikinis.

"Okay, if you just lift your right leg up to this branch, you'll be able to swing yourself up and over," Jelena instructed, already inside Hayden's yard.

I knew I should have taken gymnastics in elementary school.

"If Hayden Paris was my neighbor," Sara said from the branch above me, "I'd be sneaking over here all the time."

"If you knew the real Hayden Paris," I said, "you'd stay as far away as humanly possible."

"Come on!" squealed Sara. "Those roguish hazel eyes? The slightly curly hair that just calls out for you to run your fingers through it? Those soft-looking lips . . ."

My hands slipped and I almost lost my grip on the overhead branch.

"You okay?" Cassie called from below.

I regained my balance. "Sara, you sound like a bad romance novel."

"His manly shoulders . . ."

"Steady, there." I dropped to the ground on the other side. "If you're not careful, he'll turn up. Hayden Paris can sense a compliment from miles away."

I had to admit, he had one thing going for him, though. The lagoon-style pool glinted in the moonlight. Green palms and leafy bushes hugged its edges, and a small waterfall trickled into it at one end. We stood and admired it before leaping in. Everyone surfaced, screaming at the temperature. Jelena dived back under and grabbed at our ankles, starting a game of Marco Polo.

Cass started counting with her eyes closed. "One, two, three . . ."

We all broke away, swimming as far from her as we could.

"Eight, nine, ten!"

Suddenly a noise came from inside the Parises' house.

"Oh my god," Sara said, giving away her position. "There's someone inside."

"Don't be stupid," Jelena said. "Everyone's away for the weekend. Keep counting, Cass."

"Eleven, twelve . . ."

We heard the patio glass door slide open. We all froze.

"Someone's broken into their house!" Lindsay said in a strangled voice.

"Shouldn't we wait to see who it is before we jump to conclusions?" Jelena said, sounding convincingly brave.

"You can stay if you like," Sara said as the bushes in front of the patio rustled. "But I've seen enough horror movies to know that teenage girls and ominous noises do not lead to happy results."

At those words, everyone was out of the water and running for the tree that gave quick access to my backyard. I was in the farthest corner of the pool, so I had only reached its steps when I heard the crackling of branches and saw a figure dashing toward me.

"Oh god! Aurora! Run!" Lindsay yelled from just ahead of me.

I grabbed my towel and sprinted toward the tree. My heartbeat mixed in with the sound of heavy footsteps just yards behind me. I felt a burst of adrenaline as I reached for a branch and started heaving myself up. I was not going to die in Hayden Paris's backyard, in my bikini!

My pursuer was right below me now, grabbing at my feet. I lost my balance and fell, letting out a scream. My towel flew out of my hand and in a wide arc above me. I landed on the grass and slowly looked up at my pursuer, ready to meet my death bravely.

Hayden Paris was standing above me, smirking. "I knew you'd fall at my feet someday."

"What do you think you're doing?" I screamed, nearly hysterical. My heart was pounding like an African conga drum. "Are you trying to kill me from shock? I thought you were a psychopath!"

Hayden reached down and offered me a hand.

I batted it away. "Don't touch me!"

"Aurora, are you hurt?" my friends called over the fence.

I couldn't answer. I felt so shaky I wasn't sure of anything. Except my extreme hatred for Hayden.

I got up, shaking my fist in a gesture that would have made my mother frown. "I've had it with you!"

"She's fine, girls," Hayden called over the fence. "Back to her normal self. You head inside. I'll have her back in a moment."

I heard their voices drifting away as I scanned the yard for my missing towel. It was at the bottom of the pool.

"Arrgghh!"

"Don't worry about that," Hayden said, slipping off his T-shirt and jumping into the water in one easy motion, before I could protest.

Not that I cared about him getting wet after all he'd put me through.

He dragged the drenched towel to the surface, then pulled himself out of the pool to stand next to me. I remembered Sara's remark about his "manly shoulders." I had to admit, purely objectively, that she was right. I shook my head and pushed the thought away.

"What were you doing in the bushes? Trying to scare me to death?" I said furiously.

"I heard noises coming from the pool. I thought I'd better investigate, and I kept out of sight so as not to alert the possibly violent intruders."

"I don't suppose you could have said something once you realized it was a bunch of innocent teenage girls?" I grabbed the towel from him.

Hayden's normally teasing eyes were serious. "I honestly didn't realize it was you until you fell at my feet."

Did he have to keep putting it that way? It wasn't as if I'd intended to land there.

"What were you doing in the pool, anyway?" Hayden said. "Technically, you are trespassing."

"You weren't supposed to be home!"

"All the more reason to break in, huh? I guess pool-hopping is a regular thing for you? Come on, admit it. Now I've finally caught you in the act."

"You haven't caught me in the act of anything!" I spluttered. "Your mom asked me to keep an eye on the house. But that's the end of my neighborhood watch. From now on, your plasma TV and Xbox are fair game for thieves."

I started striding toward his house. Hayden ran to open the door for me.

"Keeping an eye on a neighbor's house usually means observing from a distance, Princess, not frolicking in their pool."

"It was firsthand observation," I insisted, as I pushed by him into his house and straight out the front door, across to my place.

Hayden chased after me, trying to put a dry towel over my shoulders.

"Ah. The fateful location of Daniel Benis's accident," Hayden said as we reached my door.

I scowled. "There'll be another accident if you're not careful."

"Breaking and entering, death threats . . . I could report you for this."

"You'd get busted for harassment," I said, tossing him back his towel.

Hayden's hazel eyes were twinkling again. "You know I'd only look sexier with handcuffs."

The front door opened, saving me from answering. Jelena, Cassie, Sara, and Lindsay peered out and took in Hayden's and my dripping bodies.

"Have you been swimming together?" Sara asked.

"It's always been you," boomed the TV from inside. That's another part of the get-over-him party. If you're going to cry, you might as well cry your eyes out at *The Notebook*. By the end of that movie, there'll be no tears left in you.

Hayden smiled. "Bonding time, huh? I'll let you get back to it. Hey, Lindsay?"

Lindsay looked at him.

"Don't worry about Tyler. I think he's been influenced by stories of freedom in our personal development class. Mr. Bridges is big on the single-man thing. I give Tyler a week before he realizes what an idiot he's been and begs you to take him back."

Lindsay smiled.

Hayden headed down the path. "'Night, girls. 'Night, Princess."

I rolled my eyes.

"Oh, and girls . . ." He stopped and turned, his bare chest glowing under the driveway lights. "You're welcome to use my pool any time. Just let me know first and I'll go swimming with you." He gave us a wink and disappeared inside his own yard.

The girls let out whistles. Sara pretended to faint.

"I was right about his manly chest," she said.

"Shoulders," I said. "You said shoulders earlier."

She sighed. "The whole package is outstanding."

"I think lack of food has gotten to you," I replied. "Let's go eat those cookies."

We headed inside and let *The Notebook* work its magic. By the end, we were all sobbing.

"I can't cry anymore!" Lindsay wailed.

She was on the road to recovery.

6   he's so into you

The rest of the weekend was a blur of get-over-him activities. There was list making—TEN THINGS I DIDN'T LIKE ABOUT TYLER—and I presented Lindsay with the breakup journal, to chronicle her highs and lows and note down all the things she wanted to scream at Tyler. There were some close calls. On Saturday afternoon I only just managed to stop Lindsay and Jelena from heading over to Tyler's and slashing the tires on his BMX bike. This made me decide to implement anger-reducing activities for Sunday, like a group jogging session and having Lindsay take out her aggression on our boxing bag (acquired before the NAD became a pacifist). By the time she'd completed all the physical activities, and I'd helped her remove all Tyler-related items from her bedroom (a massive job, let me tell you), Lindsay was too tired to consider revenge.

I have to say, I was quite happy to return to school on Monday to get away from the Taylor Swift heartbreak ballads and angry Rihanna tunes that had dominated the weekend.

"I don't know if I'm ready to deal with the stresses of single life yet," Lindsay said as we all sat down at our usual lunch table in the yard. "In math today, Jeffrey Clark yelled across the room to me, 'Is it hot in here, or is it just you?' and wiped his forehead! I've been insulated against unwelcome advances for so long I didn't even know what to do. I just sank down in my seat."

"You know Jeffrey Clark's depriving a village somewhere of its idiot," Jelena said.

"Oh, Jeffrey's not that bad," I said.

"Seriously, though," Lindsay said, tossing her newly styled hair (one of the first things to do after a breakup: get a fabulous do) out of her eyes, "you don't think I gave Tyler a hard time, do you?"

A look I knew all too well came into her eyes. She was edging into overanalytical territory.

"If guys are unhappy, they let you know, believe me," Sara said as she chomped on her lime-and-black-pepper potato chips. "He could've spoken up any time."

"Maybe he couldn't put his feelings into words. Guys have trouble with that kind of thing."

Lindsay looked like she was ready to jump up from the lunch table and go grab Tyler to interrogate him about his emotions. Which, like those of most boys, probably ran the whole gamut from "I'm hungry" to "Check out those wheels."

"He could have done a metaphorical pain dance, or pulled a face, or performed a puppet show," Sara said. "Just like *He's Just Not That Into You* says."

He's Just Not That Into You is Sara's bible. She brings it to school and reads excerpts at completely random times, like when we studied *Hamlet*. She told Mrs. Kent that Ophelia could have saved herself a lot of pain if she'd just faced facts: Hamlet was self-obsessed and rapidly descending into a spiral of self-destruction.

I think a book called *He's So Into You* would be more helpful, so girls could figure out whether their crush was exhibiting favorable signs toward them. Hey! Maybe I could write it! They say if it doesn't exist, create it, right? I could just see it on the bestseller list. The next Dr. Phil spin-off show, here I come.

"Are you saying Tyler just wasn't that into me?" There was a dangerous glint in Lindsay's eyes. Time to change the subject, stat!

"I have a fantastic idea to take your mind off Tyler," I announced. "It's time to move on."

"Hey, speaking of moving on," Jelena interjected. "Did you hear that Bradley Scott's dating Tina Vaser now? He says their charts are perfectly aligned and he's so lucky to have found his soul mate in the schoolyard."

Now I wanted to chuck a muesli bar wrapper at someone.

"Soul mate in the schoolyard? Please! It sounds like a country-and-western song." I laughed in what I hoped was a scornful way. So much for Bradley's promise to schedule another date. He'd waited, what, eight days before moving on? Not that we'd been involved enough to even call his actions "moving on."

Jelena smiled. "Somebody sounds jealous."

Jealous? I wouldn't have gone on another date with Mr. New Age. I just felt hurt that he hadn't recognized my uniqueness.

I rolled my eyes. "Tarot Card Tina's welcome to him. Anyway, as I was saying, I think it'd be great if we all got involved in the drama department's staging of *Much Ado About Nothing*," I said. "I researched the play online during computer studies, and it's got mixed-up love affairs, corruption, and a faked death! Just like any good blockbuster. And if you don't want to act, the audition poster says there are tons of backstage roles!" I looked excitedly at them for a response.

"I already saw Mr. Peterman," Cassie said, naming the head of drama, "and told him I was interested in painting sets."

I didn't have to worry about winning *her* over. Cass is a brilliant painter who takes classes in the city twice a week. I knew those sets were going to be incredible.

"Won't it be a lot of work?" Jelena looked down at her perfectly manicured hands.

I think Jelena must realize that running an international company is going to require a lot of effort but figures that she'll delegate.

"I don't know if I'm so keen," Sara said. "Do you remember when we did *Oliver Twist*? Pretending I was an orphan really affected me. I always get too emotionally involved in these things—"

"What if Tyler is there?" Lindsay cut in. "That's not going to help my recovery."

"Guys!" I felt frustrated that my idea wasn't being met with unanimous positivity. "This isn't about uncoordinated costumes or ex-boyfriends! It's about spending time together in the exciting and dynamic world of theater!"

Jelena laughed. "Jefferson High's drama department is hardly Broadway."

"Sara, I think you'd love it." I looked pleadingly at her. "Shakespeare's plays always have strong roles for women."

Sara had a thoughtful look on her face.

"So, Cass, Sara, and I are in," I said. "Lindsay?"

"Tyler's not going to be involved," Cassie said. "It'll clash with soccer practice."

"I guess it's a good idea," Lindsay said. "And hopefully distracting."

We all turned to look at Jelena.

This was completely frustrating. One word from her and she'd have everybody changing their minds again.

I sighed. "Guys, *Much Ado About Nothing*—"

"—is one of Shakespeare's best comedies," Hayden Paris said, stopping as he strolled past. "Being involved in the production means a seriously good time. I've been looking forward to it for months."

I couldn't believe that I'd forgotten Hayden was a member of the drama club. The prospect of spending more time in his presence made me want to drop the theater idea altogether. But there was no way that an independent woman like me would turn down an opportunity because of a man. I'd just have to grin and bear it.

"What's going to be a good time?" Scott Ryder said, approaching us, Alex West by his side.

At the sound of Scott's voice, Cassie took a quick, panicky breath. Because she'd been munching on a chocolate chip cookie at the time, her breath became splutters.

Alex gave Hayden a cool nod. "Alex West."

I noticed that he looked Hayden up and down carefully before deciding to come closer. Unfortunately, you can't fault Hayden's appearance. Even I have to admit that. Last year he came in second in our annual High School Hotties poll. Some of those who voted should realize that looks aren't everything—what about his pain-in-the-neck attitude?

"So, what's going to be a good time?" Scott repeated.

"A party, right?" Alex gave a confident smile. "I'm ready for that. Good music, good liquor, good-looking girls?" He sent a wink in Jelena's direction.

Jelena didn't return it, probably on account of her opinion that excessive facial gestures lead to the need for Botox at an early age.

"I haven't introduced Scott to you," Hayden said, turning to my friends perched on the lunch table.

"We've already met Aurora, Jelena, and Cassie," Scott said, waving at us three.

"Lindsay and Sara," Hayden said, completing the group.

The guys sat down at our table, Scott taking the spot next to Cassie.

"Hope you don't mind if I sit here." Hayden didn't wait for an answer—suddenly he was squished up next to me, his elbow and knee touching mine. "We always sit near each other in class . . ." he started.

"Not by choice." I pulled my hair away from the side he was on.

"So I decided I'd better stick with what I know," he continued. "You know, in case breaking the routine brings on panicky feelings."

"Don't you think this bordering-on-claustrophobic level of proximity is more likely to increase panicky feelings?"

We were practically sitting on top of each other.

"The soothing scent of your perfume is calming my panicky tendencies," he murmured in a low, mock-Harlequin-hero voice.

I leaned as far away from him as possible, virtually knocking Cassie into Scott's lap. She blushed terribly.

"Vanilla, right?" Hayden asked in a normal voice.

"Vanilla what?"

"Your perfume. Anything to do with *Cosmo*'s useful fact for the month of January that men associate the smell of vanilla with attraction?"

"I'm worried about you, Paris. How many of those magazines are you reading? Is there something you're not telling us?"

I missed Hayden's reply as I heard Jelena saying the last thing I'd ever expect: "We're all getting involved in the production of *Much Ado About Nothing*. Everyone who has the tiniest shred of attitude will be there." She raised a perfectly shaped eyebrow.

"Attitude, hey?" Alex raised an eyebrow of his own. "When's the audition?"

"Tomorrow afternoon. Are you thinking of getting involved?"

Jelena's tone was light, but I could tell she really wanted an affirmative answer from Alex.

"Well, since it seems that the most gorgeous girls at Jefferson High are involved, I'd better be, too," Alex replied.

A satisfied smile spread over Jelena's lips.

"Hey, Ryder. You into auditioning for the Shakespeare production?" Alex asked Scott.

Before he could form a reply, I spoke up. "Cassie's going to be painting the backdrops. She's a fantastic painter."

Cassie shot me a you're-being-so-obvious look. Little did she realize that guys are completely clueless when it comes to girls' crushes. You could hire a skywriter to scrawl your feelings above your crush's house and he'd still scratch his head and go "Hmm."

"You paint?" Scott's voice was suddenly excited. "That's so cool. I sculpt! Do you work in other mediums as well?"

A common passion—this was so going to up their chances as a couple!

"I like watercolors best," Cassie said, "but I also use acrylics and pastels."

At that moment, the bell sounded.

Alex grabbed his bag. "Ladies, we'll be seeing you at the audition tomorrow. Right, Scott?"

We all turned to hear Scott's reply. I had a feeling Cassie was holding her breath.

"Without a doubt." Scott gave us a wave and headed after Alex.

7   death, dragons, and dating in the medieval world

"Victims' skin turned dark gray. Their lymph nodes swelled—sometimes to the size of an egg, sometimes to the size of an apple. Then the swollen lymph glands would burst!"

Jeffrey Clark yelled the last word, making everyone in Mr. Bannerman's Tuesday morning history class jump. It was oral presentation day, and of all the medieval topics Jeffrey could have chosen, he'd decided upon the black death.

"Dead littered the streets—in doorways, on stairwells. No one, not even priests, went near the hideous carcasses."

Everyone shifted uncomfortably in their seats.

"By the time the bubonic plague ended, one third of Europe's population had died," Jeffrey finished with a flourish.

There was a stunned silence from his audience.

"Great job, Jeffrey," Mr. Bannerman stuttered. "Very . . . ah, well researched. Aurora, you're up! Our second-to-last presentation today!"

Mr. Bannerman looked relieved. Jeffrey's presentation had obviously taken its toll.

I gathered my notes and strode to the front of the room. I regard oral presentations as great practice for when I'm a wildly successful author and have to go on book tours.

"Good morning, everyone! Today I'm going to discuss courtly love. Courtly love was a system of admiration and courtship during the Middle Ages," I read off my index cards. "Just like we have rules for dating, like the timing of a post-date text, people in the Middle Ages had particular rules when it came to expressing their interest in someone. Courtly love was mostly practiced by the aristocracy—"

"Aristawhatnow?" Jeffrey asked.

"Noble lords and ladies," I explained. "According to courtly love, a knight"—I pointed to a picture (props are key when educating the ignorant)—"would form an affection for a worthy lady. This lady was often unavailable—either married to someone else or of a higher status."

"So it was unrequited love?" Hayden asked.

"Well, it was unrequited in that it was usually impossible for the man to marry the woman he loved. In medieval times, people didn't marry for love but for political or territorial gain," I replied. "So in order to explore the idea of love, a man would practice courtly love."

I'd been quite disappointed to find out the truth about medieval marriages. Just think: in a time when you had a chance to marry a real prince, you couldn't say yes without considering all the respective parties and their concerns.

"The knight would woo the lady according to the rules of courtly love." I pointed to a picture of a knight bowing to a lady. "He would write her love poems and songs, give her flowers and gifts, and perform ceremonial gestures indicating his regard for her."

"Bring on courtly love!" cried Emma Grant.

All the girls in the room let out a cheer. "Courtly love! Courtly love!" they chanted.

Ooh! I was starting a movement!

"Oh man. What are they going to expect us to do now?" a male voice moaned.

"Yeah, this courtly love stuff sounds like too much effort," another guy complained.

I craned my neck to see which two guys had spoken. They were so not future dating candidates.

"One of the main principles of courtly love was that a lady would inspire a man to do great deeds to prove he was worthy," I continued. "A knight might conquer a country, climb a mountain, or suffer intense pain, all the time hoping to win the lady's favor."

The girls in the class sighed. What woman wouldn't want to know that a man would do anything for her?

When I finished my presentation, the audience broke out in applause, several of the female contingent whistling in approval. I sat down and Cassie gave me a high five.

"Okay. Last up . . . Mr. Hayden Paris!" Mr. Bannerman sounded cheerful again. My presentation had obviously lifted his mood.

"Ready for an even better talk on courtly love?" Hayden whispered to me as he got up out of his seat.

I looked up in horror. "You wouldn't dare. You know I claimed that topic."

"Watch me," he said calmly.

I shot Cassie an outraged look. "He can't do this!" I hissed.

"'Morning, everyone." Hayden smiled his infuriatingly perfect smile.

All the girls straightened up. Some people shamelessly treated oral presentation lessons as a perving opportunity.

"I'm actually going to be discussing a topic very similar to Aurora's."

Everyone whistled.

"Did you do the courtly love research together?" Jeffrey asked in a singsong voice.

"Ooh!" the room chorused.

"All research was conducted separately!" I cried, half-standing. Cassie tugged at my arm, pulling me back down.

Hayden just smiled again. "I'll be discussing medieval knights and the code of chivalry."

"Lucky for you," I muttered.

Hayden strolled over to one of the storage cupboards and drew out a long silver sword. "I thought I'd bring this in to show you all. It's a model of a thirteenth-century sword used by English knights."

He ran his finger up the flat of the shining blade.

Travis leaped up from his seat. "Man! You've got to let me see that."

The guys all started clambering over each other to get a better look. The girls stared at Hayden like a real medieval knight had manifested before them. Great. In one short moment, Hayden had blown my presentation completely out of the water. My only hope was that Mr. Bannerman would value my great research over Hayden's blatant use of a prop. I looked over at him. Mr. Bannerman held the sword in his hand, looking as awed as a young boy.

Hayden was swamped by willing sword handlers for the next ten minutes. I was hardly impressed. Throughout my childhood I'd seen Hayden in his backyard wielding imaginary swords. So now he had a real one. Big deal. It wasn't like he'd defended a lady's honor with it or anything.

Mr. Bannerman finally managed to gain control over the class. "Great job, everyone. Especially you, Aurora."

I smiled graciously. Obviously Mr. Bannerman realized that all Hayden Paris had done was show off a boy toy.

"And you, Hayden," he added. "You two definitely would have known how to treat each other right in a medieval court. Early dismissal, everyone."

Mr. Bannerman's statement was met with cheers.

If I were in a medieval court, I would have arranged for a dragon to go after Hayden Paris a long time ago.

"The nerve!" I cried.

Cassie and I stood at our lockers, picking up our books for the next class.

"The nerve of what?" Cassie asked, pulling out her cooking folder.

"The nerve of Hayden Paris!" I cried as Sara and Lindsay joined us at the lockers. "Did you see that smile on his face when history class finished?"

"Aurora, he was probably just happy that his presentation went well. You know how he loves to get good grades," Cassie said, applying pink lip gloss.

"Believe me, it was not an I'm-happy-about-my-scholastic-achievements smile," I said. "I know Hayden's smiles. It was his Ha!-I've-foiled-you-again-Aurora! grin. Similar to his I'm-laughing-at-your-dating-disaster smirk, only with more of an upwards tilt of his chin." I jutted my chin up to demonstrate.

"Doesn't the fact that you know the minute details of Hayden Paris's smiles tell you something?" Cassie said as the four of us started walking toward our respective classes.

"Huh?"

Lindsay's cell went off. She pulled out the baby-blue phone and looked at the identity of the caller. "It's Tyler." Her voice was several tones higher than normal.

We all stopped, listening to the ringtone: LeAnn Rimes's "How Do I Live." It was so not single-girl friendly. Lindsay had to change it.

"What should I do?" she asked.

"Not answer," I said firmly.

"Not answer?" Lindsay squeaked, looking from us to the phone and back at us again.

"I'll answer," Sara said. "Give him a verbal battering."

"I can do that myself," Lindsay said, her finger paused above the Answer button.

"No one is answering!" I cried. I grabbed the phone out of Lindsay's hand. It went silent, but within a few seconds, the ringtone started up again.

I held the phone above my head. It was times like these that I was glad of my statuesque height.

"Hayden was right," Cassie said. "Tyler's already lonely, and it's only been four days."

Lindsay looked hopeful.

"Lindsay, if you talk to him now, you'll just be all flustered," I said. "What you want is cool rationality. Tyler broke up with you, out of the blue, with no real explanation. You can't let him treat you like that and then take him back right away. Plus, how do you know he's not just calling to ask for his things back?" I said as the phone finally went quiet. "That would be really embarrassing, thinking he can't live without you and then discovering what he can't live without is his rugby jersey. You deserve more than a phone call."

I pushed a few buttons on the phone, making Tyler's display come up as MEAN GUY WHO BROKE UP WITH YOU WITHOUT A GOOD REASON.

"That's why you shouldn't pick up at all this week," I added.

"What?" all three of them cried.

"When you're not picking up, Tyler will start wondering, *Hmm. What's Lindsay up to? Is she seeing another guy? Oh my god. She's seeing another guy! No!*" I said the last word like I was in an action movie and had discovered a bomb with a lit fuse. "I know it's tough, Linds, but a little bit of short-term stress will lead to long-term gains." I gave her a critical look. "So, can I trust you not to answer?"

"You can trust me," she said, in the most assured voice I'd heard from her post-breakup.

"I'm holding you to that. And change that ringtone!" I yelled after her as I headed off to biology.

8 an ill-fated audition

Mr. Blacklock entered the biology classroom, frowning. In the two years I've spent in his classes, I don't think I've ever seen him smile. Mr. Blacklock threw his books down on the desk with a heavy crash, making it clear that his ever-constant black mood had become even blacker.

"Today we'll be continuing our studies on bacteria," he said, and opened up his textbook. "Pathogenic bacteria; *pathos* being a Greek word meaning 'sadness' or 'pain'. . . . "

I guess I could say this was a pathogenic class, then?

I tuned out. The *Much Ado About Nothing* auditions were right after school, which was only about three hours away now. Last night I'd studied several of the opening scenes, making sure I was familiar with Hero's lines. But I still felt nervous. Did Cate Blanchett and Meryl Streep feel this way before an audition?

"Now, I would like everyone to make a table showing different types of bacterial diseases," Mr. Blacklock said, cutting across my audition jitters.

I took out my sparkly ruler to draw up a table.

"I want sketches of the bacteria as well," Mr. Blacklock said with a glower, before burying his head in a thick book.

I let out a sigh. At the sound, Hayden lifted his head from his work and turned to face me.

"The bacteria, right? I've taken it upon myself to make them a little more cheery." He grabbed his notebook and pointed to his bacteria, which he'd given top hats and canes. "What do you think? I was going for Fred Astaire."

I giggled. Hayden let out a laugh. Suddenly, a sense of foreboding came over me and I slowly looked up into the unamused eyes of Mr. Blacklock.

"Paris, Skye, you're both coming back here after school. The freshmen never fail to make a shocking mess of the lab, and today you can have the pleasure of cleaning it."

"But, Mr. Blacklock, the auditions for *Much Ado About Nothing* are this afternoon!" I cried.

"Be here or I'm suspending both of you." His voice was icy.

"Sir, it was my fault," Hayden said quickly. "It's not fair if Aurora misses the audition."

"Life isn't fair, Mr. Paris. Now get back to work." Mr. Blacklock walked back to his desk.

I felt like killing both him and Hayden. Now, after all the work I'd done to convince my friends to audition, I was going to miss out myself! I glared at the back of Hayden's head. I glared at my biology textbook. By the time I'd glared through the rest of my classes and the end-of-school bell rang, I felt like the Grinch. As I walked to the biology lab, ready to do slave labor for the tyrannous Mr. Blacklock, I realized that I couldn't let the girls know about my fate. If I said I couldn't be at the audition, then one by one they'd all decide not to go themselves. Then there'd be no distraction for Lindsay from the loss of Tyler, no great role for Sara, and no way for Cassie and Jelena to spend time with their crushes. No, I would suffer silently until they'd finished the auditions.

I strode into the biology lab. Hayden was already there, standing by a mountain of cleaning products.

"Aurora—"

"Don't talk to me," I said furiously. "My audition is completely ruined. Mom is going to kill me."

"Your mom's back?" Hayden asked, looking at me with a cautious expression in his eyes. "How do you feel about that?"

"I said don't talk to me."

"Look, I'm sorry." Hayden ran a hand through his hair, a miserable look on his face. "You have no idea how hard I've been working toward this audition. But if we hurry through cleaning—"

"Hurry?" I said, looking at the floor, where a river of black lapped at my feet. "It looks like there's been an oil spill in here!"

"They were doing some sort of experiment with ink," Hayden explained. "But if we rush through it, we'll still make the audition. Mr. Peterman's auditions are epic. If he could, he'd do callbacks."

"Okay, let's go for it," I said, grabbing a sponge. No one can say I'm not an optimist.

Hayden started frenetically mopping, while I tackled the benches.

When Hayden finished the floor, he joined me by the workstations. "You seemed to enjoy my presentation today. That smile you gave me, the one where your apple-green eyes sparkled with enthusiasm and your lips—"

"Are you delirious?" I splashed water in his direction.

"Why don't you take my temperature right now?" Hayden said, transferring the bottles of ink to the cupboard below the bench. "Here's the excuse you've been waiting for to get up close and personal."

I just rolled my eyes in response.

"Or perhaps you're the one with the temperature," Hayden said, tapping a finger against his lips thoughtfully. "Burning up with love. I think we should check it right now." He pulled out a lab thermometer and leaped toward me.

"We are not checking anything, Paris!" I yelled, as he tried to put the thermometer under my arm.

I pushed him away, and in the struggle Mr. Blacklock's plastic model of the human heart fell off the bench. Arteries and valves scattered across the floor.

"We're supposed to be cleaning up, not making more of a mess!" I cried. "We're never going to get to the audition at this rate."

Hayden put the thermometer away with a reluctant look on his face. I chased a runaway ventricle.

"So, a thought crossed my mind," he began.

"Must have been a long and lonely journey," I quipped, throwing my sponge into the sink.

"Very funny." Hayden put the cleaning equipment back into the cupboard. "If you have nothing to occupy your time other than coming up with anti-Hayden comments, then I feel sympathy for you."

"Sympathy?" I cried with a laugh, slamming the cupboard shut. "That's an unknown concept for you, Paris. Believe me, I have plenty of things to occupy my time."

Hayden grabbed his jacket and we headed out the door. "Oh yeah? Go on, then. I'm dying to hear about them."

He strode away down the hall. With my long legs, I was just able to match his pace.

"Okay, then," I said. "I'm writing what's going to become a best-selling nonfiction book: *He's So Into You.*"

"*He's So Into You?*" Hayden repeated, with a naughty look in his eyes. "So you think you're an expert?"

"Are you daring to question my appeal to the male sex?" I said, feeling my blood heat up.

"No. Believe me, from the guys' comments about your group's 'aesthetic appeal,' there's no question of that," Hayden replied.

"What's 'So you think you're an expert?' supposed to mean, then?" I asked, hurriedly applying pink lip gloss as we raced toward the audition room.

"Just that you're blind to what's going on half the time."

"I see perfectly!" I cried, almost stumbling on my pink heels as we dashed across the courtyard's uneven paving. The drama room was in sight now.

"So, am I right to assume you'll be doing a lot of field research for this book?" Hayden asked.

"Yes. In fact, you can help with that. What signs would you say your friend Scott displays when he's into a girl?"

"Aurora, I know what you're doing."

"Research," I replied innocently.

"You're trying to figure out Scott's feelings for a certain blond friend of yours."

"All research is for purely scientific purposes."

We dashed up the steps of the drama room. I felt jittery from head to toe. Why couldn't I have gotten here early, prepared myself, and soothed my nerves with positive affirmations as I waited for Mr. Peterman? Oh, that's right. Hayden had ruined that plan.

Hayden twisted the handle of the door, to no avail. "It's locked."

"Locked!" All hope was gone.

"We'll have to go around the back, through the backstage area."

Hayden started jogging again. I let out a sigh and dashed after him.

"Seriously, though, don't you think our friends are able to look after their own love lives?" he asked.

"In my opinion, Cupid is understaffed," I puffed. "Therefore, I'm offering a helping hand to high school couples—giving them a little nudge—"

"A shove, you mean." Hayden turned his hazel eyes on me. I met them unwaveringly.

"How do you think any goal is achieved?" I said. "You've got to have energy and drive. So, are you going to have some input into this bestselling book and tell me about Scott's romantic habits?"

"The thing I will tell you is that when Scott falls for someone, he falls hard, crediting them with incredible quality after incredible quality," Hayden replied.

I grinned. Cassie was fully deserving of such praise.

"Which is why I'm advising him to proceed cautiously," Hayden continued. "He's had his heart broken too often."

"What? You know Cassie would never do anything of the sort!"

"Yes, but slow and steady wins the race. What's it matter if he takes a while to ask her out?" Hayden said as we reached the backstage door.

"You're trying to sabotage this budding romance!" I cried. "I knew it! Just to annoy me."

"Aurora, not everything's about you," Hayden said with a maddening grin. He opened the door and gestured to me. "You first. Beauty before brains."

I stormed through the door before I realized what he'd said. My mouth opened in outrage. "Wait!" I yelled. "I'm going back out this door and you're going first."

I stepped back outside and pushed at Hayden's shoulders. He smiled, and blocked the door with his body.

"You sure about that? Isn't this a real conundrum for you? After all, if I go first, then I'm the beautiful one." He swept his free hand through his hair in an arrogant gesture. "Even though you were just stressing your good looks. And if you go first, well, then I'm the intelligent one." He lifted his hands in a no-win gesture.

I took the opportunity to elbow him in the ribs. If he was going to play dirty, I was, too.

"Oof!" he cried, and we both fought for the door. "Time's ticking by. What's it going to be?"

"Mrrrarrara!"

I had meant to say "Move out of my way," but my lips were smushed up against his shirt. This was so undignified.

I moved my head to the side so I could speak. "I've had it with your immaturity! We're both going through the door!"

I gave him a shove and we stumbled through the door and into the backstage area. We crashed into a rail holding the drama department's costumes and sent several Russian uniforms from last year's senior production of *Anna Karenina* to the floor. Hayden threw an arm up to catch them, and the button of his cuff caught my ponytail.

"Ow!" I struggled to free myself, and knocked the umbrellas from *Singin' in the Rain* from their hooks.

"I guess you have an equally high opinion of my beauty and my brains, then?" Hayden said.

"All I will say is that your looks would be greatly improved if you removed that darn smirk!"

We'd reached the backstage curtains. I tugged at my ponytail, trying to release it from his cuff. I was determined to make an elegant entrance, no matter what. Hayden tried to help free my hair, but I pushed his hands away. He'd probably claim that it was all a ruse of mine to get "up close and personal" with him. My push sent him stumbling through the stage curtain and onto the hardwood stage. My hair still caught in his cuff, I was pulled with him. My hair came free, finally, but my pink fedora, the one I'd worn today because I felt it looked *theatrical*, fell over my eyes. There went any hope of an elegant entrance. I pushed myself up from the floor, into a sitting position, my hat still blocking my sight.

"Are you sure you don't want my help on your love project?" Hayden's voice came from just near my ear. I could feel his hands on my hat brim, trying to shift it from its current position of trying to eat my face.

Strangely, the drama room was silent, except for his voice. Why hadn't our entrance been met with a chorus of laughs, or a yell of anger from Mr. Peterman about our immaturity?

"So you consider yourself an expert, then?" I asked, echoing his earlier taunt.

"I'll have you know that I'm an authority on love," Hayden said.

His hands brushed mine as I tugged at the brim of my hat. Inexplicably, a tiny shiver ran through me. Was I going crazy? Was this what it was like to be blind—everything all muddled up and your senses going into overdrive?

"In fact, maybe I should be writing *He's So Into You*," Hayden continued. "After all, I'm a guy. I know what they do when they're in love with someone."

His voice was soft and very close to my left ear. Even though I couldn't see him, I was willing to bet my most expensive perfume that he had a superior smile on his face. He was so trying to steal my Dr. Phil cameo.

"Hayden, if you ever loved anyone as much as you love yourself, it would be the world's greatest romance!" I yelled.

"Do you mind if I use that sentence for our English assignment?"

Hayden gave the hat a big tug and it finally relinquished its grip. The stage lights momentarily blinded me. I blinked and peered around Hayden, who was sitting in front of me, blocking my view of the auditorium. It was strangely dark. The only lights in the whole room were the brilliant beams lighting up the stage Hayden and I sat on. Slowly, my vision cleared and I could make out movement.

"What on earth?" I whispered, not believing my eyes.

Hayden, following my gaze, turned around. We both stared out at the auditorium. There was a silence, then the room filled with applause. The main lights flickered on and I saw fifty faces staring at us from below the stage.

"Incredible!" a voice boomed. Mr. Peterman appeared on the right-hand side of the stage with a triumphant smile on his face. "Such feeling! Such authenticity! Ladies and gentlemen, I think we've found our Beatrice and Benedick!"

9 taking the lead

I was in shock as Mr. Peterman put a wiry arm around each of us and escorted us off the stage and down to the audience.

"Excellent. Excellent!" he said. "Now, let's see if any of you gentlemen trying out for Claudio can put in as impassioned a performance."

Performance? What performance? I opened my mouth to say something, but no sound came out. A group of about fifteen guys shuffled up to the stage.

"Mr. Peterman," I said, finally regaining control of my voice, "what do you mean, Beatrice and Benedick?"

Mr. Peterman looked at me like I was crazy. "The main characters, of course. My dear, your lively audition has won you and Hayden the prime roles."

"My audition?" I looked at Hayden, who had a pleased expression on his face. Mr. Peterman somehow thought that our antics had been rehearsed! "Wait a minute. Mr. Peterman, that wasn't an audition!"

Mr. Peterman turned his attention from sizing up the heights of the potential Claudios. "Don't tell me you weren't happy with it," he said. "I can't afford for you to redo it. I've got no end of tryouts to get through today."

"I don't want to redo it," I said. "It wasn't a real audition in the first place."

"Mr. Peterman."

I turned my head to see Benjamin Zane standing behind Mr. Peterman, an outraged expression on his face.

"Your decision is completely unfair," he said. "What about my audition for Benedick? You can't just announce that these two," he glared at Hayden, "automatically have the parts without even considering the casting overnight!"

Yes! Someone else was protesting the decision. Even though it was just Benjamin Zane, wannabe Broadway star.

"Look, Mr. Peterman," I pushed my shoulders back, hoping to lend myself an air of authority, "I'm not the leading lady type. You've got this all wrong."

Mr. Peterman raised his eyebrows. Uh-oh.

"I definitely want to be involved with the play," I added quickly. "Just in a minor role."

Hayden spoke up. "I have to tell you the truth, Mr. Peterman. It wasn't a real audition."

I have to admit that Hayden is scrupulously honest. Years of pass-the-parcel at birthday parties had taught me that.

"But I really want the part of Benedick," he continued. "I'll re-audition for you, so that it's fair for everyone else."

"I knew it!" Benjamin cried. "You see, Mr. Peterman?"

I'd forgotten about the legendary rivalry between Hayden and Benjamin in the drama department. A few years ago, during a production of *The Three Musketeers*, Benjamin took a real swipe at Hayden while they were engaged in a duel on stage, because he believed that Hayden had been given a better feather to wear in his hat. In Benjamin's eyes, the golden feather was proof that Mr. Peterman favored Hayden.

"I am the director here!" Mr. Peterman cried over their raised voices. "And I know from all the roles that Hayden has played over the years that he's fully competent to take on that of Benedick."

"Thank you," Hayden interjected.

"But—" Benjamin broke in simultaneously.

Mr. Peterman shrugged. "If you have a problem with this, Benjamin, I'm sorry. But this play is full of great parts. Why don't you audition for Claudio?"

"But—"

"For Claudio," Mr. Peterman repeated.

Benjamin set his jaw and joined the group of Claudios. They didn't look happy about Mr. Peterman's suggestion. Benjamin might be obnoxious, but everyone knew he had talent. And ambition. He wouldn't stop till he had a Tony. Or an Oscar.

"Great," I said, bringing Mr. Peterman back to the issue at hand. "So Hayden's got the role."

I'm not one to sabotage another's happiness, even if it is Hayden Paris. Plus, if he was playing a main role, it meant that he'd have no time to persecute me.

"But you've realized that I'm not suitable for Beatrice, right?" I added, looking hopefully at Mr. Peterman.

"Wrong," he replied. "Aurora, I've been trying to get you to audition for years. It's always been obvious to me that you have a talent for artistic expression."

"Well, thank you, but—"

"No buts. Even if that wasn't an audition, it still showed me that you have stage presence and a real chemistry with Hayden."

I could tell that Hayden was hiding a smile. I glared at him.

"No protests, Aurora. You're Beatrice." Mr. Peterman gave a satisfied sigh. "Now, everyone auditioning for Claudio, please line up at the left-hand side of the stage."

"But, Mr. Peterman," I cried, as the Claudios nearly trampled each other to be first in line. Benjamin took a confident sip of his Evian water.

Hayden tugged at my sleeve gently. "Come on. Believe me: once Mr. Peterman gets an idea in his head, you've got no chance."

I followed him numbly into the audience. This couldn't be happening. I had no Broadway ambitions. I spotted Cassie waving at me from the crowd, and broke away from Hayden and headed toward her.

"Congratulations!" She leaped up and gave me a hug.

"Hey, great job, Aurora!" Scott beamed at me from the seat next to her. "Hayden's had his heart set on playing Benedick. It was ingenious of you to audition together—it showed what a talented team you make."

I was sure that my face was turning purple from suppressed frustration. A team? Hayden and I were archenemies. Rival gladiators pitting our wits against each other.

"A team?" I choked loudly.

Everyone around me turned to see what was going on, including Jelena and Alex, who were sitting directly in front of Cass and Scott.

"Shh!" Cassie pulled me gently down to the seat on her left.

"Cassie, why is everyone convinced that the ridiculous argument between Hayden and me was an audition?" I whispered, as the first Claudio took his place on stage and began reciting lines in a monotone voice. Mr. Peterman looked pained. Before he was a drama teacher, he used to act in a daytime soap. I couldn't even contemplate the turmoil he must feel about the comedown in status.

"Well, it all seemed so dramatic," Cassie explained. "Mr. Peterman had just finished auditioning the other Beatrices and Benedicks—"

"And let me say that there was a painful lack of talent," Jelena cut in, turning around to face us.

"Next!" Mr. Peterman gestured for the monotonous Claudio to get off the stage.

"Then we heard this ruckus going on backstage," Jelena continued. "Insults flying like mad—"

"By the time you two stumbled on stage, everyone was transfixed," Cassie finished.

"Then the scene went to a totally different place emotionally," Jelena whispered, presumably so that Alex and Scott couldn't hear. I looked at her warily.

"Hayden had his head bent near yours and—"

"Stop right there!" I put my hand over her mouth. "I can't believe this! Not only did Hayden drag me into the most embarrassing casting experience in the history of Jefferson High, but now he's got everyone convinced that there's something going on between us! I bet this was a setup of his," I hissed.

Jelena pried my hand off her mouth. Scott and Alex were looking at us with curious expressions.

I turned to Cassie desperately. "And now I'm being forced into playing Beatrice. Cass, you know I'm not one to chase the spotlight!"

Benjamin Zane took his place on the stage, his dark hair shining under the lights. Now, here was someone who loved the spotlight. Any chatter in the audience stopped immediately.

"My lord . . ." Benjamin began in a deep voice.

As I listened to his monologue, I was reminded of why he and Hayden were always in competition for the lead roles. Benjamin had a magnetic presence on stage. He even threw in some gestures, something that had been too ambitious for the previous Claudios.

"Weren't there any other good auditions for Beatrice?" I asked Cassie.

"Well . . ." Her brow creased as she considered my question.

"Saying I liked her ere I went to wars," Benjamin finished with a flourish.

"Great job," Mr. Peterman said.

Benjamin looked at him expectantly.

"Like you said, Benjamin, I'll need to consider the casting overnight."

"But—"

"I'm now auditioning Heros," Mr. Peterman announced.

"That's it!" I said, and leaped up from my seat.

Before Jelena or Cass could question me, I'd joined the lineup of Heros. I ducked behind Diana, a tall redhead who provided excellent camouflage. I tapped my foot nervously as the girls in front of me ran through their auditions, most of which were pretty uninspiring. Diana finished her piece and I stepped up. Just as I opened my mouth, Mr. Peterman gave a yell.

"My dear! What are you doing? Beatrice and Hero have scenes together. There's no way you can play both roles!"

"Talk about ambition!" the girl behind me whispered to her friend.

"Both roles?" I looked at him in confusion. "Mr. Peterman, I'm just trying to show you that I'm far more suited to the role of Hero than of Beatrice."

"Aurora, get off that stage," Mr. Peterman ordered. "I don't care if you're more suited to the part of Dogberry."

"Don't you go pinching my role, Aurora!" Jeffrey yelled from the audience.

"Mr. Peterman, I don't think I'm ready to play a man yet," I said. Why did he have such confidence in my theatrical talent?

Mr. Peterman got a pained look on his face. "Aurora, are you going to be this much trouble the whole way through the production?"

"Possibly," I answered brightly. Maybe the impression that I was a troublemaker would convince Mr. Peterman to uncast me.

"No, she won't," Hayden said, leaping onto the stage. "She's just got a good sense of humor, right?"

"Wron—"

"And that will be really useful for playing Beatrice," Hayden butted in, pulling me down from the stage.

"What are you doing?" I asked him.

"Stopping Mr. Peterman from having a heart attack." Hayden led me back to my seat. "I'm telling you, protesting his decision is useless." We reached Cassie and the others. Scott gave Hayden a grin and gestured to the seat on his right. Hayden sat down. "You're only going to make him cranky. And a cranky director is no fun," he finished.

I slumped into my own seat. Was this what the next four weeks were going to be like? Hayden hanging with our group 24–7?

Thinking of our group, I realized two members were missing.

"Where are Sara and Lindsay?" I asked Cassie, a panicky tone rising up in my throat. "Don't tell me they backed out! Maybe I can still reach them by phone and convince them to come." I rifled through my purse, trying to find my cell before it was too late.

"Aurora, relax." Cassie pointed out Sara and Lindsay sitting several rows to the left. Lindsay gave me a wave. Sara gestured at Hayden and mouthed *Hot!*, then gave me a thumbs-up. I sighed.

Alex and Jelena had their heads together over a copy of the play. Jelena pointed toward the part of Don John, the villain. Alex shook his head.

"Okay, those trying out for Don Pedro, aka Prince of Arragon, please make your way onto the stage," Mr. Peterman called out in a weary voice.

"A prince," Alex said, sending Jelena a blinding smile. "Bingo." He strode up to Mr. Peterman.

I looked at all the athletic brand labels on his clothes. "He looks more like a Nike advertisement than a prince."

"Shh!" Jelena hissed as Alex read the part confidently.

"It's in the bag, baby," Alex said to Jelena as he sauntered back to us.

"So who's going to explain what this play's all about?" Scott asked.

"Why doesn't Aurora tell us all about it?" Hayden suggested. "As she insisted before, she's the beauty and the brains of this relationship."

Now everyone had *What happened before?* written across their faces. I was never going to hear the end of this. I frowned at Hayden, but I wasn't going to refuse a challenge.

"Okay. The play begins at Signior Leonato's house, where we hear that the war is over. Leonato has one daughter, the beautiful and obedient Hero. His niece, Beatrice, also lives with him. Beatrice is lively, witty, and totally against marriage. At the very beginning of the play, we hear that the prince, Don Pedro, and two of his trustiest soldiers, Benedick and Claudio, are coming to visit Leonato.

Claudio is young and enthusiastic, and Benedick is clever and wary of marriage."

"Like Beatrice," Cassie broke in.

"Right," I said. "When these VIP visitors arrive, Beatrice and Benedick get into a fight, but Claudio takes one look at Hero and falls in love."

Scott smiled. "Love at first sight."

Was he a believer? I sure hoped so.

"We also see that the prince's bastard brother, Don John, has arrived with the group," I continued.

Mr. Peterman's voice resounded through the theater. "To interrupt the auditions for a moment, I would like to see those who want to work backstage."

"Ooh! Let's go!" Cassie leaped up from her seat and into the aisle.

Scott, Jelena, and I followed her, and joined Sara and Lindsay and the large group of volunteers by the stage.

"Excuse me, Mr. Peterman?" Jelena raised a slim arm to grab his attention. He looked over at her. "You didn't say anything about stage manager."

"Stage manager?" Mr. Peterman looked surprised. "My dear, I have always looked after that department."

"But don't you find it stressful trying to direct *and* manage?" Before Mr. Peterman could reply, Jelena continued, "Exactly! You need someone who can devote their entire attention to the stage management, thus relieving you of that heavy responsibility."

"Jelena," Mr. Peterman protested.

"Mr. Peterman, I am the girl for the job. I have excellent organizational skills and a flair for communicating with others." She sounded like she was reading off a résumé.

"Jelena," Mr. Peterman tried again.

"Does set design involve the use of spray cans?" Matt, the school's resident graffitist, chipped in, looking excited.

"Mr. Peterman, I really think that you can tell me now if I'm playing Claudio," Benjamin Zane said. "What's the point in waiting till tomorrow? I have a lot of acting obligations at the moment and I need to know how this will impact them."

Benjamin Zane's casting agency has already gotten him two carpet commercials and a crowd scene. Supposedly, the talent scouts are impressed.

Mr. Peterman looked around at everyone, not sure who to answer first. His eyes drifted to me.

"Aurora! Get out of this line!"

"But, Mr. Peterman," I protested, "you can't deny me the chance to work backstage! That was my original reason for coming here today!"

"I can! You have the female lead—"

"I don't want the female lead!"

"And you'll have no time for anything but learning your lines and rehearsing with the other actors," Mr. Peterman finished firmly.

"Couldn't I assist with costume ideas?"

"No," he replied, turning to answer an impatient Jelena.

"Mix paints for the set painters?" I tried. "Type up programs?"

"No!" Mr. Peterman folded his arms against his chest. "You are Beatrice. Just Beatrice. No costume design, no painting, no programs."

An argument started between two wannabe lighting operators.

"Backstage hostilities negotiator?" I asked.

Mr. Peterman's jaw tensed. "Hayden?"

"Already on my way," Hayden answered as he reached my side.

"Please take Aurora home," Mr. Peterman said.

"What?"

Why did I need to go home? And if I did, I so didn't need Hayden to take me there.

"There's no reason for you to be here," Mr. Peterman told me. "You should be devoting yourself to learning your lines and getting into character." He gestured toward the door.

"Come on, Princess," Hayden said, grabbing my hand.

I pulled it away and tried one last time. "Couldn't I be a line prompt?" I said in my sweetest voice.

"Home!" Mr. Peterman cried.

Hayden placed a hand on my back and guided me out the door.

"But—"

Next thing I knew, the stage door was shut firmly behind us.

10 crossing paths

The next morning I awoke from a nightmare in which Mr. Peterman had cast me in every role in *Much Ado About Nothing*, creating a one-woman show. I'd had to frantically change my costume for each character while the huge audience booed, waiting. I shook my head to clear it of the horrible images and headed downstairs for breakfast.

"'Morning, honey," the NAD said as I entered the kitchen. "How did your audition go yesterday?"

My dad works late hours, so often the only time we can catch up is mornings.

I sighed. "I'm playing Beatrice."

"Beatrice!" Dad beamed at me. "Congratulations, honey! This calls for celebration hot chocolate!"

"Dad!" I pulled the milk out of the fridge, making a face. "This is not a good thing. It's going to be a disaster."

Dad poured milk and cocoa into our special hot chocolate pot. "Aurora, you've got to have more confidence in yourself."

"Confidence isn't the problem," I said, adding the sugar. "I just don't think I have the skill to bring the genius of Shakespeare's words to life." I sighed again. "Shakespeare's like my hero. I know he's going to be rolling in his grave at this miscasting."

Dad stirred the hot chocolate thoughtfully. "Aurora, if Mr. Peterman's cast you as the female lead—"

I groaned.

"Then he obviously thinks you have talent. Just try to connect with the words of Shakespeare and you'll be on the right track."

"Hmm," I replied, as he poured the chocolate into oversize mugs. "I guess."

Later, Dad drove me to school. We passed Hayden Paris a few blocks from the entrance. He was wearing a black-and-white-striped shirt and his usual superior smile. I felt like sticking my tongue out at him. Hayden seems to bring out the five-year-old in me.

"Hey, there's Hayden." Dad slowed down. "Let's give him a ride."

"Dad! We are not giving him a ride. We're nearly there."

My foot instinctively pressed down on an imaginary accelerator. Hayden obviously heard my yell through my open window, because his head turned and he gave us a wave. I scowled.

Dad waved back. "Aurora, don't tell me you're still holding on to that old prejudice against Hayden. You two used to be such good friends—you were always over at his house when you were younger."

My dad has such a positive attitude toward everyone. It must be because of the "think good thoughts" dogma at yoga.

"Yeah, well, that's because . . ."

I was going to say "because Mom wanted me out of the way," but didn't finish. I didn't want to see Dad's eyes darken like they always do when I mention Mom. The NAD's good thoughts don't extend to his ex-wife.

"Yes, adult relationships can be complicated," Dad said.

What was he talking about? Hayden and I did *not* have a relationship. We had the opposite of a relationship—whatever that was.

"But very rewarding," the NAD finished, with a faraway smile on his face.

What was that about? I looked more closely at him.

"Dad, is there something you're not telling me?"

"Hey! Here we are—Jefferson High! Go get 'em, honey!"

"Dad, are you avoiding an answer?" I asked, getting out of the car.

"'Bye, honey!" the NAD cried, and our four-wheel-drive tore out of the parking lot.

I watched the dust settle. Dad was acting very strangely. I was definitely going to tackle him on it later.

I headed up the school's front steps and nearly crashed into a surging crowd in the hallway. What was going on? I spotted Cassie, Jelena, Lindsay, and Sara amid the swell and fought my way over to them.

"Why are you staking out the hallway?"

"We're not only staking it out, we're in the most advantageous spot," Jelena replied. She smoothed down her aqua mini.

I looked at the agitated crowd. "Is there some kind of student takeover going on?"

"Did you have a nice walk home with Hayden last night?" Sara asked, pursing her shiny lip-glossed lips in a kissy gesture.

"Yes," I said sarcastically. "It was incredibly romantic."

"What's incredibly romantic?" Scott asked, joining us. Cassie quickly stood up straighter.

"Why, me, of course," Hayden replied.

I groaned. Where had he come from?

"Hayden, you and the word *romantic* are completely incompatible," I said.

"Are you saying you know how I behave when I'm in love?" Hayden put his hands in his dark-denim jeans pockets and tilted his head.

"Fortunately, no."

"Ooh. Harsh." Alex's smooth voice came from just behind Jelena. "Cast list up yet?"

"Nope," Scott replied.

"I can't wait any longer," Sara said, tapping a foot. "Doesn't Mr. Peterman realize the stress I'm going through? If I don't win the role of Don John, supreme villain, then my talents are all for nothing—"

Luckily, her attention was diverted by a shout. "Cast list is up!"

The next minute I was being pushed forward by the crowd. Jelena maneuvered her way to the front.

"Yes! Everyone, you are looking at the new stage manager." She took a bow.

She had obviously worked her magic on Mr. Peterman.

Alex pushed in front of her. "What part did I get? Knew it! I'm princely, baby!"

He picked Jelena up and swung her around. She let out a squeal and he gave a grin as the guys around us looked at him with jealous expressions.

"Excuse me. Excuse me," Benjamin Zane called.

The crowd moved aside for him. Charisma: it can part seas. Benjamin gave the cast list an assured look, then walked away with a smile. Obviously, he had the part of Claudio.

"Sara, you're playing Don John," Cassie called out.

Sara let out a dramatic sigh of relief.

Jeffrey Clark, standing behind Cassie, punched the air victoriously. "Whoo! Dogberry!"

"Lindsay, you're working as a costume designer," Cassie continued. "And Scott, you and I are painting sets."

I shot a triumphant look at Hayden. Cassie and Scott were working together and there was nothing he could do about it!

I suddenly realized that I should check the cast list, too. Maybe I'd antagonized Mr. Peterman enough yesterday to make him recast Beatrice! I raced over. There was my name, right beside the word *Beatrice*.

"No," I moaned.

Hayden was standing next to me. "Sorry, Princess, you can't fight fate."

"Fate?" I said scornfully.

"Yeah." He grinned even harder. "We were meant to get up close and personal."

———

"Aurora!" My mother strode up to me outside the city's top beauty salon. There was more enthusiasm in her voice than I'd ever heard before.

"Let's go inside and get settled before I tell you anything," I said. She couldn't hit the roof in the serene confines of a beauty parlor, could she?

My mother gave a perfect smile as she settled into the beautician's chair. "This is the perfect setting for you to relay your fantastic news."

I gave a wavering smile and sank down into a matching creamy leather chair.

"So, Aurora, I thought we'd book you in for a facial each Friday, so your skin's glowing by the time of the performance," my mother said.

"Look, Mom, I—"

"And I've been studying up on Hero's role." Her voice was enthusiastic. "I've known since you were small that you'd be a performer."

What was going on? My mother hadn't paid this much attention to me since I was a child and she had been dedicated to ensuring that my hair ribbons matched the exact shade of my dress.

"Mom, I have something to tell you," I blurted out. "I didn't get the role of Hero. I'm playing Beatrice."

There was silence from my mother's chair. Because she was wearing cucumber slices over her eyes, I couldn't read her expression, but her jaw was tense. That could have been the tightening effect of the anti-aging mask, though.

"Beatrice," she said.

"Yes."

"Congratulations!" my beautician, Amy, crowed as she painted my nails. "Beatrice is like the star of that whole play, isn't she?"

My mother's jaw relaxed and I silently thanked Amy.

"Well, congratulations. It's not Hero, but it's still a good effort." Mom gave a smile. "And I have even better news. Remember how Bill took your portfolio shots a few weeks ago?"

"Mom, I told you that I wanted you to call the agency and tell them I'm not interested!" I said.

Last month, she'd forced me to have a series of photos taken by Jefferson's most reputable fashion photographer, and had sent them to a casting and model agency—JJ's Models. I thought she'd gotten the picture that modeling or TV or film work didn't appeal to me.

"Well, there's a huge job coming up for a vitamin water commercial, and so far they've cut it down to five models, including you."

My mother beamed, and her beautician had to push Mom's face back into a normal expression to spread the intensive moisturizer over it evenly.

"You let them send my photos off for a job?" I said, horrified.

"It's a big opportunity, darling. They called me and wanted you to go in for a casting call. I knew you wouldn't like the idea of that, so I told them you were away on a shoot."

A shoot? The only photo shoot I'd been part of lately was when Cassie, Jelena, and I decided to do crazy makeovers at a sleepover and took Polaroids of each other.

"So I had them send the audition tape you made for the agency," my mother went on. "The vitamin water people really like your look."

"But I don't want to be on TV!"

Amy and the other beautician stared at me with shocked expressions.

"I want to be a writer," I said. "I want to inspire people with my own words, not recite someone else's lines about kiwi-flavored hydration."

"Aurora, any other girl would jump at the chance."

"I'm not doing it, Mother." Now that my nails were dry, I got up and gathered my things. "I'm in *Much Ado About Nothing*, just like you wanted me to be. That's enough of an acting challenge."

"Aurora," my mother said in a warning tone, "this is an amazing opportunity."

"Yes, it is. But it's not the one that I want." I gave my mother a smile. "Thank you for the facial and the manicure."

"Aurora, I thought we'd do coffee and discuss this further. Just wait another twenty minutes. I've got to have my forehead Botoxed again."

No way was I going to stick around and observe my mother being injected with a muscle-paralyzing toxin.

"Sorry, Mom, I have a rehearsal," I lied.

"Now?"

"Yes!" I sprinted out the door.

Why was no one listening to my wishes? My mother was determined to make me the next supermodel, Mr. Peterman wanted me front and center in his production, and my friends were intent on casting Hayden as my future hubby! It felt like I had no control over any part of my life anymore.

I headed for the one place guaranteed to restore my inner peace. A bookstore.

I lost track of time as I perused the book aisles, seeking wisdom like a pilgrim visiting the Delphic oracle. After an hour or so of browsing, I headed for the checkout, laden with reading material. As I passed the Harlequin Romance section, I remembered the rumor that Mrs. Kent was a closet romance writer. This was my chance to find out. I searched for the name I'd heard she used as her nom de plume: Catherine Goldstein.

There! I grabbed the novel and looked at the racy cover. A buxom blond in a skimpy gown swooned in the arms of a broad-shouldered man. I opened it up to see if the writing resembled Mrs. Kent's style. Not that I'd really seen much of her writing beyond her comments on my essays. I started reading a love scene and my cheeks burned. Luscious bosoms?

"Enjoyable reading?" a low voice murmured in my ear.

I shrieked and whirled around to confront the pervert reading over my shoulder. As I turned, I stumbled, and fell toward Hayden Paris.

"Hey, look, we're almost replicating the pose on the cover," he remarked as he caught me.

"You scared the life out of me!"

"I see you're still wearing that vanilla scent." Hayden set me on my feet, his hands on my shoulders to steady me. "It's obvious, Princess. Consumed by desire for me, you were drawn to the romance section."

"If you take a look at my intended purchases," I said, indicating my tower of books, "you'll notice that none of them have anything to do with love."

"A cover," Hayden said. "You're an intelligent girl; you knew you'd need one."

I barely restrained myself from grinding my teeth in frustration.

"Hey, this girl looks a lot like you, Princess."

I yanked the novel from him. The girl on the cover did look like me, but was very scantily dressed.

"Why is this afternoon getting progressively worse?" I said.

"What happened this afternoon?"

"Another episode in the continuing saga in which my mother finds it impossible to accept me as I am," I said before I could stop myself. Why was I telling Hayden my personal business?

"Come on." He put a hand on my arm and guided me toward the bookshop's café. "Let's get a coffee and discuss it."

A coffee and a discussion? That's what girlfriends do together. However, I let him lead me to a table. I felt so miserable about the situation with my mother that I'd discuss it with anyone, even Hayden Paris.

"My mother wants me to be a model," I stated flatly.

"A model?" Hayden's eyes became wide and he took a large gulp of his coffee.

"So that's an unbelievable idea?" I said, feeling cross at his reaction.

"No, not at all," he said hurriedly, setting his coffee down. "You're, you know . . ."

"I'm what?" I waited to see what insult would come out of his mouth, hoping I could think of a quick retort.

"You're, you know . . ." he repeated. He looked oddly nervous. "You're . . . you'd be a perfect model," he finished, taking another gulp of his coffee.

"Why are you making a face?" I asked suspiciously.

"Just the thought of opening up a magazine and having you look out at me . . . It's . . ." He looked away.

No acerbic wit, courtesy of Paris? The world was topsy-turvy.

He turned his gaze back to me. "So you don't want to do it?"

"No. I know it sounds crazy, because any other girl would love to—"

"But you're not just any girl," Hayden broke in. He halved a dark chocolate cookie, my favorite, and passed the bigger piece to me.

"Yeah." I couldn't believe he understood. "I appreciate the talent it takes to be a model, but it's just not something that inspires me."

"What does inspire you?" He looked at me intently.

"This." I gestured at the books around us.

He leaned forward. "The way books affect us?"

"Yes!" I cried.

"I love that Kafka quote: *We need the books that affect us like a disaster, that grieve us deeply, like the death of someone we loved more than ourselves, like being banished into forests far from everyone, like a suicide.*" Hayden's eyes were glowing. "*A book must be the ax for the frozen sea inside us.*"

I have to admit that I admire people who can quote passages from books. "That's such a beautiful way of putting it."

"It's one of my favorite quotes," Hayden said, stirring his coffee. "I get it. You want to be the one swinging the ax."

"With intention, not wildly!" I laughed. "That sounds rather lethal."

Hayden winked. "Good luck explaining that one to your mom."

We laughed and sipped the last of our coffees at the same time.

"Hey, why were you here?" I asked as we parted ways, me to purchase my towering stack of books, him to go meet Scott.

"Reasons," he said mysteriously, and gave me a wave.

"You're a Harlequin Romance fan, aren't you?" I called after him.

Several curious customers turned to check out the male romance junkie. Hayden gave me a *Sure* look, but his face radiated embarrassment.

For once, I'd gotten the better of Hayden Paris.

11 undesirable aura

"Heaven," Jelena murmured as she bit into a brownie.

"If you're not careful, Ms. Carraway is going to kill you," Cassie said in a warning tone, her face almost hidden behind a Mount Everest of cookbooks. "You know how she feels about people eating in the library."

"Whatever." Jelena looked unconcerned as crumbs from the brownie fell under our study table. "If she comes by, I'll just offer her some."

"Oh my god." Lindsay looked over my shoulder. "Tyler's heading this way."

Everyone's eyes shot to the spot just behind me.

"Everyone look away from Tyler right now," I said softly. "Lindsay, remember what I told you this morning. We're playing it cool. Now, everybody laugh," I instructed.

"At what?" Jelena whispered.

"Just laugh!"

Looking like you're having a good time is one of the fundamentals when dealing with an ex. Most guys expect you to be beside yourself after losing them. Acting happy ensures they receive an ego check.

We all broke into peals of laughter. Tyler looked at us cautiously, but walked up to Lindsay.

"Hey, Linds." His voice was superlow. "Can I talk to you for a minute?"

Lindsay slowly turned to him and stopped laughing. "Sure, Tyler," she said, poker-faced. "Go ahead."

He ran a hand through his sandy-colored hair. "I sort of hoped we could talk privately?"

"Privately?" Lindsay put on her confused face, the one that we'd spent twenty minutes perfecting this morning. Call me psychic, but I'd had a feeling that Tyler would be making the approach today.

"You want your stuff back, right?" she went on. "I can drop it in your locker if you want."

Another key to dealing with an ex is to remain friendly and unconcerned. Your world continues without him.

"Lindsay, I don't want my stuff back." Tyler dropped to his knees in front of her. He took her hands in his. "I want *you* back."

"Can I ask why?" Lindsay pulled her hands away and Tyler looked shocked. "Didn't you want to . . . what was it again?" Lindsay tapped her chin, pretending to be struggling to remember. "Spread your wings and fly like an eagle?"

People at the tables nearby turned around at her words. Tyler looked embarrassed. Rightfully so. I mean, hello, talk about a B-grade movie line.

"Look, Lindsay, I needed some time apart—"

"That's cool," Lindsay interrupted. "So why are you here again?"

"Because I'm an idiot!" Tyler cried.

Half the library jumped. I saw Ms. Carraway's head jolt up from her Charles Dickens.

"We already knew that," Jelena broke in.

I frowned at her. Friends should never butt in on an I-want-you-back scene. Otherwise, things can turn hostile.

"I needed the week apart to realize that I don't need to be alone to soar, Lindsay." Tyler stroked her cheek and pulled her closer. "You're the wind beneath my wings."

I rolled my eyes behind his back at his plagiarism of Bette Midler's song.

Lindsay pulled away from him. "Well, I think it's good we've had this time apart."

"Good?" Tyler leaped up.

"It's given me some time to think." Lindsay looked at me uncertainly.

Don't give up now! I mouthed at her.

"And I'm enjoying having some space," she finished.

"Linds, we don't need space!" Tyler cried. "We're perfect together! Who needs space?"

He moved closer to her and knocked Cassie's tower of cookbooks to the ground.

Ms. Carraway strode over from her desk. "Tyler, you're disrupting a quiet study space." She attempted to usher him out the door.

Tyler gave Lindsay a pleading look and pushed back in front of Ms. Carraway. "Linds, can I meet you after school?" His voice was shrill.

Ms. Carraway nodded toward the library monitors, who walked forward and grabbed Tyler by the arms.

"Tyler, there isn't going to be any reunion," Lindsay said softly.

"Yeah, there will!" Tyler cried as the library monitors dragged him off. "I'll win you back! I have not yet begun to fight!" He shook a fist in triumph as his voice faded beyond the door.

Jelena raised her eyebrows. "Dramatic enough?"

"I hope I'm doing the right thing," Lindsay said. Her eyes were slightly teary, now that Tyler had left the room.

I looked at her. "Lindsay, remember what I told you? It's just like when mistreated workers go on strike. You're not taking the first offer. You're aiming for better conditions. Tyler will have to fight to win you back." I smiled. "And as we all just heard, he's vowed to do that."

The bell for our last afternoon class sounded.

"Yes! Forty-five minutes till the weekend officially starts!" Jelena bounced from her seat.

"I fail to understand your enthusiasm," I said. "You know our last class is interpretive dance." I sighed and picked up my handbag.

Jelena and I waved to Cass and Lindsay and headed off in the opposite direction.

"Aurora, I told you last week, Ms. DeForest is several bricks short of a load," Jelena said. "Just put a spiritual look on your face and she'll be happy."

"A spiritual look?"

"Widen your eyes and give serene smiles. Works great," Jelena insisted.

"Everyone sit down in a circle," Ms. DeForest directed as she glided to the center of the room. "Close your eyes and chant after me. Ooooooommmmm."

"Umm?" Jeffrey chirped, as we all found a place on the floor. "I say that all the time in class."

"*Ooooooommmmm!*" Ms. DeForest yelled.

Really. How did she expect anyone to relax if she shouted the spiritual mantra at a one-hundred-thirty-decibel level?

Ms. DeForest started a CD of lute music.

"Psychic intuitiveness begins with opening your mind to the universe. Soon you will be able to use tarot cards, and receive messages via dreams and willing spirits."

"Willing spirits?" Jelena sounded incredulous. I opened my eyes to see her navy-blue eyes full of disbelief.

"I know!" I whispered, glancing over at Ms. DeForest to ensure that she wasn't paying attention to us. "That sounds more like meddling with the dark side than a form of spiritual enlightenment."

Ms. DeForest opened her eyes and looked at me. "Aurora, why don't you lead our next exercise?"

Her glare made me think of Medusa—one glance from her could turn a person to stone.

"Everyone walk over to the ribbons." Ms. DeForest gestured toward a pile of rainbow-colored ribbons on sticks. "Select one, and form a line behind Aurora."

"Ribbons?" Jesse Cook sounded shocked. "Can't the guys have something more masculine?"

Tom Meyer folded his arms. "I do not do ribbons."

"Anyone who refuses to use the ribbons will be staying after school to help me dye new ones for my out-of-school classes." Ms. DeForest smiled like a cat that's caught its first mouse. "Aurora, twirl to the other side of the room, swinging your ribbon in a rainbow arc."

I was never going to talk in class again. I started twirling, and everyone followed me. At least we were united in our embarrassment.

"Become one with the light!" Ms. DeForest called. "And back again, to the other side of the room!"

"Jesse!" cried Amber Jenkins. "You nearly poked my eye out!"

"Can you blame me?" Jesse's arm waved around out of control as we continued twirling from one side of the room to the other. "All this spinning is making me dizzy."

Ms. DeForest turned up the lute music. "Faster! Connect with the divine feminine and masculine energies!"

"I can't connect with anything when I'm waving a rainbow ribbon," complained Tom.

Ms. DeForest muttered something under her breath about "the energy expended in teaching the spiritually barren" as she switched off the CD.

"I hope everyone has prepared their two-minute dance based on a traumatic experience," she said, walking around us, her hands curled into fists by her sides. "Remember, this is a nonjudgmental space."

Shane Davis leaped to his feet. "My trauma's about the moment I discovered the extent of the destruction of the world's oceans."

His CD started up and I realized it was the same one that the

NAD meditated to. Shane began leaping in the air, making high-pitched dolphin-like noises. He waved his arms like an undulating jellyfish, then threw himself onto the ground and stretched out in a starfish shape.

Jelena rolled her eyes. "This is ridiculous."

"I think it's touching that he's showing such concern for the creatures of the sea," I replied, as Shane pretended to be a turtle choking on plastic rings.

"Excellent, Shane." Ms. DeForest gave the first smile of today's lesson. "Who's next?"

I stood up. I just wanted to get this over with.

"My traumatic experience happened just recently," I announced. "It's a story of an audition gone wrong."

I threw myself dramatically to the floor, symbolizing the moment Hayden and I had stumbled onto the stage, then spread my arms out in shock as I saw the audience staring at me. I twirled in confusion at Mr. Peterman's remarks, and stopped abruptly as I figured out what he meant. I kicked my legs in the air like a Russian dancer, symbolizing rebellion. Finally, I was dragged away by an invisible force (Hayden). I finished, breathless. I'd actually gotten into this whole interpretive dance thing! I looked at Ms. DeForest expectantly.

"Pretentious," she said.

My mouth dropped open.

"No authenticity," she added. "Who's next?"

"No authenticity?" I repeated, my hands shaking in shock. "But that's what really happened."

"There was no surrender to the dance or your emotions—"

"I think it was pretty emotional," Jeffrey put in. "I observed the real event."

"Jeffrey, who is the interpretive dance teacher?" Ms. DeForest glared at him.

"The dance was what I felt," I said, looking at Ms. DeForest earnestly. "And who I am. So how can you say that it wasn't authentic?"

"Well, sometimes we have to change who we are," Ms. DeForest replied.

Change who we are? Who was she to say something like that to a teenage girl already fending off a morass of self-doubt?

"I thought you said this was a nonjudgmental space!" I spluttered.

"I don't like your aura," Ms. DeForest said icily. "Report to the office."

"You're kicking me out of class because of something the eye can't see?"

"I can see it. It's black." Ms. DeForest pointed at the door. "Report to the office."

I stormed out of the room.

"Tyranny!" I cried, as Jelena and Cassie arrived at the office an hour later.

"Were they really hard on you?" Cassie asked.

"No, but they warned me that it was my second detention in a week," I replied. I gathered my things together so we could head home. "What happened after I left?"

"Well, we had to sit through the rest of the two-minute traumatic dances." Jelena ran a hand through her long dark hair. "The only highlight was Jeffrey's strip show—"

"*Strip* show?" Cassie and I were open-mouthed.

"Yeah, he strutted over to the CD player and put on that old Rod Stewart song Do Ya Think I'm Sexy? then started making suggestive movements and ripping off his clothes."

"How far did he get?" I asked.

"He was down to his boxers by the time Ms. DeForest threw her mauve shawl over him. When she demanded to know what stripping had to do with trauma, Jeffrey replied that it symbolized his emotional nakedness."

"I can't believe this!" I cried. "Jeffrey does an X-rated dance and *I* was the one to get detention? Ms. DeForest is out to get me."

"Aurora, I'm sure she's not out to get you," Cassie said in a soothing tone.

"No, I think she probably is." Jelena smiled at two basketball players walking in the opposite direction. "After you left, Aurora, she told the class that you needed to cleanse your aura by wearing quartz crystals."

"The nerve! You know what I'm going to do?" My voice rose higher. "I'm going to get my aura photographed as evidence. At that Aquarius bookstore in town. Just wait till she sees the blatant absence of black! Just wait!"

I clenched my fists and saw Cassie send one of her change-the-subject glances to Jelena.

"Let's go get some ice cream," Jelena said. She believes sugar is the ultimate cure-all.

"Oh, I'm supposed to meet Scott." Cassie looked at us. "But I can cancel if you need counseling, Aurora."

Cassie is so self-denying.

"Are you crazy?" Jelena said.

"Yeah, Cass, I'll be fine." I smiled at her. "I think I'm just going to head home and relax."

12 the NAD's big date

When I got home, I did what I always do when I feel angry and frustrated. I began vacuuming with a fury. When I entered the living room with the droning machine, Snookums and Bebe, who had been curled up together on the sofa, leaped up, looking put out. Snookums let out a warlike yowl. For some reason he views the vacuum cleaner as his mortal enemy. If you turn your back on him, he'll pounce on it. Once he even managed to pry it open (my cats are so intelligent that I'm convinced they should be allowed to join Mensa) and shredded the vacuum bag.

Bebe started her exercise regimen, which involves running at lightning speed from the living room to the kitchen, then skidding out of control when she reaches the Italian floor tiles.

Between these two habits, it's no wonder that I worry about my cats being intellectually deprived. Like teenage delinquents, they're turning to potentially dangerous activities out of boredom.

"Aurora?" The NAD popped his head around the corner, yelling above the roar of the vacuum.

"Dad! How come you're home so early?"

I dropped the vacuum and Snookums saw his opportunity. His eyes gleamed as he pounced on his enemy.

"Snookums! No!" I yanked the vacuum away and Snookums's paws swiped thin air.

"I was wondering if you could help me," the NAD said.

"Sure thing!" I yelled, as I pushed the Off button on the vacuum and pulled it out of Snookums's line of sight. "What with?"

"I'm having dinner with someone tonight," Dad explained as I followed him upstairs to his room.

"You have a date!"

I knew his odd behavior the other morning had meant he was hiding something.

"Yes, I have a date," he admitted. "And I need some help in choosing what to wear." He gestured at the fifteen or so shirts thrown over his bed. "We're going to La Bella Donna."

I tapped my finger against my chin, like Sherlock Holmes thoughtfully surveying a crime scene. "So you want something smart but not too dressy. Something that reflects the artiness of the restaurant. And, most importantly, something that says, 'My outside is great, but my inside is even more interesting.'"

"One shirt's going to say all that?" Dad looked even more frightened at making a choice.

"That's the magic of fashion." I pulled out a shirt. "There! Perfect!"

"All right." Dad still looked slightly wary.

"Don't forget to compliment her on her outfit," I instructed. "Girls love that. And pull her chair out for her—"

"Aurora! I have dated before!"

"And don't order spaghetti! No one can pull that off till at least the sixth date—"

Dad pushed me out the door. "I'll never get to do all that if you keep stalling me."

This was so exciting! Who knew what kind of cool lady the NAD could end up with? A new woman was exactly what he needed to heal the scars of the divorce.

Twenty minutes or so later, I only just heard the doorbell chiming over the roar of the vacuum. I pushed the Off button again and shouted, "I'll get it!"

"No, I'll get it!" I heard Dad yell from upstairs.

No way was I going to let him pause in his grooming ritual. I ran for the door.

I threw it open with a beaming smile. "Welcom . . ."

The word died in my throat. Ms. DeForest was standing on our front steps.

I blinked. Maybe my imagination had gotten so vivid that I was seeing visions, like Brutus in Shakespeare's *Julius Caesar*. I stared more closely. It was definitely Ms. DeForest. That was her abundance of brown ringlets. Her sharp green eyes and narrow nose. Her mouth was a fine line as she stared back at me. A waft of sandalwood blew in on the breeze.

What was she doing here? Had she decided that I was so spiritually barren that I needed extra help?

Her gaze shifted to a spot behind me.

"Dana! You're early!"

I turned around to see the NAD, his face still covered in shaving cream. How did he know her first name?

Oh my god. I bet she'd called Dad to complain about my behavior in class. And now she'd come to have some parent–teacher meeting with him. Except didn't parent–teacher meetings only happen at school?

I looked back at Ms. DeForest. Who came for a parent–teacher meeting dressed in a royal-purple velvet minidress and a heavy pink quartz choker?

"You look beautiful," the NAD said. "I love your dress."

My eyes flashed wildly between him and Ms. DeForest. Why was my dad giving compliments before a parent–teacher meeting? Was he trying to sweeten her up?

"Thank you, Kenneth." Ms. DeForest gave him a smooth smile.

Wait a minute. I took in the NAD's appreciative gaze and the truth hit me like a wrecking ball. I felt my insides crumbling. There was no parent–teacher meeting. Ms. DeForest was the NAD's date!

My brain let out a scream. And he was using my tips on her!

"Aurora, I'd like to introduce you to Dana DeForest. Dana, this is my daughter, Aurora."

Right at that moment, a flying marmalade bundle leaped at Ms. DeForest's velvet dress. She let out a shriek and started batting at it.

"Get it away!"

She was trying to kill Snookums!

The NAD and I both raced forward, and he pried Snookums's claws from the thick material.

"Aurora! Take Snookums upstairs right now!"

The part of the NAD's face that wasn't covered in shaving cream was flushed as he passed Snookums to me. Ms. DeForest's eyes were snapping angrily.

Thank god for an escape route. I pounded up the stairs.

Dad's voice floated up after me. "I'm so sorry. Animals—who can explain them? Just give me thirty seconds to get this stuff off my face and we'll get out of here."

Snookums was more than just an animal. He was an advanced, intelligent being who just happened to wear a fur coat. Look at how he'd pounced on Ms. DeForest. He never did that to anything he didn't consider an enemy.

"Snookums! Are you okay, my baby?"

Snookums let out a pitiful meow. His kitty heart was probably pounding with confusion at what had just happened. I walked over to my window seat with him cradled in my arms like a baby.

"Aurora?" The NAD's voice echoed from the front hall. "Dana and I are leaving now. I'll be back around eleven."

The front door slammed, and the lights of what I assumed to be Ms. DeForest's car switched on and headed down the driveway.

This situation was truly pessimal; i.e., maximally bad. Ms. DeForest, my most-hated teacher, was dating Dad! How had this happened? Where had they met?

This was just like Cinderella. A girl living alone with her loving father until a new woman came into the picture. I started seeing a vision of myself sitting in the cinders, wearing tie-dyed rags. Where was my Prince? Not that I expected him to save me, but at least he would be a willing ear to listen to my sorrows.

I tried to watch a TV show to distract myself, but it was useless. Right now, the NAD and Ms. DeForest would be seated at La Bella Donna. I pictured the scene. They'd be leaning forward, smiling at each other in the candlelight. The NAD was probably using all my surefire advice on her. Why, oh why, had I given him those tips? I'd thought he was going to use them to woo some enchanting woman, not one who'd sent me off to the school office.

What did the NAD see in her, anyway? My conscience gave a twinge at this mean-spirited thought, but really? I guess she was attractive, in an alternative sort of style. But didn't he see her tendency toward cruelty? Perhaps that only came out in interpretive dance classes. Maybe outside school, she was all sweetness and light.

What had made Ms. DeForest decide to date my dad? Contact from willing spirits? There really should be a law against parents dating teachers. Talk about a conflict of interest. She could be saying anything to the NAD about my aura.

How far along was this relationship? I had to know.

Just before eleven p.m. I headed down the driveway and climbed over the fence onto Hayden Paris's basketball court. I searched the fence for a hole. Spotting one, I squatted down in front of it. This was the perfect vantage point to view the end of the NAD and Ms. DeForest's date.

"The view's clearer from the picket three down." Hayden's voice nearly scared the life out of me.

"What are you doing out here?" I hissed as I moved down three pickets.

Hmm. The view *was* better from here. I scowled. Hayden would know, seeing as he'd observed just about all of my unlucky dates.

"Taking the garbage out, my lady," he answered, and gestured toward the black trash can he was wheeling behind him. "And might

I ask you the same question? You really can't stay away from my yard, can you?"

"Hayden, I'm here out of grave necessity." I tried to arrange myself more comfortably on the ground.

"Grave necessity, hey?" He raised his eyebrows in curiosity.

"Yup."

I turned back to search the driveway for any sign of an approaching car. I heard Hayden's footsteps fade away to his front steps. Yes! Maybe he'd decided to leave me in peace. My hopes were dashed when he reappeared with two purple cushions.

"These should make your time in my yard a little less painful."

He placed the cushions on the ground and sat on one of them. I felt tempted to ask who'd invited him, but it was his yard. And he had been nice to me at the bookstore.

I noticed he was wearing new cologne. It was clean, like crisp Granny Smith apples. His red shirt was rolled up at the sleeves, showing his tanned arms.

"So what's our aim, Princess?" He leaned forward, his hazel eyes glistening in the moonlight.

I turned my gaze away from his and back to the hole in the fence. "My dad'll be back from his date in a few moments, and we're going to observe him."

Hayden tried to smother a laugh. "You criticize me for spying on you, and now you're doing it yourself? Isn't that a little hypocritical?"

"So now you're admitting that you spy on me?" Ha! He'd fallen into his own trap!

He gave me a wink. "I'm just repeating your words from last week."

"Sure." I should have known he'd never own up to his voyeuristic activities.

"Seriously, though, don't you think your dad can take care of his own love life?" he said.

"Are you implying that I'm interfering?" I narrowed my eyes.

"No, I'm just saying that maybe you should let Cupid take care of this one."

"Hayden, Cupid—"

"Is understaffed?"

"Severely." I peeped through the fence again. "Besides, Ms. DeForest isn't a good match for my dad."

"Ms. DeForest is dating your father?" Hayden whistled.

"You know her?"

"I know *of* her. Jeffrey was talking about your detention in the locker room, after practice."

Guys were discussing me in the locker room? Was there no privacy anymore?

"It's just one big gossip session in there, isn't it?"

"Not exactly. I asked him—"

"So you do spy on me!" I stood up in outrage.

"Quick!" Hayden pulled me back down as headlights turned into my driveway. "You'll miss your own spying opportunity."

"It's not spying. It's observing with an objective."

Hayden's mouth curled on one side with amusement. "It's spying. In the true double-oh-seven sense. Hey, I've always considered myself rather Bondesque."

"Well, if it's spying, we should be quiet!" I hissed.

"I think you'd make a great Bond girl," he went on. "Although you need to be aware that every one of them inevitably falls victim to Bond's charm."

I sent Hayden my most ferocious look and he shut up.

Ms. DeForest's Mazda roared to a spot about ten yards in front of us. I could see her in the driver's seat, giving the NAD a sultry smile. Talk about putting on the moves!

"I know she gave you a detention, but she might be all right if you get to know her a bit more," Hayden whispered in my ear.

"She told me I had a black aura!" I cried.

"Shh! You'll give yourself away!"

"Oh my god!" I grabbed Hayden's arm. "They're about to kiss!" I buried my head in his shoulder. "I can't look!"

"Well, he certainly likes her," Hayden reported.

I groaned. "Just tell me when I can look."

Hayden's cologne was distracting. It made me think of running through fields of freshly cut grass. I had to get him out of my space.

"Aren't they done yet?" I complained.

"Nope. It's a pretty passionate embrace."

I groaned again. "How passionate?"

"Well, they've been in constant lip-lock for three minutes now." I felt Hayden move his hand slightly to check his watch. "And he's holding her really close. She's running her hands through his hair—"

"Enough!" I said miserably.

The car door slammed.

I pulled myself away from Hayden. "I thought you were going to tell me when they finished kissing?"

He grinned. "I was distracted. And you were the one who embraced me."

"Embraced you?" I choked. "I hid my eyes. Period."

"Sure." He raised his eyebrows skeptically.

"Can you never be quiet?" I watched Ms. DeForest pull out of our driveway.

"Nope." He shook his head infuriatingly. "You know you'd be lonely without my voice."

I threw my hand over his mouth as the NAD came up the path. Hayden tried to pry my hand away, his eyes twinkling. Just as the NAD passed our section of the fence, I felt Hayden's lips gently kiss the inside of my palm.

I gave a scream. "What do you think you're doing?"

I leaped up, and Hayden fell on his back on the asphalt, his eyes wide with surprise.

"Aurora?" I turned to see the NAD peering over the fence. "What are you doing out here?"

"Aurora and I were just stargazing together, Mr. Skye," Hayden said, pulling himself up from the ground.

Stargazing? If I weren't so antiviolence, he'd be seeing stars of a different type!

"Romantic night, isn't it?" he continued.

"Very." The NAD gazed dreamily up at the sky. "So, are you coming in now, Aurora? Or do you need a few moments to say good night?"

I saw Hayden push down a smile. No! The NAD thought Hayden and I were an item. I was going to kill him for this. Hayden, I mean, not the NAD. His outrageous antics had overstressed my mind.

I leaped over the fence. "Nope. I'm coming right now."

"How was your date?" I inquired as the NAD closed the front door behind us.

"Great." He smiled. "Dana's one of a kind. She hadn't realized that the Aurora in her class was the same Aurora I'd been raving about."

The NAD gave me a hug and sprinted down the hall before I could do any more questioning.

"You shouldn't have called your evening to an end because of me," he called back. "Hayden looked very disappointed."

I stalked upstairs. I couldn't believe that Hayden had put on such an act to embarrass me! Kissing my palm so I'd give myself away to the NAD; lying about stargazing. This time, Hayden Paris had gone too far.

13 lady disdain

I used Sunday morning to interrogate the NAD. Since Friday night, he'd been locked in his office. Now was the time to use my surefire tactics. I got up at seven a.m. and started cooking pancakes with the works—maple syrup, bananas, sugar, chocolate chips, and strawberries. I didn't turn on the fan, so the smell was sure to drift into the NAD's office.

"Something smells good." Dad popped his head around the corner. "But I've got to get started on that brief—"

I flipped a golden pancake onto a plate.

"Maybe I can stay for ten minutes." He settled himself at the table and buried himself in the weekend paper. Total avoidance tactic.

"Pancakes, coming through!" I pushed his newspaper aside and placed a stack in front of him. "So, Dad, you haven't told me much about Ms. DeForest."

Dad looked anxiously at the door, his only escape route.

I leisurely poured syrup over his pancakes. "How many dates have you been on?"

The NAD's jaw tensed. I had him trapped. I grabbed my own stack and sat down in front of him, giving him my most attentive look.

"Oh, you know, a few." He shrugged nonchalantly, then started shoving pancake into his mouth.

I cut my stack into little hearts, to put off having a full mouth and being unable to interrogate him.

"So it's serious?"

"Well, it's early days yet. Dana's a very interesting woman."

That was one way to put it.

"We met at yoga, when we had to pair up for an exercise."

Darn that friendly yoga environment.

"It's nice to be seeing someone again." A small smile spread over Dad's face.

Great. Now if I said anything negative, it was going to seem like I wanted to sabotage his happiness. I played with a strawberry.

"So, what are you up to today?" Dad finished his last bite and took his plate up to the sink. "Are you and Hayden hanging out again?"

I choked on my pancake. Not only did Hayden have Dad convinced that he and I were a couple, but his kiss was still burning the inside of my palm. I had scrubbed and scrubbed and tried to block it from my mind, but I could still feel the sensation of his lips on my skin.

"Chew carefully, honey." Dad kissed the top of my head and headed for the office.

I was not going to spend the day with Hayden. My time, as always, was going to be spent productively.

By the time I turned up for the rehearsal of *Much Ado About Nothing* on Monday afternoon, I'd read through the first half of the play.

"Welcome to our very first rehearsal!" Mr. Peterman beamed at all of us seated in front of him. "I expect that everyone's prepared to have a lot of fun."

I looked at Jelena, Cassie, Sara, and Lindsay. This was exactly what I needed to distract me from the NAD and Ms. DeForest's love affair. Good friends, good times, and quality literature. Thank you, Shakespeare.

"And to work hard." Mr. Peterman's voice turned serious. "We have just three weeks to stage one of the Bard's most-loved plays. I'm sure that all of you, like me, want it to be a production of quality."

Scott and Alex popped into the seats just in front of us. Scott waved at Cassie and grinned.

"I feel nervous about working one-on-one with Scott," Cassie whispered, playing with the little yellow heart dangling from her necklace. "You know I was so jittery during our meeting yesterday that I spilled my coffee all over one of his set design sketches? I wanted to die."

"Cass, did you see that smile he just gave you? There's no way he's holding a grudge. You just need to try and relax. Focus on finding out more about him—after all, you want to be sure he's Potential Prince quality before your crush gets any more serious."

Cass nodded at me, but she didn't look any less worried.

Mr. Peterman continued, "Now, as we can see from this first part of the play, the attitudes in Shakespeare's time were obviously very different from our own. Marriage had little to do with love and more to do with social betterment and preserving inheritance. A woman's role was firstly to be a dutiful daughter, then to be an obedient wife."

"Mr. Peterman, the play is totally sexist!" Sara stood up.

Jelena rolled her eyes.

"As I said, Sara, the play was written around five hundred years ago, so the ideas are naturally outdated. However, it is still a fabulous play—"

"Yeah, sure." Sara slumped back in her seat.

"And because of those outdated beliefs, I've decided to set it in the 1950s."

An excited murmur ran through the crowd at Mr. Peterman's announcement.

"Instead of a Sicilian property, the play will take place at a fabulous estate in the American South. Leonato is a governor, and Claudio has similar political aspirations. Hero is the typical obedient daughter, but Beatrice is a Southern belle who rejects the traditional ideas of marriage. By setting *Much Ado About Nothing* in the fifties, we'll show our audience just how far we've come since then, and also how far we've yet to go toward total equality."

Sara looked pleased.

"So, all backstage crew," Mr. Peterman said, "I hope you've been listening carefully. All backdrops, costumes, and props will be fifties in style."

"This is so cool," I whispered to Cassie. "You know what this means? Cocktail dresses and pump shoes—"

"All backstage crew backstage, and all cast members up on stage, please!" Mr. Peterman called, pointing at the two areas.

Walking up to the stage, I started to get nervous. The hard part was about to begin. I took a spot next to Sara as Mr. Peterman began handing out scripts.

"Okay, all actors who are in scene one, please get ready to read."

I took my place on stage with Claire Linden, who was playing Hero, and David Murray, who was Leonato. Claire gave me a shy smile. David was studying his script intently.

"So, Leonato, Hero, and Beatrice are all sitting in the orchard when a messenger comes to tell them that the prince and his friends are on their way," Mr. Peterman said. "David, please begin."

"*I learn in this letter that Don Pedro of Arragon comes this night to Messina,*" David said, his head still buried in the script.

As I watched Cass and Scott head backstage, my mind drifted. How was I going to play matchmaker if I was on stage all the time? I was going to have to go through the script and mark all the places where I could sneak backstage.

"Aurora?" Mr. Peterman was looking expectantly at me.

"Yeah, Mr. Peterman?"

"It's your line."

"*Alas! he gets nothing by that,*" I read. "*In our last conflict four of his five wits went halting off, and now is the whole man governed with one. . . .*"

It was rather odd that my role was centered upon insulting Hayden, aka Benedick. At least I would sound authentic.

"*Don Pedro is approached!*" cried the messenger.

"Okay, I want Don Pedro, Benedick, Claudio, Don John, and Balthazar on stage," Mr. Peterman instructed.

Alex, Hayden, Benjamin, Sara, and a guy I didn't know stepped onto the stage.

"*Good Signior Leonato, you are come to meet your trouble: the fashion of the world is to avoid cost, and you encounter it.*"

Alex swaggered over to Claire, every square inch of him covered in sports logos. "*I think this is your daughter.*" He took Claire's hand and placed a kiss on it, giving her a wink. Claire pulled her hand away, blushing.

Oh my god. Alex was putting the moves on Claire while Jelena was backstage. I glared at him.

"Mr. Peterman, what kind of lighting am I going to get?" Benjamin slicked back his heavily gelled hair. "I was thinking that this scene calls for a spotlight on Claudio. He's seeing Hero for the first time."

"Benjamin, this is a first read-through," Mr. Peterman replied. "But I can assure you that no scene is going to be bright enough that you'll require those sunglasses." He pulled Benjamin's Armani shades off his eyes.

"My agent told me they give me a brooding feel," Benjamin said, taking the glasses back. "I think that Claudio should be brooding. I mean, he's a young man who's just returned from the war—"

"Could I have sunglasses, too, Mr. Peterman?" I asked. "Beatrice is a rebel. Plus, I think they would make me feel much more comfortable in front of an audience—"

"Continue the scene!" Mr. Peterman instructed. "With no sunglasses on anyone!"

Benjamin smiled at me. "Bummer."

I smiled back, and saw Hayden frowning. What was his deal?

"How come you feel uncomfortable in front of an audience?" Benjamin asked. Without his shades, I could see that his eyes were an unusual crystal blue.

"It's the first time I've been on stage," I explained.

"I could coach you if you want," he said. "I've been doing this for years. My agent says I'm a natural."

"Actually, I'm the one who should be helping her with her lines," Hayden cut in. "Since we're the ones who have all the scenes together."

"Only because of a serious error in casting." Benjamin squared his shoulders.

Hayden ignored the comment. "Aurora, I'll be happy to give you any extra help you need."

I didn't answer. Last time he'd offered to help, he'd given the NAD a false idea of our encounter in his yard. For whatever twisted reason.

"And so will I." Benjamin leaped in front of Hayden. They glared at each other.

Great. Now I was involved in some triangle of thespian rivalry between Hayden and Benjamin.

"Just read the line, Aurora." Mr. Peterman was rubbing his head wearily.

I felt slightly guilty about overstressing him, so I looked down at my next line.

"*I wonder that you will still be talking, Signior Benedick: nobody marks you,*" I read scornfully, tossing in a sarcastic laugh.

"*What! my dear Lady Disdain, are you yet living?*" Hayden replied, his usual grin spreading over his face. Why did my insults never have any effect?

"Alive and kicking!" I replied, shaking a fist for good measure.

"Aurora, stick to the script," Mr. Peterman said.

"*But it is certain I am loved of all ladies,*" Hayden said, "*only you excepted—*"

"Mr. Peterman, would Benedick really have been desired by all the ladies, or is it just an example of his overactive ego?" I interrupted.

"If he looked anything like Hayden, he'd have been desired, all right!" came a yell from a female cast member in the audience. A few whistles echoed her words.

"Looks like your question has been answered," Hayden said, and gave the audience a grateful bow. "Thanks, ladies."

I gritted my teeth. "Well, Beatrice is the one girl smart enough not to fall for this commitment-phobic egotist."

"Good character analysis, Aurora." Mr. Peterman gave me a smile. "It will be very interesting to see how you play Beatrice giving way to her feelings for Benedick."

If it was up to me, Beatrice wasn't going to budge an inch.

I got a sudden flash of inspiration. "I was thinking, Mr. Peterman, since the play's set in the fifties, maybe Beatrice shouldn't fall for Benedick. Benedick could fall for her, but she rejects him in favor of a career in publishing. I mean, she has such a way with words—four of Benedick's wits running off? Brilliant!"

"That's so clever, Aurora!" Sara broke in. "She's rejecting the female domestic slavery that accompanies the institution of marriage!" She looked ready to leap into the air with excitement.

"Sara, Aurora, the Beatrice–Benedick subplot is the backbone of the play," Mr. Peterman said. "I can't just strip away half of Shakespeare's script."

Sara paced the stage thoughtfully. "You could if you were forward-thinking. After all, if the play is set in the fifties, then the sixties are just around the corner. Everything then was about rebellion. Beatrice could be a hippie—"

"I don't know about the tie-dye factor," I broke in.

"You could wear denim flares and platforms," Sara suggested.

"Oh my god! Platforms! She could be taller than Benedick! Which would dispel the weaker-sex thing." I gave Sara a high five.

"Hey, Mr. Peterman, that means Claudio could wear the sunglasses as a whole *Rebel Without a Cause* look." Benjamin placed the sunglasses back over his eyes. "And we could get a Harley-Davidson—"

"Hey, my old man has a Harley!" Jeffrey Clark piped up. "And if it's rebellion in the sixties, let's use guns instead of swords for the fights."

"Mr. Peterman, could I have a red spotlight on me?" Benjamin asked. "I think that would be very symbolic. And red is one of my best colors."

"No spotlight!" yelled Mr. Peterman. His pale complexion was marred by the two red circles of frustration that had formed on his cheeks. "And no guns, sunglasses, Harley-Davidson, or denim flares! I appreciate your suggestions, but I've already settled on the fifties. The *early* fifties."

"You're just playing it safe," grumbled Sara.

Mr. Peterman popped two headache pills. "Can we please get back to the scene?"

"And I would I could find in my heart that I had not a hard heart; for, truly, I love none." Hayden looked at Mr. Peterman. "Why does he love none?"

"Perhaps he's hyperaware of the dangers involved in dating," I said, repeating what Hayden had said to me after my fateful date with Bradley Scott. I sent him a triumphant glance. "Rather wimpish, in my opinion."

Hayden returned my gaze unflinchingly. "Maybe he's waiting for the one."

Whoa. What was with the serious tone? Perhaps Hayden was hypersensitive about his failure to find love. The failure probably caused by (as I'd told him at our nonaudition) his love for himself being too much for any girlfriend to compete with.

"And what about Beatrice?" Hayden continued. "Why is she so anti-*amore*? Did something happen in the past to scar her?"

What was with his pointed look at me at the end of that sentence? I was all for love. Love with a carefully investigated, surefire Potential Prince.

Mr. Peterman looked excited. "We've come to an important point here. Is there a history between Benedick and Beatrice? Were they once a couple, but one rejected the other? Is that what's causing their antagonism? Or are their verbal battles disguising an intense attraction?"

"Ooh," Jeffrey piped up. "An intense attraction, hey?"

I scowled. "Love is love and hate is hate. There's no in-between."

"Well, Aurora, I think there may be in this case." Mr. Peterman placed an arm around Hayden's and my shoulders. "My view on this is that Benedick and Beatrice are crazy about each other, but to admit so would make them creatures ruled by their hearts, not their heads. Both characters pride themselves on their logic and good sense. They are, at heart, fighting against their own feelings."

"But it's unstoppable," Hayden said, and smiled at me. "Because, yet again, true love wins the day."

"Thanks, Hayden. Blow the ending," I replied.

They ended up together? From what I'd read of the play so far, they had slightly softened toward each other, but I'd been hoping for Beatrice to come to her senses and run many, many leagues away from Benedick.

"Now, let's try the scene again," Mr. Peterman instructed. "Aurora, you should be looking at Benedick in triumph—but with a hint of attraction."

"Why attraction?" I wailed.

Mr. Peterman sighed. "Aurora, it's a play. You're pretending to be attracted to each other. Work on it overnight. Next line, please."

Pretending to be attracted to Hayden? This was going to be the longest three weeks in history.

Hayden and I spoke our last two insults, and Mr. Peterman ordered everyone off the stage except Benedick and Claudio. I ran gratefully into the wings.

"You're so lucky," whispered Sara as she followed me. "All those scenes with Hayden!"

I glared. "*Lucky* is not the word for it. His voice alone infuriates me, let alone the fact that I have to pretend to be in love with him. I can't believe I'm going to spend the next three weeks having him insult me in class, in my backyard, during break, all under the guise of practicing."

"Aurora, he's not going to do that," Sara said.

Before I could roll my eyes, Cassie came around the corner, fighting back tears.

"Scott has a girlfriend," Cassie whispered.

14   cupid is understaffed

"A girlfriend?" I stared at Cass, thinking of how Scott's eyes seemed to virtually twinkle every time he looked over at her. Those eyes didn't say *I'm taken*, that's for sure.

"It's fine. I'm over it already." Her voice sounded pretty choked up for someone who was over it. "I should be, right? It's stupid to be getting upset about someone I barely know. It's just, he seemed like a great guy . . ."

"How did you find out?" I asked softly.

"Sara, I need you on stage!" Mr. Peterman shouted.

"Seriously?" Sara made a face and squeezed Cass's arm. "Let's go for pizza after rehearsal and you can tell me everything."

She ducked around the curtain and I turned my attention back to Cass.

"I thought I'd ask him about art some more . . . you know, as a whole look-how-much-we-have-in-common nudge. So he started telling me about his sculpture class and suggested that I come along. And I was so happy 'cause I thought he wanted to spend more time with me."

"And then?"

"And then he said, 'Can you give me some advice on my new piece? I'm finding it really difficult.' So I said, 'Sure. Is your model—'"

"Model?"

"The subject that he's sculpting. I asked if he was sitting or standing." Cassie's voice trembled slightly.

"Yeah?" The tension was killing me.

"And he laughed and said, 'She.' And I'm like, 'What?,' and Scott says, 'She. It's a girl I'm sculpting.'" Cassie let out a sigh. "What I can't believe is that he mentioned it so casually. Call me crazy, but I really thought he liked me. Instead, he's probably been laughing with model girl about the silly girl at school with a crush on him."

"Wait a minute," I said. "Cass. Did he actually say the word *girlfriend*?"

"No, but to sculpt a girl, well, they'd have to be really close. I just bet they have private sculpting lessons—like in *Ghost*."

I pictured Patrick Swayze and Demi Moore's steamy scene. "Cass, I really think you're getting carried away. Who says this girl is his girlfriend? It's probably a completely professional relationship! Or she's just a friend."

"What girl could be *just friends* with Scott? Plus, think of all the artists who got involved with the women they painted! Picasso, Rossetti—"

I broke in before she could list any more model-chasing artists. "Cassie, I really don't think you should get too worked up before we find out the truth. Why don't you ask him a little more about her?"

"How will I pull that off? 'So . . . Scott, how serious are things with model girl?'"

"Get onto the topic of sculpture again. If you're casual about it, he might open up."

"It's too embarrassing." Cassie sighed. "I feel pathetic."

"You can't just assume," I said. "Who knows, you could find out that you've got it all wrong and Scott's a completely free agent. He's hardly been acting like a man with a girlfriend when he's around you."

"You think?"

"Yes! So maybe tomorrow, when you're feeling a little better, you can broach the subject again."

Thank god it wasn't as bad as I'd thought. I'd been picturing some serious childhood-sweetheart thing between Scott and this "girl-friend." Cassie was just being a worrywart. Still, Scott's status was yet to be confirmed. Why couldn't guys come with ID bracelets? Like cats and dogs. A little tag saying, "This guy belongs to Amy," or whatever. Then you could just sneak a look to see whether he was available. It'd save a lot of trauma.

The next afternoon, at rehearsal, Mr. Peterman was wearing a flam-boyant orange shirt.

"Okay, next scene. Leonato and Antonio on stage, please," he called. "Anyone not involved in this scene, please work on your lines."

I looked down at my script. Then I looked at the backstage area. Had Cassie managed to find out more about Scott's availability yet? Was she exultant or sinking into despair?

I was backstage in an instant.

Cass, Jelena, and Lindsay were looking over some blocking plans together.

"Cass! Any updates on Scott?" I could hardly wait to hear her an-swer.

"I asked him what he was having trouble with and he said he couldn't capture how *cute* model girl was," Cassie said through grit-ted teeth. "That was when I told him that I had to see Jelena about canvas size and got the heck out of there."

"What?" I couldn't believe it.

Jelena frowned. "This model girl has managed to get in ahead of Cassie, which sucks, especially because we're only a few days out from Valentine's Day—"

"Valentine's Day?" I racked my brain to remember today's date.

"Friday?" Jelena looked even more frustrated.

Oh my god. Valentine's Day was only three days away! How had I totally forgotten about one of my favorite days of the year? I guess

I'd been so distracted by the NAD's dating life and the strain of playing Hayden's onstage lover that it had slipped my mind.

"Of course!" I said. "Valentine's Day is crucial. Lindsay, how are you feeling about it?"

This would be her first Tyler-free Valentine's Day in three years.

Lindsay had her head buried in a thick book of costume design. "Oh, you know," she said, looking up. "I'm not leaping around with joy, but I'm doing okay."

We all looked at her, surprised. She marked another page with a pink Post-it and kept reading.

"I wish I could say that," Cassie murmured.

"Cass, I'm going to find out the truth," I told her.

"It's pretty evident, isn't it, if he's calling this girl cute?" Jelena said, straightening her French twist.

I glared at her. Jelena was just the queen of sensitivity today.

"How are you going to find out?" Cassie played with one of her ringlets.

"I have my sources."

"Aurora!" Mr. Peterman was yelling again.

"End of this rehearsal, I'll have the answer," I called back to them as I dashed onto the stage. "Sorry, Mr. Peterman."

He nodded. "Okay, now we will be rehearsing the masked ball, then Claudio's wooing of Hero, and Don John's subsequent vow to wreck the couple's impending marriage. Anyone involved in these scenes, please be punctual with your entrances. Starting from act two, scene one. Beatrice, up!" Mr. Peterman cried. "Are we going to have to wait all day for you, Aurora?"

"*Yes, faith; it is my cousin's duty to make curtsy, and say, 'Father, as it please you. . . .'*" I paused as I read my line. This was so sad. In order to please her dad, Hero was going to deny herself her Potential Prince! "*But yet for all that, cousin, let him be a handsome fellow, or else make another curtsy, and say, 'Father, as it please me.'*"

"Beatrice is the perfect feminist!" Sara broke in. "Look at how she's showing the other women that they don't have to marry against their will!" She shook a fist triumphantly. "Tear those shackles off, Aurora! Hey, Mr. Peterman, we could have Beatrice conduct a bra-burning ceremony with the other women in the play. It could even be in alliance with Don John!"

"Yes! Nudity!" Jeffrey pumped a fist in the air. "This play is going to have an NC-17 rating! Hey, what about the sexual frustration between Beatrice and Benedick?"

"There is no sexual frustration!" I cried.

This was so embarrassing. I couldn't even look at Hayden. My face felt like it was bright red.

Jeffrey ran up to the wings and punched Hayden's arm. "Hayden, you better get up there, my man. Aurora needs a good kissing."

"Can we keep going with the scene?" I was dying. I kept blushing until the start of the ball was announced.

"The revellers are entering, brother," David said. *"Make good room."*

Mr. Peterman gestured at the stage. "Okay, Don Pedro, Claudio, Benedick, Don John, Borachio, and my other couples, please enter. In this scene, everyone's attending a masked ball. We have Don Pedro and Hero dancing together—"

"Lady, will you walk about with your friend?" Alex asked, and guided Claire away from the group. He placed a hand on her waist, so low it was almost a butt grab. Claire's eyes widened. From her expression, I could tell she felt uncomfortable. If Jelena heard about this, she was going to freak.

"Now we've got everyone pairing off," Mr. Peterman said. "Don Pedro and Hero, Borachio and Margaret, Ursula and Antonio, and Beatrice and Benedick."

"We have to dance?"

I looked at Mr. Peterman, then at Hayden. What else was I going to have to endure during this play? Why couldn't I be a Hollywood actress and have a no-physical-contact clause in my contract?

"We'll rehearse it in the weeks to come, but I'd like you all to pretend for now, so I can get an idea of the space needed for the set. Jelena?" Mr. Peterman yelled.

No! He couldn't bring Jelena out now, to witness Alex's flirtation.

"Yes, Mr. Peterman?"

Jelena popped her head around the corner and caught sight of Claire in Alex's arms. Her face turned stony.

"Could you try to estimate the space we're going to need for dancing?" Mr. Peterman asked.

"Sure," Jelena replied, her eyes flashing with what I knew to be anger. Forget the space; Jelena was going to have her eyes firmly on Alex.

Everyone formed their couples.

"May I?" Hayden held out a hand.

I nodded, knowing I had no choice in the matter. He began to guide me assuredly around the stage. I tried to frown, but as everyone turned to see us, I had to smile.

Mr. Peterman was beaming. "Excellent!"

As we whirled around the stage, Alex and Claire said their lines. Jelena sent a furious glance my way. Eek. I'd wanted to stop Alex from groping Claire, but Mr. Peterman had pushed me into dancing with Hayden.

I looked at Hayden and inspiration hit. I might not be able to do anything about Alex, but here was my chance to find out information to help Cassie's love life! Hayden was Scott's best friend. Who better to know whether Scott had a special someone?

"Hey, Hayden, can I ask you something?" I looked up into his eyes.

"Anything, Beatrice my love."

"What's Scott's status?"

Hayden's mouth dropped open. "Wait a minute. Did you just ask me about Scott's status?"

"For Cassie." I nodded toward her. "I don't want my best friend stressing about someone who's taken."

"Aurora, Scott and Cassie can take care of their own love lives!" Hayden said as he turned us to the right. "Just like your dad can."

I glared at him, thinking about the catastrophe that had been last

Friday night. "Don't bring my dad into this. You're not the one who has to deal with the consequences."

"I just believe you shouldn't stand in the way of love," Hayden said, raising his eyebrows. "What can I say? I'm a romantic."

"How can you be a romantic when you're sabotaging a romance?"

"Sabotaging?" Hayden's face was all innocence, just like the time he'd pushed me into the wading pool. "Aurora, all I'm saying is that Cassie and Scott should take it slow."

"Paris, you do realize that Friday is Valentine's Day?"

"Ah, *ma chérie,* the day of love!" Hayden said in a French accent, and pulled our linked hands over his heart.

I rolled my eyes. "That's why you need to drop the whole let-Scott-take-his-time thing. Do you realize the potential trauma that Valentine's Day holds? Do you want that trauma inflicted on Cassie, who's such a giving, loving soul—"

"I'm sure Scott can manage Valentine's Day himself," Hayden cut in.

"But with who?" I asked. "Cassie or model girl?"

"Model girl?" Hayden looked dumbfounded.

"So there is no model girl!" I cried triumphantly.

"Aurora! Is no one's love life sacred?"

I broke away from him. "You're impossible!"

"Okay, Beatrice and Benedick! Lines, please!" Mr. Peterman called.

"I'm changing this darn script," I muttered. "Benedick's going to get beaten up by a bunch of female ninja warriors."

Hayden and I finished our scene and I gratefully exited the stage. As Benedick listened to Claudio moan about how Don Pedro had stolen his girl, I snuck over to Jelena and Cassie.

"Did you find out the truth?" Cassie whispered.

I grimaced. "Not yet . . ."

"Cass, give up," Jelena said. "I don't think Aurora's concerned with either of us at the moment. She can't even keep an eye on Alex."

"What?" I looked at Jelena in shock. "Of course I'm concerned."

"Yeah, you looked really worried, waltzing around in Hayden's arms," Jelena replied. "Cass and I were racked with tension here, but you were oblivious. It's just like Claudio said: friendship can never be constant when it comes to affairs of love."

"I was trying to question Hayden about Scott's status!" I said. "Look, Jelena, what can I do to help you?"

She fell silent a moment. "I just hated seeing that whole thing going on."

"Are you really sure you want to be involved with someone who's so . . ." I paused, trying to think of a nice word. "Flirty?"

Jelena sighed. "Alex can't help being attractive. Or having obsessive girls chase him. He's defenseless."

Right. Defenseless Alex. I swallowed my laughter. I didn't want to fight with Jelena. After all, she was understandably stressed after seeing the object of her affection pursuing everyone else.

"Beatrice, up!" Mr. Peterman called.

"I'll try my best," I vowed to Jelena. "For you as well, Cass."

I tried to sound reassuring, but I felt really uneasy as I joined Alex on stage. How was I going to rein in his flirtatiousness and persuade Hayden to tell me the truth about Scott?

"I may sit in a corner and cry heigh-ho for a husband!" I read as I tried to put together a plan in my mind.

"Will you have me, lady?" Alex said. He raised a hand to my cheek and Jelena went purple.

Now he was flirting with me? Shock sent any semblance of a plan out the window.

The moment I read my exit cue, I ran for the backstage area. What was Jelena going to say? Was she going to accuse me of being one of the obsessive girls chasing Alex?

I dashed over to where she was conferring with Lindsay and Cass. Was she telling them furiously about my supposed man-thieving?

"Jelena!" I slid to a stop just in front of her. "About Alex—"

"Isn't he the most incredible actor?" she breathed.

I searched her face for any sign of anger, but her brow was unwrinkled and her mouth curved up happily.

"I can't believe that I got so upset before," she said. "His physical interactions with you and Claire are obviously his way of getting into character."

I opened my mouth, but Jelena continued, "It finally hit me while I was watching that scene where he was supposed to woo you. He was so convincing!"

Call me crazy, but to me it had seemed like genuine flirtatiousness, not Alex's attempt to channel Laurence Olivier. He'd spent most of the scene clasping my hand and staring into my eyes. I'd responded by backing away and intently studying the stage floor. Would I have felt that uncomfortable if he'd simply been reading his lines?

"Aurora, I'm sorry I was so cranky before. Can we forget it?" Jelena looked expectantly at me.

What could I say? If I pressed my point about Alex being a potential Lothario, then Jelena would be furious, whether my allegations proved false or true. I didn't want our group torn apart because of a guy. And maybe Jelena was right about Alex being in character. So far, all his flirtations had taken place during rehearsal. From now on, I was going to leave it up to Jelena herself to analyze Alex's actions and their meaning.

"Sure, Jelena." I gave her a hug.

Jelena hugged me back. "I'm never going to jump to conclusions again. And neither should you, Cass. I've got a feeling it'll all come together on Valentine's Day. Just wait and see. And Aurora, I'm sorry about the Hayden thing. You guys did look cute together, though."

Cassie and Lindsay nodded with her. I rolled my eyes.

Alex's voice drifted backstage. *"She were an excellent wife for Benedick."*

"Oh Lord, my lord, if they were but a week married, they would talk themselves mad," David as Leonato replied.

Well, at least someone else was intelligent enough to realize the prospects were dim for Beatrice and Benedick. Poor Beatrice. I really had to try to make a better future for her.

"Mr. Peterman?" I called, stepping onto the side of the stage.

"Aurora, you've already exited." He gestured for me to leave.

"Oh, I know that, sir. But I was thinking . . . Why is everyone so obsessed with Beatrice and Benedick getting together? It really seems to me like they have a toxic relationship, which is only going to result in a miserable, unfulfilling marriage."

"I think Benedick has the ability to make Beatrice happy beyond her wildest dreams," Hayden said, his head appearing through the wings on the other side of the stage. Why was he always popping up to dismiss my ingenious theories?

Mr. Peterman smiled. "Beatrice and Benedick are crazy about one another. And everyone knows it but them."

"But seriously, Mr. Peterman," I protested, "what does anyone really know about their suitability? I was thinking we should make clear the wild thinking that's led this group of people to push Beatrice and Benedick into a relationship. We could show everyone bored and thus consuming vast quantities of alcohol, which causes them to come up with this crazy suggestion—"

"Alcohol?" shrilled Mr. Peterman.

"Not real alcohol," I put in quickly. "We could just allude to it. And the destructive results it can bring about."

"We could also show the lack of power women had in the fifties," Sara cried from the audience. "Beatrice could be drugged by doctors employed by her uncle, who's worried about her unnatural lack of interest in marriage. They attempt to convince Beatrice that Benedick is a good match—"

"But Beatrice breaks free!" I cried, moving forward to stand next to Mr. Peterman.

"Is this where the bra burning comes in?" Jeffrey looked hopeful.

"And she refuses to marry Benedick!" I pumped the air enthusiastically.

"Aurora, I've had a long day," Mr. Peterman said. "Don't make it any longer."

"Does that mean you'll consider my idea?" I asked hopefully.

Hayden joined us. "How do you come up with this stuff?"

"I put my intelligence to good use."

Hayden smiled. "It's a brilliant concept, but I think you might be a little misguided about Beatrice and Benedick's relationship. Underneath all the arguing, there are genuine loving feelings."

I peered at him. "How do you know this? Were you with Shakespeare when he created the play?"

"Well, obviously not, but—"

"Exactly." I shrugged my shoulders. "So until you build a time machine and go back and become best buddies with the Bard, perhaps you should pipe down."

Hayden shook his head. "You're stripping the romance from the play!"

I laughed. "Funny you should have a problem with that, seeing as how you frequently strip the romance from other people's lives."

"Is this about Scott and Cassie again?" Hayden raised an eyebrow.

"It's about everything, Hayden." I gave him a look before I swept off stage.

15 valentine's day

"What a wonderful day to be exploring the passion of poetry!" Mrs. Kent said on Friday, gesturing at the hearts strung up around the room. I just love teachers who get into the spirit of Valentine's Day.

"I'd like to collect the assigned pieces," Mrs. Kent said as she walked down the classroom aisle. "And don't worry. All poems will be kept anonymous."

I looked over my poem one more time. I'd agonized over it since Tuesday afternoon.

The Prince

Where is the Prince who is to win my heart?
Is he forging, fighting, trying?
Or is he taking his time?
Maybe he's dawdling, crawling,
given up out of boredom?
No.
He has a blunt ax
against
an ever-growing forest
that's out to stop him.

One shred of a map
written in a foreign language.
He knows all too well
that it's a race against time
for two souls to find each other.
And that even if he reaches the castle
things are only going to get harder.
There's a rampant case of narcolepsy
to overcome.
Out-of-date fashion moments
and a dragon of doubt to fight off, too.
But if he falters, if he's unsure,
he should stop
and listen for my heart's whisper.
I'm waiting just for him.
I'm waiting for his kiss.
Hoping that he'll push on
with his mission
and come find me.

Okay, so it wasn't perfect—there were some clichés, and the rhyming scheme lacked discipline—but it was truthful. That was what I considered important.

Hayden turned around and smiled at me. "Hey, do I get to read your poem?"

I yanked it away. "Paris, haven't you heard of privacy?"

There was no way he was going to get a peek at a poem that had me calling out for a Prince.

"Privacy. That usually means you won't find your next-door neighbor and her friends cavorting in your pool, doesn't it?"

I ignored him.

"Well, seeing as poems express our hearts' deepest wishes, I won't insist on seeing your piece," he continued.

I smiled at him. Hayden saying he wouldn't interfere? How surprising.

"After all, only a brave heart could cope with the object of her poem reading it right in front of her."

"What?" I shrilled. "The poem's not about you!"

Hayden propped his elbows on my desk. "Aurora, if there's something you want to admit on this day of love, I promise I won't laugh at you."

"The only thing I want to tell you is that you're the most pompous person on earth!" I replied in outrage. If only I still had that big metal ruler.

"The most pompous person on earth . . ." Hayden looked thoughtful. "Great line, Aurora. I think I'll add that to my poem." He started scribbling on his piece of paper. "Ah, *ma chérie,* my muse, the passionate poems we could write together! Open your heart—"

"Open your mouth again, Paris, and that's it!"

Hayden fell silent. I breathed a sigh of relief. It didn't last long.

"Much as I hate to disobey a lady's request, I have to ask: Is it an ode to my looks?"

"I'm not even going to deign to reply." I tilted my desk, and Hayden's elbows slid off it.

"Sometimes there's even physical abuse," he said.

Mrs. Kent gave a big smile and turned to Jeffrey. "Where's your poem?"

"Well, Mrs. Kent, it's a tragic story." Jeffrey wiped away an imaginary tear. "You see, I suffer from metrophobia—"

"You're scared of the city?" Travis asked. "What are you even doing here, man? You're suffering more and more every moment."

"Metrophobia is not a fear of the metropolis," Jeffrey continued in a pained voice. "It's a morbid dread of poetry. So I'm sorry, Mrs. Kent, but your assignment was an impossibility."

"Can I ask why you didn't inform me of this condition, Jeffrey?" Mrs. Kent said. "I could have assigned you an essay instead."

Jeffrey buried his head in his hands. "I couldn't bear to speak of it. I am a man without poetry, without passion, without a soul."

"Well, Jeffrey, I have to say that if you don't cure your condition in the next ten minutes, your grades are going to suffer." Mrs. Kent had a twinkle in her eye.

"Doomed to walk the earth without Byron, Keats, Shelley," Jeffrey went on.

"Ten minutes, Jeffrey," Mrs. Kent repeated. "Now, would anyone like to share their poem with the class?"

"Will you admit your passion to the public, Aurora?" Hayden whispered.

"What do you think?"

I studied my poem again, checking it for spelling mistakes.

"Mrs. Kent! You've got a willing reader!" Hayden called, waving his hand in the air.

"I'm going to kill you!" I yanked his hand down.

Mrs. Kent peered at us. "Is this a physical piece?"

"No, Mrs. Kent." Hayden grinned at me. "Aurora, I was volunteering my own poem."

"Great. I can hardly wait to suffer," I muttered as he strode up to the front of the class.

"This is a poem inspired by my good friend Aurora," he said.

"Aurora's been inspiring a lot lately, huh, Hayden?" Jeffrey called out. "Your presentation on knights, poetry . . ."

Hayden sighed. "We bring out the best in each other. What can I say?"

Whistles came from around the room. My cheeks blazed. I sank lower in my chair.

"This poem is very relevant to today, being Valentine's Day," Hayden explained, "because it's about one of the most important forms of love—self-love."

He launched into a piece that echoed the beginning of Walt Whitman's "Song of Myself," with its celebration and "singing of the self." He finished to wild applause. Only Hayden Paris could make egocentricity seem an admirable quality.

"What did you think, Princess?" Hayden settled back into his seat and looked at me with an expectant gaze.

"Your focus on yourself was commendable," I replied.

He grinned. "I couldn't have done it without your suggestions."

Great. I was responsible for a poem about self-obsession. Being a muse is far from all it's cracked up to be.

"Whoever started Valentine's Day was a genius," Jelena said before biting into a heart-shaped cookie.

Every Valentine's Day, Jelena, Cassie, Sara, Lindsay, and I held a "love picnic" during lunch. We spread a huge red-and-white rug on the ground and brought Valentine's-themed food.

"The origins of Valentine's Day are a mystery," I replied, selecting a chocolate-covered strawberry from the huge platter in the center of the rug. "Some people believe that Saint Valentine was a priest who lived during Roman times. There was this emperor called Claudius who decided that single men made better soldiers—"

"Relationships *are* distracting," Lindsay said, licking the icing off a pink-frosted cupcake.

"Yeah, but this guy was really extreme," I continued. "He outlawed marriage for young men. Supposedly, Saint Valentine helped young couples to marry secretly. When Claudius found out, he ordered Valentine to be put to death."

"Wow, that's brutal." Cassie looked at me with wide eyes.

Saint Valentine was my new hero. He'd been all about risking his life in the name of true love. Just like me. Well, okay, I hadn't received any death threats, but hey, I had to put up with Hayden's abuse while trying to find out the truth about Scott. That was painful. And, like Saint Valentine, I was wholeheartedly spreading the message of love. Every Valentine's Day, including today, I ordered four roses from the school's flower booth and sent them anonymously to the four people in our year most unlikely to receive tokens of love.

"Can you believe Jeremy Webster got a rose during math class?" Jelena let out a laugh. "Who in their right mind would send him a flower?"

Jeremy had been one of my four this year.

"Jelena!" I cried. "That's not very nice. Especially from someone privileged enough to have received four cards by the end of the same class."

Half of our picnic rug was covered in Jelena's floral tributes. The rest of us had received several tokens. I had two cards, three roses, and a little white bear. Even though none of the boys were Potential Princes, I'd given them big smiles upon receiving their gifts and thanked them genuinely. I'd even managed to conjure up an embarrassed smile when Jeffrey presented me with a red novelty bell stamped with his number and the words "Ring when you want some red-hot lovin'."

"Did Alex send you a rose?" Cassie asked Jelena.

Jelena looked slightly disappointed. "Nope. But three were delivered to me during the time we spent chatting by my locker, so he's fully aware of how desirable I am."

Anyone who saw our picnic blanket would be aware of it.

"I wonder why he didn't send you something," I said.

Jelena waved a hand dismissively. "Probably some typical guy attitude about how Valentine's Day is commercial. But that's not going to stop me. Alex is like a butterfly. I've just got to pin him down."

Come to think of it, Alex *was* like a butterfly. He fluttered from girl to girl like a butterfly dances from flower to flower.

Suddenly, Cass's face went white. I turned my head to follow her gaze. Scott was standing at the edge of our picnic rug. He wore a dimpled smile and held a hand behind his back.

Oh my god. I was about to die of anticipation.

Scott extended to Cassie the hand that wasn't behind his back. She took it and he pulled her gently to her feet.

Sara, Lindsay, Jelena, and I were all silent, breathlessly waiting for Scott's next move. He slowly drew his other hand from behind his back to reveal a full golden-yellow rose. Cassie's cheeks pinkened as she reached out to take it from him. They exchanged an intense look, neither saying a word. Cass's lips parted slightly, seemingly to say something. Before she could, Scott took his hand from hers. He gave her a wink and a grin before he dashed off to the other side of the schoolyard.

16 stakeout

"Oh my god! That was so romantic!" Lindsay, sitting next to me on the assembly stands, shook her head. "And to stay silent the whole time . . . So *mysterious!*"

"Lindsay, you've been saying that for the past twenty minutes." Jelena slipped on a pair of sunglasses. "Tell me, why do they have to hold assembly out by the pool? The glare off the water is sure to give me premature wrinkling around my eyes."

"Problem is, what if model girl got a rose, too?" Cassie said, looking down at the yellow petals of Scott's flower.

"He could be giving them out like there's no tomorrow," Jelena agreed.

Cass's smile, which had been gleaming for twenty minutes, faded slightly.

I put my hand on her shoulder. "Cass, what did I tell you about not panicking till we've looked up the symbolism of the flower?"

"Which I've just found in the school library!" Sara called as she made her way up the stands to where we sat, on the second-highest step.

"Good afternoon, students and staff!" Mr. Quinten, the school principal, said over the mike. "I hope you are enjoying Valentine's

Day. I'm proud to announce that our flower booth has raised an unprecedented sum this year—"

"Probably thanks to all my admirers," Jelena quipped.

"She's a modest one, isn't she?" Sara said, and elbowed Jelena in the ribs. They both giggled.

"—which will go toward purchasing new softball equipment," Mr. Quinten said.

"Great one, Jelena," I said, putting my hands over my ears as the microphone screeched. "Now that they can finally replace the soft-balls, we'll be back to dodging the things."

"Could you try to be less attractive next year?" Sara added.

"I'll do my best." Jelena slicked on lip gloss. "But beauty is a curse as well as a blessing."

"On this day of love, I'd like to speak about student relations," Mr. Quinten continued. "As a result of the student council's bully ban, our recent student survey revealed that ninety-five percent of you feel happy and safe here at Jefferson High."

"The other five percent must have been surveyed during sports," I whispered. In my opinion, baseball bats come under the category of weapons.

"So I'd like you all to give a round of applause to the program's creator, Hayden Paris, and the other student council members who helped put it in place."

Hayden, sitting way down near the bottom of the steps, gave an embarrassed wave as everyone cheered.

Sara sighed. "He's so modest."

"Modest? This morning he was trying to get me to admit that I'd written an ode to his good looks!" I shook my head. "Can we turn our attention to what's important—Cassie and Scott?"

"Yeah, we have to find out what a yellow rose really means." Lindsay grabbed the flower symbolism book from Sara's hands.

Jelena looked thoughtful. "I wonder why he didn't send you a red rose? That's the traditional Valentine's Day flower."

"Yellow rose, yellow rose . . ." Lindsay scoured the book. "Here we go! The overall meaning is friendship."

"Friendship?" We all groaned. This was not good.

Cassie's lips turned downward.

"A yellow rose with a red tip indicates friendship turning into love," Lindsay continued.

Sara grabbed at the rose. "Does it have a red tip?"

Cassie studied the flower. "It looks more orange."

"I'd call it vermilion," Jelena argued.

"Is vermilion red?" Sara looked confused.

"Lindsay," I said, "does it say anything about a vermilion or orange tip?"

Lindsay looked down at the book. "Nope. Just red."

"So he sees me purely as a friend?" Cassie's face was pure disappointment.

"Model girl probably got the red rose," Jelena said.

"Jelena! Talk about discouraging!" Sara frowned at her.

"Guys!" I cried. "This is ridiculous! I bet Scott didn't even know the symbolism of a yellow rose! We're going to have to find out the truth of this situation instead of speculating."

"How?" Cassie sniffed her rose.

"We're going to secretly observe him," I replied in a mysterious tone.

"What, hide in the bushes or something?" Jelena laughed.

"Cassie, what day does Scott go to sculpting classes?" I asked, ignoring Jelena.

"Friday." She frowned at me. "That's today. Why? What are you going to do?"

"*We*, Cass. We're going to tail him to the class and see what's going on with model girl."

Cassie looked horrified. "We can't do that!"

"It's the only way of finding out the truth," I said. I'm all for privacy, but this was an urgent situation. "I'm sure Scott would hate the assumptions that we're making—particularly Jelena's."

"Isn't tailing illegal?" Sara asked.

"What about those investigators you can hire to find out if your husband's having an affair? That's legal," I pointed out. "And my way doesn't involve spending money that could be used on a shopping spree." I turned to Cassie. "So, are you in?"

She hesitated.

"Cass, you've tried asking him. And we've exhausted our other sources."

Hayden had been so unhelpful. If he'd just answered a simple question, we wouldn't be resorting to questionable activities.

"Oh, okay, then." Cassie's eyes still looked worried.

"So, our big playoff basketball game is happening next Thursday," Mr. Quinten announced, then broke off. "Well, this is highly unusual," he said, sounding put out. "We have a delivery boy from Flower Power here—"

"Ooh, more flowers!" Jelena cried. "My room is going to be a fragrant wonderland!"

"How do you know they're for you?" Sara asked.

"Intuition," Jelena replied. "And I saw Nick Summers hanging around outside Flower Power this morning. He's always had a thing for me."

"Can anyone see what the flowers look like?" Lindsay asked.

I peered at the assembly stage. Mr. Quinten and the delivery boy were obscured by a pole.

"Well, let's see who these flowers are for," Mr. Quinten said.

Jelena was ready to run down the steps to collect her tribute.

"Okay, ladies and gentlemen, the lucky girl is . . . Aurora Skye!"

I froze. The flowers were for me?

"Ms. Skye, will you please come and collect this over-the-top display of affection?" Mr. Quinten said.

Sara let out a squeal. "Oh my god! You are so lucky!"

I rose to my feet and shakily descended the steps. As I reached the bottom of the stands, Mr. Quinten came into sight. Next to him was the delivery boy, nearly invisible behind the gigantic bouquet in his arms.

Was that mass of flowers really for me? I barely restrained a squeal of delight.

"Here you go, Ms. Skye." Mr. Quinten gestured to the delivery boy, who stepped forward and held out the bouquet. "I really think the florist should have cleared this with me. It's held up the progress of the assembly."

I opened my arms. This had to be the most romantic moment of my life.

As I took the weighty bundle, I saw that, among the masses of red-and-pink wrapping, silver curling ribbon, and greenery, were at least fifteen long-stemmed red roses. Then I saw the rose nestled in their center. Its petals were a rainbow of deep pink, tangerine, and gold.

"Ah, true love," Mr. Quinten said wryly. "Now, to get back to the basketball game . . ."

I made my way dazedly back up the stands. My cheeks were aching from grinning so much. I sank down among my friends.

"That is the biggest bouquet I've ever seen in my life!" Lindsay's voice was hushed.

"Slight exaggeration," Jelena said.

"Lindsay's right!" Sara's voice had reached a new pitch of excitement. "You can hardly see Aurora behind it."

"Who's it from?" Cass was beaming at me.

"I-I haven't looked," I stammered.

"You haven't looked? Are you crazy?" Jelena peered at the bouquet. "Where's the gift card?"

"The flower in the center is breathtaking," Sara said.

I spotted a small envelope tucked just inside the wrapping and took it in my hands.

"What's with the delay?" Jelena asked. She, Sara, Lindsay, and Cass stared at me.

"The giver of these flowers is my Potential Prince," I said softly. "I don't want to rush the moment."

The second I opened the envelope, I'd know who my Potential Prince was. I had no candidates in mind. It could be anyone in the world.

Was I ready for this?

Ready? I'd only been waiting sixteen years and six months.

I took a deep breath and flipped the envelope open.

"What's it say?" Sara shrieked.

My eyes raced over the dark-blue script on the decorative paper.

"Aurora," I read, "you are just like this rainbow-colored rose—continually astonishing and completely one of a kind."

Cassie sighed. "That's why all the other roses are red. He's saying you're the rare rose."

"Keep going, Aurora!" Sara cried.

"The truth is, you are the center of my world. Love—"

"Who is it?" Sara shrieked.

Jelena frowned. "That's what she's trying to tell us, idiot. Shh."

"Your secret admirer," I finished, staring at the paper.

"What?" The cry was unanimous.

My Potential Prince had left off his name.

"Are you sure there's no name?" Jelena raised an eyebrow. "Is it too embarrassing to say? Is he a nerd?"

"Jelena!" Sara cried. "That's so insulting. Aurora's gorgeous. Her admirer has to be a hottie."

"There's no name."

My soul flooded with disappointment.

"I wasn't saying he *had* to be a nerd," Jelena said. "Just that Aurora's so nice, the nerds probably think they have a chance with her."

"He's not a nerd," I said. "I just know it. And anyway, anyone who can write such a beautiful message has a gorgeous heart. If he's not an Adonis, that doesn't matter to me."

"Oh, it matters," Jelena muttered.

"So who could it be from?" Lindsay said what everyone was thinking.

"Is there anyone that comes to mind, Aurora? Anyone who flirts with you?" Cassie asked, smelling one of the crimson roses.

"Everyone flirts with Aurora," Sara replied.

"Sara!" I cried. "What are you talking about?"

"Are you blind?" Sara gave an exasperated sigh. "Every time a guy gets near you, he starts flirting. You don't flirt back 'cause you have this whole unconscious-of-it thing going on."

"What?" I said, astounded. I mean, okay, I was all-right-looking, but hardly a Miss Universe clone like Jelena.

"Like I said before, you're gorgeous," Sara went on. "So it could be any of the five hundred male students here at Jefferson."

"Well, I guess that, to write a note like that, he's intelligent, articulate, and deep," I said, flattered by Sara's compliment.

"Not Bradley again," Jelena said with a sigh.

"It is not Bradley," I said.

I'd seen him giving Tarot Card Tina a book called *Scorpios' Guide to Love* this morning. Tina had given me a fierce scowl. You'd think she'd want to present a good-natured image in front of Bradley, but no.

"He's probably good at English, then," Cassie said, bringing my attention back to my own love life. "So everyone should consider the guys in their English classes."

"And try to think of guys that pay special attention to Aurora," Sara suggested.

A bell rang, signaling the end of the assembly.

"No idling," Mr. Quinten ordered. "Make your way to class in a prompt manner."

This was so frustrating. I wanted to start working on uncovering my secret admirer's identity right away.

Jelena stood up. "Everyone make a list of possible candidates. We'll talk about it on Monday."

"Monday?" I cried. "That's three days away!"

"Hey, we need time to think about it," Jelena replied from halfway down the stands.

I gathered my things together and reluctantly followed her. Even though my Potential Prince had made an appearance, it was still going to be a challenge to find him.

I spent the rest of the day toting the flowers from class to class. Frankly, I was surprised that I was allowed to keep the bouquet on my desk. The greenery alone blocked my view of the whiteboard. I was waiting for a teacher to complain that the bouquet was sabotaging my education, but they all just smiled indulgently.

When the final bell sounded, I made my way to the spot near the school gates where Cassie and I had arranged to meet for Operation Tail Scott.

"Cass!" I grabbed her by the sleeve of her denim dress. "Ready to go?"

"Shh!" She jerked her head to the left, where Scott was just ahead of us in the crowd. "Jelena's coming, too."

"What?" I looked back at Jelena. "I thought you said you didn't hide."

Jelena shrugged her shoulders. "Like you said, it's not hiding. It's tailing. Tailing's cool with me."

"Three people are much harder to conceal than two," I complained. "And you're going to be completely conspicuous with all those things."

I pointed at the two clear-plastic display bags overflowing with single red roses, various assortments of chocolates, and two teddy bears.

"Ah, hello? Person holding ostentatious bouquet talking," Jelena replied.

"Fine." I followed Cass through the gate. "You can come. But it's just the three of us. No tagalong Jelena admirers, okay?"

"Sorry, Jack," Jelena said to the boy on her right. "You'll have to walk me home on Monday."

"Hey!" Another boy, with thick blond curls, looked outraged. "You promised I could walk you home on Monday."

"Aurora!" Cassie pointed at a rapidly moving Scott. "We're going to lose him."

I grabbed Jelena's hand and pulled her away from her admirers.

"We'll sort out a roster next week!" Jelena called back over her shoulder.

"Wait up!" Lindsay was at our heels.

"Guys! I love your company, but this is hardly discreet," I pointed out.

"Oh, it'll be fine," Jelena said. "He's listening to his iPod. He won't have a clue what's going on."

I crossed my fingers and hoped she was right.

Scott continued downtown, while we struggled to maintain a distance between not being noticed and accidentally losing sight of him.

"Ooh!" Jelena spotted a pair of black stilettos in a store window.

"Oh no! We missed the light!" Lindsay cried as it changed to red.

Scott, who'd already crossed, strode ahead.

"We're going to lose him." Cassie wrung her hands. "Come on! Change the light!"

"Do you think I have time to try those on?" Jelena asked, looking at the heels longingly.

"No!" I cried.

The light flipped to green and we dashed across the road at the speed of light. We careened through the crowd.

"I didn't enjoy Valentine's Day much," Lindsay said as we dodged pedestrians.

I looked at her. Her gaze was on a lovey-dovey couple walking hand in hand.

"Much as I tried not to think about it, I was convinced that Tyler was going to pull some grand gesture to win me back—like your whole bouquet thing, Aurora." She sighed and played with one of her hoop earrings. "And he didn't do anything!"

"Linds, you just told him you didn't want him back."

"I didn't mean it!" she cried. "Do you think he thinks I mean it?"

"For someone who said he hadn't yet begun to fight, he hasn't done much," Jelena said, struggling to keep up with our fast pace due to her strappy heels.

"That's because he's still figuring out his strategy," I reassured Lindsay.

"What if he's not?" she said. "What if he's got a new girlfriend already? Oh my god. And they're on a Valentine's Day date right now—"

"Isn't Tyler at soccer practice?" Jelena interrupted.

"Which he's cut to take her on a date!"

I punched in a number on my phone. It was time to stop Lindsay's out-of-control delusions.

Sara's voice came on the line. "Hello?"

"Hey, Sara, you're still at soccer practice, right?" I said, keeping an eagle eye on Scott ahead of us. "What's Tyler up to right now?"

"Looking defeated," Sara replied. "He's been benched for kicking a guy who asked him how Valentine's Day was for him, being single and all."

"Thanks, Sara." I ended the call.

"Tyler's depressed and antisocial," I reported to Lindsay. "Extremely reactive to questions about his single status. You'll have him back within the month."

Modern technology. Genius for instant reassurance.

Just as my feet started pinching in my pointy-toed flats, we came to a large building with huge glass windows, all of which were open. Thick flowering bushes stood under the windows. We ducked behind a parked car and watched as Scott entered a room on the ground floor. Perfect.

I stepped out from behind the car. "Okay. Things get serious here. Model girl is likely to make an appearance, so we're looking for any boyfriend–girlfriend vibes between her and Scott. Just keep in mind all the body language info I've given you."

"How are we going to see Scott from all the way out here?" Lindsay asked, looking confused.

"We're not entering the art room," I replied. "The moment we do that, our cover's blown." I pointed at the bushes in front of the open windows. "We'll be observing from there. Who's with me?"

I took a look around to check that no one was watching us, then darted toward the bushes. Cassie, Lindsay, and Jelena were right behind me.

I examined the flowering shrubs. Closest to the street was a thick, golden-green hedge that ran along the entire left side of the art room. Directly beneath the art room windows was a row of bushy shrubs covered in full white flowers with red splotches.

"Okay, we're going to crawl between the hedge and those white flowering bushes," I said. "That way, we'll be able to observe the art room unnoticed and be hidden from the street. We'll leave our belongings just inside the hedge here."

I gently placed my flowers and pink handbag among the hedge's greenery, then got down on my hands and knees and crawled between the bushes. Thank god there was no chance of Hayden finding out about this. He'd never let me hear the end of it.

"I can't believe we're doing this," Jelena whispered from behind me as we made our way along the side of the building, pushing sticky, sap-coated branches out of our way. "We're getting covered in dirt." She lifted a dirt-encrusted palm and wrinkled her nose.

"Think of what CIA agents do," I whispered. "I'm sure it gets far dirtier than this."

"I doubt it," Jelena said. "Arrgghh! Ants!" She furiously brushed her shoulders.

"So, Cass—you, Lindsay, and I should all observe Scott in order to gain an accurate picture of the model-girl situation, okay?" I looked at her for agreement.

"What am I going to do?" Jelena complained.

"Keep an eye on the ants," I instructed. "Okay, agents Lindsay and Cass, are you ready to go?"

"Ready." They both gave me a little salute.

We slowly peeped over the shrubbery and through the wide window. Scott, his sun-kissed locks unmissable, was seated by the window two up from ours. He was bent over what looked like a lump of clay, and glanced repeatedly to his right.

"Okay, subject is in sight," I said.

"Model girl's got to be on his right," Cassie said, peering over the bush. "Can anyone see her?"

Lindsay and I craned our necks to see to Scott's right, but the windowsill was at an impossible angle.

I ducked back down into the bushes. "We're going to have to get closer. There's no other way."

That wasn't good. Closer meant a higher likelihood of being spotted.

"Or we could just forget it," Jelena said, her cheeks flushed, "and come back another day with binoculars and an oversize bottle of *Ant-Kil*." The last words were a growl.

Cassie folded her arms over her chest. "I'm not turning back now. Let's go."

Cassie had taken control of this mission. We followed her as she crawled two windows down.

"Everyone has to keep absolutely silent," I whispered. "Just two of us should look this time."

Cassie nodded at me. "Ready, Aurora?"

We each lifted our head, inch by inch, until our eyes were just above the top of the flowering bush. A tiny girl with pigtails sat on a stool at Scott's right, swinging her feet.

"That must be model girl's younger sister or something," Cassie whispered. "Scott's probably so serious about her that he's friends with the whole family."

I looked at the thirty earnest faces bent over their work. "And he's dragged them all to an art class? I don't think so. It's probably the teacher's daughter or something."

Scott turned to get a tool from the drawer beside him. As he moved, his sculpture came into view for the first time.

"Oh my god," I breathed. "Cass, look!"

We both stared at the sculpture of the little girl.

"That's model girl!" I cried softly. "A four-year-old! That's why he said he was having trouble capturing how cute she was."

Scott's voice drifted out the window. "How are you doing, Emily? You holding that pose okay?"

Cassie and I threw ourselves down on the ground again.

Cass shook her head. "Emily. Oh my god."

"What did you guys find out?" Lindsay whispered.

"It'd better be a breakthrough worthy of my endurance of these ants," Jelena muttered.

Cass's face broke into a smile. "Emily is his younger sister. I've been ignoring him because of model girl supposedly being his bombshell girlfriend—"

"She *is* a cutie pie," I interrupted, grinning.

"I can't believe it." Cassie let out a giggle, but I barely heard her over the eardrum-shattering roar that had suddenly filled the street.

"Scott," someone from the art room called, "could you shut your window?"

Realization hit me. "We've got to move it, now! If Scott leans out to pull the window shut, we're screwed. The bush isn't tall enough to conceal us from above."

As Scott's chair scraped back, we plunged our way through the hedge and onto the sidewalk.

"Eww!" shrilled Jelena, looking at the sap oozing down her right arm.

Luckily, her voice was drowned out by what I could now see was a motorcycle gang circling the art center's parking lot.

"Just keep going!" I said, racing to grab my bouquet and handbag. "We've got to make it to the next street before Scott sees us."

"Cassie!" The shout was just audible above the guttural roar of motorcycle engines.

"Don't look back!" I cried to Cass. "If he doesn't see your face, you can deny the whole thing on Monday."

"Cass!"

A motorcycle pulled up next to us and I realized that the shouts weren't from Scott but from the bike's rider. It was Cassie's brother.

"Andrew!" Cassie beamed at him. "What are you doing here?"

"Cruising," Andrew said.

Cass sighed. "Mom told you not to take the bike into the city—"

"Cass!" I interrupted her scolding. Things were dire! "We've got to get moving!"

"I'll give you a lift!" Andrew patted the bike's leather seat, then turned to the other riders. "Guys! Let the girls get on!"

Three other bikers handed helmets to Jelena, Lindsay, and me. I glanced back at the art building. To my relief, Scott's full attention was focused on wrestling with the window. I looked warily at the bike. Riding two-up through the city with an anonymous biker didn't seem like such a great idea. I wanted to live a long life and publish many books, not die in a James Dean–ish inferno.

"Ready to ride?"

The biker lifted his helmet and I recognized Zac O'Connell, the Shieldses' eighteen-year-old neighbor, who owned three cats. Surely he wouldn't be too reckless when the lives of several felines depended on him getting home safely.

I leaped onto the bike. "Cass, let's get out of here!"

Cass climbed onto Andrew's bike and wrapped her arms around him.

Scott lifted his head from the window and caught sight of us. His eyes widened as he took in Cassie, who hadn't put on her helmet yet. Before I could call to her, Andrew revved his bike and tore off. The rest of us followed.

When the bikers roared through my neighborhood, I saw several curtains twitching as people tried to see what the noise was. We pulled into my driveway and I jumped off the bike. "Thanks, Zac. Say hi to Buffy, Zeke, and Tom-Tom for me."

Zac took the helmet from me. "If you ever want to visit, just say the word."

Cassie followed me up the drive. "Zac's always had a little crush on you, you know."

"What?" I looked at her, then back at Zac. He had a safety pin through his earlobe. "Let's not get into that. Cass, Scott saw us!"

Cass's face fell. "You're kidding."

"I'm deadly serious. Harley-riding serious."

Andrew beeped for Cassie to hurry up.

"Don't worry," I told her. "By Monday we'll have come up with a story. You know, something like you have a twin sister who's a biker chick."

Cassie gave me a doubtful look.

"Okay, so that's somewhat unbelievable. But I'll work something out."

I waved as the whole group blasted their horns in a chorus and tore off.

What a day.

My head in the clouds, I nearly crashed into Hayden Paris, who stood on my front step.

17 there is no romance between us!

"I was beginning to think you'd never get home," Hayden greeted me. "Though that entrance was worth the wait. I haven't seen that many bikers all together in a long while."

"Hayden, what are you doing here?" All I wanted was to have a bath.

"Valentine's Day, of course."

Hayden drew three heart-shaped red helium balloons from behind his back. My jaw dropped. Hayden Paris, on my doorstep, bearing heart-shaped balloons? This day was getting even crazier.

Hayden stood there, a smile spreading over his face. "Well?"

"Is this a joke, Paris?"

The words tumbled out before I could stop them. All my rational thoughts had been knocked flat by this turn of events.

Hayden straightened the ribbon on one of the balloons. "Well, as you said in English class this morning, everyone deserves a day of love, so I thought the balloons might cheer up Snookums's and Bebe's day. I checked with the pet store to ensure they're made out of cat-friendly material."

Any moment now, Ashton Kutcher was going to leap out of the bushes and tell me that I'd been punk'd.

"The third balloon is for you," Hayden continued in a rush. "Happy Valentine's Day."

"Happy Valentine's Day," I repeated dumbly, looking into his hazel eyes. Their expression was both amused and oddly nervous. "I'm . . . I'm sure Snookums and Bebe will be ecstatic."

All of a sudden I didn't know what to say. I just kept staring from the balloons to Hayden's sincere face to the balloons again.

"So, should I hand these over to you?" Hayden asked.

"No," I said, finally finding my voice. "Do you want to come in? That way you can give them to Snookums and Bebe yourself."

Hayden stepped away from the door. I struggled with the key, my fingers shaking. What was wrong with me? I finally got the door open and stumbled slightly as I stepped inside. Hayden took my arm to steady me.

"That's an impressive bouquet, Princess."

"It takes my breath away every time I look at it."

"So who's it from?" Hayden examined the rainbow rose.

"Someone absolutely amazing," I replied. "That's all I know. It was anonymous."

Hayden lifted his gaze from the rose to me. His eyes were twinkling. Was he laughing at me? Or at my admirer? I'd kick his butt if he was laughing at my admirer.

"I have a feeling Snookums and Bebe will be in here," I announced, leading Hayden through to the living room. "The pet store brought them another Valentine's gift this morning."

Sure enough, Snookums and Bebe were clambering over the cat-climbing frame I'd bought them. It was in the shape of a tree, with scratchy imitation-bark branches and sleeping platforms shaped like elephant ear palms.

"Hey, babies!" I dropped to my knees to give them a scratch. "Someone's brought you a new treat!"

"Hi, guys." Hayden dropped down beside me and gave Snookums a rub under the chin.

"Why don't we hang the balloons from the branches?" I suggested.

Hayden wound the string of the first balloon around the lowest branch of the climber. His jeans brushed my right leg and I could feel the warmth of his calf even through the thick material.

"The red looks great against the deep brown of the branches," I commented distractedly, standing up again.

Hayden smiled. "I'd better tie them carefully. Imagine if Snookums grabbed hold of a balloon and floated away."

I laughed. "Like the movie *The Red Balloon*. He'll drift over Paris, finally landing on top of the Eiffel Tower."

"Ah, Paris. My namesake and ancestral home."

"Ancestral home? Your mom told me you come from good old-fashioned English stock!"

"Don't tell anyone else that," Hayden said. "My connection to the city of love is a fundamental part of my appeal. Along with my stellar intelligence, winning wit—"

"Reciting your poem again?" I broke in.

Hayden tried to keep a straight face but failed. "I can't help myself when I'm around you, Mistress Muse."

He held out the last red helium heart. I reached out to take it from him. Our fingers grazed. I lost my grip on the balloon and it sailed toward the ceiling.

"Oh no!"

"Aurora!" Hayden made a jump for the balloon, catching it in his left hand. "I spent twenty minutes choosing that balloon this morning, and you just let it go?"

"You didn't really spend twenty minutes selecting that balloon."

Hayden and I were now standing close to each other.

"I did." His eyes met mine. "You might have seen me at your front door holding an aesthetically unappealing balloon and tossed me in the mud."

I wanted to protest, but something about his gaze, so intent on my face, stopped me from making a sound.

"Though you look like you've been in the mud yourself."

Hayden's voice was just above a whisper as he reached forward and gently brushed my right cheek with his balloon-free hand. I suddenly remembered my disheveled state and raised my hand to the same spot, where it met Hayden's. He took a step forward.

"Happy Valentine's, sweetheart!" the NAD's voice boomed from the front door.

Both Hayden and I jumped in fright, and I stepped away from him.

The NAD strode into the living room. He visibly staggered as he took in the cat-climbing frame. "Aurora, what is this monstrosity?"

I didn't answer. I was looking at Hayden, whose cheeks were as red as the balloon he still held in his left hand. My own face felt flushed and my cheek tingled. Would Hayden have kissed me if the NAD hadn't interrupted? Well, tried to kiss me, since I would have had to stop him. I was still saving that first kiss for my Potential Prince. Despite this, I was suddenly besieged by thoughts of what the kiss would've been like. Were his lips soft—

"It's nearly as tall as I am!" The NAD reached out to feel the imitation bark. "It's verging on a redwood."

"Dad, it's Snookums's and Bebe's Valentine's present!" I finally turned my attention to the cat climber. Dad couldn't take it back! "It's a savanna tree—the kind their ancestors would have lounged on."

"A savanna tree?" the NAD repeated. "Couldn't they be content with a potted palm or something?"

"I'm trying to make them feel better about their domestic slavery."

"Those cats have their every need attended to!" The NAD pointed at Bebe's engraved silver water bowl. "If anything, we're slaves to their every meow. They need a form of entertainment that doesn't depend on material possessions."

Did his newfound Buddhist philosophy have to dominate even the cats' lives?

"Aurora's just got a big heart," Hayden said.

"Hayden! Nice to see you!" The NAD sounded thrilled. "You won't mind excusing us for a moment, will you? Help yourself to anything from the fridge in the meantime."

Dad gestured for me to follow him out of the room. Oh no. He was going to make me call the pet store and get them to take the climber back.

"Dad, I'm really sorry. But don't make me return it, please."

"Return it?"

"Isn't that what you want to talk about?"

Dad was heading up the stairs toward his room. "No. That's not necessary. Maybe it'll stop Snookums from being so destructive."

It was unlikely, but I threw my arms around him, anyway. "Thanks, Dad!"

"You can show your thanks by helping me select a tie for my Valentine's dinner with Dana." Dad threw open his closet and gestured at his tie rack.

I couldn't believe I was being asked to help him win over a woman who could only make my life more miserable. Talk about salt in a wound. Unless . . .

I stared at Dad's novelty Mickey Mouse bow tie.

"Well?" Dad looked at me. "Come on, fashionista."

I pointed wordlessly at the bow tie.

"Mickey?" Dad looked surprised. "I guess Dana might like it."

She would hate it. A Valentine's date with a man who had a cartoon mouse at his throat? I could just see her scowl. Mickey would probably convince her that Dad was really a conglomerate-loving capitalist. I envisaged her making an excuse to go to the bathroom, then sneaking out to her Mazda and driving right out of his life.

I opened my mouth to say, "She'll love it!" then saw Dad's trusting expression as he held the bow tie up to his neck. I couldn't sabotage the NAD's date. He was already scarred from my mother's sudden escape to Spain. A second escape might send him over the edge.

"No, Mickey was a joke. Wear the red tie."

"Perfect," Dad announced. "It'll match the roses."

Ms. DeForest was getting roses? Why did Dad have to be a romantic?

I chastised myself. I had received a glorious bouquet today. Who was I to deny Ms. DeForest flowers?

I plastered a smile on my face. "Get ready and I'll check you over before you leave."

I went downstairs, remembering that Hayden was presumably still in our living room. An image of his hand stroking my cheek burned into my brain. I reached the hallway and my throat went dry. What would I say to him?

I stopped at the living room entrance. Snookums and Bebe were batting at the heart balloon tied to the lowest branch. I turned my eyes to Hayden, who was looking at a sheet of paper on the coffee table. The sheet of paper that held a rough draft of my poem "The Prince."

I let out a scream. Hayden leaped in the air like he'd been shot. Snookums and Bebe bolted under the sofa.

I snatched the poem up from the table. "What are you doing?"

"Aurora, I can explain—"

"There's no worthy explanation!" I grabbed him by the shoulders and pushed him out of the living room.

"I was just looking for a piece of paper to leave you a note to tell you I had to go—"

"Why? To go break into someone else's house to read their private information?" I pushed him down the hall.

"You invited me in!" Hayden's mouth twitched in amusement.

"Under false pretenses." I threw open the front door. "Great tactic. Come bearing gifts, then go through my belongings!"

"I'm so sorry, Aurora." Hayden held out a hand. "It was a complete accident I even read it. I feel awful. I—"

"Sure!" I yelled. "I'm sure you're feeling awful. Awfully happy as you head out to tell everyone about my crappy poem—"

"It was beautiful," Hayden interrupted.

I threw the poem at him. "Why don't you just take it and make photocopies? Go on! I'm sure I couldn't feel any more embarrassed than I do now."

The NAD appeared on the staircase. He looked awkward.

"I didn't interrupt a romantic good-bye again, did I?"

I laughed in what I hoped was a scornful way. "There is no romance between us, and there will never be. Not even in your wildest James Bond–esque dreams, Hayden. Never!"

Hayden opened his mouth to reply but I slammed the door shut.

"Aurora!" Dad opened the door, revealing Hayden again. "That's incredibly rude."

"Why don't you talk to Hayden about rude?" I yelled, and ran upstairs.

"Don't worry, son," I heard the NAD say. "She'll come around."

I'd never come around. I sank to my bedroom floor, lines of the poem dancing in my head. *Where is the Prince who is to win my heart?* I wanted to cry. I could just picture Hayden's smirk as he read those lines. Now he'd probably tell everyone about my unhealthy obsession with finding a Prince.

Why had I been so honest?

Because I'd never dreamed that anyone except my romance-loving English teacher would read the poem. I hadn't planned on the bane of my life sneaking into my house!

"Aurora?" The NAD tapped at my door. "I have to leave for my date now, but cheer up. Love will reign supreme."

"Arrgghh!" What had Hayden *told* Dad?

After Dad's car had pulled out of the driveway, I started running a bath. I glanced at myself in the mirror and recoiled. I had long, angry scratches up and down my arms and legs, at least five twigs stuck in my hair, and a huge smudge of dirt on my cheek.

I remembered how Hayden had stroked that very spot, and clenched my jaw. Obviously his plan had been to distract me in order to stay in the house long enough to find my poem. I must have been delusional to wonder if he was going to kiss me. Twenty minutes selecting a balloon. Yeah, right.

I sank into the bubble bath and started to relax. So Hayden had made fun of me again. Well, what else was new? Hayden's whole existence was about tormenting me—I'd always known that.

It was time to focus on happier things. Out there, not so far away, was my Potential Prince. A guy who was pure of heart, and generous, if today's bouquet was any indication. That was what I should be concentrating on, not base things like Hayden Paris.

18 the fraud of men
was ever so

"The first scene we'll be rehearsing today is the deception of Benedick by Don Pedro, Claudio, and Leonato," Mr. Peterman announced at Monday's rehearsal.

I stood backstage with Lindsay, who was taking my measurements for my costumes, and Jelena and Cassie, who were conferring about the props needed for each scene.

"For act four, we'll need swords for Dogberry and Verges," Jelena said.

"I'd like a sword right now." I glared at Hayden. Mr. Peterman was instructing him to hide behind a hedge. Maybe Jelena could arrange for the hedge to be made of poison ivy or something.

"Murderous muttering is never a good look, Aurora," chirped Jelena as she highlighted scenes in her script.

"What's happened now?" Lindsay asked, jotting down my hip measurement.

"Just breaking and entering under the cruel guise of bringing Snookums, Bebe, and me Valentine's Day balloons—"

"Hayden brought you Valentine's balloons?" Sara interrupted. She was standing at the backstage mirror, practicing her evil Don John face.

"That's so sweet!" Lindsay squealed.

"You never told me this story." Cassie was trying to hide a smile.

"That's because it's a tale of extreme personal suffering brought about by Hayden's blatant disregard of my privacy." I could still see him, peering down at my poem. "Can we please discuss someone else's love life?" I rubbed my temples.

"Ooh!" Jelena looked up from her props list. "Let's discuss mine. I'd like to announce that Alex has been very attentive since Valentine's Day." She smoothed her ebony hair. "He called me on the weekend for—and I quote—'no reason,' and brought me coffee today. There's nothing like competition to get a guy moving."

"That's great, Jelena," I said. "Cass, how are things between you and Scott?"

"Weird," Cassie said, looking around to see that Scott couldn't overhear. "You know how you told me to act like nothing happened? Well, today he asked me how my Valentine's Day was. I managed to stammer out an okay. I don't know if he was referring to the yellow rose or the whole motorbike fiasco. He's probably realized I was spying on him."

"I wonder why he hasn't said anything about it, then?" Jelena pondered.

"Maybe he wants to spare Cassie the embarrassment." Lindsay moved over to take Sara's measurements.

"Maybe the idea of us spying on him didn't even cross his mind," I said, looking for my next cue. "We were away from the bushes by the time he spotted you."

"Here's where the song comes in," Mr. Peterman announced. "Which, going with the fifties vibe, will be a cocktail number. Music, please."

The singer began: *"Sigh no more, ladies, sigh no more, / Men were deceivers ever . . ."*

Were they ever. Hayden was prime proof of that. He might be a student council member and star student, but I knew the truth.

"One foot in sea and one on shore . . ."

"Maybe Scott's like that," Jelena whispered. "Maybe he's got one Converse in the water and the other on land. Cassie, you should just give up. Who wants an indecisive man?"

Cassie sighed. "I don't think I can. Too much of my heart is caught up."

"I'll ask Alex if he has any available friends," Jelena said, ignoring Cassie's comment. "You and I could double date!"

"I think you should give Scott a chance," I said. "He gave you a beautiful rose only three days ago."

"Sing no more ditties, sing no mo, / Of dumps so dull and heavy; / The fraud of men was ever so . . ."

This song was so not conducive to encouraging Cassie to keep the faith. I looked at Hayden on stage. He had his hands over his ears, pretending to groan at the song. He would deny the truth about himself.

"Converting all your sounds of woe into Hey nonny, nonny."

I was going to pretend that I couldn't care less about Hayden Paris. I'd just sing *Hey nonny nonny.* Whatever that meant.

"Come hither, Leonato," said Don Pedro. *"What was it you told me of today, that your niece Beatrice was in love with Signior Benedick?"*

Hayden's jaw dropped in shock.

"Excellent, Hayden," Mr. Peterman said. "Now, lean farther into the bush to try to overhear more."

"Why, what effects of passion shows she?"

"Then down upon her knees she falls," Claudio cried, dropping to his knees. *"Weeps, sobs, beats her heart, tears her hair, prays, curses; 'O sweet Benedick! God give me patience!'"*

Hayden, eavesdropping, was wearing an expression of pure delight. This was pushing it too far. There was no way Beatrice—aka I—could be on the verge of hysteria over Hayden Paris/Benedick.

I leaped on stage. "Mr. Peterman!"

"Ah, my lady love! I am blessed with a visit!" Hayden pulled himself away from the imaginary hedge.

"Zip it, Paris." I turned to Mr. Peterman. He was sitting in a director's chair with his name scrawled across the back. A left-over prop from his soap opera days, perhaps. "This play is going too far! Even for Shakespeare! In all honesty, would Beatrice dote on a man like this, Mr. Peterman? Would she?" I stared at him like a prosecutor cross-examining a witness.

"Aurora, may I remind you that this scene is showing Don Pedro's plot? It's not an indication of Beatrice's actual actions."

There were several snickers in the audience.

"Well, good," I replied. "What woman beats her heart and tears her hair out when she's in love?"

"She might if it's unrequited love." Hayden wiped away an imaginary tear. "It tears you apart."

I glared at Hayden perched at the edge of the stage. God, I wanted to push him off.

"Can we continue?" Mr. Peterman waved me away.

I hung around near the curtain as they kept reading the scene.

"Hero thinks surely she will die; for she says she will die, if he love her not, and she will die, ere she make her love known, and she will die, if he woo her, rather than she will bate one breath of her accustomed crossness," Claudio said.

"Beatrice will die?" I strode back on stage. "This is so not a family-friendly production, Mr. Peterman."

"Especially with the bra burning and sexual frustration," Jeffrey called out, rubbing his hands together gleefully.

"Enough!" Mr. Peterman roared. "Everyone get back to the scene."

I tried to calm my intense irritation at being saddled with Hayden for a future hubby, but the next scene just made it worse. Hero and Margaret tricked Beatrice into thinking that Benedick was in love with *her*. It was my turn to hide now, behind an imaginary wall, listening in.

"Okay, Beatrice's soliloquy!" Mr. Peterman said, at the end of Margaret's and Hero's lies. "Go, Aurora."

"What fire is in mine ears?" I muttered. *"Can this be true? . . . And, Benedick, love on; I will requite thee—"*

"Aurora, you're supposed to look joyful, not like you're being sent to the guillotine," Mr. Peterman cut in. "Stop there. You'll have to work on that."

"Is it really so painful being loved by me?" Hayden asked as I came off stage.

"That's one question that can be answered with a resounding yes."

His eyes dimmed slightly. "Aurora, is this about the poem?"

"It's about everything, Hayden." I folded my arms over my chest.

"It's about the poem," he said. "I can tell. You weren't reacting like this on Friday."

I clenched my fists. Was he referring to the hand-on-cheek incident, during which he'd been secretly laughing at my gullibility?

"Funny," I said, pretending to search my thoughts. "Because Friday brings back a memory of me pushing you out the door."

"Before you pushed me out the door," Hayden said. "Before your dad came home."

He *was* referring to it. He was dead.

"Can I have all the boys on stage for costume measurements?" Mr. Peterman called.

Hayden didn't budge. He just kept looking at me.

"What?" I said, throwing my arms in the air in frustration.

"Don't you have a reaction to my statement?"

"It's not worth reacting to," I replied.

Hayden's eyes dimmed even further. "You know, I don't understand why you only ever see me as an enemy, Aurora. Because the way I see you is very different." He put his hand on my shoulder. "I'm really sorry about the poem."

I pulled away.

"I never meant to pry," he said. "Like I told you, I was looking for a piece of paper to leave you a note."

"Hayden, you're wanted on stage," Mr. Peterman called.

Hayden strode out to the group of guys. Against my better judgment, I followed him. I didn't want him to have the last word.

"Whatever happened to our friendship?" Hayden asked.

"Friendship?"

"When we were younger. When we used to hang out at each other's places—"

"And you pushed me in the pool."

I turned away to join Jelena, Cassie, and Sara down in front of the stage.

"Don't tell me you're still thinking about that!" Hayden cried. "That was an accident!"

"It's always an accident with you, isn't it, Paris? You accidentally read my poem, accidentally make me think you're a burglar—"

"Are we ever going to be friends again?" Hayden cut in, so quietly I had to lean in to hear him.

I looked at him more closely. Was this an act?

His eyes were all sincerity.

I began to say that I didn't know, but I was interrupted by Mr. Peterman.

"Ms. Skye? Are you male?" he yelled.

My cheeks burned in embarrassment as I leaped off the stage. Lindsay started to take the guys' measurements.

"Why don't I make this easier for you?" Alex said to her, and ripped his shirt off, revealing a seriously toned and tanned six-pack.

There was an audible gasp from the female members of the audience.

Benjamin took one look at Alex and pulled his own shirt off.

"Here's some eye candy, ladies," Jeffrey cried, ripping off his polo shirt.

Jelena sighed. "Any excuse for Jeffrey to get nude. Couldn't he leave the shirtless thing to Alex and Benjamin? They at least have upper-body definition."

The next moment, the entire line of male cast members was naked up top. Except Hayden, even though I knew he had a chest to rival Alex's.

Jeffrey threw his socks into the audience and reached for the zipper of his pants.

"Please no," Jelena said.

We all shielded our eyes, then looked up again as the auditorium door was thrown open to reveal Mr. Quinten and an important-looking visitor.

"Mr. Quinten's reaction was kind of extreme," Cassie said the next day as we helped her carry a newly dry backdrop from the outside courtyard to the backstage area.

Jelena raised an eyebrow. "Kind of extreme? He was moments away from suspending the whole male cast."

"You'd think that being in the army all those years would make Mr. Quinten oblivious to shirtless guys," Lindsay said as we wrangled the backdrop through the door and up against one of the backstage walls. "Why did he freak out so much?"

"Probably because of the school board official with him," I replied. "Just as Mr. Quinten was promoting order and conformity to ensure future funding, there were students indulging in a free-spirited shedding of their attire."

"Which some people should never do without spending some time in the gym," Jelena said. She sat down at one of the desks and pulled out her lighting plan.

"The worst part about it is that Mr. Peterman invited the official to the play," I said. "Now he's going to be even more obsessed about the authenticity of our characters, which means I'm somehow going to have to convince everyone of my love for Hayden."

Sara got a wicked look in her eyes.

"*Don't* say it."

I was not in the mood for a defend-Hayden session. Every time I thought of him, I remembered his plea of "Are we ever going to be friends again?" After everything he'd done to me? Not a chance. Just the thought of it was exhausting.

"Let's talk about something much more interesting," I said. "The identity of my secret admirer."

"Ooh!" Lindsay joined Jelena at the table and opened up her design sketchbook. "Has anyone come up with any ideas?"

"I was thinking that it could be Tom McKenzie," Cassie said. "He's always reading the classics. Very literary. He could easily have written the message."

"Nuh-uh." Lindsay shook her head. "He's dating a girl over at Saint Mary's."

"Seriously dating her?" Jelena asked.

"They're practically engaged," Lindsay said, adding pump shoes to the costume she'd sketched out for Hero.

"Like you and Tyler," Cassie said softly.

Lindsay frowned slightly as she added details to Hero's shoes.

"The real problem is narrowing it down," Cassie said.

"Eureka!" Sara shrieked, and I felt excitement surge through me, tingling my fingertips. Had Sara figured out who it was?

"Eureka?" Jelena repeated. "Sara, who says that?"

Sara ignored her. "I've got it! We ask the florist! Your admirer would have had to pay in person or via a credit card. Either way, they'll have a name on record."

Our conversation was interrupted by a red-faced Tyler striding backstage.

"Lindsay, what's this rumor about you measuring half-naked guys? What's happened to you?"

"I don't see why you're asking me about it." Lindsay's face was oddly stony. "We're broken up, remember?" She looked back down at her sketches.

I was impressed by her convincing nonchalance toward Tyler. My pep talks must have worked.

"Half-naked!" cried Tyler again.

"Well, I can see that you didn't date him for his extensive vocabulary," Jelena muttered.

Uh-oh. Tyler's ears were virtually steaming now.

"Tyler, maybe you should discuss this later," Hayden said, appearing backstage.

"Shh!" I stopped him. "I have to hear this."

"Playing Cupid again?" he asked.

"Aren't you supposed to be on stage?"

"Why are you throwing this in my face, Lindsay?" Tyler's voice had gone up an octave and he paced back and forth in front of us. "Are you auditioning my replacement already?"

"Is it my imagination or is this getting melodramatic?" Hayden whispered.

"You idiot!" Lindsay said, poking Tyler in the chest. "I was measuring them for costumes. In no way was I responsible for the spontaneous strip show."

"Well, I'm sorry, then!" Tyler yelled.

"Good!" Lindsay yelled back. "And let me remind you *again* that this is none of your business."

"It is when I want you back!" Tyler said. "What have I got to do? Do you want me to beg?"

He threw himself at Lindsay's feet.

"Excuse me?" Jelena waved the lighting plan in the air. "Some of us are trying to work?"

"Reconciliation is on track," I said to a bemused Hayden.

Lindsay held the scepter of power now. Tyler would never try a "fly like an eagle" line again.

"I'll sing!" Tyler said, breaking into "How Do I Live" by LeAnn Rimes. His voice wasn't exactly melodious as he thumped his chest hard.

"Tyler, I'm not taking you back." Lindsay's voice was very quiet but very serious.

"What?" I whispered. This wasn't the way the script was supposed to go. Feigned nonchalance was good for a while, but I'd told Lindsay that once Tyler reached the point of begging, the path to reconciliation was open.

Tyler, Jelena, Sara, Cassie, Hayden, and I all stared at her in disbelief.

"Lindsay . . ." Tyler's voice was choked.

Lindsay turned away. "I don't want to hear it."

Tyler continued staring at her in shock.

"Come on, buddy." Hayden took Tyler's arm. "Let's talk about this outside of rehearsal." He led him away.

"Lindsay, what happened?" I said softly. "We've passed the two-week point, and Tyler knows he was in the wrong."

My tone was almost pleading, which surprised me. I was all for my friends being independent women. But Lindsay and Tyler—they'd been crazy about each other forever. I'd never even considered the possibility they might not reconcile. Weren't they meant to be together?

"I don't know if I want to be the person that I was with him," Lindsay said. "Focused on just one thing: Tyler." She took a deep breath. "On Monday, I was looking through a costume book and I realized how much fun I've had being involved in the play. And it hit me: I never would have done all this if Tyler hadn't broken up with me. Maybe this whole thing was meant to be."

19 seeing stars

"I can't believe they won't give out personal information!" I groaned at the following day's rehearsal. "Since when did florists start behaving like the CIA?"

"Well, I guess if you send flowers anonymously," Jelena said, "you want to stay anonymous. I still say he's a nerd."

I ignored her. "What if this amazing, one-of-a-kind guy never reveals himself?" A shiver of horror ran through me. "Or worse. What if this is all a practical joke? What if it's just Tarot Card Tina trying to get even with me or something? And she's going to reveal the truth and humiliate me in front of the entire school?"

"Aurora, no one would spend that much money on a joke bouquet," Jelena said as she checked off items on her props list. "What's happened to you? You're getting paranoid."

"I know," I moaned. I felt guilty about accusing Tarot Card Tina of deceiving me. "I guess so many of my emotions are invested in this that I can't think straight. I mean, what else can I do? I've tried asking the florist and making a list of suspects."

"The only thing you can do," Cassie said, adding shadowing to a cardboard column that was to become part of the Southern plantation set, "is wait until he makes his next move."

"Okay!" Mr. Peterman called. "Act two, scene three. I need Don Pedro, Claudio, Benedick, and Leonato on stage, pronto! In this scene, we have a very image-concerned Benedick being teased by the others because they know his newfound vanity is all to do with being in love with Beatrice. Okay, begin scene!"

There was a long silence on stage.

"Where's Alex?" Mr. Peterman cried. "It's his line! We've got to do better than this, people. Opening night is less than two weeks away now!"

"Uh-oh." Jelena winced and stuck her head around the stage curtain. "Mr. Peterman? With all the stress of being stage manager and coordinating a cast of twenty-two actors and countless backstage crew—"

"Just get to the point, Jelena."

"I neglected to mention that Alex has a health-related emergency and can't be here today."

Mr. Peterman let out a loud sigh. "Jelena, let Alex know that if he misses any more rehearsals, we have a perfectly proficient understudy to replace him."

"Mr. Peterman, I can assure you that Alex will be fit as a fiddle for tomorrow's rehearsal," Jelena said quickly.

Mr. Peterman didn't answer, just took another swig of his Bach flower tincture.

Jelena rolled her eyes in his direction. "God, talk about overdramatic." Luckily, she was behind the curtain again by that point.

"Is Alex sick?" Cassie's eyes were concerned.

"Of course not," Jelena said as she went back to checking props. "He's at the athletic equipment sale downtown."

I stared at Jelena. "He asked you to lie for him?"

Jelena shrugged. "Aurora, you're making a big deal out of nothing."

"What if you got in trouble for it?" I pressed.

"Just drop it. Did I tell you that we're going on a date Friday night?"

I gave up. It wasn't like I didn't stretch the truth myself some-times. Still, something about Alex troubled me. I couldn't put my fin-ger on it, but the closer Jelena got to him, the more concerned I felt.

I decided to work on my lines to distract myself. I walked over to my handbag, which I'd left in the wings. I opened the back pocket and as I lifted my script out, a silver envelope danced to the floor. My name was typed on the front, like the note that had accompanied my bouquet. I gave a gasp and snatched it up. As I went to rip it open, I realized that I couldn't have a secret admirer–related moment without my besties, so I dashed back to Jelena, Cass, Sara, and Lindsay, who'd just turned up with rolls of material in her arms.

"Eee!" I squeaked, grabbing Cassie and Jelena by the shoulders.

"Okay, she's officially lost the plot," Jelena said.

I ignored her and waved the envelope in front of them. "It's an-other note from my secret admirer!"

"What's it say?" Lindsay dropped the material on the floor and raced to my side.

"Let's find out."

I carefully broke the seal and pulled out a sheet of delicate paper scattered with silver stars, covered with dark-blue writing.

"Check the bottom first," Cassie begged. "I can't wait another moment to know his identity."

I couldn't, either. As my eyes swept down the page, I felt giddy with joy.

My face fell. "It's just signed 'Your secret admirer,' like last time."

Sara peered over my shoulder. "Maybe there's a clue in the note."

I looked at the beautiful script again. "It's a poem!"

My secret admirer had written me a poem. This was like some-thing out of a movie. There was a simultaneous shriek of excitement and we all started jumping up and down. Everyone crowded in on me and grabbed at the note.

"Wait!" I cried above the pandemonium. "I'm going to put it on the table so we can all see it."

I placed the delicate sheet of paper on the table and we all stared at the poem.

She's Like the Stars

Aurora,
she's like the stars, far above me.
I stand transfixed.
She's
my Alpha,
radiating light across my world of sky
on a collision course with my heart and my mind.
The light of this one star
distracts me
from earth, words, everything else I've ever seen or heard.
I'm a victim of her gravity.
Yet I can only skirt
the periphery of her existence.
It will take light-years
to travel
to this spectacular star.
But I'm up for the journey.

Love,
Your secret admirer

"That is so beautiful," I said softly.

"*My Alpha? Spectacular star?* This guy is like the next Lord Byron or something!" Sara cried.

Cassie was grinning. "Whoever he is, Aurora, he's infatuated. You're the center of his universe."

My whole body felt like it was bubbling over with joy. I hardly minded the fact that the writer of the poem hadn't given his name—he was sure to, sometime in the future. I was just completely blown away by the poem.

"Wait a minute!" Sara snatched up the letter. "I can't believe we've been so stupid! Here's our clue to his identity right in front of us!"

We all looked at her blankly.

"The poem, guys." She gestured at it.

"But he didn't sign his name," Lindsay said.

"I've got one word for you all," Sara said. "Fingerprints."

Jelena arched a brow. "That's ridiculous."

"Daughter of a cop talking," Sara replied. "I've got all the equipment at home. It's easy."

"But, Sara," I asked, hating to destroy her enthusiasm, "won't his fingerprints have been destroyed by all of us handling the note?"

"You never know. Mr. Secret Admirer could have left a rogue print." Sara's voice was full of confidence. "Plus, he only just put the note in your bag, didn't he?"

I nodded. "I went to get my water twenty minutes ago."

"And we've been at rehearsal for an hour now," Sara cried triumphantly. "So he's obviously part of the production, which makes the investigation easier, because it's a closed environment."

I wasn't completely convinced. "Okay, say we even find a fingerprint, are we going to demand to fingerprint the whole cast and crew?"

"That's not exactly subtle," Jelena chimed in.

"Don't you want to find out his identity?" Sara pleaded.

I smiled at her. "I think I'll wait a little bit longer. He might have a romantic plan to reveal himself to me. I don't want to spoil it."

Jelena went back to her lighting plan. "What if he doesn't? What if he's a nerd?"

"What is it with you and the nerd thing?" Sara asked.

"*She's like the stars, far above me,*" Jelena quoted. "Hello. He's saying that she's out of his league."

"I don't think he's saying that," I said, dropping dreamily onto a stool and studying the poem again. "I think he's just being complimentary."

"Maybe there's another reason why he can only skirt your periphery," Cassie said. "Maybe there's something keeping you apart."

"Maybe you and he are like Romeo and Juliet." Lindsay sighed. "Perhaps he belongs to a rival social group at school."

"Well, let's hope love will conquer all!" Cassie said.

I could tell that Cassie and Lindsay were thinking about their not-so-fairy-tale situations with Scott and Tyler.

I felt slightly guilty. With all the excitement about my secret admirer, I'd lost my focus on my friends' love lives. Well, that had to change.

There had to be some way of fixing the cracked romances around me. Even if it meant questioning Hayden again.

"All right! Act four, scene one!" Mr. Peterman boomed. "The ill-fated wedding of Claudio and Hero. I need Don Pedro, Don John, Leonato, Friar Francis, Benedick, and Beatrice up here as well, please."

"I'm on." I tucked the poem carefully into my script folder and handed it to Cass. "Take care of this for me, please."

I still felt like I was dancing on air as I took my place on stage.

"Hey, there." Hayden took his spot next to me, at the side of the wedding altar. This was my chance to repair the shattered remnants of TylerandLindsay.

"So, in this scene," Mr. Peterman took his seat again, "Claudio jilts the innocent Hero because of Don John's lies."

Sara gave a devilish laugh and rubbed her hands together eagerly.

"You come hither, my lord, to marry this lady?" the friar asked Benjamin.

"No," Benjamin said, sweeping his hair back off his forehead. "Mr. Peterman, I'm thinking that my right is my best side. Can I change spots?"

"So what happened with Tyler?" I whispered to Hayden, trying not to sound too eager.

"Well, we just had a little talk," Hayden whispered back, his breath tickling my ear. Its warmth seemed to heat my whole body. I tugged at the collar of my shirt. Was there some problem with the air-conditioning in here?

"And?" I pressed.

"And we tried to come up with some solutions."

Hayden was going to make this difficult for me, I could tell. But I had some tricks up my sleeve.

"Solutions, hey?" I repeated. I'd recently read that echoing someone's last few words encourages them to open up to you.

"He's dealing with a lot at the moment," Hayden said.

"What's he planning to do? I was thinking that some flowers would really help the situation." Anything but another singing attempt. Or a string of movie clichés.

"Aurora, Tyler's feeling pretty embarrassed about what he's going through. I can't break his confidence."

I should have known that Hayden would still be riding the keep-quiet train.

"I thought you had this whole Aurora–Hayden friends thing going on," I said.

"Yes." He looked confused. "But what's that got to do with Tyler?"

"Well, friends share," I said. "Friends confide in each other."

Hayden smiled. "Aurora, confiding in each other doesn't mean sharing Tyler's private business. He needs to speak to Lindsay himself."

"So once again you're going to sabotage a romance." I felt like screaming with frustration. I could never get anywhere with Hayden Paris. It was the story of my life, playing over and over again. "Well, I'm sorry, but I can't be friends with someone who doesn't want the best for others."

"I do want the best for others. That's why I'm not spreading their private information around!" Hayden replied. "Come on, Aurora, you're being a little overdramatic."

"Overdramatic!" I huffed. "So is this what it's like to be friends with you, Hayden? Receiving continuous insults?"

"I wasn't—"

"Because it doesn't seem all that different from being enemies with you."

Hayden smiled gently. "Aurora, we were never enemies."

It was all I could do not to snicker. Hayden certainly had a warped recollection of our past.

"There, Leonato, take her back again: Give not this rotten orange to your friend," Benjamin said.

"See!" I cried. "This is a prime example of what happens when people choose not to get involved in others' love lives! Claudio's calling Hero a rotten orange and everyone else at this sadistic excuse for a wedding is just standing around doing nothing."

"Okay, so in extreme situations, like when a woman's honor is at stake, I'm all for breaking a confidence," Hayden said. "But Tyler and Lindsay are hardly on that scale."

"What if they never get back together?" I cried. "And you're the one that stood between them? Just like you're standing between Scott and Cassie!"

"Scott and Cassie are fine!" Hayden said.

I gave a snort. "Scott and Cassie are not fine. Sure, to an unperceptive eye like yours, everything might look okay, but underneath the surface it's a murky mass of confusion."

"It seemed very clear to me on Valentine's Day that things were going great—"

"What about that afternoon, though?" I interrupted.

"Valentine's Day afternoon?" Hayden looked confused.

"Maybe you should ask Scott about it," I said. "Because Cassie's completely lost as to why he's hardly spoken to her since then."

"Aurora, your desire to help others is one of your best qualities, but it's a little extreme at times. People are perfectly capable of falling in love on their own, you know. What about destiny? Call me romantic but—"

"Believe me, Hayden, there's no chance of anyone calling you that."

A twinge ran through me at making such a mean-spirited statement, but I ignored it.

"Mr. Peterman?" Benjamin's voice said before Hayden could reply. "As one of the leading men of this production, I really need a space of my own to mentally rehearse as well as physically prepare myself. I think a dressing room is necessary."

A snicker ran through the auditorium.

"A dressing room?" Mr. Peterman looked incredulous.

"Or a trailer," Benjamin suggested. "My agent says that on the set of a blockbuster—"

"Could I have a trailer as well, Mr. Peterman?" Sara cut in. "Playing an evil character is really putting a strain on my nerves. If I had a soothing space—"

"I think Dogberry and Verges need a trailer," Jeffrey called out. "For a postproduction party space. Lovely ladies drinking champagne—"

"*No one* is having a trailer!" Mr. Peterman's face was purple. "Sorry to disillusion you, but this is not a blockbuster with A-list stars, million-dollar sets, and personal assistants. It's a high school play. *High school.*"

My guess was that Mr. Peterman was feeling the contrast between his former soap-star life and his present situation.

Hayden turned back to me. "It's rather hurtful to hear you constantly repeating how impossible it is for me to be romantic."

"Well, why don't you prove your credentials and help me reconcile two couples?" I said in my most persuasive tone.

Hayden let out a sigh. "I know I keep saying this, but I don't believe in interfering in other people's love lives."

"Fine, then," I shot back. "Forget I ever asked for your help. I'm more than capable of looking after this myself. Not only will I get Cassie and Scott together, but Tyler and Lindsay will be back in love within two weeks."

"All right, Friar Francis, Hero, and Leonato, off stage. Beatrice and Benedick, are you ready for your big love scene?" Mr. Peterman's voice was hopeful.

I stomped to my spot before Hayden could say anything more. Love scene. I shook my head. This play was sick.

"This is the moment when Beatrice and Benedick finally admit their true feelings to each other," Mr. Peterman said. He had a big smile on his face. Obviously he was counting on some riveting chemistry from his best actor and his novice actress.

"Oh yeah!" Jeffrey yelled from the audience. "Sexual tension coming up!"

"It's obviously a huge turning point for the couple," Mr. Peterman continued. "Culminating in the kiss. But don't worry, we won't be practicing that until next week—probably Tuesday."

My heart stopped. I opened my mouth to say something, but nothing came out. The kiss? Was Mr. Peterman hallucinating? Maybe he meant a kiss between Hero and Claudio. Yes, it had to be that.

"The k-kiss?" I stammered, my whole body willing him to say it was Hero and Claudio who kissed.

"Between Benedick and Beatrice, of course!" Mr. Peterman said. "When we do rehearse it, Hayden, you'll need to take Aurora into your arms and kiss her passionately—"

"There's no kiss written in this script!" I said, ripping through the pages of our scene.

"Well, no, but this is where the kiss always comes in the production," Mr. Peterman said. "Don't worry, you've got a while to practice it."

I stared at Mr. Peterman and an embarrassed-looking Hayden. My life was over.

20   the depths of despair

"This can't be happening! I can't kiss Hayden Paris. I can't!"

I sat hunched over at a lunch table with my head in my hands. After Mr. Peterman had effectively told me my life was over, I'd pushed blindly outside with Jelena, Cassie, Sara, and Lindsay at my heels.

"Aurora, it might not be that bad," Lindsay said, rubbing my back reassuringly. "I mean, okay, it's going to be slightly embarrassing having to get intimate in front of everyone, but it's just a play."

"Plus, it's Hayden," Sara said. "Think of the positives. Every girl in the school is going to be jealous. And Hayden is sure to be a divine kisser."

"I can't kiss him!" I wailed. "This whole *Much Ado About Nothing* thing has been cursed from the beginning. First I have to play Hayden Paris's lover. And just when I finally—and, can I say, reluctantly—get to grips with that, I'm told I have to push my limits to a whole new level and kiss the bane of my life!"

I took a deep breath. I was feeling dangerously dizzy. Kiss Hayden Paris? Kiss him? Oh god.

"Okay, he might be the bane of your life," Jelena said. "But he's also really popular. And hot. I just don't get the big deal."

"I'll tell you the big deal." I buried my head in my hands again. "All these years . . ."

"All these years what?" Lindsay prompted.

"All these years you've been secretly crazy about him?" Sara leaped up from the seat next to me. "That's what you're trying to say, aren't you, Aurora? And now that you have to kiss him, you can't hold back your feelings anymore."

Was she insane?

She was right about one thing. I couldn't hold anything back from my friends now, not when I'd been plunged into the depths of despair.

"All these years I've been saving my first kiss for a Prince, getting into no end of embarrassing situations to ensure that it would be a beautiful, life-changing moment."

Jelena's elegant jaw dropped, just as I'd expected. "You've never kissed a guy? Are you serious?" She looked at my expression. "Oh my god. You are serious."

"All that effort, and Hayden Paris is going to be the one to get it." I took a shuddering breath. "*Hayden Paris.* My next-door neighbor who's effectively made the past ten years of my life a complete misery. I can't kiss him. I can't. This is like some sort of nightmare."

"First kisses aren't always all they're cracked up to be, you know," Sara said wryly. "You need a good kisser. Which Hayden is sure to be. You never know, smooching him could be beautiful."

"How can it be beautiful if I'm kissing the wrong person?" I said. "Letting go of the idea of saving my first kiss for my Potential Prince is like letting go of a dream. That's why I'm so upset."

I couldn't believe that a school play was about to destroy such an important romantic goal.

Cassie knelt in front of me and squeezed my hands. "Hope isn't lost yet. There's got to be a way to fix this. Think of how many kisses you and I have stopped so far! I'm going to do everything I can to make sure your first kiss is with a Prince."

"Me, too," Lindsay said, placing her hand on ours. "I was lucky enough to kiss the right person, so I want you to as well."

I watched her face soften as she remembered her first kiss with Tyler.

"I so would have jumped at Hayden Paris being my first kiss, but hey, I'll promise, too." Sara slapped her hand down on Lindsay's.

We all looked at Jelena.

"I still can't get over the fact that you've never been kissed," she said. "But if that's what you're set on, Aurora, then I promise, too." She placed her hand on the top of the pile. "One for all and all for one!"

"Okay." Cassie sat back down at the table and got out her notepad. "Anyone got any ideas on how to prevent this kiss?"

"Talk to Mr. Peterman?" Lindsay said. "You could say that your family's extremely conservative and morally objects to public displays of affection."

"Or pretend that you've got a really bad cold and tell him you're worried that making out with Hayden will pass the germs to his lead actor," Sara suggested.

"Guys, has Mr. Peterman ever listened to any of our objections? About script changes, costume suggestions, or character motivation?"

Sara frowned. "You've got a point."

"There's no way he'll let me get out of the kiss," I said.

"Okay, what about something more dramatic?" Jelena said. "You get 'sick' on opening night and miss all the performances."

"I can't do that," I said. "We've all worked so hard on this play. If I pretend to be sick, Mr. Peterman will either drive to my place and demand that I get out of bed, or he will use my understudy, who's completely uncommitted." I pictured gum-chewing Felicity playing my role. "Then the whole mood of the play will be wrecked, the school board official will cancel the school's future arts funding, and Mr. Peterman will have a mental breakdown." I let out a sigh. "I can't do it."

"Even to protect your first kiss?" Lindsay asked.

I shook my head. "There's got to be another way."

"I've got it!" Sara cried. "You want your first kiss to be with your Potential Prince, right?" She didn't wait for my answer before plunging on. "Well, that's got to be your secret admirer. So, if we find out his identity, you can confront him. He admits it; bang, you fall in love; and boom, he kisses you. Or you might have to kiss him, if he's not moving fast enough."

I pictured myself lunging at my secret admirer. It was so not how I'd imagined things. "Sara, I don't know."

"It's your best chance," Cassie said thoughtfully. "Once you've had your first kiss with a Prince, Hayden kissing you won't mean anything."

"I guess . . ." I still felt uneasy about kissing Hayden.

"So, for the sake of speed, can I fingerprint everyone?" Sara looked pleadingly at me.

Jelena frowned. "How are we going to do it?"

"I've got it!" I leaped up from the lunch table.

"Free soft drinks!" Jeffrey exclaimed, and grabbed a cup of lemonade.

Virtually the whole cast and crew of *Much Ado About Nothing* was crowded around Jelena and Sara's hurriedly assembled refreshments table. Cassie, Lindsay, and I had raced down to the corner store to buy liters of Coke, lemonade, and other drinks.

"Everyone drink up!" Sara announced. "Benjamin, Travis, everyone! Drink! Drink!"

She sounded like some sort of peer-pressure drinker at a keg party. However, I wasn't going to protest. I quickly filled paper cups with fizzing soda.

"Has everyone got a cup? Let's have a toast!"

"To the success of *Much Ado About Nothing*!" Jelena cried. "And to your fabulous stage manager!"

"Hear, hear!" Alex, who'd just arrived and reassured Mr. Peterman of his "miraculous recovery," picked up a lemonade and toasted Jelena.

"To *Much Ado About Nothing!*" everyone chorused.

And to finding my secret admirer, I silently added as I watched Hayden take a sip of his lemonade.

"Remember to write your name on your cup to get a refill later!" Sara shouted.

"A refill?" Jelena looked at our dwindling supply. "We don't have enough for refills."

"Believe me, I'll have this baby packed up and smuggled out the moment Mr. Peterman restarts rehearsal," Sara whispered. "But if we don't have names on the cups, then we've gotten nowhere."

She was right. We needed to be able to match the prints on a cup with those on the poem. I passed a marker around. "Make sure you put your names on your cups!"

"That's not your cup, it's mine!" someone said.

"It's not like it matters!" his friend shot back.

"Don't mix them up!" I cried, unable to believe people could be so blasé about my romantic future.

"Back on stage!" Mr. Peterman cried.

People threw down their cups and raced off, leaving the five of us with around fifty fingerprint samples.

"Okay." Sara slipped on a pair of plastic gloves from the box we'd bought. We all followed suit. "We can chuck out all the girls' cups, except our own. I'll need them to identify the other prints on the poem."

"What do we do with the guys' cups?" I asked.

"Handle them only on the rim and put them very carefully into my evidence box," Sara said, brandishing a large cardboard box.

I placed the cups in one by one, wondering which would reveal my Potential Prince.

"Isn't your dad going to wonder why you're using his equipment on all these paper cups?" Lindsay asked.

"He won't mind," Sara replied, halfway out the door. "I think he hopes I'll follow in his footsteps."

"Are you sure you don't want any help with the analysis?" I asked, picturing Sara surrounded by dozens of used paper cups.

"Nope. You can leave it to me. But it's going to take a good couple of hours tonight. Do everyone a favor and go home early, Aurora. You're looking completely frazzled."

"So not a good look," Jelena added.

Since I had no more scenes that day, I took Sara's advice.

Unfortunately, going home early did nothing to calm my nerves. When the phone rang at eight p.m., I nearly knocked over my bedside table in my haste to answer it.

"Hey, Aurora." Cassie's voice was excited. "Have you heard anything from Sara yet?"

"No. Have you?"

"No."

"God, I hope she finds a fingerprint. I'm going crazy." I drew my knees up to my chest. "Distract me! How did the rest of rehearsal go?"

"Well, there was a slight hitch when Tyler turned up on stage, quoting lines from a poem he'd written in memory of Tylerand-Lindsay."

I groaned. "Was it bad?"

I heard a giggle in Cassie's voice. "Let's see, from what I can remember, it ran something like, *Black, black, my soul is black. My twin flame has snuffed the light. . . .*"

Everyone was turning to poetry. Look at what Mrs. Kent had started.

"*Striped, striped,*" Cassie continued, "*my soul is striped. Black despair and white hope. I am a zebra—*"

"Tyler is a zebra?" I shrieked. "Oh my god. How many people heard it?"

"Well, he'd arranged for James in lighting and sound to give him a microphone and a spotlight, so everyone at the rehearsal."

"I'm going to kill Hayden. This must be his and Tyler's big plan to win Lindsay back."

"Maybe you should hold off on killing him," Cassie said, "because I think it might have worked."

"Lindsay said she wants Tyler back?" My tone was ultraexcited.

"Well, she didn't say that. But she got this funny look on her face. And now that Tyler's working on costumes with her—"

"He what?"

"Oh yeah. I forgot to tell you. He pledged his never-ceasing assistance to Lindsay, so she's got him stitching crystal beads onto Hero's wedding outfit."

Tyler, sewing? "Wow, Hayden's actually given Tyler some good advice. I can't believe it."

"Well, it's no surprise to me," Cassie said. "Hayden's a really smart guy."

For once, I didn't try to argue with her. I was in shock. Hayden Paris encouraging a romance instead of sabotaging it with advice about taking things at a snail's pace? Unbelievable.

"He asked me to call you and tell you about TylerandLindsay—"

"He what?" I said, incensed. "I can't believe him! You know why he asked you to do that, don't you?" I didn't give Cassie a chance to answer. "Because of the fight we had today about TylerandLindsay and you and Scott—"

"Me and Scott?" Cassie's voice had gone up an octave.

"And how he didn't want to get involved at all because he's a romantic," I continued. "Talk about skewed logic. So I vowed that I'd have everything straightened out within two weeks, and now he's beaten me to the punch by putting TylerandLindsay on Reconciliation Island." I let out a frustrated growl.

"'Reconciliation Island'?" Cassie's voice was skeptical. "Aurora, don't you think you're getting a little bit overdramatic?"

I gasped. "That's what *he* said! Has he been talking to you, Cassie?"

"Briefly . . ."

"Oh my god! He hasn't been talking to you about Scott, has he?"

"Well, a little."

"Arrgghh! He's trying to propel himself onto the bestseller list before me!"

"He's what?" Cassie sounded confused. "Aurora, he's only trying to help. Maybe he wants to show you that he *is* romantic—"

"Hardly." I let out a laugh. "Oh my god, he hasn't got you and Scott together as well, has he?"

I no longer doubted Hayden's ability to achieve anything. Thank god I hadn't said I'd have Cassie and Scott engaged or anything, or Hayden would have had them at the altar by now.

Cassie sighed. "No, unfortunately not. I just don't understand. Things have been weirder than weird since Valentine's Day. I don't want to sound vain, but before that, I could tell he liked me—"

"Cassie, that's not vain. It was obvious to everyone."

"Even when the whole model-girl thing was going on, he was still smiling at me all the time and making excuses to touch me."

"And he gave you a rose!" I added. "Which we know now, due to model girl being his little sister, meant something."

"But did it?" Cassie said. "Maybe all he wanted to be was friends." I heard her sigh. "Ironic. Since Valentine's Day we haven't even been that."

"I don't think he figured out that we were spying on him," I said, considering Scott's vibe around Cassie since then. It definitely wasn't accusing.

"Then why is he acting so weird? What other explanation is there? He doesn't like girls who ride motorcycles?"

"All I know is you've got to talk to him," I said. "That's the only way you're going to unravel the twisted yarn that's Scott's brain."

"Oh god."

"At least break the ice. If you get him laughing, he may start spilling his soul to you."

"You think?"

"I'm sure," I said, even though I wasn't in the least.

"Okay!" she said firmly. "I'm going to do it. I'm going to break the ice."

"Go for it!" I said, and we hung up.

As the evening stretched on, I tried to study my lines, but my thoughts stayed on Sara and whether she'd found any clues. Next Tuesday was the rehearsal of the Beatrice–Benedick lip-lock. That meant I had less than a week to get my secret admirer to kiss me. I couldn't believe that after sixteen and a half years of patiently waiting for my first kiss from a Prince, I was having to rush into the whole thing!

Sara's fingerprinting was my only hope. Without it, Hayden was guaranteed to be my first kiss. This was a time for prayer. I leaped out of bed, threw myself onto my knees, and prayed with all my might: *Please, please, please let me find out the identity of my secret admirer.*

The phone broke into my dreams the next morning at 7:05 a.m.

"I know who your secret admirer is!" Sara shrieked into my ear.

"What?" I mumbled, still half asleep.

"Your secret admirer!" Sara sounded impatient. "It's Jeffrey Clark!"

21 the chain of destiny

Jeffrey Clark was my secret admirer? No matter how many times I turned the idea over, I couldn't make sense of it. It was like being told that the earth really was flat.

"So have you talked to him yet?"

Lindsay's face was all expectation as we sat down at a booth at the local coffeehouse. After hearing Sara's fingerprinting results, I'd dazedly texted everyone, requesting an emergency meeting on the way to school.

"How could she have talked to him?" Jelena said, ripping open two sugar packets and sprinkling them into her already sweet caramel mocha. "School hasn't even started yet."

"She could have called him," Lindsay said.

"Called him?" I gripped my mug of hot chocolate. "It's hardly something I could talk about on the phone. I'm only just coming to terms with the revelation."

I felt terrible, but I was kind of disappointed about my secret admirer's identity. Call me naive, but I'd imagined him as a mysterious stranger at Jefferson High that I'd happened to miss noticing. But it wasn't like that at all. Far from being a stranger, Jeffrey was in all of my classes, and I'd never felt a spark of attraction for him.

I mean, he was great for a laugh, but I just couldn't picture him as a Potential Prince.

I'd never seen him show any signs of *amore* toward me, either.

Wait a minute . . . He *had* admitted to looking at my butt in Ms. DeForest's class. And he'd given me that bell on Valentine's Day . . .

"I just can't get it into my head," I said.

"Well, you'd better get a move on," Jelena said. "There are only five days till the Beatrice–Benedick smooch session. And seeing as you don't want to kiss Hayden . . ."

"Sara, is there any way that you could have gotten this wrong?" I asked.

"Well, I can't guarantee one hundred percent accuracy," Sara replied. "There were obviously a number of variables involved. However, the prints match up."

I could tell that the frown on her face wasn't because I was questioning her fingerprinting skills; it was because she was just as confused as I was about the results of the test.

"Are you sure you want to do this whole approach-the-secret-admirer thing?" Cassie asked me. "I mean, do you have any feelings for Jeffrey?"

Jelena burst out laughing and we all turned to look at her.

"I'm sorry," she said. "But this is Jeffrey Clark we're talking about. Jeffrey with a penchant for stripping and a fascination with the plague. Oh god, this is too funny."

"Thanks, Jelena," I said dryly. But she had a point. When I'd included "unique" in the list of my Potential Prince's qualities, I hadn't *quite* meant Jeffrey's degree of specialness.

Cassie stirred her latte. "If you don't have any feelings for him, then maybe you shouldn't tell him that you know the truth. There's no point in hurting him."

"You could just ignore the results," Lindsay added.

Could I do that? Could I just keep quiet if Jeffrey sent me more and more heartfelt messages?

"What if Jeffrey confronts you?" Jelena's crimson mouth was

smirking. "And what about the kiss? That's the whole reason we did the fingerprinting. Don't tell me the refreshment stall was all for nothing."

I sighed. After all the trouble we'd gone to, it did seem cowardly not to speak to Jeffrey. Plus, I couldn't ignore the fact that he'd sent me a highly expensive, visually spectacular bouquet, a heartfelt note, and an amazing poem.

"I'm going to talk to him," I said. "I mean, if he wrote that poem, then there's more to him than we think." I paused. "Like they say, you can't judge a book by its cover."

It would be spiritually shallow of me to reject Jeffrey on the grounds that he didn't appear to fit my Potential Prince image. The notes I'd received indicated a deep, poetic soul. Maybe Jeffrey really did have another side to him.

"I have to give him a chance. It's only fair, after he's put his heart and his wallet on the line."

"Oh my god," Lindsay whispered.

Oh no. Not another emotional plea from Tyler in a public place.

Lindsay's eyes were huge. "Jeffrey and company just sat down at a booth."

I glanced pseudo-casually to my right and saw that she was correct.

Jelena was nearly purple from suppressed laughter. "Well, Aurora, are you going to go talk to him?"

"I can't do it here!" I whispered.

Jelena smirked. "Sure you can. If you don't, I'll call him over myself."

"You wouldn't."

Her face was all grinning resolve.

"Okay, I'm going," I grumbled.

I made my way over to Jeffrey, who was building a tower of salt and pepper shakers. I took a deep breath. "Jeffrey?"

Jeffrey turned his head away from the wobbling tower and the whole thing collapsed.

Travis laughed. "You suck, man. Let me try."

"No way!" Jeffrey snatched the spices away from him.

"Jeffrey?" I already had a headache. "Could I talk to you for a minute?"

"Go ahead, babe," he said.

He, Travis, and Jesse all grinned at me expectantly. Oh god, did they all know about the secret admirer thing?

"I was hoping I could talk just to you?" I said quietly.

Now I knew exactly how Tyler had felt when he approached Lindsay in the library.

"Ooh!" Jesse said. "You hear that, Jeffrey? She wants to talk to you privately!"

"'Privately' is code for a make-out session," Travis piped up. "With Aurora Skye! Man, you got it going on!"

Both Jesse and Travis elbowed a grinning Jeffrey in the side. Several tables around us fell silent.

"Right, that's it." I started to walk away. No Potential Prince would allow his friends to hassle me in a public place.

"Wait!" Jeffrey leaped up from his seat. "Aurora, we can definitely talk privately! Shut up, you guys!" He glared at a tittering Travis and Jesse.

"Let's get a booth," I said, and pointed to one that wasn't too far back, in case Jeffrey tried to get passionate or something. Yes, I was on a deadline with the whole first-kiss thing, but I needed a few dates to ascertain Jeffrey's Potential Princeliness first.

Jeffrey stretched out on one side of the booth. "So, babe, what did you want to talk to me about?"

I paused. Couldn't Jeffrey just admit that he was my admirer? He obviously knew that I'd figured it out. Why else would we be talking privately?

He gave me a grin, and I took a long look at his face, something that I'd never done before. Did I find him attractive? Well, he did have a nice smile—white and bright and brimming with the promise of fun. And his eyes were a lovely blue that contrasted with his golden hair. Maybe kissing him wouldn't be so bad.

Wouldn't be so bad? I didn't want to kiss someone I considered *not bad*. I wanted to kiss someone out-of-this-world incredible. But maybe once Jeffrey's real identity was revealed, I *would* feel that way about him.

"Jeffrey," I tried again. "I know that . . ."

"You know what, babe?"

He leaned across the table toward me. Oh god. This was moving too fast.

"I know that we're very different," I said slowly, not wanting to say the wrong thing. "That's why I have to admit that I was very surprised to find out that you thought of me in that particular way. . . ."

"Oh yeah! Babe, you're gorgeous," Jeffrey said.

So there it was: his confession of his regard for me. It was official now.

Jeffrey pulled a sandwich from his backpack. He'd just declared his love and he was eating a sandwich? Call me oversensitive, but I'd kind of expected him to be less blasé about his feelings. Perhaps he was eating out of nervousness? I should be focusing on the important thing: he was my admirer. I gave him what I could tell was a wobbly smile and continued.

"Obviously there's a lot more to you than I realized. Your poem was so beautiful—"

"Huh?" Jeffrey sat up straight. "Poem? I've never written a poem in my life."

The interior of the coffeehouse seemed to whirl around me. Jeffrey hadn't written the poem?

"Are you serious? You've never written a poem? Not even, say, for a girl you like?"

"Nope." Jeffrey took a bite of his sandwich. "But don't let that discourage you, babe. I have other talents. Humor; a great body."

"But you've never written a poem?" I pressed. "You swear?"

"What is it with chicks and poetry?" Jeffrey asked. "No. I can't stand the stuff."

I stood up, giddy with relief. I should have remembered Jeffrey's claim in English class about suffering metrophobia. There was no way he'd choose to woo a girl using poetry.

"Fantastic!" I cried. "Thanks, Jeffrey!" I grabbed my bag and threw it over my shoulder. "I'm sorry about this whole misunderstanding. I had you mixed up with someone else."

"Someone else?" Jeffrey dropped his sandwich. "Now, wait a minute, Aurora. I could try my hand at poetry if that's what you really want. Some of those poems are pretty sensual—"

"Gotta run, Jeffrey!"

I dashed back to my friends.

"How did it go? Did you arrange a date?" Cassie asked.

"Did he seem any deeper?" Lindsay asked.

"No and no! And yay!" I cheered quietly, hoping that Jeffrey couldn't hear.

"And that makes you happy?" Sara stared at me.

"I'm happy because it wasn't him!" I whispered. "He didn't write the poem."

"But what about the fingerprints?" Sara said. "I spent hours on the analysis. I can't be wrong."

"It was wrong," I said quickly. "Let's get going. I'll tell you the whole story once we're out of Jeffrey's earshot."

"You know what this means, don't you?" Jelena said when I'd finished my explanation. "It means that we're back to square one with this whole damn secret admirer thing! We have no clue who this nerd is—"

"Jelena!" I said.

"We have no clue who this supposedly fabulous guy is," Jelena went on. "And no way on earth of finding out!"

"Sara, is there any way you could try the fingerprint thing again?" I asked. "Obviously Jeffrey's fingerprints got mixed up with someone else's somehow. Maybe the secret admirer accidentally used Jeffrey's cup."

"I don't have the cups anymore!" Sara said. "They went out with this morning's garbage."

"We are not going through the garbage!" Jelena cried.

"Of course we're not!" I said, though it had crossed my mind. "Jeffrey had lemonade, didn't he? If we can remember who else drank lemonade, we could narrow it down."

"I hate to tell you, Aurora, but almost everyone drank lemonade," Cassie said. "It was the first to run out."

"It's impossible," Jelena said. "There's no way we're going to find out this guy's identity by next Tuesday! You have to give up."

"It's not impossible." I was trying to stay positive. "There's got to be something we can do."

"I've got an idea," Lindsay said. As I whipped around to face her, her eyes dimmed. "Oh no. That won't work."

"What won't work?" I cried. "Come on, Lindsay, at least say what it is."

"You're not going to like it," she said.

I made a pleading gesture. "Lindsay, please!"

"Well, all the magazines say that jealousy will usually motivate a man to make his move," Lindsay said. "So, if we get your secret admirer jealous, then he might pop out of the shadows and claim you."

"How would we do that?" I asked, wondering why Lindsay would think I had a problem with the idea.

"Well, as we know, you have a big moment coming up on Tuesday," Lindsay said.

My face flushed as I thought of the upcoming rehearsal.

"If your secret admirer heard that you were going to be getting cozy with Hayden Paris—"

"Total high school hottie," Sara added, taking in my look of horror.

"Then he might get all worked up over another guy kissing his dream girl and reveal himself before it happens!" Lindsay finished.

"Technically, if he's part of the production, then he already knows," Jelena said. "Sorry, Lindsay, but the jealousy idea is no good."

Lindsay shrugged. "We have no actual proof that this guy's part of the production. He could have an inside man who does his deliveries for him, which means he could be completely unaware of Tuesday's rehearsal."

"But how are we going to get the information to this guy if we don't know who he is?" Cassie asked.

Lindsay smiled. "We inform everyone in the school about Aurora and Hayden's kiss."

"No!" I cried. "Everyone's going to give me hell about it!"

"But it won't matter if it results in you finding your secret admirer and kissing him before Tuesday, will it?" Cassie said.

She looked closely at me and I remembered how, the night before, I'd urged her to take a risk. I had to answer truthfully.

"Okay, I admit that it sounds worthwhile in the long run."

The sacrifices a girl has to make for love.

"Okay. Well, we've got to do this properly. . . ." Jelena said. "I know. I could announce it over the loudspeaker!"

"No!" I'd die of embarrassment if the announcement happened in a class where Hayden sat right in front of me.

Jelena pouted. "Fine. I'll just start the rumor mill, then. As you know, I'm the expert in that area."

More than ninety-six hours later, I stood with Jelena outside the interpretive dance room. Since Thursday, I'd done my best to smile at every guy I set eyes on, just in case he happened to be my secret admirer. I'd kept my phone within arm's reach the whole weekend, praying for a call or a text. Nothing. Now it was Monday afternoon, only twenty-five hours till the rehearsal, and there was absolutely no sign of my love on the horizon.

"You're going to have to face facts," Jelena said, removing her silver sandals. "The rumor's all over the school and this guy still hasn't revealed himself. This first kiss with your fantasy Prince isn't going to happen."

Her words burned, but I was all too aware of the reality of the situation.

"I can't give up!" I threw down my pink peep-toes for extra emphasis.

Jelena shrugged. "Just get the first kiss over with."

I glared at her. My first kiss wasn't something to get rid of!

"Everyone inside," Ms. DeForest called, holding open the classroom door.

The room had had a makeover. The walls were now purple, and gold drapes fell from the ceiling and covered the windows. God knows how she'd gotten permission from the school board to turn the classroom into an oil sheik's retreat.

"Look at this place!" Jeffrey ran into the center of the room, with Travis and Jesse following.

"Feel the vibe, man!" Travis twirled one of the drapes around himself.

"Come join us, my beautiful woman!" Jeffrey shimmied my way.

Obviously he was still under the impression that he and I were a possibility.

Ms. DeForest slammed the door shut. "Stop sullying this sacred atmosphere! Today's lesson is about soul growth. Please find yourself a spot on the floor."

She switched on the stereo. Suddenly the room was enveloped in darkness. Several girls let out earsplitting shrieks—including Jelena, right next to me.

"Blackout!" I heard Peter Guinness cry excitedly from somewhere to my right.

"What if there's a fire?" Amber Jenkins sounded hysterical. "What if that's the reason the power's gone off?"

I couldn't smell smoke, but I leaped to my feet. From the sounds around me, I guessed everyone else had done the same.

"To the fuse box, gentlemen!" Jeffrey cried.

There was a thunder of feet as the male members of the class tried to follow Jeffrey's order, then the thumps of people running into walls.

"There is no blackout!" I could hear someone clapping— presumably Ms. DeForest trying to restore order. "I turned the lights off. The darkness is a metaphor for your spiritual ignorance."

I doubted that my spiritual ignorance was this extreme. I couldn't even see my hand in front of my face.

"The darkness is swallowing you up," Ms. DeForest said. "You are confused. Disorientated. Terrified."

Someone let out a piercing scream.

"Mr. Clark!" Ms. DeForest boomed. "What is the meaning of that outburst?"

"You can't see anyone!" Jeffrey said, sounding hurt. "How do you know the scream came from me?"

"I am all-seeing and all-knowing," Ms. DeForest said. "Explain yourself immediately."

"It was primal," Jeffrey said. "You said we were terrified, and the terror rose up in my throat and burst out."

"You are tumbleweeds blowing in the hurricane that is life," Ms. DeForest continued, obviously deciding not to respond to Jeffrey. "You ask yourselves, why do certain things happen to certain people? Today, I have the answer for you. Today, we will explore the mystical force that controls all events: fate!"

Suddenly, light flooded the room. I blinked, feeling slightly stunned.

"Two lines of fifteen people," called Ms. DeForest.

Everyone formed two lines, facing one another, then linked hands with the person opposite at Ms. DeForest's command. Jelena and I made sure we were a pair.

"Okay. As you may have noticed, we have an extra person." Ms. DeForest pointed at Kelly Ryce. "Your hands are forming a platform that will propel Kelly from the start of the line to the finish." Ms. DeForest pointed at the end closest to me.

"Propel?" Kelly looked at the line, then back at Ms. DeForest. "I don't know about this."

"The chain of destiny will support you," Ms. DeForest said, gesturing at the line of our linked hands. "Now, run and leap!"

Kelly closed her eyes and dived onto our linked hands, which sank suddenly under the weight.

"Propel her! Propel her!" Ms. DeForest shrieked.

"This is ridiculously hard work," Jelena said, rolling her eyes.

"Next!" Ms. DeForest pointed at Tom Meyer, who was at the head of the line. That side had to move down one person, which meant I was now holding hands with Shane Davis.

"Feel the chain of destiny throwing you this way and that!" Ms. DeForest called to Tom.

"Like a theme park ride!" he said.

Ms. DeForest frowned. "Fate is not a friendly theme park ride! It is out of control, throwing the possibility of destruction constantly in your way. You have no power to alter its effects."

As ridiculous as this exercise was, I couldn't help wondering about Ms. DeForest's claim. Was fate real? Was that why my secret admirer hadn't turned up? Because he was destined not to?

Oh my god. Surely it couldn't be destined that Hayden Paris should be my first kiss?

The idea seemed ridiculous, but it also seemed to fit, in a weird way. Ever since I'd heard about this onstage kiss, I'd done everything in my power to put a stop to it. I'd fingerprinted fifty people, confronted Jeffrey Clark, started a school-wide rumor, and racked my brain trying to discover my Potential Prince's identity. But none of it had changed anything.

"The chain of destiny is locked in, controlled by forces set in place millennia ago!" Ms. DeForest said, as Amber Jenkins rode the chain of destiny with an unimpressed look on her face.

Millennia ago? What had happened way back then that had made the Aurora–Hayden kiss a locked-in outcome?

I closed my eyes with a groan. Once again, I needed a time

machine. If I could just stop Hayden from moving to Jefferson— or, more simply, stop myself from auditioning for *Much Ado About Nothing*, much as I loved being a part of it now—then the kiss would never happen.

Or would it? Was it locked in, like Ms. DeForest was saying? Even if Hayden hadn't moved to Jefferson, would I still have crossed paths with him somehow and ended up being forced to kiss him?

Fate was too cruel. The whole of my life I'd been living under the happy misapprehension that my first kiss was mine to give away. Meanwhile, destiny had been laughing to itself over the truth. Hayden Paris was going to have the pleasure of kissing my virgin lips.

"Let yourselves go with the flow!" Ms. DeForest stretched her arms out. "Say, 'Fate, I accept you and your whims. I give my assent!'"

My thoughts whirred. Could I accept fate? Could I assent to its whims? Could I give Hayden my first kiss?

I made myself consider the idea unemotionally. Hayden was an academic achiever and a student council member. He wrote poetry and participated in the dramatic arts. He cared about animals and he had charisma and confidence. He also was honest (too honest sometimes) and, I had to admit it, honorable. Based on this description, he sounded right for the part. But all of this was based on logic. Logic could only apply so far when it came to a kiss. Kissing was wrapped up in emotions and attraction and other scary, sticky things.

I pictured Hayden's twinkling hazel eyes looking into mine, imagined him lowering his dark head. I waited for his lips to make contact . . . then felt them touch mine. My heart thudded. For a moment, I wasn't in Ms. DeForest's class. I was in Hayden Paris's arms.

Oh my god, I *could* kiss him. I could see it as clear as crystal in my head—and it seemed almost . . . My breath caught. Appealing?

The memory of us standing so close together on Valentine's Day floated into my mind like the helium balloon he'd given me.

Then I saw him reading my poem. Refusing to help me with TylerandLindsay or Cassie and Scott. Observing all my horrendous dates.

The helium balloon of good thoughts popped.

Could I consent to giving my carefully preserved, all-important first kiss to the bane of my life? Was I the type of person to let the wind of fate blow me around without protest? No, I was not. I was Aurora Skye, and I believed that one person could make a difference. While there was still time and opportunity and breath in my body, I was going to fight fate.

"Ms. Skye!" Ms. DeForest's exasperated call broke into my personal triumph. "Please ride the chain of destiny."

I looked at the line of linked hands that would throw me out of control.

I sprinted toward it, dived underneath the line of hands, and slid out untouched. I let out a whoop as I exited.

"What is the meaning of this?" Ms. DeForest demanded.

"I'm making my own destiny," I said, with all the resolve in my soul.

"*Out!*" Ms. DeForest boomed. "Your energy is disruptive and destructive!"

"Are you ever going to come up with a reason other than invisible forces for kicking me out?" I asked, getting to my feet.

Ms. DeForest glared at me. "Get to the office, before I decide to suspend you for two days."

"Technically, only the principal can suspend people," Jeffrey chirped. "I should know."

"Both of you, *out!*" Ms. DeForest pointed to the door.

"But I wanted to see Aurora ride the chain of destiny!" Jeffrey complained.

I raced out the door before Ms. DeForest could explode.

I couldn't believe that I'd gotten detention again. My academic record was a shambles.

To make it worse, Jeffrey spent the time composing stanzas in my honor, obviously believing that poetry would improve his chances of a hookup. I never thought I'd be anti-poetry, but phrases such as "Oh, the fantasies I have" and "Curves, curves that stir my soul" were mortifying.

I blocked him out and focused on constructing my battle plan against fate. It was time to take Operation Stop Kiss to a whole new level.

22 fighting fate

The next morning I woke up in an upbeat mood. Life was a sweet prospect, now that I knew I was in control of this afternoon's event. I was dancing down the hall toward the door when the NAD stopped me in my tracks.

"Aurora, can we talk?" His brow was crinkled. "Dana called yesterday and told me you'd been disrupting her class."

Ms. DeForest had told on me? Some spiritually advanced soul she was. She must have gone directly from her class to phone Dad.

"Not only that, but she told me that this has occurred before— both in her class and in Mr. Blacklock's."

Ms. DeForest was keeping tabs on my classes?

The NAD let out a sigh. "I couldn't believe it. I've never known you to be in trouble before."

"Dad," I protested, "it was completely unfair!"

His face softened. "I know that you're probably going through a lot, with falling in love for the first time. That's natural."

"What?" I gaped at him.

"But even if your romance with Hayden is playing with your emotions, I still want you to give Dana the respect she deserves, both in class and here at our home."

"When have I not given her respect?"

"Well, she seems to feel that you're a little standoffish—"

"That's only because she called me—" I stopped.

"She called you what?" Dad looked closely at me.

There was no point getting into how she'd accused me of having a black aura. The NAD was infatuated with Ms. DeForest and wouldn't hear a word against her. Love truly was blind.

"Never mind," I said. "I'll be polite."

"That's my girl."

The NAD gave me a squeeze, but I pulled away, annoyed that he was so willing to believe that I'd behaved badly.

Rehearsal was even more crowded than usual that afternoon. It seemed like half the school had volunteered their assistance for the day, not wanting to miss the much-talked-about lip-lock between Beatrice and Benedick.

"All right!" Mr. Peterman rubbed his hands together. "The time has come for the big moment! Yes, everyone knows what I'm talking about!"

Jeffrey feigned ignorance. "Could you remind us, Mr. Peterman?"

I groaned from my place backstage.

"The rehearsal of the kiss between Benedick and Beatrice!" Mr. Peterman cried. "So, Hayden and Aurora, please come on down!"

Mr. Peterman sounded like the host of *The Price Is Right*. I watched Hayden make his way on stage, waving good-naturedly at the catcalls and ribbing. I slowly slid off the stool, afraid that my shaking legs wouldn't support me. Maybe I could just run out the backstage door.

"Aurora?" Mr. Peterman called. "Kissing takes two. Please make your way to the stage."

I took a deep breath and turned to the girls, checking that Tyler, who was embroidering Hero's nightgown, couldn't overhear. "Is everyone clear on their roles?"

"There's no way we couldn't be," Jelena said. "You've been reminding us all day."

Cassie elbowed her. "Don't worry, Aurora. Everything's going to go exactly as planned."

Her words bolstered my spirit.

"Ms. Skye?" Mr. Peterman was now on the megaphone. "Hayden is waiting for you."

I dashed onto the stage as fast as my shaking legs would let me. There was no turning back now.

"Okay! We're ready to go!" Mr. Peterman said, taking his place on the director's chair.

I looked at Hayden, who was wearing a deep-blue shirt and a slightly nervous smile, and my legs became even more jellylike. To try to calm myself, I glanced at Cassie and Scott's amazing set, which suggested the inside of a church. A stained-glass window stood behind an altar with a font of holy water next to it. In front of Hayden and me was a long aisle—and an audience of at least fifty cast and crew, all wearing smug expressions.

"Mr. Peterman?" My voice came out slightly tremulous. "Are all these people necessary? They're heightening my performance anxiety."

Mr. Peterman swallowed a sip of guava juice. "My dear, if this is causing you performance anxiety, you're really going to be in trouble on Friday, when the house is packed. Don't worry about today. It's going to be very start and stop, because I'll be directing you with the megaphone to build the most effective mood."

Megaphone? Mr. Peterman was going to be booming instructions like "Run your fingers through his hair!" across the whole auditorium? This had to be the most embarrassing moment of my life.

"Now," Mr. Peterman said through the megaphone, "Aurora, you are praying in front of the altar."

Thank god I was on my knees in this scene. If I'd had to stand, I would have collapsed. I suddenly found myself praying for real: *Oh, please let me go unkissed. . . .*

"Excellent, Aurora!" Mr. Peterman boomed. "Now, Hayden, Benedick is halfway up the aisle, looking with affection upon the beautiful Beatrice but not sure whether to approach her. Begin scene!"

"Lady Beatrice, have you wept all this while?" Hayden's voice was gentle.

"Now, Aurora, turn to him with desperate eyes."

I turned my head slightly and looked up to where Hayden stood by the pews. My clasped hands shook slightly.

"Yea," I answered bitterly, *"and I will weep a while longer."*

"Can't we just get to the kiss?" Jeffrey called out.

Part of me agreed. It was torture, waiting for the moment when the plan would fall into place.

"No interruptions." Mr. Peterman's voice was firm.

"Surely I do believe your fair cousin is wronged." Hayden took another step forward.

I turned my back to him. *"Ah, how much might the man deserve of me that would right her!"*

"Passionately, Aurora!" Mr. Peterman said. "Beatrice is giving Benedick a clue here. This is how she wants him to prove his regard."

Hayden dropped to his knees beside me and grasped my hand, which suddenly stopped trembling. For a moment I forgot about the fifty pairs of eyes in the audience. I was Beatrice, in a church, with Benedick's knee brushing mine.

"I do love nothing in the world so well as you: is not that strange?"

Hayden's voice was a mix of nervousness, resolve, and a sprinkling of joy. I had to admit that he was a talented actor. A wide smile spread over his face as if he was relieved that he'd finally confessed, and I felt my own lips turning upward in response. For a moment we were six years old again, grinning at each other in the sandbox.

"Aurora?" Mr. Peterman's megaphone brought me back to reality. "Your reply?"

"As strange as the thing I know not," I stammered, looking down

at Hayden's hand in mine. *"It were as possible for me to say I loved nothing so well as you: but believe me not; and yet I lie not; I confess nothing, nor I deny nothing—"*

"What's she talking about?" Jeffrey yelled.

Beatrice was muddled up with feelings. Just as I was at that moment, minutes away from the start of Operation Stop Kiss.

"Okay, Hayden," Mr. Peterman boomed. "Place your hand on her cheek."

Hayden slowly lifted his palm to my cheek, which was now burning. This was all too familiar.

I had to stay focused on the script. Three lines until the plan went into effect.

"You have stayed me in a happy hour: I was about to protest I loved you." My voice shook slightly.

"And do it with all thy heart." Hayden moved in closer, and an odd expression crossed his face.

"I love you with so much of my heart that none is left to protest," I said.

Hayden's eyes flickered slightly. What was wrong with him?

"Okay, Hayden, I want you to gather Aurora in your arms—"

The auditorium was plunged into darkness.

Screams echoed around the auditorium, but all I was aware of was the warmth of Hayden's body as he held me in his arms, and the funny feeling in my stomach.

"Fire! Fire!"

"Where's the exit?"

Crashing sounds came from the seating area. I was glad I wasn't down there.

"I can't smell any smoke, can you?" Hayden's voice was very close to my left ear. "It's probably just a blackout."

I restrained a giggle. I knew it wasn't a blackout. It was Lindsay, who had flicked the switch at the fuse box while Sara kept watch for any teachers. Operation Stop Kiss was a success!

The idea had come to me in detention. If Ms. DeForest had

caused so much chaos by simply turning the light switch off in our interpretive dance class, then it would probably work just as well during the kiss scene. I felt terrible about sabotaging the rehearsal, but this was a dire situation.

"Everybody freeze!" Mr. Peterman's voice cut through the blackness. "I will not have anyone trampled to death during my rehearsal!"

Silence fell.

"Jelena?" Mr. Peterman called. "Find the emergency flashlights!"

"I don't know where they've gone," Jelena wailed.

I knew she was lying, since I'd instructed her and Cassie to hide the flashlights right at the back of the storage cupboard. I was giddy with relief. There'd be no time now to rehearse our "big moment," and the rest of the week's rehearsal schedule was already squashed tight with other scenes. By the time opening night arrived, my admirer would have turned up or I'd have come up with another plan. I was safe!

"Silence!" Mr. Peterman boomed. "We'll light the candles."

"Candles?" I repeated.

"There are dozens of them set up for the church scene," Mr. Peterman answered.

I hadn't realized I'd voiced the question out loud. Why hadn't Jelena briefed me on the props?

"Mr. Peterman . . ." Jelena's voice was strangled. "Do you know how many candles we'll need to light this place up?"

"Think of the waste of materials!" I called in the direction where Mr. Peterman's voice seemed to be coming from.

"There'll be an even worse waste of materials if we don't rehearse this scene," he called back. "Jelena, start lighting them now."

"With what?" I could tell Jelena was stalling.

"A lighter?" Mr. Peterman sounded like he was talking to an idiot. Poor Jelena.

Please don't let anyone have a lighter, I prayed. If we didn't have a lighter, there'd be no light. If there was no light, there'd be no rehearsal. If there was no rehearsal, there would be no kiss.

"I've got a lighter!" a voice called.

"Me, too!"

I bit back a groan. Did these people have any idea of the chain of events they were setting up?

"Me, too. We can't let this scene go unrehearsed," someone added with a snicker.

Okay, obviously some people were aware.

"Let there be light!" Mr. Peterman boomed.

Little flames appeared all over the room, and the lighters' owners, their faces weirdly illuminated, made their way up onto the stage. I pulled away from Hayden before our embrace became evident and people assumed we'd been "rehearsing" in the dark. Hayden went to assist Jelena and Lindsay with lighting the long white candles by the altar.

What are we going to do? Lindsay mouthed to me.

I don't know! I mouthed back frantically as the church aisle lit up with tiny lights.

"Everyone not involved in the scene, off stage!" Mr. Peterman said, as the last of the candles was lit. "We're running out of time."

Hayden took his position next to me again. The candles twinkled all around us, enveloping the stage in a warm glow. Instead of stopping the kiss, I'd simply heightened the romance of the situation! Talk about irony.

"Let's go!" Mr. Peterman said. "Hayden's lowering his head. . . ."

We weren't even going to run our lines through again? We were going straight into the kiss?

"Ready, *ma chérie*?"

Hayden placed one hand on my waist and drew me near. His face slowly moved toward mine, and the scent of freshly cut grass surrounded me. He was twelve inches away.

Eight.

Six.

"Stop!" Sara screamed, leaping onto the stage.

Hayden's head whipped around to her, and I nearly collapsed with relief.

"What is going on?" Mr. Peterman was incensed. "I said no one else on stage!"

"But this is important!" Sara cried, standing above Hayden and me. "Look at this!" She gestured wildly at the backdrop.

"Yes, Sara, it's a stained-glass window," Mr. Peterman said with a sigh. "Hardly of vital importance compared with the rehearsal of this *crucial scene*."

"It is of vital importance," Sara said weakly. I could tell she was stalling for time. There had to be only about ten minutes of rehearsal left. "Look at this! Beatrice is about to kiss her love in a church! This window is a symbol of thousands of years of oppression of women by the Catholic religion! It's just wrong!"

Mr. Peterman rubbed his temples. "I don't want to hear this."

"Of course you don't!" Sara cried. "You're a man!"

"Sara doesn't mean to get personal, Mr. Peterman," I cut in. "She's just making the very valid point that the Beatrice–Benedick union is already under a black cloud, and so—"

"This kiss can't happen here!" Sara said.

"No, it can't!" I agreed.

Hayden was looking at us like we'd gone crazy.

"Hayden, please place your lips over Ms. Skye's so she can't talk anymore," Mr. Peterman said.

"Well, I don't know." Hayden's eyes were twinkling. "I've learned to always let her have her say."

Mr. Peterman held up a hand. "Hayden, I'm looking to you as my lead to complete this scene. You're in love with this woman. What do you do?"

Hayden's eyes turned serious. He lifted his hand and traced the side of my face, his touch like the whisper of a breath on my skin. He gently cupped my face in his palms, tilted my lips up, and stared straight into my eyes. His eyes were dark and full of emotion, sending my thoughts spinning back to the question I'd asked myself yesterday: Could I kiss Hayden Paris?

Something inside me whispered yes, drowning out my protests

that he was the bane of my life, that I didn't like him, that my first kiss was meant for a Prince—the Prince who'd sent me the flowers and the poem and . . .

I couldn't breathe. I was frozen, mesmerized by Hayden's eyes, his full lips, the tiny distance between us that he was swiftly closing. *Yes.*

Then he paused, four inches from my lips, and met my gaze. I saw in his eyes an unwillingness to keep going, and my senses came back to me.

There was no way that someone who didn't want to kiss me was going to get my first kiss. Someone who was only acting out a scene in front of fifty pairs of greedy eyes. No. This whole ideal of mine had started long ago, in my childhood, when I'd first heard the Sleeping Beauty story and had prayed for a Prince of my own. It was worth whatever I could do to save it.

Before Hayden could move any closer, and before Mr. Peterman could butt in, I yanked my hands away—and knocked over one of the long candlesticks. Out of the corner of my eye I saw it fall and hit the font of holy water, which wobbled under the impact—and fell toward me.

I knew how heavy it was, having helped Jelena and two of her flunkies carry it onto the stage.

I let out a scream. Oh my god! I was going to be killed by a falling font!

As the huge prop bore down on me, Hayden threw himself over me and rolled us both out of the way. The font hit the floor with a thud that shook the whole stage, its water splashing out.

I lay flat on my back on the wooden slats of the stage, with Hayden pressed on top of me, sheltering me from harm. I looked into his eyes, which weren't just hazel, I noticed, but shades of the most brilliant brown, green, and auburn, like a late-autumn leaf. But even more striking was the expression in them: fear and concern and reassurance.

I felt our heartbeats merge. There was no time anymore. There was no sound except our breathing. I felt the vibration of people leaping onto the stage to check if we were okay. I wanted to stay here, where it was safe, in the warmth of Hayden's arms, breathing in his scent.

I reached up and touched the side of his face.

"Oh my god! I was nearly killed!" Sara shrieked.

23 friends?

"My life flashed before my eyes!" Sara said as soon as the waiter at the wood-fired pizza restaurant had left the table with our order. "My mother, my father, my four brothers—and that horrible *Oliver Twist* costume. Can you believe that was almost my last thought?"

She thumped the table, making our glasses and cutlery jump and nearly causing me to fall out of the booth. An hour after Mr. Peterman had dismissed us—saying that because there was holy water all over the stage, the power was out, and his two leads were shaking, we'd better leave the rehearsal where it was—I was still on edge.

"I can't believe you're only thinking of yourself!" Jelena said, glaring at Sara. "Mr. Peterman looked like he was going to strangle me for not making sure everything was safe on stage. How was I to know that Josh hadn't screwed the stupid thing down?"

My silly impulse to yank myself away from Hayden had caused chaos for everyone else. "I'm sorry," I said. "It's my fault, guys. If I wasn't such a clumsy idiot . . ."

"Hey," Cassie soothed, passing me some napkins to dry my eyes. "Accidents happen. We're not here to lay blame." She frowned at Jelena and Sara, who were still glaring at each other.

I nodded, trying to stop my chin from trembling. I couldn't block out the image of the font bearing down on me.

"Thank god for Hayden," Lindsay said as the garlic bread arrived. "He was incredible. He looked at the font, looked at you, and the next thing I knew he was launching himself into the air and rolling you away from harm."

I remembered Hayden's body shielding mine, and my heart started racing again.

"That just ups his appeal even further," Sara said, pulling apart the buttery bread. "You know, for a minute there, before the font thing happened, I was almost convinced that you were going to kiss him."

The sip of water I'd taken went down the wrong way.

"It must have just looked that way," I spluttered as Lindsay pounded my back.

I felt bad about lying to my friends. For a moment there, in the magic of the candlelight, I had actually been about to surrender my first kiss to Hayden. Until that expression had appeared in his eyes.

I realized the anger I'd felt about his hesitation wasn't there anymore. It had been wiped away by the way he'd thrown himself into danger to protect me. Plus, his hesitation had brought me back to my senses in the nick of time. Otherwise, my first kiss would have been gone by now and I'd have been regretting that momentary hypnotism I'd been under.

Wouldn't I?

I was still pondering that question as I arrived home after dinner and heard the phone ringing.

"Hello?" My breath was coming fast after the rush to unlock the door.

"Aurora?" Hayden's voice was in my ear.

I froze. This was the first time I'd spoken to Hayden on the phone since we were twelve, except for a series of prank calls Jelena and I had pulled a few years ago.

"Hayden, h-hi," I stammered.

"Hi." His voice was warm. "I just wanted to check up on you. I threw you down on the stage pretty hard this afternoon—I could have given you a head injury."

Hayden had saved my life and he was worried that he'd given me a bump on the head? I couldn't believe it.

"No, I wasn't hurt at all. Thanks to you, Hayden."

"It was nothing." He sounded embarrassed. "I just saw that font coming toward you and knew that I'd better do something."

His voice was soft, and suddenly I was back there, on the stage, looking up into those autumn-leaf eyes, in that odd place where time hadn't existed. . . . Suddenly I felt very glad that those same eyes couldn't see me now.

"So anyway," Hayden said, "I was calling to say that I spoke to Mr. Peterman, and he doesn't think we'll be able to rehearse the scene again before dress rehearsal—"

Oh my god. Just like I'd hoped.

"—but he trusts us to go through it ourselves."

What?

"So I was thinking, it could be fun to rehearse it in a fresh environment," Hayden said. "We might get some inspiration. What do you think?"

"Great, great," I managed.

Hayden and I, practicing the kissing scene one-on-one? How would I subtly maneuver my way out of that? But what could I do? Refuse to rehearse? That wasn't very professional.

Okay, so I'd hardly acted professionally today, what with cutting the power and all, but still.

"Great!" Hayden's tone was total enthusiasm. "Why don't we meet at the front gate after school tomorrow?"

"Tomorrow it is," I said.

What drastic measure was I going to have to resort to now?

———

"You ready to go, Princess?"

I jumped at Hayden's voice. My nerves were completely shot after yesterday's misadventure.

Hayden refused to fill me in on the chosen rehearsal spot, even as we boarded a ferry and took seats outside in the sunshine.

"The zoo?" I gasped as the ferry approached the boardwalk.

Hayden burst out laughing. "Okay, I admit it's not the first place you'd think of to run through lines. But I recently saw this documentary where Shakespearean actors took to the streets—"

"Hayden, you're not serious!"

"Sure am." He stepped up onto the jetty and held his hand out to help me across the gap.

"So we're going to be quoting ye olde English by the chimpanzees?" I said. "What's that going to be like?"

It was hysterical. Hayden made a rule that each scene should take place in a different animal area. We played out our first fiery exchange by the polar bears; our waltz at the fancy-dress party by the meerkats; and instead of our love scene taking place in a church, we ran through it as we rode the skyrail over the park to the seals.

"I love you with so much of my heart that none is left to protest."

Before I'd realized it, we'd reached the part where the kiss was supposed to happen. We looked at each other awkwardly.

"So . . . this is where the kiss comes in," Hayden murmured.

"Yeah."

We still had several minutes before we'd reach the exit platform. Oh god. What had I gotten myself into? I was stuck in a tiny carriage up in the air with Hayden, who was about to steal my first kiss. My only escape was to leap out and plunge twenty feet into the alpaca pen.

"Which we haven't rehearsed yet," Hayden said slowly.

"No . . ."

I looked down and saw that my hands were clutching the safety rail so hard that the knuckles were white.

"Maybe we could leave it till the dress rehearsal," Hayden said quickly. "I mean, now's not exactly a private moment." He cocked his head toward the carriage full of crying toddlers behind us. "I'm sure we'll be able to pull it off convincingly as long as we have a sense of the blocking."

"Sure," I said quickly, feeling embarrassed.

"So, Mr. Peterman wants it to be passionate." Hayden looked away, his cheeks slightly pink. "So after that line, I'll put one hand on your waist and the other on your cheek, like we rehearsed yesterday, and then I'll—"

"Shouldn't we gaze into each other's eyes for a minute or so, to heighten the tension for the audience of 'will they, won't they'?" I offered.

I was dying of mortification, but as a fellow actor, I wanted to at least look like I was providing input.

Hayden turned back to me. "Definitely. So we're looking into each other's eyes . . ."

Our eyes met for real.

Right then, our carriage set down and we both jumped in surprise.

"Hey," Hayden said. "We've been pretty diligent with the rehearsal. Why don't we catch the tiger show?"

"Great," I said, thankful for the change of topic.

"They're so cute!" I clapped madly as Sita, one of the female Bengal tigers, leaped into the pool.

Hayden, sitting next to me on the stands, laughed. "Kind of fiercely cute."

"When I see them playing," I said, "they remind me of a larger-scale Snookums."

"I think I'd be a little scared of Snookums the tiger," Hayden said, "what with all the pouncing he does."

"I wish he had an area like this." I looked over the expansive tiger enclosure. "I just know that he and Bebe are bored at home alone all day."

"Hey," Hayden said, "I've got an idea! Have you seen that ad about DVDs for cats?"

I nodded.

"Why don't we make our own?" Hayden pulled out a camera. "I could get some footage of the lions, the leopards . . ."

My face broke into a smile.

We raced around the zoo, filming not only the lions and leopards but also the elephants, giraffes, antelopes, and birds of prey.

"This will make a pretty good savanna scene," Hayden said, reviewing the footage on the ferry back to the city. "I'll edit it a little, add some music, and transfer it to DVD for you."

"Hayden," I looked at him seriously, "thank you for the whole DVD thing, and for today, too—a totally unusual but very fun rehearsal. But most of all, thank you for what you did for me yesterday."

Hayden smiled. "It was nothing."

I took a deep breath. "What I'm really trying to say is, I want to be friends with you."

"Friends?" Hayden repeated. "How can I say no to that request, Princess?"

"So you and Hayden are friends?" Jelena said as she pasted copies of the script onto the backstage walls for any actors who might want a last check of their lines before they went on stage.

I'd stopped by rehearsal to see if my friends wanted to get dinner afterwards. "Yeah. I decided that life's too short to hold grudges."

"So what happens with the kissing scene, now that Hayden's your new best friend?" Sara waggled her eyebrows suggestively.

"We've decided to just go for it on the day of the dress rehearsal."

Sara, Jelena, and Lindsay all gaped at me.

"Well, *he* thinks we're just going to go for it," I said. "But I'm going to skip to my next line, which is 'Kill Claudio.' Hayden can't kiss me after a highly unromantic statement like that. And since we're doing the dress rehearsal in front of a live audience, Mr. Peterman can't stop us and make us go back to the kiss. Easy."

My words were swallowed up by shrieks from the stage.

Jelena closed her eyes and grimaced. "Not another falling prop."

The shrieks drew closer and a paint-splattered Cassie ran toward me, with an equally paint-covered Scott in hot pursuit. Both of them were laughing their heads off.

"I've broken the ice!" Cassie breathed as she tore by me.

"I can't believe we're spending the time we should be at dinner cleaning up paint from the courtyard!" Jelena huffed ten minutes later as she put lids back on paint cans. "What on earth possessed you to start a paint fight, Cassie?" Jelena wrinkled her nose.

Cassie grinned happily. "Sorry, Jelena. When Scott and I finished the last backdrop, this wild urge came over me. I was so sick of everything being polite and formal between us, so I flicked my paintbrush at him."

"What did he do?" Lindsay asked with a horrified look on her face.

"He stared at me for a moment and I got really scared that he was going to be furious," Cassie said, brushing a purple curl away from her face. "Then he gave this big grin and said, 'This is war!'"

"Cass, I am so proud of you." I threw a bucket of soapy water over a particularly paint-splattered section of the courtyard.

"You're proud of her for making a mess?" Jelena shrieked as droplets hit her shoe.

"Oh, be quiet, Jelena," Sara said. "Let Cass tell us her story."

"Scott dipped his fingers in the yellow paint and dabbed them on my face!" Cassie laughed. "Then we were flinging paint at each other. That's why the courtyard is the way it is." She grabbed a scrub brush and attacked a forest-green stain.

"It's a waste of materials!" Jelena said, shaking her head, but everyone ignored her.

"Anyway, it was the most fun I've had in ages, and now Scott's totally normal around me!"

Cassie's voice was triumphant. I hugged her, paint stains and all.

The ringing of my cell interrupted our joyous jumping up and down.

"Just let me get that," I said. "Hello?"

"Hello, darling."

"Hi, Mom!" I said, grinning as Scott returned and threatened to spray Cassie with the hose. "I bought your ticket for the play today. You've got a seat in the third row for Friday."

"Listen, Aurora, about that," Mom said.

My smile faded.

"I'm not going to be able to make it. I've got a business dinner with a client we've been courting for six months."

"You can't come to the play?" I cried out.

My distress was drowned out by Jelena, who'd accidentally been sprayed with the hose and was screaming her head off about her dress being dry-clean only.

"No, of course not," Mom said. "I want you to change the ticket from Friday night to Saturday."

"And you'll definitely be there, right?" I couldn't keep the anxiety out of my voice. I'd only just realized how much I wanted my mother to see the play.

"I promise," Mom said. "This is only the beginning, Aurora. Bright things are ahead of you."

"I love you."

It was the first time I'd said it since the week before she left for Spain. The words felt funny on my tongue.

"We'll talk Saturday," Mom answered.

Thursday was one long blur of play rehearsals, lighting cues, and last-minute run-throughs. Without a minute to spare, I was very glad that I had my plan for Friday's dress rehearsal set up.

The rehearsal, in front of the whole school, was a nightmare. During the opening scene, Byron, who was playing the messenger, forgot his lines and spent the rest of the scene hiding behind a tree. By the time Hayden's and my big moment arrived, two actors had tripped over the Oriental rug that was part of the Southern plantation house's furnishings, the cocktail singer's backing music had gotten stuck, and Jeffrey had pulled out a real knife for his law enforcement scene. The audience's enthusiasm didn't seem affected by the mess-ups, however. The air was virtually humming with anticipation as the kiss scene approached. I could see half the cast grinning in the wings. By the time Hayden had one hand on my waist and the other on my cheek, they looked like Cheshire cats.

Hayden gazed deep into my eyes, exactly like we'd planned.

Was it my imagination or was the whole auditorium leaning forward expectantly?

I gazed back at Hayden, but instead of saying, *"I love you with so much of my heart that none is left to protest,"* I narrowed my eyes and hissed, *"Kill Claudio,"* as menacingly as possible.

Hayden's eyebrows shot up in surprise, but he managed to go seamlessly into his next line as someone in the audience yelled, "What happened to the kiss?"

At the cast meeting, an hour later, Mr. Peterman was asking the same thing.

"Not only were the scene changes a shambles and people completely negligent about their upcoming cues," he shouted, pacing up and down in front of us, "but the Beatrice–Benedick scene, which should have been a saving grace in this joke of a dress rehearsal, also died an excruciating death."

Mr. Peterman stopped his frantic pacing and spun around to face me. "*Kill Claudio?* What happened to the kiss?"

"I panicked," I said in my best apologetic tone. "I forgot my line."

"You didn't think it might have something to do with telling Benedick you loved him?" Mr. Peterman said. "As you were heading toward a *kiss*?" He hissed the word like a cobra spitting venom.

"Aurora was doing her best," Hayden said. "Everyone forgets a line at least once."

He looked sympathetically at me, and I felt a twinge of guilt at his unfailing belief in my honesty.

"Well, I think it was pretty weak of you to just give up on the kiss, Paris." Benjamin arched an eyebrow. "Being the male lead is all about taking charge. You should have just kissed her."

"Being an actor," Hayden replied archly, "is about authenticity. Don't you think it might have seemed *slightly* odd to kiss Beatrice after she'd made a murderous statement?"

"You know what I think?" Jeffrey piped up. "It's weird that Aurora could forget the kiss. I mean, who forgets a piece of action like that? Maybe it was intention—"

I was thankful that Mr. Peterman interrupted before Jeffrey could finish. "That's enough!" he bellowed. "Let me just say one thing. Tonight is opening night. And *nothing* is to go wrong. *Nothing*, do you hear me?"

I nodded, feeling sick. It was obvious that if I pulled the "Kill Claudio" trick again, Mr. Peterman was going to have my head. Plus, it was highly unlikely that anyone would believe I could forget the same line twice. My actions were already being called into question by Jeffrey, who wasn't the most alert person.

Alex's cool voice broke into my thoughts. "I think we need a good party, once this thing is over."

Jelena looked at him, her eyes gleaming. "I could arrange a cast-and-crew party for Saturday night."

Alex smiled his Mr. Perfect smile. "Babe, you are one cool woman."

"I know," Jelena said. "Mr. Peterman, could we have a cast party in the gym? I'll do all the organizing, of course."

Mr. Peterman was slumped in his director's chair. "While Rome was burning, Nero played," he muttered, shaking his head.

Obviously he'd progressed from angry to morose.

"I'll take that as a yes," Jelena said, and winked at Alex.

"Oh, Mr. Peterman?" Benjamin called out in his deep stage voice. "I have a suggestion."

"Yes, Benjamin?" Mr. Peterman's voice was weary.

Benjamin turned to face me. "Aurora needs brighter lighting whenever she's on stage. You know, so she can shine like a star."

I stared at him in shock.

"Do you think we could have this all wrong?" I asked, feeling strangely disembodied as Jelena fussed with my hair and Sara straightened my necklace.

"All wrong?" Jelena looked at me like I was crazy. "He said it loud and clear. Aurora needs to 'shine like a star.'"

"Just like in the poem," Sara chimed in.

"The poem's phrase was 'She's like the stars,' not 'She needs to shine like a star,'" I said.

"She shines like the stars, she is a star, same difference." Jelena appraised me from head to foot.

"Oh, I can't believe that Benjamin Zane is your secret admirer!" Lindsay beamed at me. "How exciting!"

"But why would he announce it in front of everyone? Why not tell me in private?" I said.

"He's an actor," Lindsay said. "He likes having an audience."

But if he liked an audience, why had Benjamin been a secret admirer? Why hadn't he just wooed me publicly from the beginning? Something felt odd about the whole thing.

"I think the way things have worked out is perfect," Jelena said. "Benjamin is rich, good-looking, and talented. Just think, if his career takes off, you could end up dating a Hollywood actor."

"Yeah."

I couldn't work out why I wasn't happy. My secret admirer had turned up and he was a guy half the girls in school would die to go out with.

"So what are you waiting for?" Jelena and Sara were looking at me expectantly. "Go talk to him!"

"Now?" I said. "I mean, I have lines to look over and—"

Jelena interrupted my admittedly feeble protests. "When else? Do I have to remind you that the Hayden–Aurora kiss is this very evening?"

"And I just found out that Benjamin's in his dressing room," Sara said. "So you'll be able to talk to him privately."

I couldn't help feeling apprehensive as I headed toward Benjamin's dressing room. I had no idea how I felt about him. I thought he was a talented actor. And he did have amazing crystal-blue eyes. But beyond that?

As I reached what had formerly been the supplies cupboard but now had a huge gold star with Benjamin's name on the door, I paused. Could we have this all wrong? If I'd spent so little time with Benjamin that I'd barely formed an opinion of him, then how could he be so enamored of me?

Unless it was some kind of love-at-first-sight thing. Maybe he'd taken one look at me and decided that I was his soul mate! Come to think of it, the secret admirer messages had started not long after we'd begun rehearsing the play. Benjamin had offered to coach me. Maybe that had been his way of suggesting a date!

Maybe he was my secret admirer after all. I owed it to myself to find out.

I knocked tentatively.

"I'm trying to focus!" came the exasperated reply.

"Sorry!" I yanked my hand away from the door. "I'll . . . I'll come back later . . ."

"Aurora?" The door swung open and Benjamin looked out with surprise. "You should have said it was you. Come in!"

I paused in the doorway.

"Well, come on." He flashed a set of perfectly straight pearly whites at me. "I know why you're here."

Well, there was my answer. He'd obviously said the "shine like a star" thing on purpose, knowing that I'd confront him.

"You do?" I stepped inside, folding my arms to disguise how my fingers were trembling.

"Of course."

He shut the door behind me, accentuating how small the dressing room was. Benjamin and his crystal-blue eyes were now a foot away from me.

Benjamin looked me square in the eye. "It's about the kiss, isn't it?"

I jolted. How on earth did he know that I was on a deadline? Sara. Had she said something while finding out he was in his dressing room? I could feel my cheeks going pink.

"You shouldn't be embarrassed," Benjamin said, like he was reading my mind. He moved closer to me. "Not at all."

His voice was very low and his hand was heading for my cheek.

Was he going to kiss me now? In this supply closet? I so didn't feel ready. Then again, how much more ready was I going to feel in a few hours?

"Hayden's the one who should be embarrassed."

Benjamin's hand missed my cheek. I turned to see him grab a comb from the shelf behind me.

"Hayden?" I repeated. Why should Hayden be embarrassed about the fact that I'd never been kissed? What on earth did it have to do with him?

Benjamin shrugged. "He should have just kissed you."

"He what?"

Why was my secret admirer all for Hayden kissing me? My head spun.

"Hayden is far from being the lead actor that this production needs," Benjamin said, running the comb through his ebony hair and looking in the mirror. I vaguely noticed that he'd strung little lights all around it.

"The line you forgot was so close to the kiss that Hayden should have just gone directly into it," Benjamin went on.

I stared at him, suddenly comprehending. He'd been referring to the Beatrice–Benedick kiss, not my own love life!

Benjamin shook his head and examined his reflection carefully. "I have no idea how Mr. Peterman could have cast him as Benedick instead of me. Anyway, do you want me to run through the scene with you? I can show you some great techniques to create emotion. On my most recent carpet cleaning ad I had to be dismayed at a wine spill, and the director said it was the most emotionally honest reaction to a stain he'd ever seen."

I felt so confused. Benjamin wanted to give me acting tips? I'd thought by now he'd have gone into a spiel about how long he'd loved me and why. Well, he might have all the time in the world, but I didn't. I had only a few scarce hours to get to know him and force him (nicely) to kiss me.

"Benjamin, did you write me a poem?" I blurted.

He turned to face me. "A what?"

I had to repeat it?

"A poem," I managed to squeak out.

Benjamin raised an eyebrow. "Aurora, I'm an actor, not a poet. I don't write lines, I speak them."

"It's just that I got this poem," I continued. "And you said something really similar to one of the lines when you were talking to Mr. Peterman—that I should shine like a star?"

Benjamin nodded. "Yeah, I think that Mr. Peterman should put the spotlight on you, to take the focus off Hayden's inadequacies."

All at once I could see that any signs of interest Benjamin had shown in me—like wanting to be Hayden's stunt double in the waltz scene—were linked to his rivalry with Hayden.

I pretended to look at my watch. "Oh! Is that the time? I just remembered I have a dress fitting."

Benjamin wasn't listening. He picked up two head shots of himself—one front on, one in profile. "Could you give me an opinion on these? Which do you think is better?"

"The one on the right." I pointed at the shot where he was posed, chin in hand, à la Rodin's *The Thinker*. "It's very . . . commanding."

Benjamin looked thoughtfully at the head shot. "Thanks. I'm going to be signing them at a booth outside the auditorium this afternoon."

I realized how silly I'd been to think Benjamin might be my secret admirer. He had no time for a girlfriend; all his energy was devoted to self-promotion.

"You know, it's funny," he said, turning his gaze from the photo to me. "You and I have way better chemistry than you and Hayden do. Are you sure you don't want to run through that scene? I'm no kissing wimp."

I gave him a no-thanks wave and shut the door behind me.

Better to be safe than sorry.

"He said you and he have great chemistry?" Jelena shook her head as I nervously hopped around backstage. It was less than an hour till curtain call, and not only was I on the verge of making my stage debut but also I had no feasible way of preventing the kiss.

"You had a clear opportunity for a date there," Jelena continued as she checked off items on the props table.

"Jelena!" I cried. "He wasn't my secret admirer! I can't go accepting dates with whoever."

Sara, wearing part of her Don John costume—a leather jacket and a boy's black wig—rushed up. "Was it amazing?"

"Was what amazing?" I rubbed my temples.

"Nothing was amazing," Jelena said. "Benjamin wasn't the stupid secret admirer."

"I hate to say it, Aurora," Sara said, examining her wig in the full-length mirror, "but I don't think the secret admirer's going to be making an appearance tonight."

I tried to push down my panic. "What am I going to do, then? The kiss is coming up and I've run out of options. The way things are looking, I'm going to have to knock over the holy water font again."

"Sorry to tell you, but the font isn't budging from its spot," Jelena said. "It's got a good fifteen screws in it. I had to come up with all these ideas for using it as a permanent prop—like making it a birdbath in the orchard scenes."

"You see? What am I going to do?"

"I'll tell you what you're going to do," Jelena replied, looking completely frustrated with me. "You're going to go and get your makeup done and leave me to focus."

Half an hour later, I had fifties-style pale pink lips and black eyeliner, but the agitation was still prickling me. I went in search of Cassie and finally found her running through a last-minute order-of-backdrop schedule with two crew members.

"Cass!" I dashed toward her in a Chicken Little the-sky-is-falling panic.

Cassie, like a true bestie, immediately turned all her attention to me.

"I've run out of ideas," I told her. "Benjamin wasn't my secret admirer, I'm still unkissed, and I'm looking at having to use the 'Kill Claudio' line again."

Cassie's eyes widened at the frenzied bombardment of bad news.

"I know, I know!" I continued. "I feel terrible about messing with the play yet again, but if Mr. Peterman would just listen—"

"There's no way he's going to let you get away with skipping the kiss again," Cassie interrupted. "Not on opening night. He'll use the megaphone to demand that Hayden goes for it."

"I doubt he'd go that far."

"He's not a rational man right now, Aurora," Cassie said, sounding like Jelena. "The whole kiss thing could push him over the edge." She placed a hand on my arm. "You've got to talk to Hayden about this. Just explain it to him."

"Talk to Hayden?" I repeated in a strangled voice.

Cassie smiled. "You guys are friends now."

"We're not close enough for *that*."

"Look, I know Hayden," Cassie said. "If you explain it to him clearly, I'm sure he'll have no problem forgoing the kiss. Then, even if Mr. Peterman goes for the megaphone option, Hayden won't comply. He'll probably think it's sweet. I know! Tell him about the Sleeping Beauty thing!"

I stared at her, horrified. Tell him about the Sleeping Beauty thing? Was she out of her mind?

"All actors to the left wing! I repeat, all actors assemble for pre-show cast check!" Mr. Peterman bellowed through the megaphone.

As Mr. Peterman led us through vocal warm-ups, Cassie's suggestion played through my head. Much as I hated to admit it, it did make sense in one respect. The only surefire way to prevent the kiss was to get Hayden to promise not to go for it.

As I crossed the room to where Hayden was looking over one of Jelena's scene prompts, he gave me a huge smile. My vocal cords seized up.

"How are you doing?" he asked.

"Fi-i-i . . ." My vocal cords were still on strike. My resolve to get this talk over with was nowhere to be found.

"I'm buzzing!" Hayden said, and gestured for me to follow him to the stage curtain. He pulled the heavy velvet aside slightly. "Look. It's a full house."

I gaped at the rows and rows of faces stretching across the auditorium. There was a roar of sound as people found their seats and consulted the programs that Cassie had designed. For the first time it hit me that these people had paid to see the production. And in less than ten minutes, I was going to be up there in front of all those expectant faces. My heart plummeted fifty stories.

Hayden dropped the curtain and took in what I presumed to be my expression of blatant terror. "Uh-oh. I probably shouldn't have shown you that. I've made you nervous, haven't I?"

I nodded like a still-buzzing electroshock therapy patient.

I finally found my voice. "It sounds stupid, but I'd sort of forgotten that all these people were going to be here. Well, not forgotten—that's idiotic. I mean, all our practices and today's dress rehearsal sort of felt like playacting—not that serious. But this," I gestured toward the masses gathering behind the stage curtain, "this is the real thing. Everyone here is expecting a great show and I'm so not going to deliver."

"Aurora, your natural vivacity comes through on stage," Hayden said. "All you need to do to be truly great up there is relax!"

"You think?"

"I know!" he said. "Every actor gets nervous. I'm shaking in my shoes right now."

"You are not!" I said skeptically.

"I am!" He grinned. "Do you want to feel my heart racing?" He pulled my hand onto his chest.

My own chest began thumping faster as I stood there with my hand over Hayden's briskly beating heart. "Okay, I believe you."

Hayden lifted my hand from his chest, but instead of dropping it, he held it in his and gave it a squeeze. A glimmer of reassurance appeared. We stood there, hand in hand, as the rest of the cast assembled in the wings. It struck me that we were feeding the school rumor mill with more juicy gossip, but, strangely enough, I didn't care.

As the auditorium lights dimmed and Mr. Peterman gestured for us to take our places on stage, Hayden gave me a gentle push. "Go get 'em, Princess."

Then the curtain was up and the stage lights were on and it had begun.

"*I learn in this letter that Don Pedro of Arragon comes this night to Messina,*" David as Leonato said, remembering his line this time. He broke into a smile and I relaxed slightly.

As the scene continued, I found myself getting caught up in this world of the 1950s. Claire, sitting beside me in a pink-and-white polka-dot sundress and ballet flats, really was my innocent cousin, Hero. As we sat among the trees that Jelena had wrangled out of the local nursery, it felt just like we were having a picnic on the grounds of a Southern plantation. Suddenly I was living the lines, not just saying them.

At the end of the scene, I floated back into the wings.

"What are you dillydallying for?" Jelena dragged me toward the costume department. "Have you forgotten that you've got to don a ball gown before your next scene?"

Lindsay stood waiting with an amazing creation in her arms. I gasped as I took in the strapless bodice sprinkled with tiny crystal beads, the narrow waist with its thick red satin sash, the longest, fullest taffeta skirt I'd ever seen. This was the first time I'd seen the dress; it had still been under construction until late this afternoon.

"Lindsay!" I gasped as she began zipping me into it. "You created this?"

"You like it?" She smiled modestly as she changed my wrist-length gloves to elbow-length crystal-detailed ones.

"Linds, it's amazing! It's like a Dior or something!"

"I keep telling her that her career in fashion is in the bag," Tyler said proudly as he handed me a pair of red peep-toe heels.

I smiled as I sat down to slip them on. Lindsay and the newly devoted Tyler (who'd barely left the costume department all week, aside from last-minute runs to the sewing store) were back on track.

"It's totally in the bag," I said as I stood up and took in my appearance in the mirror. The dress sparkled in the light, cascading down my body in perfect lines. "How do I look?"

As I spun around from the mirror, Hayden walked in. He stopped in his tracks and stared.

Lindsay, Tyler, and Sara all stopped what they were doing and looked at Hayden. The silence was deafening. For some reason, I suddenly really cared about Hayden's reply to the question I'd unintentionally asked him.

His eyes took me in for what seemed like an eternity. "You look *exquisite*," he said.

His reverent tone made something inside me start shaking. I took a step, and one of my heels wobbled dangerously.

Hayden took my arm and we swept by Lindsay, Tyler, and Sara. I didn't dare look back, because I knew Sara would be feigning a faint and mouthing the word *Hot*.

Hayden stopped in the wings and stared at me again. "Aurora, I need to—"

"Aurora!" Lindsay ran after me. "We forgot to change your lipstick! It needs to be red to match the dress."

Lipstick? Oh my god, I'd totally spaced on Operation Stop Kiss! How had that happened?

Hayden's eyes met mine as Lindsay fussed over my lips, and he smiled. Suddenly I knew he wouldn't make fun of me. Surely I could talk to him now?

But the school orchestra struck up a big-band tune and the moment was lost.

25 the big moment

Being on stage for the ball scene was like being in an enchanted world. Tiny fairy lights twinkled all around, and couples in fifties finery and delicate masks bowed to each other and began gliding around the stage.

Hayden's eyes never left mine as we danced. I vowed that in the next scene change I'd speak to him.

No, I wouldn't.

Yes, I would.

No, I *couldn't*.

As I watched the glowing fairy lights dancing their own waltz in Hayden's eyes, a question jumped into my brain: I didn't subconsciously *want* this kiss to take place, did I? I didn't actually want to experience a kiss from Hayden Paris's lips, which had told me that I looked exquisite and seemed so soft and . . .

Oh my god! I tore my eyes away from Hayden's mouth.

The fairy lights and the waltzing were getting to me. That explained why I felt so giddy, and why I was feeling this weird affection toward Hayden. That and the fact that he'd saved my life. It would be totally abnormal not to feel a fondness for your rescuer.

Oh my god! That was why I was experiencing such a lack of resolve when it came to the Stop Kiss conversation. I didn't want to hurt Hayden's feelings!

I looked into his eyes and guilt hit me like a sledgehammer. It would be impossible for him not to take it personally. He'd wonder if he was unattractive or had bad breath or, worse, that word had gotten around that he was a terrible kisser.

As the scene ended, I exited the stage, feeling like the worst person in the world.

Sara grabbed me by the shoulder. "So . . . *exquisite,* hey?"

I gave her a look.

"It's going to happen," she said, "you and Hayden locking lips. I say after all that's gone on this evening, it's a certainty."

"It's not going to happen!" I hissed, even though my guilt over Hayden's upcoming emotional breakdown was hitting me hard.

"It is," Sara said in a singsong voice.

"You won't believe what just happened!" Cassie flew over to us, her cheeks scarlet.

"Hayden's come up with more compliments for Aurora?" Sara asked.

"What?" Cassie looked confused.

"I'll fill you in later," Sara said. "It's juicy news."

"Sara, he was just being nice—"

"He was just being 'Oh my god, I'm in love with Aurora!'"

I reeled around to face her. "Sara, stage nerves have turned you loony. It was a compliment, not a declaration."

"Scott tried to kiss me!" Cassie cried, then clapped her hand over her mouth as the actors on stage went quiet.

Sara's eyes goggled, and I knew my jaw was virtually touching my chest. We must have looked pretty comical.

The onstage lights dimmed as Hero and Claudio's betrothal scene ended.

"Finally!" I threw my arms around Cassie. "Wait a minute. Did you say 'tried'? As in, it didn't happen?"

"Next scene!" Jelena appeared behind us in stage manager mode. "Sara, you're up."

Sara looked pleadingly at Jelena. "But Cassie's kiss . . . I have to hear the details."

"Get on that stage, Sara." Jelena's voice was no-nonsense. "I'm not going to tell you again." She gave Sara a push and she disappeared. Jelena turned to us. "So what's going on? Are we talking Scott and Cassie?"

"Shh!" Cassie pulled us to a quieter spot in the wings. "Okay, we were shifting one of the trees off the stage. I'd just put it down when I realized that my necklace had caught on one of the branches." Cassie fingered her gold locket. "Before I could say anything, Scott was on his knees next to me, trying to free it. He was this close." Cassie put her hand eight inches from her face. "His hands were touching my neck, and he glanced up at me, and his face went all serious—and he went to kiss me! I thought I was going to pass out with anticipation!"

"Good!" I cried. "I mean, not the passing out part but the kissing part."

Cassie's expression changed to bewilderment. "And then he stopped! Two inches away from my lips! He whispered, 'I can't do this!' and rushed off!"

"'I can't do this'?" Jelena repeated. "Why couldn't he do it?"

"Maybe he had performance anxiety?" I suggested. "Knowing that he was about to kiss the girl of his dreams."

"What a wimp!" Jelena scoffed.

"Jelena!" I cried. "It's touching that he's nervous!"

"He didn't look nervous," Cassie said. "Well, not until the whole I-can't-do-this comment. There's some other reason—I don't have bad breath, do I?" She looked horrified.

"Never, in the ten years I've known you, Cass, have you ever had bad breath," Jelena reassured her. "He's just a wimp!"

"Maybe he was worried about *his* breath?" I said, knowing how lame it sounded. "Or maybe he thought that the moment wasn't quite right?"

"If the moment wasn't right, then why did he start moving toward her in the first place?" Jelena asked, lowering her voice.

"Cass, there's some perfectly good reason why he pulled away," I said. "Maybe he remembered something he had to do for the next scene—"

"Oops! I'm needed in props!" Jelena said, and dashed off.

"How am I going to face him?" Cassie asked me. Her face was creased with tension.

"He's the one that backed out of the kiss," I said. "Right now he's going to feel seriously emasculated. So if you play it cool—"

"I can't."

"You can. Because once we discover the reason for this odd behavior, you'll be so happy that you didn't get worked up about it." I crossed my fingers behind my back, hoping my words would prove true.

Cassie gave me a resigned wave, looking as though she were heading to the gallows instead of just backstage. Poor Cass. If only I could read Scott's mind. Maybe I could try asking Hayden again. . . .

Hayden! The whole Cassie–Scott debacle had totally distracted me from the fact that I had to talk to Hayden *soon*. Like within thirty minutes.

Okay, it was time to brainstorm. Ways to tell Hayden to keep his mouth to himself *without* hurting his feelings.

Wait a minute. What if I made it about *me*, not him?

Hayden's soliloquy drifted into my thoughts: *They say too that she will rather die than give any sign of affection*. . . .

My mouth dropped open. Here was the reason: I had issues about PDAs. This kiss was a *very* public display of affection (hello, three hundred people in the audience) and I was uneasy with it. Hayden would hardly want to make me go against my principles, being a stay-true-to-your-beliefs individual himself.

I would tell him just before Hero and Claudio's wedding. That way I could say it firmly but quickly and Hayden wouldn't have time to try to reason with me before we got pushed on stage.

As everyone in the wedding party assembled by the front entrance of the auditorium (Mr. Peterman wanted us to use the auditorium aisle as the church aisle), I frantically looked for Hayden. He hadn't turned up yet. Jelena began arranging the bridal party in order of appearance.

"Aurora, is something up?" she asked. "You seem very on edge."

"On edge? Me?" My voice was unsteady.

Recognition dawned on her face. "Have you made up your mind what you're going to do?"

"I . . . I've just got to talk to—Hayden!"

Hayden raced up to me. "Sorry!" His breath came in short gasps. "My shirt for the wedding was missing—Lindsay had to tear the costume department apart. We finally found it underneath Jeffrey's saddle. Can I talk to you, Aurora? Privately?"

It was like he'd read my mind. "Let's go."

"Where are you going?" Jelena cried. "You're on in eight minutes!"

I took off before she could say anything more. Eight minutes should be long enough for a hurried I-have-a-problem-with-PDAs speech, shouldn't it? I dashed around the corner and pulled Hayden into the privacy of the archway that led to the school garden. We were both breathing heavily—him presumably from the mad dash to find his shirt, and me out of panic that I might not have time to talk to him.

"Hayden, I—"

"Aurora, I have something really important to say to you." Hayden looked at me intently.

"Aurora!"

Someone laid a hand on my shoulder. I whirled around to see Benjamin standing behind me. I felt his eyes taking in my yellow bridesmaid's dress.

"You were great in that last scene," he said. "I wished I'd been dancing with you myself." He smirked at Hayden. "I don't suppose you could give us a few moments? I have some suggestions for some of Aurora's scenes."

Hayden shook his head. "Benjamin, I have a suggestion for you—"

"Benjamin," I said, stepping between the two guys, "now's not really a good time for tips." I flashed him a smile. "Hayden and I are trying to discuss something important."

"Ménage à trois in the garden, hmm?" Jeffrey's voice came from behind us.

"There's nothing going on!" I cried.

Who knew what rumors this whole thing could start? I looked at my watch again. Three minutes to go.

Hayden, as if reading my mind, grabbed my hand, and we were running away from Benjamin and Jeffrey before they could react. Hayden pulled me behind the auditorium's side wall.

"Hayden, I—"

Hayden stopped me. "Aurora, I have to tell you something before this next scene."

Based on his urgent tone, it had to be about the kiss. Maybe he had issues with PDA, too.

"I have to tell you something, too."

"I've been meaning to tell you for a while now," he went on.

"You have?" I couldn't believe this was turning out to be so easy. "So have I!"

"But I was afraid you would react unfavorably."

"So was I!"

"But now that things have changed between us and we're friends—"

"I'm so glad we're friends," I cut in. Having this conversation with an enemy would have been impossible.

Hayden's face melted into a smile and he squeezed my hand, which he still held. His chest rose as he took a deep breath. "I want to tell you that I—"

"What are you two doing?"

Hayden leaped about a foot and I let out a startled gasp. Jelena stood in front of us, her whole face a scowl.

"The cast is lined up and the audience is sitting in there waiting!"

She yanked both of us around the corner before we could say a word. Any chance of me talking to Hayden had just been destroyed.

"Hayden, you're at the front with the other best man and the groom," Jelena ordered.

Hayden paused. "But—"

Jelena ignored him. "Aurora, you're next to the bride." She pushed me toward Claire, who stood shimmering in her wedding gown and veil.

Jelena turned to Benjamin, Alex, and Hayden, who was still looking at me urgently. "Boys, you're up," she said. "Scene start!" And she threw open the auditorium door.

I walked slowly up the aisle in front of Claire, smiling serenely at all the wedding guests/audience members, but secretly panicking. Hayden and I might have agreed on the PDA thing, but we had no plan in place for what would happen at the moment of the kiss. Would we just skip over it, or look at each other lovingly, or . . .

I had to talk to him. If we made a mess of the scene, Mr. Peterman would commit himself to a mental institution.

As we assembled at the altar—girls on the left, boys on the right—I tried to get Hayden's attention by waggling my eyebrows.

"You come hither, my lord, to marry this lady," the friar said.

I gave Hayden a subtle wave, then glanced nervously into the audience to see where Mr. Peterman was sitting. I hoped he hadn't noticed my attempts at non-theater-related communication.

"No," Benjamin said strongly, stepping away from Hero.

The wedding party stared at him in surprise.

"Psst!" I hissed.

Hayden's head finally turned my way.

I have to talk to you, I mouthed.

What? Hayden mouthed back, looking shocked. He took a step toward me.

Wait! I mouthed.

If he waited till everyone reacted in shock to Claudio's foul accusation of Hero, then his movement closer to me wouldn't be as obvious.

Claudio glowered at Leonato and his daughter. *"Would you not swear, all you that see her, that she were a maid, by these exterior shows? But she is none: she knows the heat of a luxurious bed; her blush is guiltiness, not modesty."*

Claire wavered in an almost faint, and half the wedding party rushed forward.

Hayden edged over to my side. "Thank god. I really have to tell you something."

"Don't worry. I know it's about the PDA," I murmured, doing my best to look concerned about Hero.

"PDA?"

"Yes. What are we going to do about it?"

"Do?" Hayden's eyes registered complete confusion. "What on earth does a public display of affection have to do with what we were talking about?"

"What?" It wasn't about the kiss? What on earth was so important, then?

Just then I saw an outraged Mr. Peterman staring at Hayden and me. Uh-oh.

"Never mind," I said.

"But, Aurora, you have to know that I—"

"Mr. Peterman is watching us!"

Hayden glanced at the director, whose eyes were bulging at our audacity for talking during a pivotal moment in the play. Hayden quickly moved back to Don Pedro's side before Mr. Peterman could have a megaphone moment.

What on *earth* was I going to do? For once, my mind wasn't working fast enough. I spoke my lines and tried my hardest to look convincing, but time sped by and my idea slate was still sickeningly blank.

Before I knew it, Hayden and I were alone in the candlelight once more.

"Lady Beatrice, have you wept all this while?"

Oh god, I felt like weeping. Why hadn't I discussed this whole thing with Hayden earlier? I should have been straight up from the beginning, instead of assuming that my Stop Kiss stunts would work.

I could ad-lib. Say something like, "Stop, my love, I have the flu—a terrible malady—do not commit your sweet lips to mine."

No way was the audience going to buy my version of Shakespeare. It had to be more subtle. Maybe if Hayden registered how unwilling I was, he'd pick up my subliminal "no kiss" messages.

As I looked up at him to communicate unwillingness, the fire in his eyes reduced my thoughts to ashes.

I registered myself reciting my lines, but all I knew was Hayden. His dark hair and the way the locks in front swept over to the left, like a wave falling above his eyes . . . eyes that were alight and holding a thousand secret messages. As my eyes traced his straight nose and cheekbones, I felt I'd never really seen him before.

Hayden gazed into my eyes, just as we'd planned. Here was my last chance to pull away.

"I love you with so much of my heart that none is left to protest," I whispered.

Hayden put his hand on my waist and I knew I wasn't going anywhere. I wanted to be close to him, closer than anything, in his arms. I wanted to give in to this fainting falling feeling that had possessed me. This was it.

Hayden's eyes searched mine for several centuries. My heart drummed.

He slowly lifted my right hand and drew it to his lips, and placed the softest, most tender kiss upon it.

26   no-show

The NAD beamed at me. "You were wonderful!"

I smiled and used all my willpower to focus on the scene around me. I wasn't going to think about what had happened on stage.

Cassie and I stood with her mother, father, and brother, along with the NAD and Ms. DeForest, in a swelling crowd of similarly enthusiastic parents.

"The chemistry between you and Hayden was wonderful," Mrs. Shields said to me.

"Yes, the boy next door," the NAD said. "Much as I hate to say it, that chemistry was already—"

An excited-looking Sara and Jelena raced up. "Sorry, Mr. Skye, but we have to drag Aurora away for a moment." Jelena gave my dad a smooth smile. "Important production information."

I gave a sigh. I knew what she wanted to talk about. It was either go with Jelena and Sara and discuss the non-kiss or stay and listen to the NAD discuss Hayden's and my supposed relationship. I followed Jelena. Cass came, too. I'd rather talk reality than fiction.

We were barely ten rows away before the onslaught started. I dropped into a seat, unable to cope standing up.

"So what happened with the kiss?" Sara sat down next to me and gripped my arm like the device that doctors use to measure blood pressure. "It obviously didn't happen, so—"

"How do you know it didn't happen?"

The moment the scene had finished I'd steered well clear of my friends, curious cast members, and Mr. Peterman. I hadn't wanted to discuss anything.

"I was watching. Everyone in the cast and crew was," Sara said matter-of-factly.

"Travis even pulled out his cell phone to film the big moment, which I smartly confiscated," Jelena said, propping her legs up on the empty seat next to her.

"The big moment that was incredibly disappointing," Sara added.

Cassie shook her head. "No way was it disappointing. It was the sweetest moment in the whole play."

"So what story did you spin to Hayden?" Jelena took a jumbo bag of jelly beans out of her purse and opened them without taking her penetrating gaze off me.

"I didn't spin anything," I said, breaking her gaze.

"But how did Hayden know not to kiss you, then?" Cassie asked.

"He didn't know. He just didn't kiss me." I shrugged in what I hoped was a nonchalant way and took a red jelly bean from the bag.

The three of them stared at me. Jelena dropped the jelly bean bag.

"I can't believe it!" She squatted in the aisle, trying to round up jelly beans. "That's two guys who've backed out of kisses tonight. Is there something in the air?"

"Look, I don't get the big deal," I said impatiently. "I got my wish—the kiss didn't happen. So let's drop it, okay?"

I got up from my seat and stalked back to the NAD and Cassie's family.

"Sweetie," Mrs. Shields asked Cassie, who was right at my heels, "who's that nice-looking boy who keeps looking over here? Do you know him?"

We all turned to see who she was talking about. Scott gave an embarrassed smile.

"Oh, that's Scott," Cassie said quickly. "I worked with him on the backdrops."

"Why don't you call him over?" Mrs. Shields said.

"Yeah, Cass." Andrew winked at his sister. "Let's meet the boy who can make you blush that much."

"Andrew!" Cassie frowned at him, but gestured at Scott to join us. "Scott, I'd like you to meet my parents," she said.

"Nice to meet you, Mr. and Mrs. Shields," Scott said, and shook their hands with a genuine smile. But as he turned toward Andrew, the smile became slightly forced.

"And my brother, Andrew," Cassie said.

"Your brother?" Scott's wary look fell away and was replaced with a big grin as he pumped Andrew's hand enthusiastically.

Suddenly I knew why Scott Ryder had been acting so strangely for the past two weeks.

"Scott thought Andrew was your boyfriend!" I whispered to Cassie as we headed for our parents' cars.

"No!" Cassie looked horrified.

"He saw you get on Andrew's bike that day we tailed him to his sculpture class." I grinned. "And presumed you and Andrew were dating."

"What?" Cassie yelped, looking at Andrew in horror.

I laughed. "That's why he was so odd around you. He thought he'd made a fool of himself by sending you a rose when you were already attached. That explains the non-kiss, too. That's why Scott said, 'I can't do this!' and raced off. But now that he knows you're single, I bet my left arm there's going to be some K-I-S-S-I-N-G going on soon!"

Cassie grabbed my hand and we joyfully skipped past the adults.

"Aurora, I know you said you didn't want to talk about it, but how are you really feeling about Hayden not kissing you?"

I stopped skipping. "Dad's starting up the car. I'd better get going before Ms. DeForest convinces him to leave me behind."

"But, Aurora, I can tell you're feeling—"

I jumped into the backseat, cutting her off with the slam of my door.

"So, where to, future Academy Award–winning daughter?" the NAD asked as he pulled out of the parking lot. "Shall we stop for celebratory ice cream?"

I saw Ms. DeForest, in the front passenger seat, frown. "But, Kenneth, you promised me you'd come to the moonlight gathering up on the headland."

I imagined the NAD in druid attire, battling the coastal winds as he took part in a chanting circle.

"We've already been to the play. I'm sure Aurora won't mind if you and I have *some* personal time this evening."

"We could make it a very quick stop," I suggested.

I didn't mean to be insistent, but I did want to spend some time with Dad. I'd hardly seen him during the madness of rehearsals over the last month.

"I'm sure you don't mind." Ms. DeForest turned in her seat to give me a sharp look.

"Well, I guess not," I said.

"Fabulous!" Ms. DeForest said, reaching for the NAD's right hand. "So it's back to your house, Kenneth, to drop off Aurora, and then on to the gathering."

"Well, I feel kind of bad about taking Aurora straight home," Dad said, looking at me in the rearview mirror. "There's that drive-through ice-cream shop. Aurora, pick the most decadent sundae you can think of as a reward for that fabulous show. Wasn't it great, Dana?" He turned to smile at Ms. DeForest.

"Well, I suppose it could be considered entertaining," she replied, tossing her long brown ringlets. "But it was completely devoid of any real *message*. In my opinion, theater should address issues."

"But it did address quite a few," I said. "Mr. Peterman set the play in the fifties to highlight male–female power dynamics, then and now. He was asking the audience to consider how far we've really come—"

Ms. DeForest let out a laugh. "Oh, you can't really believe that piece of fluff actually made the audience think!"

"It might have." I tried to keep the edge out of my voice. "And I don't see the problem with theater being enjoyable."

"Well, you wouldn't, would you?" Ms. DeForest said. "You're a teenager. Life is all about enjoyment. None of you worry about anything beyond your own little world."

I felt the seat belt tighten as my chest swelled with barely repressed indignation. "That's kind of an assumption. And Shakespeare's work is hardly fluff."

"Well, you're entitled to your opinion." Ms. DeForest sniffed. "Not that I expected anything revolutionary from an overindulged teenager."

A *what*?

The NAD looked with concern from Ms. DeForest to me and back again. "Now, girls . . ."

"You probably shouldn't call Ms. DeForest a girl, Dad." The words shot from my mouth like a charging army. "Seeing as she's eons away from being mistaken for an overindulged teenager."

"Aurora, you will not speak to Dana like that— Damn it!" the NAD yelled. I jumped in my seat. "I missed the exit for the ice-cream shop."

"Don't worry about it," I muttered. "I'm more than ready to go home."

I leaped out of the car the moment it pulled into the drive, and stomped up the stairs to my room. If Ms. DeForest was going to call me an overindulged teenager, then I might as well act like one.

As I threw myself down on my window seat, a flash of headlights caught my eye. The Parises were arriving home. The mood in their car would be joyful, I was sure, not sickeningly tense like my ride home.

I shut my curtains but I couldn't shut off my thoughts. Now that

I was alone, the autopilot mode I'd been in since the end of the Beatrice–Benedick confession scene dropped away. Why hadn't Hayden kissed me? What had stopped him?

Like I'd told my friends, I'd gotten my wish. I'd escaped the kiss. And, as I'd heard Mr. Peterman raving to Hayden about the "beautiful delicacy" of the kiss on the hand, it was safe to say that the scene would stay the way it was and my first kiss was once again mine to keep. I should have been dancing around the room in delirious happiness. But all I felt was confusion.

How had I gone from being so vehemently against the kiss to *accepting* it?

Hayden's eyes . . . the burning way he'd said, "I love you," to Beatrice . . . It had been like getting too close to an actual fire—I'd started melting inside, transfixed by Hayden's face. And then the heat had consumed me and I'd given myself up to its intensity, allowing it to transform me into someone who wasn't Aurora Skye at all. Someone impulsive and reckless; someone who leaped off cliffs without hesitation. Someone whose face had probably screamed, *Kiss me! Kiss me!*

I buried my face in a cushion. My embarrassment was colossal. Could Hayden have seen this abandonment of reason? Oh my god! Was that the reason he hadn't kissed me? Had he backed off because he was terrified by my wild, all-consuming passion?

I let out a shriek and tossed the cushion in the air. It landed on my bed, and Snookums, who'd been snoozing on the quilt cover, let out an outraged meow.

"Sorry, Snookums!"

I had to get a grip on myself. Okay, so I might have gone slightly silly and momentarily thought I wanted to kiss him—but who could blame me? Just about any girl would have felt the same if she'd heard him making wildly romantic statements in that deep voice of his.

"Get a grip, get a grip, get a grip!" I cried, as Hayden's face flashed up before me again.

But my mind wasn't listening to common sense. It was running away, down treacherous trails, crying, *You can't catch me.*

Maybe he finds you unattractive, it called back to me in a singsong voice.

I felt like I'd been punched in the stomach. No, he couldn't think that. He'd told me this very evening that I was "exquisite." Hadn't he meant it?

This was ridiculous. What did I care if Hayden Paris found me attractive or not?

I let out a laugh, suddenly realizing how stupid the whole thing was. I was asking myself the very questions that I'd been terrified of inducing in Hayden by rejecting his kiss. Another moment and I would be wondering if I had bad breath!

I grabbed my imagination by the scruff of the neck and shoved it firmly back in its box. Then I walked over to my pajama drawer. I needed rest. No way were thoughts of Hayden Paris going to make me lose sleep.

"Are you okay, Aurora?" Cassie asked me the following evening at six o'clock.

"I'm great!" I stifled a yawn. "Raring to go."

"It looked like you were nodding off."

"Cass, how on earth could I fall asleep in one of these impossibly uncomfortable backstage chairs?"

I was secretly asking myself the same question. Obviously, when a person had suffered insomnia all the preceding night, involuntary lapses into unconsciousness were to be expected. I'd managed to block Hayden out of my thoughts, but not my own mortifying "kiss me, kiss me" reaction.

"So, any news on the Scott front?" I changed the subject.

Cassie blushed slightly. "We just went for coffee down the road."

"And?" I asked, feeling more awake as my curiosity kicked in.

"And he held my hand," Cassie whispered, sounding ecstatic.

"I told you!" I cried. "Oh, this is the best thing that ever happened!"

Now that my worries about the kiss were over, I lived it up on stage. I put all my energy into telling Shakespeare's story—about two enemies who fall in love, one innocent girl, two bumbling law enforcement officers, a prince, and a world of grand balls and fun times. I tried several times to spot my mother in the audience, but the lights were too bright. I really hoped she was enjoying it. I sent my best smiles to her section of the audience, knowing that even if I couldn't see her, she'd be able to see me.

I was grateful that my stage fright had completely disappeared. I felt heady, like all my senses were enhanced. I never wanted the play to be over.

"Man, I can't wait for this play to be over," Alex said during intermission.

He, Jelena, Cassie, Sara, and I stood in the backstage kitchen, which was a hub of excitement.

"Why?" I asked.

"Claire Linden—she's so self-righteous. When I dance with her, she holds herself at a distance like I've got cooties or something. Talk about juvenile. I figure she has a thing for me."

I noticed Jelena's paper cup of Coke was compressing dangerously in her left hand.

"And is put out that I'm dating the hottest girl in school," Alex finished, wrapping his arm around Jelena's waist. Her grip on her cup relaxed.

"I think Claire's just a little bit shy," I said.

Alex snickered. "'Socially impaired' is another way to put it. She's a little bit of a freak. She has this huge book called *Shakespeare: The Invention of the Human* that she carts around with her all the time.

She probably sleeps with it at night." Alex snickered again. "It's probably the closest thing she's going to get to a boyfriend. She hasn't got a lot going on in this department." He pointed at his chest.

"Tell me about it!" Jelena gave a tinkling laugh. "Ever heard of a push-up bra?"

"Jelena!" I cried.

"Ever heard of a plastic surgeon?" Alex laughed along with Jelena. "We should use the profits from the play to set up a breast-job fund."

To my horror, I realized Claire was standing just to our right, her eyes brimming with tears. She turned and dashed away.

"She just heard you!" I pointed at Claire's rapidly retreating figure.

Alex shrugged. "Maybe it'll inspire her to start saving for surgery."

I felt like slapping him. Instead, I dashed after Claire, with Cassie and Sara at my heels.

"I can't believe you let him get away with saying those things," I told Jelena, when we ran into her outside the women's bathroom ten minutes later. "I only just managed to get Claire to stop crying."

Sara glared at Jelena. "She not only let him get away with it, she encouraged him. How could you, Jelena?"

Jelena shrugged. "What was I supposed to do?"

"Uh, not join in?" Sara suggested.

"Maybe you could get Alex to apologize," Cassie said as we walked back into the kitchen.

"Apologize?" Jelena took an unconcerned sip of her drink. "She was asking for it, going after *my* boyfriend."

I remembered the way Alex had behaved around Claire at the beginning of rehearsals—grabbing her around the waist, stroking her arm. She'd been the one resisting him, not the other way around.

"I don't think she was going after him, Jelena—"

I stopped as Alex came back. He slung an arm around Jelena and me. "How's crybaby Claire?"

I pulled myself out from under his arm. "You really hurt her feelings."

"Oh, relax, Aurora." Alex slung his arm around me again. "There's nothing wrong with reminding people like Claire that she's dreaming if she wants to hang out with or date people like us."

"I'd hang out with her," I said.

"Yeah, she's probably more fun to hang out with than you and your elitist attitude," Sara muttered under her breath.

I tried to push away the growing uneasiness I felt about Alex and got ready to go back on stage.

The rest of the play raced along, and before I knew it, we were all linking hands and giving a bow. As I stepped forward, rows of people stood up.

"A standing ovation! Well done, Princess!" Hayden said.

Of course, he nearly brought the house down.

Just as I thought to look for my mother, the curtain fell.

I pushed my way through the throngs of people in the audience, searching for my mother. After ten minutes of being crushed like a grape in a winepress, I decided to give up on my search till the crowd had thinned out a little. I'd use the time to change into my dress for the after-party. Inspired by my secret admirer's poem, I'd chosen a dress that twinkled with silver sequins, like a sky full of stars. I slipped it on, along with delicate silver heels, and headed back into the almost empty auditorium. Most of the parents had headed out toward their cars, so I made my way outside, passing groups of chattering parents, searching for Mom.

Before long, the early spring air was nipping at my bare arms, so I retreated inside, taking a seat on the stage, where it would be easy for her to spot me. She'd probably gotten caught up talking to someone—she loved socializing. Several people walked by and looked at me curiously, likely wondering why I was all dressed up and sitting on an empty stage. I made a show of looking at my watch.

Thirty minutes later, the auditorium was empty except for a janitor sweeping the garbage from the aisles.

"Aurora." Hayden walked across the stage from the wings. "What are you doing here? Wow." He took in my dress. "That's a showstopper of an outfit."

"Thanks. Listen, have you seen my mom?"

Hayden frowned. "No. Do you think she could have gone backstage to meet you? Do you want to go look?"

He offered me his arm, and I slipped my arm through his, the tense feeling in my stomach relaxing slightly.

We walked through the backstage area, which was virtually deserted.

"How about the party?" Hayden said. "I know it's a long shot, but several parents showed up earlier, much to Jelena's horror."

I forced a laugh. "What did she do?"

"Marched over and demanded that they leave."

Hayden's words were drowned out as we entered the gym. One of Jelena's many admirers was acting as DJ, and electro music dominated the room, reverberating through the floor. Jelena, wearing an amazing backless red dress, was dancing with Alex. Cassie and Scott were gliding in each other's arms, completely oblivious to the music's frantic pulse. Tyler and Lindsay were pulling silly dance moves. Jeffrey was dancing on a tabletop.

"I'll check the perimeter; you check the dance floor!" Hayden yelled over the music.

Jelena glided over to me. "Aurora! How do I look?"

"Like a siren," I said. Her hair fell in long black waves and her lips were the same scarlet as her dress. "Look, my mom didn't happen to be one of the parents you turned away before?"

Jelena blinked. "No. Hey, Alex is the best dancer!"

I smiled distractedly, still searching the crowd for Mom. A moment later, Hayden arrived at my side, shaking his head.

"No sign of her. Have you checked your cell?" he asked.

"No." I pulled it out of my handbag, feeling like the stupidest person ever. I'd turned it off during the play so I'd be free from distractions.

"Well, there's your answer. She's bound to have left a message about where to meet you."

I switched on my phone.

Can't make it to the play. Wooing the developers is taking longer than expected. Sorry, Mom.

I thrust the phone at Hayden and dashed toward the exit. I needed air.

"Aurora, wait!"

Hayden caught up with me as I stumbled out onto the grass.

"I'm such an idiot," I choked. "It never occurred to me that she just wouldn't show up."

I sank to my knees on the grass, feeling sick, as I remembered how I'd smiled my brightest smiles on stage, thinking that she was there in the audience.

"I sat in the empty auditorium for *half an hour* after the show finished. Anyone else would have started getting suspicious, but not me." I gave a bitter laugh. "Idiot."

"She's the idiot, for not coming," Hayden said, his voice harsher than I'd ever heard it. For some reason, it made me feel slightly better. He knelt down beside me.

"I wanted her to be there." It was hard to get the words out past the lump in my throat. "I don't know why, because she was gone for four years and she missed all sorts of things. But for some reason, I really cared this time."

"Of course you did." Hayden squeezed my shoulders. "I mean, I get embarrassed about my mom's enthusiasm—she videoed the play twice."

I gave a hiccupy laugh.

"But if she didn't show up," he continued, "I know I'd be crushed."

"I just wanted her to see it." I shook my head. "I wanted her to see Cassie's backdrops, and Lindsay's costumes, and you and me on stage."

"Your world," Hayden said softly.

It was as if he'd reached inside me to find a truth that I hadn't been able to see for myself. A sense of being completely and utterly understood fell over me, and for some reason the lump in my throat became even bigger.

Oh no. I wasn't going to cry. I hadn't cried when she'd left. I'd forced myself to stay strong for the shattered NAD. No way was her failure to show up to a play going to cause me to lose it now.

I pulled myself up off the ground. "Hayden?" I forced my voice to stay steady. "I'm going to call a cab."

"You don't want to go to the party?"

I shook my head. "I'm not really in a partying mood."

"Okay, no party," he said. "But I can't let the star actress go home without celebrating. How about we go into the city?"

I glanced at his concerned face. And found myself agreeing.

27 it's a date

"I can't believe we only have Monday's matinée before the play is over," Hayden said as we sat eating ice cream on a bench by the harbor.

"God, you're right," I exclaimed, my spoon halfway to my mouth. "While I was on stage tonight, I was wishing it would never end! I felt so alive."

"And excited, right?" Hayden took a big bite of his hazelnut ice cream. "God, there's no better feeling. I'm kind of hooked on it."

"I was really surprised to feel that way." I licked the back of my spoon. "I've always thought that writing was what made me deliriously happy, but this was pretty close."

"You could always combine the two," Hayden suggested. "Be a playwright. Or a scriptwriter. That way you could write yourself great parts."

"Hmm." Interesting idea.

"You could write me a part, too." Hayden grinned wryly. "You know, hugely spunky guy with a colossal intellect."

"Yeah, right, Paris." I punched his arm. "You'll be A-list within five years without my help. If I write you a part, you'll win a damn Academy Award. Just think of what that'll do to your ego."

Hayden chased after me with a dripping cone and I ran along the boardwalk, shrieking.

"Thanks for a great evening, Hayden," I said with a smile, as the cab dropped us off in front of my house.

"No problem." Hayden's eyes turned serious. "I hope it made you feel a little better."

"It made me feel fantastic."

Unbelievably, the ice cream and Hayden's silly quips had actually made me temporarily forget the whole Mom no-show thing.

"Listen, Aurora, about what I was trying to tell you last night . . ."

"Yes?" For some reason I was holding my breath.

Hayden ran a hand through his hair. "I was—"

The Parises' backyard floodlights switched on.

"Oops," Hayden said. "Mom's probably waiting up. I'd better go. 'Night, Princess."

"'Night," I replied, and turned up my driveway.

How weird was it that an evening with Hayden had been about a thousand times more enjoyable than any of my dates had been?

I stopped short when I saw Ms. DeForest's car in the drive. After our altercation last night, things were likely to be tense. Perhaps the best thing for all of us would be for me to sneak upstairs.

I quietly entered the house and took a careful look around. No one was in sight. I peeped into the living room for one last check, and froze, unable to believe what I was seeing.

Ms. DeForest was on her knees in the living room, the lights dimmed, swinging a long pendulum in front of Snookums, who was transfixed by the hypnotic movement, an odd look in his yellow eyes. I felt like I'd stumbled upon a voodoo ritual.

"You're hypnotizing my cat?" I shrieked, and before I knew what I was doing, I'd dashed into the room and snatched the pendulum out of Ms. DeForest's fingers.

Ms. DeForest's face was creased with irritation. "I'm using an external stimulus to create a more symbiotic relationship between cat and owner."

"By hypnosis?" I snapped my fingers in front of Snookums's face. He didn't react.

"Yes," Ms. DeForest said firmly. "This animal's behavior is appalling."

The NAD entered the living room with two cups of tea. "Here, Dana. Dandelion for you—" He froze when he saw Ms. DeForest and me in a standoff.

"Did you know about this?" I asked him. "That she was in here messing with Snookums's mind?"

"Honey, Dana was just trying some behavioral work. I said she could."

"You said she could *hypnotize* him?" I cried.

"Hypnotize?" the NAD repeated, looking bewildered. He turned to Ms. DeForest.

"Kenneth, I was just trying to get him into a state where we could work on his issues."

"His issues? He's a cat, not a psychiatric patient!" I choked, staring at Snookums. What if he never snapped out of this stupor?

"Aurora, you're overreacting." The NAD's voice was stern.

My jaw dropped as the NAD blatantly took Ms. DeForest's side.

"It's for the animal's benefit," Ms. DeForest said, taking her tea from the NAD. She looked completely unconcerned about Snookums's state of paralysis.

"He was hardly a willing participant." My voice quavered.

I dashed out of the room, grabbed a can of tuna from the cupboard, and opened it. I raced back to Snookums and waved the opened can in front of his face. The glazed look in his eyes disappeared. I gave a sigh of relief.

"I don't want her near Snookums or Bebe again," I said to the NAD as I scooped Snookums up.

"Aurora! You will not be rude to Dana. And staying up in your room all evening ignoring us isn't right, either."

"What are you talking about?" I stared at him. "I just got in."

"You just got in?" The NAD looked at his watch. "It's two a.m."

"I'm glad to see that you've noticed one thing this evening." I ran for the stairs.

I've always been glad that the NAD is so easygoing. But for him to forget about my whereabouts completely—well, it made me feel that our relationship was becoming as distant as the one I had with Mom. My chin trembled slightly.

No. I'd worked hard at distracting myself this evening. I wasn't going to spoil all that now.

I sat down on my window seat and scrutinized Snookums, glad to see that the glazed look in his eyes was gone. From the outside, he looked like his usual furry-faced self. I stroked Snookums's head as we sat together on the window seat. Part of me felt that our hug was giving me more comfort than it was giving him.

I snuck out of the house at an ungodly hour the next morning to avoid a potentially volatile NAD and Ms. DeForest, who'd obviously slept over. I whiled Sunday away browsing through stores. Amid my window-shopping, I made about fifteen calls to my mother's cell, hoping she might be able to come to the matinée performance on Monday. She never picked up.

When the curtain fell on Monday's performance, any chance of her seeing the play was gone. And I was left with a permanent ache in my chest.

"I guess it's back to real life again," Jelena said as she began storing props away in big plastic containers.

"It's weird that it's all over," I said, watching as the stagehands pulled down pieces of the set. "No more costumes, no more rehearsals."

"No more maniacal Mr. Peterman." Jelena rolled her eyes.

"But don't you think it was worth it?" I said, helping Lindsay carefully place Beatrice's ball gown in a dress bag. "All the things we wished for actually happened. Sara, you got the part you wanted. Cassie, you and Scott got to know one another."

And some really unexpected things had eventuated, like Hayden and me becoming friends. Who would have thought?

"Alex and I got together," Jelena added, stacking shoe boxes.

Sara turned away from the mirror. "I don't know if that's such a great thing."

"Excuse me?" Jelena stopped stacking.

"I don't think he's good for you," Sara said. "Look at what happened at intermission."

I thought of Claire's teary face. "You don't have to date Alex," I reminded Jelena. "You've got masses of admirers, none of whom need to be convinced how cool you are."

"Alex is the only one in my league," Jelena said.

Sara snickered. "Oh yeah, he's in a whole class of his own."

"It's my love life and I'll date whoever I want." Jelena put the lid down on a shoe box and stalked off.

Sara rolled her eyes. "She won't listen to a word against him."

"Let's change the subject," Cassie said. "Jelena has a good heart. She'll come to her senses."

She and I began helping Lindsay sort through the costume jewelry.

"I have some news," Lindsay said, looking worried. "Tyler and I are back together."

"Linds, that's—"

She rushed on before I could say anything more. "He was so dedicated to helping me last week, and so sweet, that I fell back in love with him. But don't worry—we're not going to get all claustrophobic again. I don't want to go back to TylerandLindsay. We're on a trial basis for a while."

She was obviously afraid that we might disapprove of her decision.

"That's great, Linds." I meant it wholeheartedly. Tyler's commitment to assisting Lindsay had turned my opinion of him around.

Cassie threw her arms around Lindsay for a congratulatory hug. I did the same.

"Tyler will never pull that 'I need to soar' line again," Sara said, joining the mass embrace.

"Oh, I wish the play wasn't over!" I said. Such great things had come out of it.

"We've got a committed thespian now!" Hayden said, smiling at me as he entered the room with the holy water font in his arms. "Despite the fact that this thing threatened her life."

"Luckily you saved her." Sara winked at him. "She owes you a favor now. Maybe dinner."

Sara! I mouthed as Hayden walked past us. Even though he and I were friends, I felt embarrassed by her teasing.

"Dinner sounds great." Hayden placed the font down carefully, out of the path of any backstage crew. "I've finished the DVD for Bebe and Snookums, so why don't I bring it over tonight? I'll pick up some Thai food and we can give the movie its premiere."

"Let me cook," I said. "You saving my life renders me grateful enough to get out the pots and pans. I'll make something Moroccan to go with the savanna scenes."

"It's a date." Hayden gave my arm a squeeze as he headed back toward the stage. "I'll see you at seven."

Sara started a dance of triumph the moment he was out of sight. "It's a date, it's a date, it's a date!" She shook my shoulders with delight. "I knew it. I've been watching you guys the past few days— the chemistry between you has skyrocketed."

"Sara, we've been playing lovers. Of course we've had to create some chemistry."

"I'm talking about off stage, not on." Sara gave me a knowing look. "A romantic clinch is so coming up. I think you'd better set up some candlelight tonight."

"Sara, I've done everything in my power not to kiss Hayden." I turned away from her, trying to hide my warm cheeks. For some reason, thinking of candlelight had brought back how I'd felt as I'd gazed into Hayden's eyes after the near miss with the holy water font. "Avoiding his lips was a full-scale operation. For the last time, nothing is going to happen with Hayden Paris." I said the last words firmly, trying to shake the spacey feeling that had infiltrated my body.

Sara didn't reply. She'd actually taken heed of my protest.

"Thank you. You've finally listened," I said, feeling steadier.

I turned around to see Cassie, Sara, and Lindsay staring at the backstage curtain.

"What are you staring at?" I asked.

Sara's face was horrified. "I think Hayden was standing there."

"You think or you know?" I cried.

"Well, we only saw him when the curtain shifted slightly," Cassie said, looking upset. "He seemed to be pulling down the orange tree backdrop."

"Why didn't you tell me he was there?"

My words ran through my head: *I've done everything in my power not to kiss Hayden.* I'd be point-blank traumatized if he'd said that about me.

"You spoke so quickly that it was too late," Sara said.

"He might not have overheard," Lindsay said.

Sara shook her head. "Linds, her voice was really loud."

I darted toward the stage. I had to explain my words to Hayden. God knows how, but I had to. I couldn't bear the idea of hurting his feelings.

I pulled back the curtain. Hayden had gone.

28   revelations

I gave the pot of couscous a good stir before returning to the kitchen
bench to slice the orange for the salad. It was 6:45 p.m. and I'd almost finished preparing the Moroccan meal. The dining table was
ready to go. I'd put out a jug of iced mint tea, and the green liquid
shimmered in the light of the flickering tangerine and black ylang-
ylang candles placed on either side of it. I'd added the candles, even
though Sara's teasing words kept echoing through my mind. I hoped
an ambient atmosphere would ease the difficult conversation I was
about to have with Hayden.

My hands shook slightly as I tried to cut the orange into even
segments. The doorbell rang and I dropped the knife, scattering orange pieces to the floor. I scooped the knife up and tossed it into
the sink before dashing to the front door.

"Hayden." My words sounded close to a sigh of relief. A part of
me had been frightened that he wouldn't show. "How are you?"

I crossed my fingers behind my back and hoped that his answer
wouldn't be "Traumatized."

"Tired." Hayden gave me a small smile.

I suddenly got a crazy urge to do something, anything, to make
that smile stretch to his eyes like it usually did.

We stood looking at each other through the open door. Hayden wasn't making a move to step inside.

"Aurora, I'm not sure . . ."

Was he canceling now, on my doorstep?

Suddenly the smell of burning filled the air.

"No! The couscous!" I ran to the kitchen, Hayden behind me.

"No, no!" I pulled the smoking pot off the element. As I turned to put it on the marble board, my feet slipped on a segment of orange that I'd dropped earlier and I stumbled backwards. "Whoa!"

Hayden grabbed me around the waist with one arm and seized the smoking pot with his other hand. "Little bit of an impromptu tango dip, Princess."

He placed the pot down on the board next to us and carefully pulled me back up toward him. I couldn't read his expression. His tone was serious, not teasing, as I'd normally expect.

"Is it ruined?" I asked, trying to fill the silence.

"Is what ruined?"

Our friendship, I wanted to say. The thing I'd always shunned but now couldn't bear to lose.

"The couscous. It's supposed to provide a contrast to the deep-fried dates."

"You made deep-fried dates?" Hayden suddenly seemed to take in the table and candles. "Princess, you've gone all out."

His eyes were warmer, the golden flecks of his irises dancing. They reminded me of the fireflies the NAD and I used to watch out on the veranda.

"Is it ruined?" was all I could manage. The golden flecks were distracting.

Hayden slowly let me go and picked up the couscous pot. "Recoverable. It's only the bottom that's a little burned."

"Let's take it to the table." I needed to sit down before my shaky legs caused me to slip again.

———

"This is fantastic." Hayden grinned at me as he took a bite of the cumin potatoes. I grinned back. I was so relieved to have him sitting across from me.

"It's great being here with you," he said, reading my mind.

"It's great to be your friend again," I said. "I want us to stay this way, always."

Okay, the plan was under way. Step one: emphasize my positive feelings for Hayden.

"Always?" Hayden stopped eating.

"Of course."

Why did he look unhappy?

Hayden looked seriously at me. "I don't feel like we're friends."

"You don't?" I was horrified. This confirmed it: he'd overheard my Stop Kiss rant.

"I mean, we were, but something's changed—or I think it has—"

"You've got the wrong idea!" I blurted. "I'm your friend, always."

Hayden, instead of smiling, sat very still, his gaze on the table. I felt sick. Could one statement, uttered out of stupid embarrassment, destroy things between us forever?

"I can explain it," I said. "I can tell you the reasons why I couldn't kiss you."

The words came tumbling out. He had to understand my motivation.

"I don't want to hear it." Hayden lifted his eyes back up to mine, and I was shocked to see the depth of hurt there. "I thought maybe I'd been wrong about this afternoon—"

"It's not you, Hayden. It's me. I can't—"

"I know you can't." Hayden shook his head. "I can't do this, either, though. I'm sorry."

"Hayden, please let me explain—"

I dashed after him as he strode down the hall.

I grasped his hand. "Let me apologize. I know we can fix this."

"I can't be your friend right now," Hayden said. "You need to give me some time."

He pulled his hand from mine. I felt like he'd pulled a part of me away with it.

He walked out the door, shutting it softly behind him.

I stayed up till three a.m. that night, my fingers creeping to my phone, creating and erasing texts that all said the same thing in a dozen different ways: *I'm sorry, please let me explain.* But every time my finger hovered over the Send button, I remembered Hayden's request for time. My need to be forgiven had to come second to his wishes.

The next day, at school, I waited to see whether Hayden would say something to me. If he just gave me a smile or made eye contact, I could take that as permission to go ahead with my apologies. He never once turned around in any of the five classes we had together that day.

By Wednesday morning I'd decided that I couldn't wait for permission to apologize. I staked out his locker before class, hoping he'd need to pick up a book. He came down the hall, just as I'd hoped, saw me standing there, looked at me for a brief moment, then dropped his gaze and walked right by.

He obviously didn't want to have anything to do with me. I'd blown it.

I tried to focus on other things, like helping Cass shop for an outfit for her all-important date with Scott on Friday, but even when I succeeded in distracting myself, thoughts of Hayden eventually slipped in. I attempted to focus on my studies, but instead of looking at the board, my eyes kept drifting onto Hayden.

After not registering a word of my Thursday morning English class, I had to ask myself: What if Hayden and I never resolved this misunderstanding? What if I finally got what I'd once wished for— for Hayden to disappear out of my life?

By Friday I wasn't sleeping properly, my appetite had faded, and I was obsessed with thoughts of Hayden. Was this guilt? Did guilt stop you from functioning like a normal person?

"So, last night's homework—five hundred words on feudal farming," Mr. Bannerman said, getting up from his desk to collect papers. "Jeffrey? Where's your homework?"

"I know this seems highly unlikely—"

"Just tell me, Jeffrey."

"Aliens took it back to their planet as an example of fine Earth literature?"

The whole class cracked up.

"God help those aliens." Mr. Bannerman shook his head. "Have the paper to me by the end of the day, Jeffrey."

"But it's already several light-years away by now!"

There was a crash as Travis, who'd been balancing on the back legs of his chair, laughed, lost his balance, and fell backwards.

And, right then, the thing I'd been both dreading and hoping for happened. Hayden turned around, and our eyes met.

I felt myself give a small gasp, and then I was tumbling. Tumbling down into the depths of his gaze, to a place where only Hayden and I could go—like the place between dreaming and waking. A tremulous connection that could be lost in a millisecond by the simple breaking of eye contact. And I couldn't break it. I couldn't move a muscle or whisper a word. I was lost in its intensity. A weird terror came over me that Hayden would be the first to look away, leaving me alone with this feeling.

But it was neither of us who broke the spell—it was the end-of-class bell.

And then I was grabbing my things and running from the classroom in a daze. My feet didn't seem to touch the ground, and my whole body was trembling. An earthquake had hit me, and I knew that things would never be the same.

I was in love with Hayden Paris!

In love with his beautiful eyes and his teasing smile, with his softly curling hair, with the way he made me laugh, with his bordering-on-irritating level of intelligence, with the way he lit up the stage. In love with his passion for a cause, his integrity, his honesty.

Madly, crazily in love. Oh god!

I finally stopped running when I reached the archway where I'd attempted to talk to Hayden on the opening night of the play. I tried to catch my breath, along with the thoughts and feelings flying around inside me like butterflies. In love! Where had that come from?

I laughed. How could I have been so stupid? It had been there all along, like some kind of ticking time bomb. Jelena's comment came back to me: *One of these days, you're going to discover why Hayden Paris gets you so worked up.* The reason I got so worked up was because I *cared* about what he thought of me.

The trembling in my knees when he got really close to me, the kiss I'd almost given in to twice—it was obvious now. I was in love!

I paced up and down, saying it to myself like a hymn: *In love. In love. I am in love. With Hayden Paris.* I was lost in the exquisite feelings.

Half an hour later, after I'd registered that I had a biology class and made it with two minutes to spare, the exquisite feelings had become misery. Why did they call it love? It was *torment.* It was a thousand flaming arrows striking you in the chest. Hayden wasn't speaking to me. He didn't want to spend time with me. This was un-requited love.

Just then, out of the corner of my eye, I saw Hayden dash in the door. My heart became a jackhammer and I snapped my eyes down to my textbook. This had to stop. Hayden's heart wasn't doing any reciprocal hammering when he saw me. To hope for his forgiveness was one thing; to hope for more was madness.

I kept my eyes lowered as Hayden took his seat in front of me. Oh god, I was going to hyperventilate. And yet I felt headily *alive.* Being near Hayden was intoxicating. I felt like my chest would burst with adoration.

I gazed at Hayden's hands, which were scribbling something on a sheet of paper. He had beautiful hands.

Those same hands tore the sheet of paper from the notebook, folded it over twice, and placed it on my desk. Before I'd even glanced up, Hayden was facing forward again. I stared at the note. Part of me desperately wanted to know what it said, and part of me didn't dare touch it. What if it just said something like *I want my jacket back*? Or worse. That moment in history class, that *look* we'd exchanged—my realization of love must have been written all over my face. The way I'd dashed off—I was transparent. He must know! I couldn't bear to read an *I don't feel the same way* scribble.

But what if it didn't say that? What if it said he was ready to forgive me? Even if love was out of the picture, I'd still have our friendship—he'd still be in my life. I grabbed the note, but just as I began unfolding it, another hand closed over mine. Mr. Blacklock's!

"Hand it over, Ms. Skye."

"But . . ." I clutched the note, which was oh-so-temptingly almost unfolded. I didn't know what it said yet!

Mr. Blacklock wrenched the paper from my clasp. "I will not have illicit communications in this class." In one swift motion, he crushed the paper in his fist, along with my hopes. "Count yourself lucky that I'm in a good mood today and have decided not to read it aloud to your classmates."

My mouth was an O of outrage.

Thankfully, before my revenge fantasies got too out of hand, the bell rang. I dashed for the door.

"Aurora!"

Hayden was calling me! I almost spun around in delight. But then I stopped.

A note was one thing, but face-to-face communication? If what he had to say was bad, there was no way I'd be able to hold it together. I kept running, without looking back, and didn't stop till I was at home, safe in my living room.

I'd always imagined that falling in love would be enjoyable. Not a mad seesaw of emotion that plunged me from euphoric to terrified, hopeful to hopeless, energized to exhausted. Even now, absurd hopes filled my mind—that there might be the tiniest chance that he felt the same way about me.

Could he?

My palm tingled as I remembered the soft kiss he'd given it while we were spying on the NAD. He'd bought me those beautiful balloons on Valentine's Day, and there'd been that odd moment when he'd stroked my cheek and looked all intense. The expression on his face when he'd seen me in the ball gown, the way he'd breathed "exquisite." That had to be good!

I gave a twirl on the living room carpet.

Then I remembered how I'd thrown him to the ground after that palm kiss. I'd pushed him out the door on Valentine's Day. I'd threatened to throw him off the school stage! I moaned as I heard myself saying, *There is no romance between us, and there never will be.*

I'd sabotaged any feelings Hayden might have thought about having!

Misery hit me with full force then. Hayden had kissed my palm, not my lips, even though he'd had the chance. I'd been right there in front of him. There was no way he had feelings for me. No way.

I groaned and collapsed into an armchair. Love truly was torment.

29 facebook fiasco

"Aurora!" Sara yelled to me as I arrived at school the following morning, heavy heart in tow. She, Lindsay, Jelena, and Cassie signaled frantically for me to join them at their table. "Is there a reason you've been keeping this a secret from us?"

They knew about my feelings for Hayden. Was I so obvious?

Sara turned her laptop around to face me, tapping the screen for emphasis. Facebook?

My jaw dropped and I pulled the laptop closer. Right there, on the Facebook page for Get High (Heels!), were the words "Could Aurora be autumn? Who's the girl you want to see wearing the heels? Click 'Like' to cast your vote for our four new seasonal faces from the fifteen finalists." Alongside the text was one of the shots that my mother had sent to the agency two months ago. I blinked. It had to be a mistake. But there was my name and photo, along with information about the label's new look for autumn.

"You're in a competition to be the face of my favorite shoe label and you didn't even think to tell us about it?" Sara shrieked.

"That photo of you is gorgeous!" Lindsay sighed. "I've already voted!"

"Congratulations!" Cassie threw her arms around me.

Jelena didn't say anything, just stared at me.

"So . . . spill!" Sara demanded. "How did this happen?"

"I-I don't even know myself," I stammered, feeling completely overwhelmed. I needed to call my mother. "Excuse me for two minutes, guys. Sorry."

I stepped away from the girls and punched in the number.

"I was expecting your call," Mom said smoothly. "The Get High (Heels!) voting page launched today."

I paced up and down by the school gate. "Why has the agency entered my photos in a Facebook competition?"

"It's the label's competition, Aurora, not Facebook's." Mom's voice was matter-of-fact. "Don't worry; it's legitimate. The label contacted various agencies looking for girls—"

"Since I've told you that I don't *want* to be a model, and specifically asked you to get the agency to take me off their books, why am I now in the position of having my entire high school able to Like me on a public Web site?" I said, trying not to grit my teeth.

"Well, I was about to inform the agency, but then I heard that Get High is intending to run TV commercials, and now that you've got the acting bug—"

"I got the acting bug to please you!"

"I thought it was a fantastic opportunity, and as your legal guardian, I okayed them to enter you into the competition."

My legal guardian? I barely saw my mother, much less lived with her!

"And how long have you known that they'd chosen me as one of the finalists?" I asked, taking deep breaths to keep my cool.

"Oh, well, since Monday—"

"Monday!" I cried. "And now it's Friday, four days later?"

"Darling, I've been virtually cut off from all modern civilization. I've been to the Keys with clients, completely uncontactable."

"I've noticed!" I said, thinking of my dozen phone calls.

"I couldn't call you," Mom said. "Believe me, I wanted to. I was excited."

"If you were uncontactable, how'd you find out about the competition?" I asked suspiciously.

"By e-mail, of course."

"So you could receive e-mails but you couldn't *call* me?" I said, gripping my phone tighter.

"Don't be difficult, Aurora." Mom's voice was stern.

"Difficult? I'm the one being voted for on Facebook! I want you to call the agency right now and retract your permission."

Mom laughed. "Darling, don't be ridiculous. The four girls chosen win a sizable amount of money, along with a year's contract with Get High. It's money you can put away for college—"

"Then I'm calling the agency myself."

"Don't disappoint me, Aurora."

"You disappointed me! What about Saturday night?"

She hung up without responding. I felt like screaming.

My friends surrounded me. They'd obviously overheard my heated conversation.

"You didn't know about any of this?" Sara asked.

I sighed. "Completely clueless. How did you all find out about it?"

"I'm a Facebook fan of Get High," Sara said. "I woke up, scrolled through the news page, and there it was. I started freaking out and messaging everyone I knew."

"It's spread remarkably quickly," Cassie said. "You've got one thousand, two hundred and sixty Likes already."

"Oh my god." I shook my head. "I have to stop this."

"Oh, you're so lucky!" Lindsay said. "Think of the shoes!"

"The money," Jelena added.

"The male models!" Sara said. "Get High had some really hot guys in its last catalog."

I barely registered their words, or the next few hours: Jeffrey waggling his eyebrows and asking if I was going to move into lingerie modeling; Benjamin accosting me after my first class to tell me that my next step was to join a television casting agency and asking

if I wanted to go for a coffee this evening to discuss it with him;
my classmates openly discussing their opinions of my photo and
whether they intended to vote for me.

At lunchtime, Cassie, Sara, Lindsay, Jelena, and I found a quiet
spot to lay out our picnic blanket. Alex and Tyler joined us, but so
did a horde of other people, all bombarding me with questions. When
would they announce the winner? Was it a national ad campaign?
What magazines would I be appearing in?

I kept repeating that my photo would be taken out of the running
once I spoke to my agency later this afternoon, but no one was listening.

"Do you think you'll be on billboards?" Alex asked.

Billboards? Oh god, I hadn't even thought about billboards. I
couldn't be legally locked in to this, could I?

"Hey, I was thinking," Alex said, before I could respond, "why
don't you come with Jelena and me to the club tonight? I know the
guy on the door, so the age thing isn't a problem. Hell, it probably
wouldn't be, anyway. You totally look over eighteen, Aurora."

Jelena frowned. "Alex, it's supposed to be a date."

Alex shrugged. "Yeah, so?"

"A date's usually just two people?"

"Oh, come on, babe." He took a swig of his drink. "You and me
and Aurora on the dance floor? It'll be fun."

"I, um, I've already got plans," I improvised. It would be totally
wrong to crash Jelena's date, even if I felt like going out clubbing.

"Cancel them," Alex said.

"Alex, she's got plans," Jelena said firmly. "Give it up."

Alex frowned at her. "I don't get the big deal. Can't we have a little
fun?"

"Are you saying that being with me isn't fun enough?" Jelena's
eyes were dangerous.

"Really, guys, it's fine," I said.

Neither of them took any notice of me.

"Aurora?"

My breath caught in my throat. Hayden was standing at the edge of our picnic blanket.

"Hey," he said.

"Hey," I replied.

He wasn't smiling. Wasn't he happy about talking to me? But why would he have come over if he didn't want to chat? He didn't say anything, though, and I was equally mute. This was getting uncomfortable.

"Did you—" I started.

"Aurora, I—" he began at the same time.

We both fell silent and I blushed. Thank god everyone else was focused on Jelena and Alex's quarrel instead of the ice age between Hayden and me.

Hayden gave an embarrassed laugh. "Listen," he said slowly, "I want to say congratulations on the competition."

Thank god the silence was filled. Even if what filled it was related to my completely implausible new career prospect.

I shook my head. "My mom. It's a long story, but let's just say no one will be able to Like me for much longer. It's inconceivable things even got this far."

"It's not inconceivable in the slightest," Hayden said. "The company recognizes how special you are."

He thought I was special? My heart was dancing like the daffodils in Wordsworth's poem. "Th-thank you," I stammered.

"So . . ." Hayden seemed to take a deep breath. "I was wondering if you wanted to watch the savanna DVD with me tonight? I know it's short notice, but I owe you, after running out on dinner the other night. We obviously need to talk. . . ."

Yes, yes, yes! But just as I was working out a friendly, not-bordering-on-obsessive reply, Alex interrupted.

"Sorry, Hayden, but she's got plans. And seeing as she wouldn't cancel them to come to the club with us, there's no way she's going to drop them to watch some DVD."

My smile faded. My fictitious plans, constructed to save Jelena's love life, were destroying my own! If I said that I had no plans, then

Alex would get all insulted, or pressure me further about going out with him and Jelena.

"So, who's the lucky guy?" Sara teased. "Benjamin? I heard him asking you out after math class."

Hayden's face clouded over.

"N-no," I stammered, trying to think what my plans might be.

"Half the guys in the school are after Aurora." Alex laughed. "She's hot property!"

"Okay, well, maybe some other time, then, Aurora," Hayden said. "See you." He dashed away.

"Hayden, wait!"

I didn't know what to say, but everything felt wrong and I desperately wanted to fix it. But he didn't look back.

"Ooh!" Lindsay, who'd been studying the fashions in the latest *Vogue*, clapped her hands together, an expression of delight on her face. "Are your plans with your secret admirer?"

Alex's eyebrows shot up in surprise. "She has a secret admirer?"

"I told you," Jelena said, still annoyed. "He's the one who sent her those roses and the poem—'She's like the stars, blah blah blah.'"

I jumped. My secret admirer! Had the past twenty-four hours rendered me stupid? Not only had I completely forgotten he existed, but I'd fallen in love with someone else. I was a traitor! Fickle! Unfeeling! My secret admirer had been pursuing me for weeks and I'd just carelessly turned my mind to another.

Oh, why was everything so messed up? My life was *Much Ado About Nothing* on steroids.

Since I was supposed to be "out," I spent the evening at the city library, perusing the poetry stacks for other writers' advice on love—except my attention kept drifting from the page. Right in the middle of writing a poem of my own (which, much as I hated myself for it, actually referred to Hayden's "smoldering eyes"—was I becoming a walking cliché generator?), my cell lit up with Cassie's number.

"Cass," I said, "you're supposed to be on your date now! Why aren't you there?"

Cass giggled. "I am. I'm calling you from the restaurant's bathroom!"

"Then, what's up? Are you calling for advice?"

"No, it's going great!" Cass sounded enthusiastic. "The art show was really inspirational. And you know what he told me? He's been crazy about me since he first saw me in history! Can you believe it?"

"Yes, Cass, I can." I smiled, thinking of the way Scott's eyes lit up whenever he looked at my best friend.

"And the rose? Well, it turns out he chose yellow because it reminded him of my blond hair!"

I laughed. Sometimes things could be absurdly simple.

"Anyway, I wanted to tell you about the date now, because Jelena and I are leaving really early in the morning."

"Where are you going?" I asked.

"Oh. Well, Jelena was all dressed up to go to the club with Alex, and then he canceled—"

"He what?" I couldn't believe it.

"Jelena was furious and hung up on him. She called me, just as I was leaving to go to the art show, and said that she was going to show Alex that she wasn't Ms. Always Available, and so she'd asked her mom if they could go to that spa down the coast for the weekend and did I want to come along?"

"She didn't ask me," I said, feeling a little hurt.

"She said her mom was bringing a friend, so there was only space for one of us."

"She's not mad at me, is she?"

Cass paused. "She was a little annoyed about Alex inviting you on their date, but that was all. Anyway, I'd better go. I've been in the bathroom for a while now."

"Okay, Cass. Hope the evening gets even better."

"Hey," Cass added, "is everything okay with you and Hayden? It seemed a little strained at lunch."

I'm in love with him and he doesn't feel the same way.

I put on a cheerful voice. "Yeah, everything's fine. Have a great time at the spa!"

If only I could believe my own lies. I slumped in my chair, feeling utterly miserable.

30 i don't exist to you

As the weekend progressed, my anxiety level continued to rise. I worried about Alex's cavalier attitude toward dating. I despaired over my own fickleness when it came to my secret admirer. I was grateful that at least one worry disappeared: the agency, once informed that I hadn't agreed to being part of the Get High (Heels!) social media campaign, promised that they'd remove me from the competition. They weren't thrilled, but at least my picture would be off Facebook in the next forty-eight hours or so.

Unfortunately, my other problem wasn't so easily fixed. My thoughts, hopes, and dreams about Hayden were incessant. I tried to tell myself that I shouldn't be having these thoughts about someone who wasn't my secret admirer, but even though I knew it was the honorable thing to do, I didn't *want* to stop loving Hayden. I kept hoping that he would text me, or call me, or knock at the door.

My jitteriness increased when my mother sent me a text on Sunday morning asking me to meet her for a late afternoon coffee. Since the Get High (Heels!) Facebook page was still running my photo, she might not have heard yet that I was no longer in the running for the contract. A very unpleasant conversation was awaiting me.

I headed outside to wait for the taxi that Mom was sending for me, and hoped it would arrive before the rain did. While I waited, I heard footsteps crunching up the drive.

"Aurora."

"Alex!" I started with surprise to see him, athletic attire and all, on my driveway. "What are you doing here? Jelena's away for the weekend. Didn't she tell you?"

Maybe she wasn't speaking to him. It could be part of her Ms. Unavailable tactics.

"I'm not looking for Jelena. I came to see you." Alex gave one of his wide, white smiles. "About something very important." He gave me a wink and stepped closer to me. "Can I give you a clue?"

He pulled a hand from behind his back, revealing one long-stemmed crimson rose.

Oh. My. God.

Alex grinned. "I'm your secret admirer, Aurora. Surprise!"

"But you're Jelena's boyfriend!" I stared at him in horror. There had to be a mistake!

"Hardly," he said.

"But you've been on dates."

"Dates during which I grilled her about you. You know, subtly, so she wouldn't pick up on it. I had to find out what you like in a guy."

"No!" I shook my head violently. "This doesn't make sense. If you liked me, why didn't you talk to me or hang around with me, instead of Jelena?"

"Aurora, I learned from Jelena that you're a girl who's impressed by what's under the surface. That's why I decided to do the secret admirer thing. I wanted you to get to know the real me instead of judging me right off the bat."

"But you acted so crazy about Jelena!"

Alex shrugged. "I had to play the part, make it so I'd be the last person you'd suspect. Asking you to the club was part of the plan. Once you said yes, I was going to tell Jelena I couldn't make it, so she'd decide not to go. Then, when you and I were alone, I'd give you the rose and you'd be blown away. But then you couldn't go, so I decided to come over this morning to tell you."

My head was spinning. "I can't believe it."

"Aurora, I'm mad about you." Alex stepped closer to me again. "You're the most beautiful girl in school."

"You said the same thing about Jelena last Saturday night!" I cried, stepping backwards to put space between us.

"Forget Jelena!" He grabbed me around the waist and pulled me to him. "I want you."

"Alex, stop it!" I tried to push his hands away. "You might be my secret admirer, but there's no way I'm going to date a guy Jelena's crazy about. It would be a total betrayal!" I looked him straight in the eye. "You knowingly used one of my best friends. I'm sorry, but that proves you're not the guy for me."

I expected Alex to look mortified, but he just laughed and grabbed me around the waist again. "Come on, I'm a man who's infatuated. We do stupid things." He pushed his lips toward mine.

"No!" I wrenched my head back and gave him a ferocious shove.

Alex's eyes popped open as he lost his balance and fell backwards. The next second, he landed in the ever-present driveway puddle with an enormous splash.

I was a little frightened he might try something else, even when soaked to the skin, but at that moment the taxi pulled up.

Alex got to his feet, wringing muddy water from his sodden Adidas T-shirt. "You know what your problem is, Aurora Skye?" he spat. "You think you're too good for anyone." He turned and stormed off down the drive.

I stood there, shaking, until the taxi driver blasted the horn. I dazedly got in. I didn't dare look out the window as we passed Alex.

As the taxi headed toward the city, I kept seeing Alex's furious, dripping face. How could he have thought I'd betray one of my best friends and take up with him? He'd been so confident that I'd fall at his feet, grateful for the honor of his attention! As for trying to force his kisses on me—I shouldn't have just pushed him into the puddle; I should have thrown some judo kicks into the mix, too.

I couldn't believe Alex was my secret admirer. Suddenly, the thought of the poem made me feel ill. He must have plagiarized it. And how had he managed to get so crazy about me? It wasn't as if he'd spent enough time in my company to appreciate my personality or my mind or anything! Was it my looks he was infatuated with? If so, the whole thing made even less sense, because Jelena was phenomenally beautiful.

Jelena! How on earth was I going to break this to her? I'd never seen her so crazy about a guy. I had to call her ASAP. She needed to hear the news from me instead of through the grapevine. The rumors would probably be flying by the time she and Cass got back from the spa.

I bit my lip and called her cell. It rang and rang before going to voice mail. Why wasn't she picking up?

I tried Cassie's number and got the same response. Was there no cell reception at the spa? How far from civilization was it? I couldn't leave a voice mail—I had to speak to Jelena personally.

Maybe I could reach her through the spa itself. I dialed information and got the number.

"Hello, Oasis Spa, Mandy speaking. How may I help you?"

"Hi, is there any way you could put me through to the Cantrills?"

"Is it an emergency?"

"Well, technically, no."

"We encourage our guests to switch off during their time here, since we have a no-calls policy except in the event of an emergency—"

"Okay." I struggled to maintain a pleasant tone. "It's just really important that I speak to Jelena Cantrill. Is there any way you could make an exception?"

"I'm afraid not," Mandy replied firmly. "Unless it's an actual emergency, I can't put you through."

"She'd want to take this call!"

Mandy was unrelenting. "The Cantrills are returning to the city tonight. You'll be able to chat then, dear."

"It can't wait—"

Mandy said a swift good-bye.

I called several more times, hoping to reach a different staff member who might be more lenient about the no-calls policy. But it seemed that Mandy was the only one manning the desk.

The taxi finally reached the coffee shop. I headed inside and saw Mom sitting with her back to the door. As I headed toward her, I realized she was on the phone.

"Carlos, it was wonderful." She gave a tinkly laugh. "We need to get away for romantic weekends more often. The Keys was just perfect."

I froze.

"Okay, I'd better get going, but I'll see you at Michaela's at six for drinks."

I stared at her back, unable to take a step.

She turned around, as if feeling my trembling presence behind her.

"Aurora! What's this nonsense about you telling the agency to remove you from the competition?"

My pulse was roaring in my ears. "You were with him last weekend," I said. "You weren't with clients. You lied to me."

"Aurora, I didn't exactly lie. I had a meeting there for the new development, but I stayed—"

"Admit it!" The words ripped from my throat. "You lied because you didn't want to come. You knew you weren't going to fly all that way and come back hours later for the play." My voice quavered slightly. "You're not interested in my life."

"How dare you say I'm not interested," Mom snapped. "I'm meeting you here today to discuss your future opportunities."

"But that's the only time I see you, isn't it?" I said. "When there are 'opportunities' for me. You want me to be in the public eye so it reflects back on you. And you know what? I wanted your approval—no, your *love*—so much that I auditioned for the play, then waited on pins and needles for you after curtain call the other night, hoping you'd be proud." I could feel the lump in my throat pressing down on my vocal cords. "Hoping for something—anything—from you."

I'd never seen Mom look so angry. "Stop that nonsense right now."

"You want me to stop?" I said. "Tell me, then, if you love me so much, why didn't you cancel that weekend with Carlos?"

My mother didn't respond.

"Why didn't you just tell him you'd made a promise to me and couldn't break it?"

"Because he doesn't know about you!" Mom burst out.

Something inside me crumpled. "What?"

"I haven't told him. I don't know how he'd react." She gathered her handbag up, ready to leave. "He's never had kids."

"No," I whispered. "You haven't told him because, in all honesty, I don't exist to you."

They were the last words I managed before my throat closed up and I ran for the door. This time I'd be the one to leave first.

Somehow, I made it onto the busy city street and into another taxi. All I wanted was to hold back the flood of tears until I got home.

As I stumbled up the driveway, I ran into the NAD dashing out of the house, briefcase in hand.

"Aurora." He put his hand on my arm and his voice sounded tight. "I have to tell you something."

A sudden terror came over me as I looked at his serious expression.

"Snookums has gone missing."

"How?" I choked.

"Dana let him out after seeing that he'd scratched the new Tibetan rug." The NAD's tone was cautious. "She didn't know he was an inside cat. I called out for her to grab him, but Snookums was already halfway down the drive by then."

Instead of a reply, a choking sound burst out of my throat. Snookums was gone. Out onto the road, where people didn't always brake in time for animals.

A roll of thunder sounded. The sky was like a bruise now, black and blue.

"I'm really sorry, honey," Dad said. "I've been looking for forty-five minutes, but I have to leave now."

"You what?" My voice cracked.

"I've got a plane to catch, and I'm in danger of missing it. I have to be in New York for a meeting tomorrow morning. I only found out at lunchtime that I have to go."

"You're leaving?" I gasped.

As if in answer, a taxi pulled up at the end of the drive.

"Aurora, it's Sony. I have to be there." Dad pushed a bag of Crispy Treats, Snookums's favorite, into my hand. "Give this a shake when you call out for him. He'll come home soon. I'm sorry." His voice was distracted.

"But . . ."

My voice faded as I watched him race away from me. Once again, I was completely invisible to a parent. I tore after him, panic rising in my chest.

"No! You can't leave me here alone." I clung to his jacket sleeve like a toddler being dropped at day care.

Dad twisted away from me. "Aurora, I've got to go!"

"I can't believe you're doing this," I babbled, stumbling as I tried to keep up with him. The sky was dark with the approaching storm.

"Aurora, stop being unreasonable!" Dad yelled.

I stared at him. Something deep inside me quivered.

"I'll be back tomorrow night," he called through the taxi window. Lightning flashed behind him.

Just go! I screamed.

I saw his face drop as the taxi pulled away.

The sky opened up—a deluge of water that slammed through my clothes and drummed at my skin. But I didn't care. I ran up and down the deserted street, calling Snookums's name and listening with all my might for the meow that would make everything all right again.

I desperately shook the box of Crispy Treats, which had become a soft, soggy cardboard mess. "Here, kitty!"

Silence.

My voice broke. "Snookums! Come back, please!"

I stumbled through a vacant lot, the long grass a blur through the tears that burned my eyes. I was trying desperately to hold back the flood that threatened to overwhelm me.

"Snookums!"

I tripped and fell, my palms slamming into the muddy ground. Half a dozen Crispy Treats tumbled out of the carton onto the grass.

"Aurora, wait!" There was a loud shout from behind me.

As I stumbled to my feet, I saw who was calling. And finally the tears came.

Hayden's eyes were heavy with concern. "Aurora, what are you doing out here in this storm?"

I just cried harder. And then Hayden was pulling me to him, drawing me into his arms, sheltering me under the white umbrella he carried.

"Snookums is gone," I sobbed. "And if I'd been home today, then he wouldn't have annoyed Ms. DeForest and she wouldn't have let him out. But I wasn't. I was off trying to please my mom, yet again, and I couldn't, and I'm so sorry, Hayden, I'm so sorry!"

"Sorry?" Hayden pulled slightly away from me and looked at me intently. "For what?"

"The day before she left . . ." The words rushed out of me. "The day before Mom left, you invited me over to your place to go swimming. Remember, when the pool was finally finished? I was just heading out the door when Mom's car pulled up. I was surprised, because she never came home early. She said she wanted to spend the afternoon with me, but I wanted to go over and see you, so I said no. And she looked at me with these disappointed eyes—I'd never seen her look like that before. And then the next day she was gone! And I thought . . . I thought that it was my fault, that maybe if I'd spent that afternoon with her she might not have left. And every time I saw you after that, I was so angry at myself. And so I dropped you!" I sobbed. "I dropped my best friend and acted like I hated you! Just so I could cope! I'm so sorry!"

"Hey . . ." Hayden gently pulled me into his arms again. "You don't have to be sorry at all. I knew how much of a hard time you were going through."

"I'm so sorry!" I whispered into his tearstained blue shirt. Even though he said it was okay, I needed to repeat the words. "For the other day, too, for what you heard—I've wanted to explain it to you since Monday. And . . . and I can't stop crying for some reason—"

"Shh," Hayden soothed, stroking my back. "You cry as long as you like, okay?"

I clung to him, the steady rise and fall of his chest guiding my own shaky breaths, his heartbeat reminding mine to keep time. The rain thundered down on our umbrella, but Hayden's arms were a stronghold.

After what seemed like a century, I pulled away and looked up at him. "I have to keep looking," I said softly, wiping my eyes. "Snookums is out there in this storm. I have to find him."

"I'll help you," Hayden assured me. "Let me go grab a flashlight. It's going to be pitch black any moment."

In Hayden's arms, I'd been oblivious to the creeping shadows all around us.

"Wait here." Hayden handed me the umbrella. Before I could stop him, he dashed out into the downpour.

I stood under the umbrella, feeling oddly numb, listening to the happy croaks of the neighborhood frogs, until Hayden raced back to me.

"All right." He switched on the heavy-looking flashlight. "Let's start the search."

And search we did. Under hedges and parked cars, in people's front yards, along bike trails, up trees. As it grew later and later, I felt myself panicking. What if I never saw Snookums again? What if my furry family member, the one who had seen me through endless trials and tribulations, was gone forever?

"We're going to find him." Hayden answered my unspoken fear.

"What if it's too late?" I whispered, looking fiercely at the ground so I wouldn't cry again.

"Aurora." Hayden took my hand, and I looked up. "We're going to find him. I *promise* you that."

I stared into his earnest eyes, at the droplets of rain glistening in his hair, and I believed him. Hayden would search with me for as long as it took. He squeezed my hand, and a realization hit me like a thunderbolt. I was free to love him. There was no secret admirer anymore. I was free to hand him my heart.

And wait for his reply.

Suddenly I started shaking. My responsibility to my secret admirer might have fallen away, but I was terrified. What if Hayden did feel the way my soul ached for him to feel, and I let him in, and he ended up hurting me? Turned me away, like my mother had? He would become yet another scar on my heart, another warning to slam the door, turn the key, and live out my days in solitary confinement.

"Hey, you're trembling," Hayden said softly. "I think I should get you home."

"No, I'm fine." The concern in his eyes made me shake even more.

Hayden began guiding me home. "You've been drenched for two and a half hours."

"But Snookums . . ." He was counting on me to come through for him. I just had to get a grip on myself.

"It's going to be really difficult to find him tonight," Hayden said. "He's probably hidden somewhere to get out of the rain. I think we'll have more of a chance once the storm clears. We can start looking again at dawn."

"But—"

"And that will give me a chance to create some Missing Pet posters to put up," Hayden continued, as he gently steered me up the driveway. "It'll increase the odds of finding him."

I knew he was right.

"You go take a hot shower right away," Hayden said as I unlocked my front door. "I'll make you some tea."

I stood in the shower, feeling the hot water sink into my skin, wishing the warmth could permeate my insides. I got out, got dressed, and numbly tried Jelena's number. Still no answer.

"Feeling better?" Hayden asked when I joined him in the kitchen.

I nodded absently as I watched him pour water from the kettle into a mug. He carefully spooned two teaspoons of honey into my herbal tea. How had he remembered that, after all these years?

"I should get started on the posters as soon as possible," he said.

"I could help you."

He shook his head. "You look exhausted." He handed me my drink.

"But I need to do something."

I needed a distraction or else I'd go nuts.

"Why don't you find a photo of Snookums for the posters?" Hayden suggested.

He left the room and returned with several bound albums. Our family photos. I hadn't looked at them in years.

"Wait a minute." I ran upstairs and grabbed a copy of the shot of Snookums in a Santa hat. "This one's nice and clear."

"I'll head home and do the posters right away." Hayden squeezed my shoulders. "Don't get up. I'll see myself out."

"Will you help me look tomorrow morning?" I asked.

I knew he would, but I needed to hear him say yes. I needed the certainty.

"I'll see you at six thirty a.m.," he called back as he headed for the front door. "Good night, Princess."

His voice was so full of reassurance that I felt like crying again.

I sat at the kitchen table, staring at the family albums in front of me. Before I knew what I was doing, I reached for them.

Here was my family history—laid out on the pages of these rust-brown albums. A run-through of the past sixteen years. Photos of Mom and Dad with radiant faces and eyes that were full of love for each other. Studio photographs of me as a baby, carefully posed. The three of us on a vacation at the beach. Hayden and me, grinning at the camera. Snookums as a kitten. Then my parents' smiles, so loving only pages before, became forced-looking. There were pictures of my mother's many dinner parties, with a tense-looking Dad sitting at the head of a table that had long since disappeared. Shots from a trip to Tahiti, which Mom and Dad had taken alone. I'd stayed with the Parises. I remembered the strained look on my parents' faces when they'd returned two days early to pick me up. I hadn't understood—wasn't Tahiti supposed to be relaxing?

Then the shots stopped and the record got messed up. The person who'd taken charge of the camera had left the picture. The camera lay in a drawer, unused, because Dad and I didn't want any reminders of how we felt then—like zombies, going through the motions of living, with dead eyes and locked hearts.

A year later, when time had somehow started again, there were photos of my thirteenth birthday. The NAD had gone all out with a party at a roller-skating rink, and I stood among a huge group of grinning girls. No Hayden in the photo. He'd left a present on the doorstep, but I'd hidden it away in a drawer, unable to bear the reminder of our friendship.

Mom had forgotten my birthday that year.

I slammed the album shut. But the camera in my mind, which recorded and stored everything so carefully, was streaming images frenetically.

Me, gazing up at my mother in awe when she was all dressed up to go out—this beautiful, mysterious mother, who looked so happy as she headed downstairs, wearing her wide smile, not the tight one she wore on weekends.

Me, waiting by the school gate long after everyone else had left, making up stories for myself so I wouldn't count every car that went by that wasn't hers.

Me, listening to her sighs when I was at home on school breaks and Hayden wasn't there to play with me. She'd announce that we were "going visiting," which meant sitting patiently on other people's couches, then getting bored and wandering around an unfamiliar house, hoping to find a bookshelf so I could escape into a new world. Feeling angry about how long the visits took, but also feeling guilty because you weren't supposed to get angry at your mother, were you? You were supposed to love her. And she loved you back.

Me, sitting in my room, trying to do my homework while I listened to Dad and Mom fight. Holding my breath each time one of them slammed the front door and drove away, yelling that they were leaving.

And then one day, Mom had.

I opened the album back up, looking at the empty pages, and photos from my mind filled them. The NAD presenting me with a key so I could let myself into the house after school. Getting home one day and realizing that I'd left the key inside on the kitchen table. Panic coming over me. Beating at the door until my fists were red and realizing that I had to be my own mother now. Going to the library to get books that taught me how to cook, how to take care of things in the house, how to cope with growing up. I became the girl with the answers to everything, the girl who was confident and didn't cry. Only it hadn't worked, because here I was, sitting at a cold marble table, feeling lost and scared.

Why didn't my mother want to know me, even though I did everything I could to be agreeable, likable, lovable? Why had my father dashed out on me this afternoon? Was my whole family destined to leave me? Even Snookums?

The tears came again. I cried for all the times I'd called out for my mother and she hadn't come; for all the times I'd tried my best to make her love me but couldn't. I cried for all the things she didn't know about me and didn't want to know, and the ache I felt inside when I looked at her. For how pathetic it made me feel to want to be loved so badly.

I cried for the twelve-year-old girl who'd believed that her mother's sudden disappearance was her fault. I cried for my father, and how his life had changed. I cried for the way I'd treated Hayden, for the hurt I must have caused him, for the lost years of friendship. For the new way I felt about him and the terror that had me crippled and unable to risk telling him I loved him. I cried for the news I had to tell Jelena that would make her cry, and the way it would make her more cautious about giving *her* heart away. I cried until I couldn't see, until I was exhausted, until four years of feeling had drained from me.

What was the way out of this? How did I lift the heaviness from my heart to try to forgive my mother, to make peace with the past, as impossible as it seemed? How could I learn to look forward, to let myself experience love, affection?

The thoughts spun around and around in my head as the night went on and the rain spilled down outside. Finally, I laid my head down on the cool marble of the table, overwhelmed.

And then I heard a pounding noise. I lifted my head off the table and realized, from the faint light in the kitchen, that the night had ended. The pounding was someone at the door.

The kitchen clock read 6:57 a.m. Hayden hadn't come!

The banging at the door came again. Was it him? Why was he so late? I rushed down the hall, feeling hurt that he'd broken his promise.

I pulled open the door. "Oh!" I gasped.

There on the doorstep was an exhausted-looking Hayden, with a bedraggled Snookums in his arms.

He'd found him, just as he'd promised.

I threw my arms around the both of them, laughing and crying as Hayden grinned at me and Snookums yowled in protest at being squashed between the two of us.

"But how . . . ?" I asked, staring at Hayden.

I could hardly believe that Snookums was right here with us, that last night's storm had vanished and the sky was a heavenly blue. I felt like a new person.

"I kept looking," Hayden said, as I rained kisses down on Snookums's damp head.

"But you went home."

"I only said that so you wouldn't insist on coming with me. You looked so exhausted. Finally, at six thirty a.m., I found Snookums in the park, scaring some geese."

"You rescued him!" I cried, thinking of the hours he must have spent out in the rain. "You stayed up the whole night. . . . Why?"

"Because I wanted to see you smile again," Hayden said softly.

And I did smile, as the three of us stood in that embrace in the early morning light, feeling the cool breeze tickle our skin.

It was a new day.

31 rumors

When I'd said as many thank-yous as humanly possible, Hayden raced home to shower and have breakfast, while I bathed and blow-dried a protesting Snookums. He settled down happily, once I filled his food bowl and gave him a pat.

I made it to school five minutes before the bell rang. As I walked in the school gate, a hush fell among the groups in the courtyard and heads began turning my way.

What was going on? Was it still the Facebook thing? I'd have thought that everyone was over it by now, but maybe not. Whatever it was, I couldn't worry about it. I had to find Jelena. There she was, standing with her back to me, by the fountain. As I walked over to her, I felt even more heads turning my way. I suddenly had a very bad feeling.

"Jelena . . ." I began.

She turned around, her eyes fierce. "I don't want to talk to you."

She knew. Somehow, she'd heard about what had happened.

"Please, Jelena, just let me explain—"

"Explain what?" she interrupted. "How you ruthlessly set out to steal my boyfriend?"

The crowd let out an outraged "Ooh."

She couldn't think I'd intentionally gone after Alex! "Please, Jelena, if we could just talk about this privately—"

She let out a laugh. "You want to talk privately with me when the whole school knows about your off-the-Richter-scale kiss with him yesterday?"

"My *what*?"

"Oh, don't play innocent, Aurora," Jelena snapped. "How do you think I felt, coming home last night to find dozens of messages about my boyfriend and my best friend kissing on her driveway?"

"Jelena, y-you've got this completely wrong," I stammered. "The only thing Alex kissed was the ground, because I—"

"Pushed him away?" Jelena said scornfully. "You really expect me to believe you pushed away your secret admirer, the one you were *destined to be with*?"

"Alex was Aurora's secret admirer?"

I turned to see a shocked-looking Lindsay standing behind me, an even more dumbfounded Sara with her.

"You must be the last two people in this whole school to find out the truth," Jelena told them loudly. "Besides me, of course. Yup. Alex sent the roses, and he wrote the gushing poem. And Aurora's standing here, trying to deny the whole thing!" She let out a sarcastic laugh.

Jelena's words stung like crazy, but it was the devastation in her eyes that was killing me. I had to get her to believe me.

"Jelena, somehow the truth has gotten mixed up," I said. "Yes, Alex came to my house and told me he was the secret admirer. But I told him that there was no way I'd go after a guy you liked—"

"'Cause I'm your friend," Jelena said in a singsong voice. "Spare me the story."

"There was no kiss!" I cried. "I don't know how this whole crazy story started, but there was no kiss. I swear!"

"Sorry, Aurora, but I don't believe you." Jelena looked away. "And I don't think anyone else here does, either."

I looked at the faces in the crowd. Half the girls gathered in the courtyard were glaring at me already.

Lindsay took a step toward me. "I believe her."

"Lindsay, are you sure you want to do that?" Jelena said quietly. "She's stolen my boyfriend. Who's to say yours won't be next?"

Lindsay looked uncertainly at me.

"Remember how insistent she was about you not taking Tyler back?" Jelena pressed. "Don't you think it might have been for a different reason? She obviously gets a kick out of this sort of thing."

"It was so Tyler would feel truly sorry about the way he behaved—" I started.

Jelena cut me off. "You don't want to lose him again, do you? Lindsay?"

Lindsay stepped over to Jelena's side.

"Lindsay, please believe me . . ." But I knew it was hopeless. Jelena had hit Lindsay's weak spot.

Sara took my arm. "Well, I believe Aurora. The whole story's a bunch of crap. She would never touch anyone else's man."

Thank you. I smiled at her, my only ally, as the first bell sounded.

"Come on, Lindsay, let's go." Jelena swept away, a muddled-looking Lindsay in tow.

The crowd around us disappointedly broke up.

"I can't believe everyone's listening to this ridiculous story," I said, as a group of girls walked by with their noses in the air. "I mean, I've never looked twice at anyone's boyfriend, and they know it."

Sara rolled her eyes. "They just love the idea of a juicy rumor. Don't take any notice of them. The whole thing will blow over. Let's get to class."

I sat in my math class under the glare of accusing looks, surrounded by whispers.

"How low can you get? Taking your best friend's boyfriend!"

"Now she's a *model*, I guess she thinks she can have anything she wants."

How was everyone so ready to believe that I'd do what they were accusing me of? Not only Jelena but also Lindsay *and* the whole school body? If they could believe this, who was to say that Cassie—who was at a dental appointment—would be on my side when she got back? Or Hayden?

I felt like crying. This wasn't just going to blow over. I had to take action.

"I'm going to do something about this," I said, when Sara met me outside the classroom at break.

"What?"

"Talk to Alex. Somehow, the story about us has gotten completely mixed up, and maybe he can tell me how."

I marched outside, Sara behind me, and headed for the table where Alex was sitting with a group of guys.

One of them nudged him. "Ooh, Alex, look who's coming over."

Alex gave me a wink. "Hey, babe. Come for another kiss?"

"You." The truth dawned on me. "You made up the rumor."

I couldn't believe it. I'd thought maybe he mentioned the incident to someone, who'd then gotten the story twisted, but I'd never considered that he might have spread the lies himself.

"Rumor?" Alex grinned lazily. "I wasn't aware of any rumor. Just some people discussing the mind-blowing kiss we had."

The guys gave him high fives. I bunched my fists, struggling to keep my cool.

"I want you to tell everyone the real truth about what happened yesterday," I said, pointing at the gathering crowd behind me.

Sara snickered. "Yeah, not the Alex-wishes version."

The crowd tittered.

"All right, I'll admit that I haven't exactly been honest," Alex said, holding up his hands. "The truth is, Aurora kissed me."

"I what?"

The crowd exploded in whispers. I felt like hitting him.

"She planted one right on me." Alex laughed.

"You—"

"Don't feel embarrassed, babe," he cut in. "I like a girl who goes after what she wants."

"You're lying." Hayden pushed his way through the crowd and stood beside me.

Hayden believed me! I shot him a grateful look.

Alex let out a snort. "What would you know about it, Paris?"

"I know that you were in the guys' locker room on Friday when everyone was discussing how they'd never been lucky enough to kiss Aurora," Hayden replied. "And I know that you bet some of the guys in there, including the ones sitting with you now, that you'd be the one to actually do it."

My jaw dropped.

"Yeah . . . so?" Alex said, looking unworried. "I knew that I had the best chance of scoring a kiss, being the secret admirer and all. Why not make some cash out of it?"

"Are you for real?" Sara spluttered.

I saw Jelena join the outskirts of the crowd.

"Okay," Hayden said flatly, "if you are Aurora's secret admirer, why don't you quote a few lines from the poem you wrote for her?"

I looked at him, feeling confused. How was Alex reciting the poem going to prove anything? Then I noticed that Alex's smile had faded slightly. The crowd had gone very quiet.

"Go on, then," Hayden said. "We're all waiting."

"She's like the stars," Alex began loudly. "White, shining high in the sky—"

"Wrong," Hayden said. "The lines are *Aurora, / she's like the stars, far above me.*"

I gasped. How did he know the words?

Hayden continued, without looking at me. *"I stand transfixed. / She's / my Alpha, / radiating light across my world of sky . . ."* He paused. "Care to go on, Alex?"

Alex laughed. "What does that prove, anyway?"

"It proves that you were lying about being her secret admirer," Hayden said. "And if you were lying about that, then I'd say it's pretty likely that you were lying about the kiss, too. In fact, I know you're lying, because I saw Aurora push you into a puddle when you went to kiss her."

The crowd burst into laughter. I knew no one would believe Alex's story now.

I felt dizzy from all the revelations. Alex wasn't my secret admirer? That meant he was still out there somewhere. . . .

"I know who sent Aurora those things," Hayden said, "and it wasn't you."

I was going to pass out. I was going to sink down onto the courtyard stones. . . .

"Who is it?" I dimly heard Lindsay ask, above the roaring in my ears.

"It's someone who sees her as more than a fashion model who can up his status," Hayden said, looking pointedly at Alex. "Someone who meant every word of that poem, and the message."

"Who is it?" the crowd roared.

My own heart shouted the same question, then went into overdrive as Hayden turned to face me.

"It's a friend of mine," he said.

The bell rang and the crowd dispersed. I vaguely noticed Alex slinking off.

I stared at Hayden. "A friend of yours?" I whispered.

I wanted it to be you, my heart said.

"I can't tell you right now," Hayden said. "The whole thing will be revealed to you really soon—I promise!" He grasped my hand briefly, then let go. "I've got to get to a student council meeting. We'll talk later."

"But—"

He dashed off before I could say another word.

I stood staring after him, then caught sight of Jelena, ten yards away. Her gaze met mine.

"Jelena!"

Before I could take a step toward her, she broke eye contact and rushed off.

"Hi!" Cassie called. She came bounding through the school gate, hand in hand with a beaming Scott. "I just got out of the dentist's. Scott came with me to hold my hand—isn't that sweet? Did I miss anything?"

32 the world's greatest romance

"How could Alex make up such a lie?" Cassie gasped at lunch.

"Such a horrible lie," Lindsay added.

Lindsay had come up to me first thing at lunch, a massive apology bouquet (which she'd obviously cut class to get) in her arms. Her eyes had been so distraught that I'd forgiven her instantly.

"Male ego." Sara rolled her eyes and took a bite of her sandwich. "He obviously wanted to date the most popular girl in school—who, up until last week, was Jelena. When that looked like it was going to change, he ran after Aurora."

"The awful thing is, everyone believed him." I shivered as I remembered the accusing looks.

"Even me," a cool voice said. "How stupid was that?"

"Jelena!" I turned around to face her.

She gave me a small smile and pulled off her sunglasses, revealing eyes that were red around the edges. She looked at me uncertainly. "I'm sorry I didn't talk to you right away, but I was embarrassed. I just felt so stupid for believing Alex's lie and accusing you in front of everybody! There's no excuse for it, but I liked him *so much*—I've never felt that way about anyone. So, when I heard all those messages on my phone, I just lost it. What killed me the most was thinking that you'd betrayed me." Her eyes misted up. "'Cause you're my best friend and, despite all my ambition, I would *never* do that to you. Loyalty is everything to me."

We looked at each other for a moment before throwing our arms around each other.

"Can you forgive me?" Jelena cried.

"Jelena, she's hugging you," Sara responded. "What do you think her answer is?"

It would obviously take us both a while to get over our respective hurts, but I wasn't going to let Alex's stupidity destroy something as important as our friendship.

"How are you feeling about Alex?" Cassie asked as she handed Jelena a cup of lemonade.

"Pretty upset," Jelena replied. "But the fact that his social standing has plummeted is some consolation. His lie about being Aurora's secret admirer has shown the entire female population of Jefferson High just how desperate he is to look good. No one's going to go near him for a long time."

We all burst into laughter.

Lindsay sighed. "What a morning. Alex's accusations, a schoolyard showdown, the revelation that Aurora's secret admirer is a friend of Hayden's—"

"What?" Cassie cried. "How do you feel about that?"

I couldn't answer. My feelings were too jumbled up to put into words. My secret admirer was one of Hayden's friends, but it was Hayden himself I wanted to throw my arms around and never let go. Hayden Paris, who'd helped right my world twice this morning, whose smile made my heart leap. But he obviously didn't feel the same way. Why else would he willingly help his friend to woo and win me?

The walk home that afternoon was a miserable one. As I trudged up the driveway, I saw the NAD sitting on the front step, waiting for me.

"Dad . . ." I wasn't sure what to say. I was mortified to remember myself screaming after his departing taxi. "You're back."

"Yes, honey." His face looked tired, not angry. "I shouldn't have gone."

"Dad, no. You had an important presentation. I was just so upset about Snookums that I wasn't myself."

"I wasn't myself, either." Dad frowned. "Dana broke up with me minutes before you arrived—"

"Oh no!" I cried. "Dad, I'm so sorry!"

He gave me a skeptical look. "Aurora, you were hardly her biggest fan."

"No," I admitted. "But I am sorry that she hurt you. What was her reason?"

"She broke up with me because of a tarot reading." Dad's voice was bitter.

"A tarot reading?"

"Stupid cards," Dad muttered. "Anyway, honey, I'm sorry I was insensitive about Snookums. I know it's hard on you, with me being away all the time. I'm going to try harder to spend more time with you."

I felt a lump rise in my throat. My dad wasn't going to leave me. It was time to let that old fear go.

As Dad headed inside, my phone jangled with a text: *I told Carlos about you. We both want you to come for dinner next week. Mom xx.*

It wasn't perfect, but it was a start. Perhaps my mother would never love me the way I wanted her to—my heart gave a squeeze as I considered it—but maybe there was some kind of dynamic there that was worth keeping and working on. She *was* reaching out, in her way, and I still wanted to close the crevasse between us, even if certain cracks in the surface always remained.

"Aurora," a voice called.

I looked up to see Hayden dashing up my drive.

"I have a message for you from your secret admirer. He wanted me to deliver it personally, to ensure there are no more cases of mistaken identity."

He handed me a silver envelope. I looked at it uncertainly. How could I tell him that my heart was breaking?

"He wants you to open it as soon as possible," Hayden said.

"I . . . Okay." I slowly unsealed it and pulled out another creamy sheet of paper written on with deep-blue ink.

To the beautiful Aurora—I want to tell you who I am and exactly how I feel. Just like Much Ado About Nothing, *all will be revealed in the end. Meet me on the school stage at 6 p.m. Love, your secret admirer.*

"He wants to meet me tonight?" I stared at the message.

"He has a surprise for you," Hayden said. "Don't worry. He's a friend of mine, so it's safe. I got permission for him to use the stage after hours. I pulled a few strings with the school board."

"Hayden, I . . ."

The one I want to be with is you.

"He wants you to be there more than anything in the world." Hayden's voice was low.

If I said no and hurt his friend, I'd also be hurting Hayden. I couldn't bear to do that.

"I'll be there," I said, somehow managing to conjure up a smile. "I promise."

He smiled back and headed down the driveway. I went inside, feeling like I wanted to cry.

I needed support. It was time to confide in someone.

"Cass!" I cried, as soon as she answered my call. "My secret admirer wants to meet me tonight."

"Oh my god! That's fantastic!"

"No, it's not, because—"

"You need help getting ready, right? I'll be right over!"

The line went dead. I stood clutching the phone in the living room. I guessed the whole I-know-you-won't-believe-this-but-I've-fallen-for-Hayden-Paris thing would probably be better said in person. Just in case she passed out from shock.

Ten minutes later, there were excited thumps at the door.

"Surprise!"

Cass, Lindsay, Jelena, and Sara stood on the front step, grinning at me.

"Your secret admirer's revealing himself!" Sara shrieked.

"We brought hair curlers *and* straighteners!" Lindsay said, wielding one in each hand.

"And perfume. You've got to have an intriguing scent," Jelena said. "Are you going to let us in?"

She didn't wait for an answer. Next thing I knew, the four of them were pushing me inside and upstairs, past a gaping NAD.

Sara bounded into my room. "Let the makeover begin!"

"Okay, first decision: outfit." Jelena whipped open my wardrobe door. "We want something eye-catching."

"Guys—"

"How about this?" Sara tossed me the tiniest black tube top.

Cassie looked at the garment doubtfully. "It's slightly revealing."

"Sexy, you mean," Sara said.

Lindsay looked at me. "I've never seen you in that."

"That's 'cause it's mine," Sara explained. "I brought it over."

Jelena shook her head. "Yours, hers, she's *not* wearing it."

"Are you trying to say I don't have taste?" Sara pouted.

"Guys—" I started again, then stopped.

I couldn't tell them. Telling them would mean a barrage of advice. Well meant, but advice all the same. The decision I made about tonight had to be mine alone, because it was my heart I was risking.

I was going tonight not only because I'd promised Hayden but also because it was the right thing to do. After all the effort the secret admirer had gone to, I owed it to him to be there.

But what I'd do once I was there was a complete mystery to me right now.

One hour and forty minutes later, I was standing at the door of the auditorium.

"You look perfect." Cassie squeezed my hands.

I wore a floaty white dress, a silver locket on a fine chain, and simple white heels.

"Thank you, guys," I said. "For helping me get ready, for being here . . ."

They all hugged me, and the weight on my shoulders lightened slightly.

"What are you going to do now?" I asked. The taxi that had brought us here had taken off.

"Observe, of course." Jelena was matter-of-fact.

Sara grinned. "We're going to duck around the back and hide in the wings."

"You *what*?" I gaped at them.

"For precautionary reasons," Sara said. "No way are we going to let you meet some unknown guy alone. Even if we are on school property."

"And we can rescue you if he's a nerd," Jelena said.

I got a mental image of the four of them tearing through the side curtains and scaring the life out of some not-so-attractive guy.

"For the last time, Jelena, he's *not* a nerd!" Sara stamped her foot on the gravel path. "He's a friend of Hayden's, for god's sake!"

Hayden. I closed my eyes, saw his immeasurable gaze holding mine.

"Is it okay that we stay?" Cassie asked. "We'll get going as soon as we know he's okay."

"Sure," I answered. They did have a point—there were risks with meeting someone who could be a stranger, and I wanted my friends looking out for me.

"Arrgghh!" Sara screamed. "It's five fifty-nine p.m.!"

Jelena gave me a last spritz of perfume. "You'd better open that door, Aurora."

I looked from them to the door but didn't move.

"It's going to work out." Cassie's voice was full of reassurance.

Something in me believed her, even though, logically, I knew there was no possible way it could be true. I was meeting the friend of the guy I secretly loved.

I placed my hand on the doorknob.

"Good luck!" my friends called, their giggles fading as they dashed around to the back of the building.

My heart was in my throat as I readied myself to turn the handle. I was just as clueless about what to do as I'd been when I'd first gotten the message this afternoon. If I told my secret admirer the truth—that the only one I loved and ever could love was Hayden—he'd be incredibly hurt. Not to mention that his relationship with Hayden would be completely messed up, too. I risked destroying their friendship, with no guarantee that I'd even be able to win Hayden's heart, anyway. Not when he'd helped his friend to woo me. But I couldn't just deny my feelings and date this other guy! He didn't deserve someone whose affections were elsewhere.

I couldn't put this off any longer. I had to have the courage to face what was waiting for me and to do what I felt was right, whatever that would be.

I turned the handle and pushed the door open—and let out a gasp.

A line of tealight candles ran all the way down the auditorium aisle; hundreds of them lit up the otherwise dark room. Pink, yellow, and orange rose petals were scattered alongside them, as well as thousands of tiny silver stars. I held my breath as I walked slowly down the magical path, feeling like I was in a dream. Piano music was playing through the auditorium speakers.

On the stage, inside a giant heart of tealights, stood two champagne glasses and a picnic basket. I glanced around breathlessly. The place was deserted.

I turned my eyes back to the heart and my eyes fell on something glinting near the edge of the stage. It was a scroll of silver paper, scattered with more stars.

A message, intended for me.

My fingers trembled as I walked up onto the stage and picked up the scroll. Here was my answer.

My breath caught as I unraveled the tightly curled paper.

Your secret admirer is standing behind you.

I turned, ever so slowly . . . to see the last person I'd expected.

"Hayden?"

"Aurora." His voice was hushed as he stepped toward me. He held out a rainbow-colored rose, identical to the one that had been in the Valentine's Day bouquet.

"I . . ." My vocal cords wouldn't work. All I could do was stare at him—everything I'd wanted and thought I couldn't have.

"Shh." Hayden held a finger to his lips. "Please let me explain before you say anything." He pressed the rose into my hand.

"You're—"

"Please. I've been waiting forever to say it—or what feels like forever, anyway." His chest rose and fell as he took a deep breath. "I'm your secret admirer."

"But how? Why?"

I felt like he was a mirage that would disappear if I blinked.

"Why?" He looked amazed. "Because I'm crazy about you!"

I felt like I was going to faint. Was I even hearing right?

"Aurora, I've been in love with you for as long as I can remember," Hayden exclaimed. "Years! You couldn't see it?"

"You never acted like you were in love with me," I said. "You seemed more intent on driving me crazy!"

"And you never wondered why? Teasing you was the only way to get you to pay me any attention!" Hayden laughed, shaking his head. "You didn't catch on to all my hints about us as a couple? You playing Bond girl to my Bond?"

"No," I said. "I just thought it was the Hayden Paris ego out in full force." I blushed. "Oh god, I'm sorry! That's not an insult—"

"No, I understand. Admittedly, because of that ego I *was* a little blind, but it took me a while to realize that my tactics weren't working."

Hayden's words were spilling out, like he was worried I might be offended or upset. I desperately wanted to reassure him.

"Hayden . . ."

"Sorry. I know I'm making a mess of this." He laughed nervously. "I think you're just going to have to let me stumble through it. Anyway, I knew that if you were ever going to see me as anything other than your pain-in-the-neck neighbor, I needed to up the ante. That's where the whole secret admirer idea came in. Or rather, you inspired it—I wasn't kidding when I said you were my muse."

"I inspired it? How?"

"Your presentation in history class. You talked about a knight wooing his lady love with messages and gifts. It seemed like a great idea, and Valentine's Day was coming up, so it was perfect timing. Do you remember that day I ran into you at the bookstore? I was there to buy the stationery for the messages. After we had coffee, I met up with Scott to order the flowers."

"But why didn't you put your name on the bouquet?"

We would have avoided so much misunderstanding, our terrible fight, the agony of the past week.

"You didn't seem ready for that. I was worried you'd think it was a joke—that I was trying to make fun of you or something."

"You really thought I'd react like that?"

He gave me a look. "Aurora, you threw me on the asphalt when I dared to kiss you on the hand."

I cringed, remembering the night we'd staked out the NAD's date. "I didn't realize you were making a move!"

"Exactly. I didn't trust that you'd take the bouquet the right way, so I sent it anonymously. But when I came around with the balloons

on Valentine's Day, I was bursting to tell you. I wanted to kiss you—
I was going to kiss you—"

I put up a hand to stop him. He didn't need to say any more, do
any more. "Hayden, I—"

"Please let me keep going." He rushed on, looking embarrassed.
"Then your dad arrived. You went off to help him, and while I was
waiting I caught sight of your poem, and I'm ashamed to admit that
I read it. You caught me, and I was so angry at myself because I'd
wrecked everything between us. The only good thing was that I realized what you were looking for. You wanted a prince, someone
who would fight against the odds for you. So I wrote the poem and
hoped, in the meantime, that with us being thrown together in the
play, you might grow to like me a little better."

I wanted to break in, to tell him about my own feelings, but I also
wanted to hear more. Every sentence he said made me even happier than the last.

"And then I found out about Benedick and Beatrice's kiss,"
Hayden said. "I'd been dreaming about kissing you for so long that
it seemed wrong for it to be something that happened in the play. I
tried to convince myself that it was all part of being an actor, so that,
on the day, I'd be ready to go for it." He took another deep breath.
"But at the moment I bent down to kiss you, I realized that I didn't
want our first kiss to be in front of everyone. I wanted it to be real,
not put on."

"So that's why you paused," I breathed. "I thought you weren't
attracted to me."

Hayden's eyebrows shot up. "How on earth did you come up with
that? It was completely the opposite—so much so that I was worried
you would see it in my eyes. I meant to tell you the truth on opening
night, but the moment felt so rushed. So I went for a kiss on the
hand." He smiled. "And then I was free to plan how I'd reveal my feelings for you in private."

"But you were so odd around me after the play!" I cried.

Hayden looked embarrassed. "I feel terrible, but that afternoon, when I invited you to watch the DVD, I overheard what you said to Sara."

"I know," I said. "It was a mistake. I wanted to explain things over dinner."

"I'd hoped that was the case. But then you started talking about our friendship and how you wanted to stay exactly as we were. I couldn't handle it. I spent two days avoiding you, feeling completely miserable."

I remembered how miserable I'd felt myself.

"And then, in history class, when I turned around and you looked at me, I saw something in your eyes. I decided to try again. But the very next day the Facebook thing happened and all the guys were going crazy over you. I didn't want you to think that was all I cared about, so I thought I'd wait. Imagine my surprise when I arrived at school on Monday to hear that Alex was your secret admirer!"

"And so you said it was a friend of yours instead. You had me so mixed up!" I thought of the agonies I'd suffered this afternoon.

"I didn't want Alex's stupid bet spoiling the surprise I'd planned for you." Hayden stepped closer and took another deep breath. "Aurora, I know it's a long shot, and you've only just started seeing me as a friend, so it's a huge shock for you, but if you'll just give me a chance, just one chance—"

I reached for his hand.

"What are you doing?" Hayden's voice was very low.

"Do you know why I couldn't kiss you?" I said, squeezing his hand. The sense of relief I felt at this simple touch was astounding. "As old-fashioned and ridiculous as it sounds, I was saving my first kiss for the one who was supposed to be worthy of me. I thought that was my secret admirer. Which turned out to be you! So, that kiss I was trying like crazy to save is yours." I laughed, tears in my eyes, and lifted our joined hands to my heart. "Yours as my secret admirer, but most importantly, yours because I . . . I feel as strongly as you do."

Hayden stared at me, disbelieving. "You feel the same?"

"I only figured it out in that history class. For someone who considers herself a dating guru, I'm surprisingly unaware of my own heart!"

I let out a jittery giggle, and Hayden started laughing, too. And then he stepped closer and took me into his arms and we stopped laughing. At that moment, the first few chords of my favorite song, Des'ree's "I'm Kissing You," began playing. We stood at the edge of the stage, closer than we'd ever been during rehearsals, so close that I felt his heart beating against mine.

I took a shaky breath. "I wanted you to kiss me then, and I want . . . I want you to kiss me now."

"Are you sure?" he whispered.

I nodded, not trusting myself to speak. Time seemed to slow down to the speed of our heartbeats. My legs trembled. This was it.

Hayden stroked my cheek and bent his head slowly, his gaze still locked on mine. Closer and closer he came, until the space between his lips and mine, between not kissing and kissing, was infinitesimal. This was the last moment. One second, one tiny movement, and we'd be there, over the edge. I couldn't breathe. I closed my eyes.

Hayden's lips met mine. Gently, like the brush of a butterfly's wing, the lightest of touches. I let out a soft gasp before our lips met again and the kiss grew stronger. I wrapped my arms around his neck, pulling him deeper into this new place where only we existed. It was just Hayden and me, our lips parting and meeting again, his hands cupping my face. No distance between us; just the exquisite joy of discovering each other. Lights burst in my head and my heart, and I knew why kisses were such a big deal. They were a moment of perfect happiness in an imperfect world. This was why I'd waited.

"Perfect," Hayden whispered against my lips, echoing my thoughts. The word melted into another kiss.

Suddenly, ecstatic shrieks ripped through the silence.

"What on earth?" Hayden pulled away.

I grinned, remembering my friends hiding in the wings. "I think we've got witnesses."

Hayden laughed. "Another stakeout? You know, that kind of reminds me of our story, which is seriously starting to shape up like a Bond film."

"Hayden! How many times do I have to say—"

"Think about it," he mused. "We did some spying, defeated a bad guy, *and* had a romantic scene."

He did have a point.

"Hey," he said, with a playful look in his eyes, "do you remember how you said that if I ever loved anyone more than myself it would be the world's greatest romance?"

"Hayden! You know I didn't mean it."

"Well, I think we may just be in for the world's greatest romance," he said, laughing.

"I think we just might."

I grinned as he picked me up in his arms and spun me around, kissing me again and again.

acknowledgments

my US team:

Kat Brzozowski—I'm so thrilled to have the opportunity to share Aurora with more of the world—and to be publishing with St. Martin's. Thank you for embracing the books with so much enthusiasm from day one, and for your general hard work on this project—this has been such an exciting experience for me and I feel hugely blessed to have this opportunity. I cannot wait to do this all over again for *How to Convince*!

A big thank-you to Jessica Katz in production, and Todd Manza, who is responsible for the American copyedit. To Karen Masnica, and Michelle Cashman, who look after the all-important publicity and marketing for the book. I'm so lucky to have experts on my side when embarking on this US adventure!

my australian team:

Elizabeth O'Donnell—Libby, I can't thank you enough for your dedication and hard work in securing me my contract with St. Martin's. I have been dreaming of a US contract since the age of twenty-one, when *How to Keep a Boy from Kissing You* was just a manuscript saved on a floppy disk—and I still pinch myself that this is happening! As an author, you always hope your work will go on and connect with large audiences from all different places—and that wouldn't be possible without your help, so I owe you infinite thanks!

Big thanks as always to my publisher from HarperCollins Australia, Lisa Berryman, who instantly embraced and understood Aurora Skye and has been an instrumental part of bringing her and the Find a Prince™ program to life.

The gorgeous Gemma Fahy (who was probably the very *first* person besides myself to read Aurora's story in full) and the incredible Cristina Cappelluto—thank you so much for all your hard work. This goes for everyone on the HarperCollins Kids team—you are absolute superstars!

My wonderful wordsmiths who took on the original editorial work for the Australian publication: Elizabeth Kemp—many thanks for your suggestions on trimming one very hefty manuscript; Nicola O'Shea, who made my first experience of the editing process supremely smooth (one look at those first few pages and I knew Aurora and Co. were in safe hands); and Emma Dowden, who ironed out a very confusing time line. I'm in awe of the contribution good editors make to a manuscript.

Kate Burnitt, it was such a pleasure to have you calmly and expertly guiding it all.

A final (and no less worthy!) thanks to Fiona Pearson, for taking a risk so early on.